Praise for

spoiled

★ "A pitch-perfect satire of the glitz-and-glam world of the rich and famous...With deftly interwoven humor, hyperbole, and poignant, authentic moments, this is a wholly entertaining, thought-provoking offering." — *Booklist* (starred review)

"Fashion bloggers Cocks and Morgan...bring humor, heart, and formidable writing skills to this exuberant debut.... The fashion knowledge, eye for Hollywood ridiculousness, and wicked humor that the authors are known for is on full display." — *Publishers Weekly*

"The Fug Girls (of fashion snark blog GoFugYourself.com) move seamlessly into the world of fiction. Their YA debut is a fluffy, excellent treat.... Try this one on!" — *Romantic Times*

"Readers hooked on celebrity culture and fashion will enjoy this behind-the-scenes, fun-filled romp." — *VOYA*

"*Spoiled* really is such a FUN read! I love it: It's dishy, it's girly, it's L.A.... everything I love." — JOE ZEE, Creative Director, *ELLE* magazine

spoiled

a novel

by heather cocks &
jessica morgan

poppy

Little, Brown and Company
New York   Boston

Authors' Note

This is a work of fiction. Characters, places, and events are the product of the authors' imagination and are not to be construed as real. Any resemblance to actual events or persons (living or dead) is purely coincidental. Although some celebrities' names and real entities and places are mentioned, they are all used fictitiously.

Poppy • Hachette Book Group
237 Park Avenue, New York, NY 10017
Visit our website at www.lb-teens.com

Poppy is an imprint of Little, Brown and Company.
The Poppy name and logo are trademarks of Hachette Book Group, Inc.

The publisher is not responsible for websites (or their content)
that are not owned by the publisher.

First Hardcover Edition: June 2011
First Paperback Edition: May 2012

Library of Congress Cataloging-in-Publication Data

Cocks, Heather.
Spoiled / by Heather Cocks and Jessica Morgan.— 1st ed.
p. cm.
Summary: When her mother dies, sixteen-year-old Molly moves
from Indiana to California, to live with her newly discovered father,
a Hollywood megastar, and his pampered teenaged daughter.
ISBN 978-0-316-09825-0 (hc) / ISBN 978-0-316-09827-4 (pb)
[1. Sisters—Fiction. 2. Fathers and daughters—Fiction. 3. Preparatory schools—
Fiction. 4. Schools—Fiction. 5. Theater—Fiction. 6. Los Angeles (Calif.)—
Fiction.] I. Morgan, Jessica, 1975– II. Title.
PZ7.C6473Sp 2011 [Fic]—dc22 2010043181

10 9 8 • RRD-C • Printed in the United States of America

For Fug Nation

one

"ARUGULA, PUT THEM DOWN. You know thigh-high sandals give you cankles."

Brooke Berlin snatched the seven-hundred-dollar Gucci gladiator shoes out of her friend's hand and threw them back onto the display table, knocking over five and a half pairs of boots in the process. Choosing not to notice the shoes strewn across the floor—Brooke, in life and in shopping, rarely cleaned up her own messes—she cast a concerned frown at the Tyra Banks clone at her side.

"Relax, Brooke, I was just looking," Arugula said. "Those are *so* 2008."

Satisfied that she'd helped save yet another soul from style self-sabotage, Brooke turned and surveyed the modern, high-ceilinged store—shirts crisply folded on tables illuminated from within; white walls lit by metal pendant chandeliers as skinny as the clientele; gleaming chrome benches for those clients' tired plus-ones—and inhaled deeply. She loved the smell of retail. Shopping was her Xanax, her Red Bull, her cure for the common cold: Brooke truly believed anything could be fixed by flexing the trusty plastic rectangles in her wallet. Some might have called it excessive consumption (like her father, if he ever noticed the bills), but Brooke preferred to think of it as philanthropy. Those poor schmoes wearing name tags pinned to last season's blouses all worked on commission, and minimum wage wouldn't even buy half a sushi roll at Nobu. Shopping was practically her patriotic duty.

Today, though, the central display was underwhelming. Inferno was the trendiest boutique in Los Angeles, the kind of place where paparazzi "caught" people like Nicole Richie buying maxi dresses, and tourists waited outside behind velvet ropes. But inconveniently, a mere week before the most important night of Brooke's entire life, Inferno's management decided the next hot fad was an exhumation of Seattle's 1990s grunge scene. Even Katy Perry, riffling through the racks across the way, seemed dismayed. Through the window, a paparazzo snapped her scowling at a flannel romper. Brooke felt a flare of envy and turned away.

"What lunatic thought this was a good idea?" she whined, poking at an oversize plaid button-down. "I can't show up at this party dressed like a lumberjack."

"We could go across to Chanel," Arugula offered.

"And look like an old lady? I don't think so." Brooke cleared her throat and raised the volume a few decibels. "Daddy and I just want everything to be perfect. Brick Berlin doesn't do anything halfway."

"Dude, that's Brick Berlin's kid?" someone whispered as a spate of heads jerked in their direction. "He's, like…Oh. My. God. Those *abs*."

Brooke beamed. Just because she wasn't a household name—yet—didn't mean she was totally anonymous.

"We haven't even been here five minutes and you've already played your trump card?" Arugula whispered.

"I can't help it if tourists have excellent hearing."

"I know you better than that," Arugula said. "You're clearly anxious. I *told* you not to skip power yoga this morning."

"I just couldn't handle ninety minutes of looking at people's crotch sweat," Brooke said. "And I don't believe in anxiety. It gives you wrinkles. But I do have to look exactly right on Saturday. A girl only turns sixteen once."

"Technically, this is *your* third time in a few months," Arugula replied. "Remember, you let the football team cook you a birthday meal to count toward its community service, and on your actual birthday in May your dad bagged on Spago to scout a location…."

"Details," Brooke said dismissively. "This is the one that *counts*."

She scanned the rest of the store, bypassing spandex

bodysuits, vegan shoes — a trend Brooke couldn't wait to see die; to her, fashion wasn't cruelty-free if it was ugly — and one very alarming jumpsuit covered in spikes. Her shining moment was too important for an outfit that belonged on VH1 Classic being worn by a big-haired tart writhing on the hood of a pickup truck. Brooke Berlin was many things, but tarty wasn't one of them.

Across the room, she spied a familiar pair of bifocals peeking out from a messy lump of dresses near one of the changing rooms.

"Brie!" Brooke called. "Find anything good?"

"I thought her name was Martha," Arugula said.

"Martha is a name for old people with suspenders for their socks," Brooke said. "I'm doing her a favor. Cheese is so *in* right now. Brie!"

A fist poked out from the teetering heap and gave Brooke a shaky thumbs-up.

"At least she's got better taste than the last underclassman you hired," Arugula noted. "Remember those Hot Topic coupons?"

"I know," Brooke shuddered. "As if I shop at the *mall*, much less the store that costumed my dad's zombie eating-disorder movie."

"Was *Chew* any good? I couldn't bring myself to see it."

"Don't," Brooke confided. "Daddy dumped the lead actress in the middle of filming and you can totally tell. She stops purging with conviction halfway through the second act. *So* disrespectful."

They walked over to Brie, who was sticking out a pasty leg to keep patrons from snagging the lone empty dressing room. Brooke patted her sophomore assistant on the head— it was important to be gentle with the help—scooped up a layer of dresses, and closed the curtain behind her.

"I'm surprised Brick actually agreed to let the tabloids document this party." Arugula's voice floated through the velvet drape. "Mother said the agency decided the single jet-setter image did more for his profile than 'doting father.'"

"Actually, Daddy's just *very* protective," snapped Brooke, shimmying out of her sundress. "But once he saw how important it was to me, he couldn't say no."

He had, in fact, said no several times. It had been ten years since Brick Berlin let his daughter make any sort of public appearance with him. He claimed it was for her safety, but it wounded Brooke; she liked showing off her father, plus it seemed like a tremendous waste of his connections. But after three crying jags, one expertly rendered fainting spell, and a bunch of brochures scattered around the house with titles like "Twenty Myths About Manual Labor," Brick caved and agreed to throw Brooke a sweet-sixteen party that would introduce her to Hollywood the way she'd always dreamed: as his daughter, the budding actress. It was about time. What was the point of being a celebrity legacy if it didn't open doors? Nepotism was only a dirty word if you had no talent.

"Ugh. I look like a Hells Angels reject in this," Brooke complained, throwing a studded leather skirt through the curtain in Brie's general direction. "Seriously, if we can't find something decent for me to wear, this whole cover story will be ruined and I'll have to abandon Hollywood and make my living as a"—Brooke paused, then shuddered— "a *doctor*, or something."

"God forbid," snorted Arugula as Brooke emerged in a gold textured sheath. "Too scaly," she added. "Also, don't disparage premed before you've tried it. My own independent study of anatomy textbooks has been engrossing."

"You are so weird," Brooke said fondly. "Good thing you punched Magnus Mitchell for gluing my hair to the swings when we were five, or else you might be spending Saturday night reading the thesaurus instead of being fabulous with *moi*."

"Please. Even geniuses like to party. Here, try the green one."

"Ooh, Daddy *does* love anything money-colored," Brooke bubbled, grabbing the dress.

Alone again behind the curtain, Brooke felt a wave of excitement. Since Brick had gone from action star to busy actor-director-producer with unfettered access to studio jets, they rarely did anything together. She didn't begrudge his success—in addition to all the money, being Brick Berlin's daughter had even the teachers at school treating her like a queen. But Brooke missed the days when her father would come home every night, scoop her up with a grin, and make her tell him a story. Now, *if* he had time to call from the road, he just absently asked her stuff like whether they still taught gymnastics in PE. It was like he wasn't quite paying attention.

Well, that will change, Brooke thought, casting an appraising look at her reflection. The tart green silk wove around her in a series of perfect pleats, making her waist look tiny (it was), her light tan look natural (it wasn't), and her legs seem ten miles long (a theory that several seniors on the cross-country team had offered to test). Brick would be pleased and proud.

A disembodied voice punctured her thoughts.

"Poor Arugula. Last season's YSLs? *Really?* Do I smell an exclusive? Is Brick Berlin stiffing your mom on her commission?"

Brooke froze. Shoving her feet back into her Louboutins—*this* season, naturally—she charged outside and stopped dead in front of the one person who truly made her skin crawl.

"Hello, Shelby," she said, infusing two years' worth of contempt into each syllable.

"Brooke. Of course. I *thought* I smelled drugstore perfume," Shelby Kendall said, tossing her overabundance of shiny black hair as if she were in a Pantene ad.

Brooke focused on her rival's annoyingly flawless face and prayed a zit would appear and spontaneously burst all over the Diane von Furstenberg shirt that was slipping off one of Shelby's smooth shoulders. Ever since Shelby had arrived for freshman year having renovated herself suspiciously quickly from a mousy, forgettable teacher's pet into

7

a tat-free Angelina Jolie, she'd set her sights on using the school's TV station to usurp Brooke's queen-bee status, and the two girls had gotten along about as well as a pig farmer at a vegan restaurant. It boggled Brooke's mind how easily people bought into Shelby's popularity ploy and vaulted her up the social hierarchy. At least Brooke's own charms were natural (well, except for her tan, but it was a fact that bronzer saved lives). Beauty bought with the money Daddy made digging for scandals in half of their classmates' own backyards seemed like it ought to be a tougher sell.

Shelby met Brooke's eyes with barely a blink. The paparazzo hovering outside waved at her and pointed at them questioningly, and Shelby shook her head with a very dismissive wave.

"One of my father's guys," Shelby explained. "For a second he thought you were somebody."

She punctuated this with a sparkling laugh, throwing back her head and clutching Brooke's upper arm as if they were besties who'd just shared the most spectacular joke. Brooke knew better than to let Shelby provoke her, especially in front of the tourists who'd just heard her bragging about Brick. But she couldn't resist pushing back a little.

"I see your dad's coverage of the *American Idol* scandal bought you another nose job," she said, with equally false cheer.

"And I see your boobs still haven't come in," Shelby said. "Luckily, nobody knows who you are—you could still get them done and no one would notice."

"We both know I'm going to get plenty of attention after *Hey!* covers my party."

Shelby patted Brooke's shoulder. "I'm sure you're right, darling."

Brooke narrowed her eyes suspiciously, but Shelby's attention had shifted elsewhere.

"Sweetie!" she squealed.

Abandoning Brooke and Arugula, Shelby signaled the *Hey!* photographer, who obligingly started snapping her as she ran over to a table where one of the lesser Kardashians was autographing a pile of three-hundred-dollar tank tops from her new line, Klothes. The girls shrieked, then hugged without actually touching.

"Something about that makes me uncomfortable," Arugula warned in a low voice.

"I know, right?" Brooke rolled her eyes. "That family needs to buy another consonant."

"No, I mean with Shelby. She didn't even call you a drag queen. That almost never happens."

"Oh, whatever," Brooke said. "I'm sure she's just off her game because her father is putting me front and center in *Hey!*, and there's nothing she can do about it."

In truth, though, Shelby's victorious expression had made Brooke queasier than a carb binge. She'd seen it often enough to know that it never led to anything good.

Worse, it cast a pall on her shopping day to know Shelby was lurking around, as annoying as the old tube of lip gloss currently leaking at the bottom of Brooke's handbag. She darted back into the dressing room, scooped up a stack of dresses she figured she'd just buy now and try later, and swanned back into the store.

Shelby had returned, and she was scrutinizing Brie with anthropological fervor. "What is *this*?"

"I'm Mar—" Brie began.

"Brie is my personal assistant, and I'll thank you to treat her with respect," Brooke said, drawing herself up to her full five feet eleven inches to look as imposing as possible. "You know the underclassmen always look to me as a wise big sister."

"What an appropriate choice of words," Shelby said, snapping her fingers as if she'd just remembered something important and pulling an issue of *Hey!* out of her purse. She tossed it at Brooke. "Page fifteen."

Arugula subtly shook her head, but Brooke couldn't resist.

BRICK BUILDING A BIGGER FAMILY? screamed the headline. The story read:

> Is Hollywood's biggest himbo hunk hiding a deep family secret? A source close to Berlin confirms that next week, he'll unveil a love child. When asked if there was truth to the rumor, Berlin said cryptically, "Children, like protein shakes, are God's greatest present." We assume that's a yes.

Brooke didn't realize she was shaking until Arugula nudged her back to consciousness. Gossip about Brick never failed to chafe, especially because at least eighty percent of it usually turned out to be true—and she almost never heard it first.

"*Surely* he told you…?" Shelby asked, the very picture of concern. "I can't imagine my father keeping something this huge from me. Maybe Brick thought the shock would cause a relapse of your tanorexia. That summer you were the color of a traffic cone hurt us *all*."

Brooke ignored this and gritted her teeth. She was pretty sure none of Brick's girlfriends had ended up pregnant—unless the most recent one's *Elle* spread was heavily airbrushed, but considering the photo shoot featured her riding a bull, it seemed unlikely. She plastered a smile on her face and met Shelby's sharp green eyes.

"Juicy," she said, with all the nonchalance she could muster. "Too bad it's not true."

"That's right. Stay strong, sweet pea," Shelby said, drifting toward a display of fringed ankle boots. "But why don't you hang on to that anyway? Might be fun in your family album! No mom in there means *plenty* of room for a new sibling."

Ari sucked in a breath. "I'll get the car," she whispered.

Swallowing bile, Brooke nodded stiffly and turned to Brie.

"Tell the manager to put this all on my tab," she announced. "And tell him the clientele here has gone disastrously downhill. I am *way* skeeved."

11

Brooke brushed past Shelby—with a hint of an elbow jab—and exited Inferno with her head high. Once outside, though, she bolted down Robertson and around the corner onto one of the residential streets to hide, so she could have her mini breakdown far away from the photographers waiting for Nicole Kidman to come out of Chanel.

Her eyes burned, and not just because of that stupid tabloid story. Even after the letters stopped coming, Brooke never imagined she would turn sixteen without so much as word (or a car) from her mother. And it pissed her off even more that Shelby could push the Kelly Berlin button so effortlessly. Getting upset over her absentee mother seemed almost too obvious, like something from a bad soap opera but without hot, shirtless men everywhere to distract from the pain.

After a few calming yoga breaths, Brooke decided to reject her anger. Kelly's absence and Shelby's noxiousness only made it that much more important to make a huge impression on the Hollywood bigwigs at her party. Topping her mother's feat of being the first hand model ever to wear a Lee Press-On Nail would be tricky—but winning an Oscar at eighteen would be a decent start. Shelby may have gotten the last word today, but Brooke wasn't going to be derailed by some vague blurb in a magazine.

It will happen, Brooke told herself. *Be calm. There is nothing in your way.*

Brooke's funk returned as soon as Arugula dropped her off at home. For all her bravado, something about the *Hey!* blurb nagged at her, and she needed to talk to Brick.

She trudged up the ten stone steps to her front door and let herself into the house, which was vast and silent as a library. The stillness only added to her irritation. She felt like the building was shushing her when she hadn't done anything wrong. Petulantly, she hurled her house keys at the nearest surface; unfortunately, that surface turned out to have a face.

"Whoops! Sorry, Stan."

Her father's assistant rubbed his bald head. "What happened? Is this what amnesia feels like?"

"I wish *I* had amnesia." Brooke moaned for maximum melodrama. "Any idea where he is?"

"The usual—in the library reading Tolstoy."

"So which is it, gym or pool?"

"Got it in two, hon."

Brooke blazed ahead to the living room, across the solarium's parquet floors, through the French doors onto the patio, and down the sloping, verdant grounds to the Olympic-size pool, where Brick's bright red swim cap gave him away. She tore off her shoes, plopped down on the mosaic tiles that fanned out from the diving board, and stuck her feet in the water.

Brick stroked toward the ledge. Brooke couldn't resist kicking out at him.

"H-h-hey!" he sputtered, surfacing with a mouthful of

water. "Oh, hi, honey. Didn't recognize your foot. How was your day?"

"It was…interesting," she said, arranging her features into a mighty pout.

Brick didn't take the bait; he was too busy hauling himself out of the pool to notice. Brooke winced. She hated his embarrassingly snug racing Speedo, but he swore it was his trademark. It never worked to point out that there was no need for a trademark when he was hanging out alone at the house.

"Hey, Sunshine, since we're here together, there's something I need to tell you, okay?" Brick said, peeling off his cap and shaking out his thick russet hair. "And I think it's going to be super great, but it's also going to shock you a little."

"Let me guess," Brooke spat. "That stupid protein-shake quote was real?"

Brick hung his head. "Let *me* guess: *Hey!* wrote something, and you saw it?"

"Shelby basically shoved it up my nose."

"Those bastards weren't supposed to say anything yet," Brick cursed, slapping the cement ringing the pool.

"It was hideous, Daddy," Brooke wailed. "I can't believe Shelby Kendall knew about this before I did! Can you imagine what that felt like? I want to run away to Europe and get a face transplant!"

This had worked well on the most recent episode of Brooke's favorite soap, *Lust for Life*, although for some reason Bobbie Jean had also woken up in Dr. Hedge Von

Henson's Swedish sanitarium three inches shorter and a redhead.

Brick sighed. "Listen, Sunshine, I'm sorry," he said. "I didn't mean for you to find out that way. But before you get angry, hear me out. A sibling could be fantastic. Think what it'll be like to have someone who looks up to you and needs you."

A calming voice in Brooke's head (that sounded eerily like Tim Gunn) chimed in that celebrity babies were dominating the tabloids—as were the people holding them. She imagined a "Famous People Feel Things Too" feature in which she tickled the chin of a tot in tiny designer sunglasses while Brick looked on with adoration. Embracing her father's random spawn would make her look so modern and open-minded.

"And just think how cool it could be!" Brick was continuing. "Someone to shop with, someone to help you with your math homework..."

Brooke snorted. "A baby helping me with math? I know I flunked my geometry final last year, but come on."

"A baby? Who has a baby?"

The thought bubble containing Brooke's daydream began to deflate. "Wait, what are *you* talking about?"

"Your sister. Molly. Well, okay, she's your half sister, but I don't want to dwell on that distinction. It might make her feel unwelcome."

"And this *Molly*"—Brooke pronounced the name as if it tasted like earwax—"isn't a baby?"

"She turned sixteen a few days ago."

Brooke's mouth went dry. "How...*what?*"

"Well, Sunshine, you've always known your mom and I weren't exclusive when we first started dating," Brick began. "I didn't even know she was pregnant until I got back from the *Rad Man* shoot. But what I never told you is that on set I met Laurel, and"—he got a faraway look in his eyes— "she worked in wardrobe, and we just connected, you know?"

"*What* wardrobe? You wore a bodysuit for three months," Brooke muttered.

"She was an artist with spandex!" Brick huffed. "Anyway, by the time Laurel told me about the baby, I'd already married your mother. Laurel didn't want any drama, so she went back to Indiana."

Brooke's eyes narrowed. "She's from one of those *middle states?* Dad, why would you *ever* let a tabloid hear about this? She could've just stayed hidden in her cornfield or whatever!"

"That's just it, sweetie, she can't. See, Laurel got sick, and she...she's..." Brick's voice broke, which Brooke might have found touching if her world weren't crashing down around her. "Long story short, Molly's coming to live with us. In two days. She'll be here for the party. I was waiting to tell you until all the arrangements were final."

For a second Brooke thought horror had stolen her voice. She imagined the grief in Brick's eyes when he realized his indiscretion forever silenced his child, and pictured him laying her on a chaise longue, a single tear falling from his cheek as he whispered, "Sweet Brooke, I *will* hear your song again."

Instead, Brick pleaded, "Come on, Sunshine, say something."

"Something," Brooke mumbled. Damn, so she wasn't mute. It was just as well; she couldn't sing anyway. She made a mental note to learn.

"I should've told you from the start. It's a lot to deal with."

"A lot to deal with?" Brooke echoed. "Math is a lot to deal with. A crater-faced half sister from the sticks crashing the most important night of my life is a total *nightmare*."

"There's one more thing," Brick said, a hint of unease in his voice. "I thought we could use the party as Molly's big debut. You know, make her part of the story."

"*My* story?" Brooke gasped.

She gazed at Brick's blazing white grin and wanted to punch him. This thunder-stealing she-devil was shaping up to be the worst catastrophe since high-waisted jeans.

"Now it can be grand and important and meaningful," Brick said, losing himself in his thoughts. "It's such a powerful angle — how in losing her mother, Molly's gained a family." He paused. "Wait, that's kind of good," he said, reaching for his BlackBerry.

Stung, Brooke stumbled to her feet. Her father's muscles blurred before her as he typed away on his stupid phone, a stupid smile on his stupid face. Without knowing what she was doing, almost as if the foot belonged to somebody else, Brooke kicked Brick back into the pool and bolted up to the house.

She burst inside her palatial top-floor suite (panting slightly; the hilly lawn and two flights of stairs were a lot of ground to cover at tantrum speed) and slammed the door as hard as she could—mostly out of habit, since she knew Brick was still outside shaking water out of his ears. But the explosion of noise felt good. It matched what her brain was doing. All those fantasies of standing at Brick's side while he called her the light of his life, anointing her the next jewel in the Berlin acting dynasty, were dissolving like mascara at the Drama Club car wash. It wasn't fair.

Brooke heaved herself into the plush pink wing chair by the window. Her gaze fell on a framed tabloid page from when she was seven and Brick took her to the premiere of his kids' film, *Diaper Andy*, about a stay-at-home dad who invents a baby-changing robot. It was her first and last public event with him, before he'd decided he needed to protect her from people's prying eyes.

"There's no sunscreen for the limelight," he'd intoned. Then they'd split a PowerBar.

Her eyes drifted beneath the tabloid page toward another treasured memento: a proof from a Vaseline campaign showing a graceful pair of hands tenderly moisturizing themselves. Brooke stared down at her own identical fingers, then grabbed her laptop. Her e-mail account's Saved

Drafts folder flashed onto the screen: 198 unsent messages, one for every week since she'd gotten her own computer. Brooke opened one at random from when she was fourteen. It read:

Dear Mom,

Do you still meditate? I tried to do it the way you always used to, but it didn't work. There's too much to think about. Like how I don't have any lace-up boots. And Jake Donovan didn't ask me to the dance. I wish you were here to talk to. I gave you my cell number, right? Maybe you wrote it down wrong....

Brooke slammed it shut. "Stupid," she hissed.

Since Kelly left and Brick's career took off, Brooke could count on one hand how many birthdays she and Brick had spent together, or how many of her performances he'd been able to attend—people *still* talked about the courageous death monologue she'd improvised when she played a tomato in her fifth-grade play about cooking. But Brick had been in Cannes. This party was supposed to be her moment. *Their* moment. Instead, some warty love child was horning in, and not only didn't he get it, but he didn't even seem to mind. How could a guy who'd given himself Lasik as an Arbor Day present be so blind?

So as much as she knew the world expected her to

embrace her tragic half sibling, truth be told, Brooke was angry at her.

No, not angry. Furious. Brooke Berlin was *furious*.

Dear Mom,

Where the hell are you?

two

"YOU KNOW, you kind of have his eyes."

Molly was supposed to be packing, but instead she and Charmaine were doing exactly what they'd been doing for months, ever since Molly's mother had dropped the bomb: watching every Brick Berlin movie they could get on Netflix. Today's choice was the fourth installment in the Dirk Venom series, *Deadly When Prodded*.

Squinting at the screen, Molly mentally compared her eyes to Brick's. But it was hard to spot any similarities when he had blood, dirt, sweat, and—for plot reasons best ignored—traces of clown makeup all over his face.

"Don't taunt the snake," Brick-as-Dirk rasped, "or you'll get the venom." Then he shot a cape-wearing man in the face.

"They really should've stopped after the third movie," groaned Charmaine. "This is embarrassing. By which I mean awesome."

Molly glanced at her watch. It was seven o'clock already. By this time tomorrow, she'd be in Los Angeles, living with a man she'd just seen wield two machine guns on a tightrope while Megan Fox clung to his back. It was too surreal to absorb.

My dad is a movie star. My dad is a movie star.

Molly had repeated this to herself five hundred times since she'd found out, and it still hadn't sunk in yet. Maybe number five hundred one would be the charm.

My dad is a movie star.

Nope.

Shaking her head, Molly hopped up and hauled her dilapidated avocado green suitcase onto the bed. If she didn't hurry up and throw some stuff into it, she'd be boarding the plane to L.A. without any luggage and probably ring some kind of alarm with the feds. A long-lost daughter on the No-Fly List sounded like a twist worthy of one of Brick's movies.

She began rooting through her dresser for things to pack that wouldn't get her crucified in Los Angeles. Compared with all the über-trendy people she'd seen on *90210* episodes, who looked ripped out of the pages of *Lucky*, all Molly's favorite stuff suddenly seemed tatty and plain.

"I have no idea how to do this," Molly said, blowing out her cheeks. "Are running shoes even legal in Los Angeles?"

"They must be. I just read in *Hey!* that Jennifer Lopez is starting a sneaker line called Flan, where they're all named after different desserts," Charmaine said.

"Well, *Hey!* wouldn't lie to you." Molly grinned at her friend. "You're its best customer."

"Isn't Fancy-Pants Private School going to make you wear a uniform, anyway? Like on *Gossip Girl?*"

"Oh, God, I have no idea." Molly chewed on her bottom lip. "Should I bother bringing a coat, do you think? Does L.A. even *have* seasons?"

"Maybe Brick will buy you a whole new wardrobe," Charmaine said, a faraway expression on her face. "That's what he'd do in the movies. You'd get there and you'd have an entire closet full of Prada that fit you perfectly."

"Too bad this is real life."

Except it didn't feel real. Seven months ago, Molly had been the daughter of a long-dead army captain she'd never known and a very much alive seamstress, and the only time she ever paid any attention to the celebrity rags was when Charmaine thrust one at her, usually accompanied by a frenzied query about whether or not Brody Jenner seemed like he would make a good starter husband. Now her mother was gone, and her father turned out to be a living, breathing tabloid regular with his own cologne at Walmart. It felt like having ten minutes to digest a ten-course meal: queasy-making and strange. (That could also describe Trick by Brick, which she'd snuck to the store and smelled.) Life-changing deathbed confessions happened on soap operas, not to a regular girl from West Cairo, Indiana, who ran a six-minute mile and didn't care about her split ends.

And change generally wasn't Molly's thing. She'd dated the same guy since they were old enough to panic about whether kissing would make their braces lock together, she'd slept in the cozy bedroom tucked under the eaves of her grandparents' house since her mother brought her home from the hospital as a newborn, and she'd eaten a peanut-butter sandwich for lunch almost every day since she was twelve. Even her old gold shoelaces never changed, a good-luck charm she'd gotten in eighth grade and threaded superstitiously through every new pair of sneakers she bought. Given all that, Molly couldn't quite believe what she was about to do. In fact, secretly, she felt a little impressed with herself for deciding to go live with the dude who'd just killed Bruce Willis in the summer's biggest blockbuster—even if this move had been basically her mother's dying wish. Because as weird as it felt to be leaving the only home she'd ever known, Molly was excited. A fresh start after months of misery sounded like exactly the right choice. Possibly the only choice.

"Los Angeles is going to be so cool." Charmaine sighed. "I wish I could jet off and live in a mansion. I'd make the *best* rich person. I'd have an electric car, like Cameron Diaz, and a butler like in *Batman*. I'd never empty the dishwasher again. You're so lucky."

Then Charmaine caught herself: "Oh, God, obviously, I don't mean—"

"It's okay," Molly said. "I know what you meant."

She sat down again on the bed.

"What do I *do?*" she asked. "Like, what do I say to him?"

"You say, 'Papa, open your arms and let me in,'" Charmaine instructed.

"I can't quote one of his own movies at him!" Molly laughed. "Especially not *Diaper Andy*."

"Maybe you should ask him if you can have your own wing of the Bavarian castle he just bought from Nicolas Cage."

"Good idea. Or I can ask for a job aboard his new seaworthy replica of the ship from *Pirates of the Caribbean*," Molly said.

"That one actually might be true," Charmaine said. "It was in the same *In Touch* where they said he insured his abs for seven figures, and that *definitely* sounds real."

"I just don't want to look like an idiot, you know?"

"You're going to be fine, I promise," Charmaine said. "Brick is going to be so stoked to have you there, he won't even notice *what* you say. He seems really nice every time I've seen him on Letterman."

Molly's few conversations with Brick *had* been nice, if bizarre. The first time, he'd seemed gutted about Laurel's death, offered Molly his condolences and then his home, and sniffled through a strange digression about the merits of Krav Maga versus karate. Molly had been too numb to say much, and she didn't feel emotionally able to make decisions about anything other than which jeans to put on in the morning. But she'd been tempted. Moving meant escaping the ghost of Laurel that haunted her in West Cairo, where everyone knew and loved her as a happy extension of her mother. And when the doctors announced that Laurel's chemo had failed, Molly had overheard a whispered conversation between Ginger and Miltie in which they agreed not to take the round-the-world trip they'd saved for all their lives, in favor of helping with Molly's expenses. So after two months of people walking up to her in the street and hugging her unbidden, and watching Ginger absently caress her hopeful collection of guidebooks when she thought no one was looking, Molly had called back and accepted Brick's offer. Her grandparents needed to escape, and so did she. For his part, Brick's glee reverberated through the phone line so loudly that she'd had to put down the receiver for a few seconds. She'd never heard anyone whoop before.

"Do you think famous people hang out at his house all the time?" Charmaine wondered, absently rolling up pairs of socks and shoving them into Molly's shoes. "Like, are you going to come down for breakfast, and there's Samuel L. Jackson, eating a bagel?"

"Like Brick gets within ten feet of a carbohydrate."

"Of course he does," scoffed Charmaine. "Those biceps need fuel. I bet he has a chef. And a Bowflex machine."

"Awesome! I'll be buff in no time."

"You know, you're going to need that positive attitude when Brick's other kid tries to turn you into a Scientologist."

"I'm sure she won't be that bad...?"

Molly couldn't keep the question out of her voice. Brooke

Berlin was the most mysterious variable in this entire scenario. Laurel had known nothing about her, and in the few short chats Molly had with Brick to discuss logistics, all he'd said was that Brooke asked for a sister for Christmas when she was eight.

"Her Wikipedia page was hilarious," Charmaine said. "But that had to be accidental."

"You mean, 'Brooke Ophelia Mayflower Berlin is the regal daughter of one of Hollywood's most cherished actor-directors, known throughout the city for her tiny ankles and tremendous talent'?" Molly recited from memory.

"You'd think anyone who allowed the Internet to say that about her would've thrown in a picture," Charmaine complained.

"I wish she had," Molly said. "She'd seem a lot less mysterious if I knew what she looked like."

"Maybe she has a dark secret," Charmaine said. "Like a disfiguring scar. Or a man face."

"She might turn out to be fun," Molly offered. "Anyone whose initials spell *bomb* has to be kind of entertaining, right?"

The girls giggled. Molly was hit by a wave of nostalgic, melancholy fondness for her friend. *Can you miss someone before you've even left them?* But Molly knew the answer. She'd started missing Laurel, in a hundred tiny ways, the day of her cancer diagnosis. Her eyes moistened.

"You'd better text me every day," Charmaine said. "What did people *do* in the Dark Ages before cell phones?"

"Forget cell phones. We'll need Skype," Molly said. "I'll be crying about whether it's social suicide to wear this."

She held up her favorite shirt, a tee with a hole in the collar that read "J. C. Mellencamp High School Cross-Country Hurts So Good."

Charmaine frowned, then shrugged. "Just pack it. Be yourself," she said. "Most of Lindsay Lohan's closet is way worse, anyway. Just try not to turn up on Perez Hilton with your bra showing through your top."

"I am not going to end up on Perez Hilton," Molly said.

Charmaine cocked an eyebrow.

"Oh, my God. Am I going to end up on Perez Hilton?" Molly gasped.

"The real question is whether he writes anything on your face."

Molly buried her head in a throw pillow.

"What am I doing?" She half laughed, half moaned. "My father is more famous than God! I'm going to have to start wearing *makeup*!"

"Don't forget tooth-whitening strips," Charmaine added.

"Do I have time to wax my forearms?"

"Yeah, and pick up some Restylane while you're at it. You're not truly a celebrity until you look like you've been punched in the mouth."

Still giggling, Molly giddily started dumping entire drawers full of shirts into her luggage. But eventually her attention wandered out the bedroom window, where, through the dusk, she saw a beat-up truck pull in across the street at the two-story clapboard house nearly identical to her own. A lanky boy leapt out, clutching a Big Gulp. He made a beeline for Molly's front door.

Charmaine joined Molly at the window. "Is it time?"

"It's time."

"Go," Charmaine said. "I'll…just start throwing all your random shit in boxes. You have so much stuff, I'm reporting you to *Hoarders*."

Molly left Charmaine alone in her garret bedroom and plodded down the narrow, curving stairs, her good mood evaporating. She wished *she* could do the packing and delegate this conversation to Charmaine. If only she were already in Hollywood, she could enlist a screenwriter's help to make sure she didn't botch it. This was so much more than saying good-bye to some boy. This was *Danny*. He'd been her savior during Laurel's chemo, bringing her mom Slurpees when they were all she could keep down, and hiding sunflowers where they'd surprise Molly just when she needed it most. They'd been together since their sandbox days, and the relationship was as comforting as the cardigan Laurel hung on the back of the chair in her sewing room. Molly was packing that sweater, but she had to find a way to leave Danny behind.

She wished she could ask Laurel what to do. Laurel always had advice. Sometimes the advice was weird—like the time she'd told Molly never to buy yellow underwear—but at least it was always worth pondering.

"How's the packing going?" Danny greeted her when

she opened the door. As always, Molly was struck by what a perfect, stereotypical swimmer he was—tall and lean, with an adorable grin, like he'd just leapt off the front of a Wheaties box.

"Charmaine's on it," she said.

"You know she's just throwing out all the stuff she thinks is ugly." He sat down on the front stoop and looked up at her. "Take a breath, Molls."

She closed the door and took a seat next to him. The concrete was warm through her cutoffs. "I am breathing. Sort of."

"We don't have to do it," he said, taking a slurp from his Big Gulp.

"Do what?"

"Have this whole weird good-bye talk. I don't want to have it."

His blue eyes met hers and then quickly flicked away.

"Denial," she said. "Interesting strategy."

"I think it could work," he said, running a hand through the strawberry blond thicket of hair she knew he'd shave off right before the first regional swim meet.

"Danny…" Molly began. "The last few months…I mean, did I even say thank you?"

"No need," Danny insisted. "You're my best friend. And I didn't do anything you wouldn't have done for me."

He slung a long arm over her shoulder. "Look, I know things haven't always been perfect. But we're Molly and Danny, you know? It's gonna be okay. We're always okay," he said. "Just remember, I love you like Homer Simpson loves beer."

"Like a mean kid loves dodgeball."

"Like a dog loves a fire hydrant."

This was their ritual. It could go on for as long as forty-five minutes, and once made Charmaine threaten to stab them both with a fork.

Danny leaned in and kissed her, his mouth warm and familiar and tasting ever so slightly of Dr Pepper. Behind them, in the house, Molly could hear Charmaine screech, followed by a loud crash.

Danny pulled away. "You'd better go rescue her."

"I don't know how to do this without you." Molly choked, feeling that familiar pricking sensation behind her eyes. At this rate Indiana would put a water conservation ban on her tear ducts.

Danny stood and pulled her to her feet. He kissed her once more, hard and fast on the mouth.

"Call me when you get to L.A.," he said.

"I will."

Danny dropped his arms. With one last look, he crossed her front lawn as quickly as he ever had.

Molly turned to go back inside and saw a sunflower poking out of the mail slot in the front door. She hadn't noticed it, didn't even know when he'd done it, but it was perfect and perfectly heartbreaking. She turned around to wave it at him, to clutch it to her chest and thank him, but Danny was already gone. Another ghost.

three

MOLLY SETTLED INTO the soothing buttery leather of
seat 3A and instantly understood all the fuss over flying
first class: It was like therapy without all the intrusive
questions.

Right now, Molly's particular ailment was nerves. Excessive ones. The chaos theory kind where a butterfly flaps its
wings in your stomach and it causes your ears to ring and
your left toe to swell up enough that your Converse don't
fit. Yesterday, she'd been excited; today, without Charmaine to distract her with jokes, the monumental signifi-
cance of this move was turning her brain to mush. She
needed soothing wherever she could find it, and being able
to recline fully with a container of warm nuts—and drink
Diet Coke out of a crystal glass—really did help a little.

"Going on vacation?" asked the aggressively mustachioed man sitting next to her.

"I'm going to visit my dad," Molly told him.

It sounded so profoundly *normal* coming out of her mouth. Natural, even, despite the fact that she'd gone sixteen years without saying anything remotely similar. The butterflies gave way briefly to a pleased warmth. She flipped open the magazines she'd purloined from Charmaine's stash. *People* showed Brick beaming as part of a story about him buying an alpaca farm for a costar who'd expressed a passing yearning to make sweaters, and he was in *Us*'s "Stars…They're Just Like Us!" section as someone who "loves sandwiches," illustrated by a grainy photo of Brick coming out of a Subway restaurant.

Away from the prying eyes of family and friends—who all seemed fixated on interpreting her body language as a way of gauging her emotional well-being—Molly stared intently at Brick and searched for something, anything, of herself. Charmaine said their eyes were the same. A shadow of Molly's dimple seemed visible on his cheek, and from his gym shorts Molly could tell they had the same runner's quads. She wondered if his hair stuck up in the back as much as hers did in the mornings, and if he also liked strawberry Pop-Tarts better than actual strawberries. Was he allergic to pomegranates, too?

The sheer force of her interest in the subject surprised her. Molly had never thought much about what it would be like to have a father. In fact, she'd never thought much about the one she'd believed she had. An orphaned college fling of Laurel's who'd died in Iraq before Molly was born, Army Captain Hank Walker had been a picture painted only with words, because, as Laurel used to say, Molly was the only memento he'd left behind (which of course made a whole lot of sense *now*, given Laurel's confession that he was actually an invention based on the novel she'd been reading when she went into labor). At first Molly had pressed for more details, but as she got older, Laurel's answers got more vague, and her expression increasingly sad and remote. So Molly stopped asking. And after a while, she stopped wondering. Aside from the odd curiosity brought on from watching the neighborhood dads play catch with their kids, Molly had never felt anything lacking in her life—especially because her grandmother Ginger had enough stern looks and abstinence lectures in her arsenal to raise sixty teenagers. But here was this big bear of a man, grinning broadly at the camera, seeming familiar to her in a way she'd never noticed before. It was tangible, breathing proof that her tastes, her eyebrow furrow, or the fact that her big toe always seemed twice as big as it should be had an origin outside Laurel's DNA.

Molly's eyes stung. Thinking about her mother was like slamming her hand in a car door: It hurt too much to consider doing it on purpose. She especially didn't want to dwell on how Laurel had almost chosen to die without telling Molly that her father was arguably the most famous movie star in the world. Focusing on *that* made Molly kind of angry at Laurel, and then she felt terrible for being angry, and then she resented feeling terrible....

The memory came anyway: Laurel setting aside her ever-present knitting needles and beckoning for Molly to sit next to her on the bed, her face almost lost beneath her favorite chemo turban. It was exactly thirty-two days before she took her last breath.

"I'm so sorry," she'd said as her opening gambit. "I lied. I'm selfish, and I lied. Here, I knitted you another scarf. It's green. I love you in green."

The story poured out of her mother like she'd turned on a faucet, and the scarf hadn't helped Molly absorb it any faster: how Laurel had fallen in love on set; how she'd discovered she was pregnant after the actor had married someone else; how she'd moved home and had Molly and then, impossibly, kept quiet about this whole incredibly dramatic series of events.

Afterward, Molly spent the entire night staring at her bedroom ceiling, trying to put herself in Laurel's place and wondering how it was possible that her free-spirited, bubbly mother, who never had a thought she didn't blurt out, could've spent the last sixteen years holding on to the most mammoth secret Molly could imagine. Her father was *Brick Berlin?* Whom she'd just seen on *Access Hollywood* talking about a fund-raiser for hearing-impaired dogs? How was it possible that one minute you could be giggling at someone for mispronouncing the words *cochlear implants*, and the next, be that person's daughter? And how could *anyone* refrain from sharing something that monumental, that crazy, at the first opportunity? Charmaine, for example, couldn't keep to herself what she spent on shirts at Forever 21, much less anything legitimately juicy.

"Molly, you have to understand that I truly thought this was for the best," Laurel had said, her wan face showing the strain. "I saw what Hollywood did to people. I didn't want to raise you in that world. And Brick *is* Hollywood."

"What does that even mean? Is he *evil*, or something?"

Laurel sighed. "Brick is not a bad person. I promise. Please don't blame him for this," she said. "He always wanted to be a part of your life. And he's always said you'd be welcome there when we were both ready."

"You've been talking to him?" Molly squawked.

Laurel covered her face with a thin hand.

"He calls to check up sometimes," she admitted. "I know I should have told you. I know I handled this about as wrong as a person can handle anything. But I was so tired of the showbiz rat race. I didn't think that would be much of a life for you, especially with his other family and something like three big film franchises to distract him. So I talked him into thinking you'd be better off with me in Indiana until...well, I don't know. Until the time was right. He didn't love the idea, but he agreed. For me." Her eyes misted. "And then somehow I guess the time never *was* right."

"You guys could've let me make that decision," Molly had pointed out.

"Yes. I could have. I *should* have. But I kept telling myself I was saving us both from something. I was young and I was an idiot. I know that's impossible to imagine." Laurel laughed without humor. "But he's your father. I wish I hadn't been so cavalier about ignoring that. I wish… well, I wish a lot of things. But mostly I wish I'd come clean sooner so this transition might've been easier for you."

Molly hated the word *transition*. Laurel used it countless times to describe what would happen after her death, like Molly was just switching lanes on the freeway.

In the end, Danny had been the one to remind Molly that she had a limited amount of time left with her mother, and that Laurel hadn't kept that secret out of malice. So Molly had laid down all her resentment and accepted the situation as well as she could, so their last months together wouldn't be any more terrible. But all that suppression left Molly feeling as if she'd grown a very nosy five-year-old inside her brain who refused to stop shouting: *How much does he know about me? Does he really want me? Or is he just doing this because he thinks he has to? Is that why I'm doing it, too?*

Deep down, she knew the last one wasn't true. Molly hadn't truly appreciated the intangible aspects of having a parent until she'd lost hers, so knowing there was one more of them out there felt an awful lot like a life raft. And Molly did think she detected sincere warmth in Brick's eyes. Having plowed through his essential filmography, Molly suspected Brick wasn't a good enough actor to fake friendliness that well during his off-hours—especially for the paparazzi. But it also seemed like ninety percent of celebrities came across as relaxed and stable, and then inevitably the *Enquirer* would unearth photos of them playing naked mini golf at the Playboy mansion with three call girls, a chocolate fountain, and a chimp.

What if he turns out to be crazy like that? Molly thought. *Wait, maybe I don't care, as long as he likes me. Oh, God, what if he doesn't like me? What if he thinks I'm this ridiculous, unsophisticated obligation and everyone at my new school thinks I'm totally lame, and I end up a miserable outcast in really old sneakers?*

Sometime in the last five minutes, Molly's thumbnail had found its way between her teeth, and she'd gnawed at it unconsciously until her hangnail began to bleed. She wiped it on the hot towel sitting next to her glass. She had to calm down or else she'd show up in Los Angeles with hands that belonged on a horror-movie poster. This was scary, but it was all going to be okay. It *had* to be. Laurel wouldn't have pushed this if she hadn't believed it would work out, and if Molly excluded the rather enormous lie regarding her parentage, Laurel had been a great mom. Besides, surely she wasn't going to lose her mother *and* get rejected by her father in the same three-month period. Wasn't that statistically improbable?

Molly decided to make the thrill of anticipation unseat her nervous energy. She closed the magazines and let out a shaky, cleansing breath that drew the attention of the flight attendant (everyone seemed to care way more about your feelings in first class).

"Would a chocolate chip cookie help?" the lady asked. "Fresh-baked."

See? The positive attitude was already working.

Molly's feet were on the ground barely fifteen minutes before her life took another Hollywood turn. A uniformed driver whose sign read MS. CHANANDALER BONG grabbed her at baggage claim and escorted her to a glossy Escalade with tinted windows—one of which was cracked enough for her to see a man wearing a deeply fake beard in the backseat.

"Sorry for the cloak-and-dagger stuff," the guy said, leaning out the window and peering at her over a pair of reading glasses with the lenses removed. "I didn't want the paparazzi to ruin this moment. Get in!"

Brick Berlin ripped off his chin fuzz with the gusto of a *Mission: Impossible* spy and threw open the door. His voice was every bit as deep and rich as it was in the movies—if it could have a flavor, it would be chocolate—and he looked exactly the same, right down to the unrealistic accessories.

Molly froze. When she'd pictured meeting Brick for the first time, she'd thrown herself into his arms (and Brick hadn't been wearing a beret). Instead, her legs abandoned her, so Brick scooted toward the edge of the seat and scooped her inside the car practically with one hand, while she did nothing but stare.

Hazel. Like hers. She *did* have his eyes.

As the driver slammed Molly's door shut, Brick hugged her so hard she felt a few ribs quit on her. He felt as densely muscular as he looked on film, and he smelled like spray tan and expensive cologne (definitely *not* Trick by Brick). Molly was torn between being touched and wondering if he was acting, since this was exactly what his character did in *Tequila Mockingbird* when he rescued his fiancée from South American sex slavery. It made the moment that much more surreal.

Brick pulled away and ruffled Molly's hair.

"You have Laurel's freckles," he told her. "Molly, I'm so sorry she's gone. She was a wonderful woman."

"It's okay," she said, her voice trembling. "I mean, thank you. I mean..."

"This is an emotional time for us all," Brick said kindly. "Cancer is a vicious thief."

He paused to let that sink in and then grabbed her face. "I've been waiting to meet you all your life, Molly. And now that you're here, I hate to look into those eyes and see an ounce of pain, sweet child of mine!"

Molly's heart skipped as she noticed she'd been right about their shared cheek dimple. She blinked back fresh, unexpected tears. Maybe it was the effect of being comforted by her father for the first time in her entire life, maybe it was that meeting a new parent reminded her of the one that was gone, or maybe it was the fact that he was gazing searchingly at her through fake Harry Potter glasses, giving him an air of permanent surprise. Probably, it was all three. Molly had gotten used to feeling every possible thing at once.

Brick gave her damp cheeks a firm pat.

"Let it out," he advised. "Tears are full of toxins. If you hold them in, they'll flood your brain."

Molly chuckled in spite of herself. Brick frowned and then took off his glasses.

"That does sound kind of ridiculous," he admitted with a grin. "My trainer told me that. But I'm sure it's true on a deeper level. I'll ask my hypnotherapist."

The driver started the car and pulled out of the parking garage, at which point twenty or so photographers descended upon the Escalade, yelling and shoving one another.

"Damn, I thought we'd lost them back on Sunset," Brick said, shaking his head. "This disguise sucks. I *told* Stan I should wear the headdress."

Molly had seen footage of paparazzi scrums on TV, but it was ten times scarier in person. A woman getting her hair pulled by a cameraman slammed against the window, begging Brick for "the goods." The guy closest to Molly, who couldn't have been much older than she was, wore a trucker cap that read PORN STAR IN TRAINING.

"Molly, open up," he shouted, jiggling the door handle.

Molly grabbed the nearest object she could find—which turned out to be an ice bucket—and tried to hide behind it.

"How do they know who I am?" she gasped.

"Well, here's the thing, Sunshine," Brick began. "There's going to be a tiny little story in *Hey!* about this. About you, I mean. Being my love child."

"What?"

Molly was reminded of the time she belly flopped off the high dive at the local pool: The wind was knocked out of her, and she thought she would drown. The entire student body of both her new *and* her old high school might read some sordid tabloid story about *her?* How was that even possible? She'd only been in Los Angeles fifteen minutes.

"I'm sorry," Brick said. "But fear not! It's not a smear job. Here's what already ran."

Molly scanned the crinkled magazine Brick handed her from his back pocket. The weird breathless feeling eased up when she realized the blurb didn't actually use her name.

"'Children, like protein shakes, are God's greatest present'?" she read, trying to sound cheerful. "I've never heard that one."

"Well, protein shakes are delicious," Brick said. "And they make you a better version of yourself."

Molly stared at him. "Okay," she said, after a beat. "But how did those guys know my name? It's not in this article."

"I almost forgot!" Brick evaded. "I brought you an ice-blended from the Coffee Bean!" He opened a mini cooler set into the console at his feet. "I got vanilla. Laurel loved vanilla."

42

Brick handed her the drink. Molly took it silently and cast another uneasy glance out the window as they crept along. A photographer was trying to climb up the trunk. The driver finally found a spot of open road and floored it toward the airport exit.

"Sunshine, this is just how it works around these parts," Brick said. "Everything gets out eventually, so we decided, hey, let's leak it on our terms. So I'm sure they know your name because of the party."

"What party?"

"Well. *That* is a long story," Brick said. "Why don't we talk about it when we get home?"

"Sure," Molly said, wanting to seem agreeable. She took a long sip of her drink and privately hoped a crippling brain freeze would shove her into a coma before that conversation, or the mysterious party, ever even happened. Suddenly, it seemed awfully naive to think she could drop into her world-famous father's life without anybody caring but him. As if to underline the point, they passed a building bearing a giant poster from Brick's latest movie that read BRICK. BRUCE. BEYONCÉ. *BERGERAC.* The shoot-'em-up remake of *Cyrano* made $98 million its first weekend. Molly and Charmaine had seen it twice. For research. Obviously.

"Oops, almost time for *E! News,*" Brick said.

He clicked on the TV in the back of the limo and cranked up the volume. In what Molly found was a welcome and pressure-free silence—she could let her emotions settle down a notch—they watched a story about Ed Westwick shaving his head to play Howie Mandel in a biopic called *No Deal,* and then a piece about Chris Pine hurting his hamstring doing a stunt for the next *Star Trek.*

"Oh, no," gasped Brick. "He can't play the second lead in *Avalanche!* if he can't climb!"

Brick whipped out his BlackBerry, then boomed frenzied instructions at whatever poor sap from his office was unlucky enough to have answered his call. So she wouldn't sit there and just stare dumbly at her father, Molly gazed out the window. It was a relief to see L.A. had McDonald's and Starbucks and supermarkets and crappy bumper sticker–covered cars, just like West Cairo. But it also had a brilliant azure sky unmolested by anything except sky-high palm trees ruffling in a gentle breeze—so Californian that it almost seemed fake—and about ten tons more traffic. It was 2 p.m. on a Monday. Didn't anybody have a job? Where were all these people *going?*

After about an hour, during which Brick made four more phone calls and arranged to send a ham to Chris Pine, the car exited onto Sunset Boulevard. The concrete jungle vanished, replaced by a winding, tree-lined road dotted with palatial houses lined up like beads in a necklace, broken only by UCLA's redbrick campus. Eventually, the Escalade pulled up to a huge set of wrought-iron gates set between two tiled outbuildings, one of which was marked in cursive with the words *Bel Air.* A man inside the security kiosk waved them through with a smile.

"Almost home," Brick chirped, stowing his phone back in his pocket. "Look, that's the country club. Maybe I should send *them* a ham. They think I use my phone on the golf course too often. Crazy!"

The car began its climb up a curving road. Molly hadn't realized the term *Hollywood Hills* was actually *descriptive* — for some reason, in her mind, the city was all sand and blazing heat bouncing off flat pavement. But Bel Air was lush and green and rolling.

"That's where the crown prince of Saudi Arabia used to live," Brick said, pointing at yet another gate, behind which was a driveway so long Molly couldn't see the house at the end of it. Her nosy days of staring out her bedroom window at the neighbors across the street were probably over, which was a shame, as these neighbors were doubtless way more interesting. No offense to Danny.

"That guy threw the craziest parties," Brick said wistfully. "But my pool is nicer."

They pulled up to an ivy-covered brick wall and robust fuchsia bougainvillea bushes. The gate swung open to reveal a gravel driveway running through a tunnel of trees and across a green and perfect lawn, up to a white house larger than Molly's high school in Indiana. As they parked, someone wearing a gray workman's jumpsuit hurried past toward a spherical chrome-and-glass greenhouse that looked suspiciously like the bad guy's laboratory in *Rad Man*.

Whoa, Molly thought. This place was no house. It wasn't even a mansion. It embarrassed mansions.

Brick hopped out and opened Molly's door with a flourish. "Welcome to Casa Berlin!"

Molly slowly climbed out of the car, making the most of this first chance to take in all of her father in one go. Divested of his disguise, Brick was even better-looking than he was on-screen: well north of six feet tall, with thick red-brown hair and familiar hazel eyes surrounded by long lashes Molly wished she'd inherited. They crinkled warmly at the edges when he smiled, like the kind of candy wrapper his muscles suggested he hadn't actually untwisted in years. He also had the whitest teeth Molly had ever seen.

I am Brick Berlin's daughter. Somehow, standing right in front of him, it was both easier and harder to believe than when she was back in Indiana.

Molly followed Brick up the steps, through a midnight blue front door with a snarling half-man, half-lion doorknocker, and into a marble foyer flanked by two identical wide, curving staircases, meeting underneath a crystal chandelier. It made her feel very small. She had joked to Charmaine that her first seconds in the Berlin house would play out like in *Annie*, when Daddy Warbucks's staff bursts into song and dance upon her arrival. Molly now had to admit a little choreographed welcome sounded much more appealing than the echo of footsteps on chilly marble.

The driver lugged in her bags and disappeared up the left flight of stairs. Molly started to follow him, but Brick stopped her.

"You'll have time for the tour later," he promised. "First, your sister is really excited to meet you."

For the next ten minutes, Molly trailed after Brick through room after empty room. They wandered through an enormous kitchen (where Brooke was not, as Brick had hypothesized, baking flaxseed muffins), the plush screening room (where Brooke was not watching *Diaper Andy*), and Brick's gym (where Brooke was not doing squat thrusts), only to end up back in the cavernous foyer.

"I can't believe this!" Brick said. "She swore she was going to be here."

"It's okay. Something probably came up," Molly said, to allay his distress. "We have ages to get to know each other. I'm not going anywhere."

This brightened Brick, who actually clasped his hands together with glee.

"That is true!" he said. "And this way, we can have some private bonding time. I want to hear everything that's ever happened to you."

He was slinging a beefy arm around Molly when she felt something in his pocket buzz. Brick disengaged and pulled out his phone.

"Tell me you have good news, Mitch," he said. "What? No, we can't shoot in Key West. The movie is called *Avalanche!*"

Molly took a seat on the staircase and watched as Brick walked in ever-tighter circles.

"There are no polar bears at large in Key West," Brick shouted. "That will ruin the last half hour. Do not call me back about this."

He hung up with a dispirited punch to the phone.

"Sorry about that," he said, turning to Molly. "My lead actor is a *yutz* and so is his manager. I mean, we can't do it without polar bears. White fur is the apex of fear. Everyone knows that."

"And it's probably hard to find mountains off the coast of Florida," Molly attempted, sensing the situation demanded sympathy even though she felt a bit out of her league in this conversation.

Brick frowned. "My God, you're right. This will not stand. I don't care how much he spent on his bungalow. Just give me a minute to call him back."

He scuttled down the hallway, leaving Molly totally alone. She paused and rubbed her forehead, vainly hoping that would help make sense of what just transpired. This day was getting more surreal with every moment that passed, and it made her want to lie down for a second. She assumed the driver had gone in the general direction of her room—so, upward—but Brick said he'd be right back. Should she just sit there and wait?

The air conditioner whooshed on right over her head. Molly broke out into goose pimples.

"Home sweet home," she whispered to the cold and empty room.

four

TWENTY MINUTES AFTER BRICK DISAPPEARED, Molly cursed herself for sucking down that coffee drink in the car with such abandon. Now she was stuck in a stark white entryway with nothing to distract her from her screaming bladder but a potted ficus, an elaborately carved antique table (whose sole purpose was holding a perfectly centered bowl of mint green Tic Tacs), and a midsize knockoff of Michelangelo's *David* near where the two staircases met—which seemed less like the taste of a single action hero and more like the decision of an interior designer who hoped he'd find it a flattering comparison and invite her to move into his pool house.

She felt rude going rogue to find a bathroom but decided Brick probably wouldn't mind, so Molly hopped up and tiptoed around the room. A house this big ought to have tasteful wall-mounted placards with arrows pointing to the ladies' room, like a hotel lobby. After a few dead-end peeks through open doorjambs, Molly noticed the faint outline of a knobless door to the left of the Tic Tac table — the kind of thing that matched the molding so perfectly you could barely tell it was there. Molly had seen doors like these only in the movies, so it was almost logical that she'd encounter one here. She smacked it with her palm, and the ease with which it sprang open almost knocked her off her feet.

It wasn't a bathroom, but it was arguably even better: The closet was the size of her living room back home, and teemed with sporting goods — two snowboards, a jai alai basket, three tennis rackets, an archer's bow and arrows, surfboards, what looked like a polo mallet, and a fishing pole with a tag still hanging from it. The right hanging bar was stuffed with women's coats of every color and fabric imaginable, including fur, while the left featured twenty-five versions of what looked like the exact same black jacket. Molly whipped out her cell phone and snapped a photograph. Charmaine was going to love this.

"Documenting your new home?" a voice asked behind her.

Molly whirled around and came face-to-face with a bespectacled guy holding a clipboard and sporting more scruff on his chin than on his entire head. She held her breath. Snooping through the closets before she'd even unpacked probably didn't make her look very good.

"Don't worry," he said, his eyes twinkling behind round wire-framed glasses. "I've worked here for seventeen years and every day I see something I want to photograph, just to prove that it happened."

He stuck out his hand. "I'm Stan, Brick's assistant and expert orderer of custom-made black coats for every temperature between fifty-two and seventy-six."

Molly broke into a relieved smile. "Back home, fifty-two can feel downright balmy."

"Give it a couple of years." Stan grinned back. "We'll make you a thin-blooded California girl in no time. Come on, let's get you settled. I bet your friends in Indiana are going to be way more interested in your new room than the coat closet, anyway."

Molly grabbed her backpack and trailed Stan up two flights of marble stairs to the top floor. He was not the kind of person she'd imagined would work for Brick. She'd pictured an aggressive twentysomething wannabe drinking smoothies in borrowed Louboutins; Stan was middle-aged, lean with a slight potbelly, and wore a thumb ring. He was a turtleneck and a clove cigarette away from reading poetry at open mike night in a coffeehouse. Still, he seemed smart and genial—the perfect concierge.

When they alighted on the third floor, a sunbeam from the domed skylight hit Molly in the face with such bright force that she reflexively pushed her sunglasses down from the top of her head onto her nose. Apparently, she was going to need to wear SPF even inside the house. To her right, past the mouth of the other staircase — was one for up, and one for down? — was a door with a large velvet "B" hanging from the knob.

"Welcome home," Stan said, leading Molly to an unmonogrammed door across the way and ushering her inside.

The vastness of this room, *her* room, was so great that Molly almost tripped on the carpet fibers in her hurry to digest it all. Everywhere she turned, there was something to admire: In the corner, a well-stuffed chair sat by a fully stocked bookcase; a flat-screen TV hung over the desk, which had a shiny red laptop on it; across from the bed was a vast fireplace, presumably for those brisk fifty-two-degree nights. Ahead of her, French doors led to a balcony overlooking a flourishing rose garden, and to her left, yet more sunshine spilled onto a mahogany four-poster bed outfitted with a cream linen canopy and illuminated what looked like a spa-quality bathroom (and thank God for *that*, since Molly's bladder wasn't quite as enchanted as she was). It was a dream room, the kind of place she'd only ever seen sit empty in the pages of a catalog, inviting you to find happiness by spending two grand on throw pillows and chalkboard paint. Molly wished Laurel were there to see it. *Of course, if Mom were alive, I wouldn't even be here to see it.*

"There's a linen cupboard in the bathroom and a mini fridge in the closet," Stan said, ticking off items on his clipboard. "Dinner is at six thirty sharp because Brick doesn't like to metabolize anything after seven. If you run out of towels, soda, snacks, term paper ideas, whatever, this is the household intercom. Push one for me, two for the cook, three for housekeeping. Double-oh-seven buzzes Brick's study, but he never hears it, so don't even bother. Brooke doesn't have a code. She said it's demeaning."

Molly cracked a tiny smile. "I can't wait to meet her," she said. "Is she home yet?"

"Nope. She said something about a fashion emergency and ran out of here about an hour ago," Stan said. "From experience, I know those can take anywhere from five minutes to five days. Now, is there anything else I can do for you? Any questions, concerns, dietary restrictions, conscientious objections?"

"I think I'm all good, for now," Molly said. Stan's briefing had been so thorough, she wondered if she was meant to tip him.

"All righty. Settle in, unpack, take some photos," Stan winked. "From the balcony, if you look left, you can see half of the tennis court. And if you stare really, really hard at the right side tree line, you'll see Britney's roof. Honest to God."

Stan began to close the door but stuck his head back in the room at the last minute. "Brick is really happy you're here," he said. "I know sometimes he's a little larger than life, but he means everything he says. He's been looking forward to this ever since you called."

Molly blushed a bit and stared down at the floor. "I'm glad I'm here, too," she said.

"Also, Molly... *Rad Man* was my first job with Brick, so I

knew your mom," Stan said, his tone dropping a notch. "Laurel was one of the coolest people I've ever met."

Molly's throat tightened.

"And you should also know that Brick adored her," he continued. "I saw it myself. She wasn't just some random woman to him. It was real."

Molly stood there in silence for a moment, trying to come up with the words to express how tremendous it was to hear that.

"Thanks, Stan," was all she could manage.

Stan smiled at her with supreme understanding, then shut the door and left Molly alone in her new kingdom. She swallowed a few times, hard, to regain her composure. Her heart wanted to call Danny or Charmaine, her head wanted to busy itself with unpacking, her body wanted to go jump in the pool, and her bladder...well.

This is too good to be true, she thought a few minutes later as she ran her hand along the edge of the giant Jacuzzi bathtub. Even the walk-in, beige-tiled, glass-walled shower had four jets in the walls aimed at all angles and a large shelf stocked with about twenty different Kiehl's products.

Her suitcases had already been wheeled into the walk-in closet, but before getting to work, Molly decided to follow Stan's advice and head out to her balcony. The air smelled faintly of jasmine, and her terrace was so large it contained two chairs, a glass-topped table, and a chaise longue. In the distance, she could indeed see red Spanish tile, and she wondered if Britney was under it somewhere doing the "Baby, One More Time" dance that Molly and Charmaine had tried (and failed) to master back in elementary school.

Molly pulled out her phone and took a picture, then texted it to Charmaine with a note that read,

GUESS WHO MY NEW NEIGHBOR IS? HINT: SHE'S TOXIC.

The reply came back two seconds later:

!!!!!!

Molly had to agree: Brick seemed nice, Stan was cool, this house was a palace, and it was August and there wasn't even a hint of humidity in the air. Okay, so she hadn't met the mysterious Brooke yet, but as Molly closed her eyes and let the fragrant breeze play on her face, even that didn't feel like a problem. It turned out optimism was pretty easy to muster on her own private balcony overlooking a peaceful Southern Californian paradise. She'd waited this long to find out about Brooke Berlin; it wouldn't kill her to wait a little longer.

"So then I said to Wolfie, 'I think the Puck stops here!'"

Silence.

"The Puck!" Brick repeated. "Get it?"

Molly realized too late that this was Brick's punch line. She wasn't surprised that, based on his résumé, he was better at landing *actual* punches.

"That's hilarious!" she mustered. "Um, I love Wolfgang Puck's frozen pizza."

"He lives up the street. This steak is from his restaurant, you know," Brick said proudly. "And my cook did the sushi. He used to be an Iron Chef." He shot her a sheepish smile. "I wasn't sure what you'd like."

Molly gazed at the juicy filets mignons and beautiful, precisely wrapped sushi rolls on the plates before them. She was starving. But the food sat untouched. Molly's eyes flicked up to the empty seat across the dining table and wondered which was eating at her more: hunger or curiosity.

"I'm going to call her," Brick said, frowning at his watch.

Molly's good mood from earlier had devolved back into nerves. She'd sworn she would greet Brooke with a relaxed and positive attitude, no matter what, but that vow was a lot easier to make when their meeting was just an abstraction. In the two hours since Molly's arrival, which she'd spent putting approximately one shirt in each of the zillion drawers in her walk-in closet and watching a marathon of *Teen Cribs*, Brooke's continued absence became a silence that was very loud indeed. Brick seemed so anxious about it that Molly wondered if she should be offended by the vanishing act.

Suddenly, the echo of a large door slamming reverberated through to where they sat.

"That must be her now," Brick said, relieved.

"Sorry, Daddy!" a voice floated in from the foyer. "Ari had a Prada emergency."

Brisk footsteps clacked closer and closer toward the dining room door. Molly sat on her hands to keep from chewing her fingernails. Despite her best efforts, her foot, which had begun bouncing manically five minutes ago, would not stay still. She forced herself to make eye contact with the threshold Brooke Berlin was about to cross, and, for the second time that day, felt goose bumps push up through her skin.

Here we go, she thought.

five

"YOU MUST BE MY NEW SISTER!"

A tall blonde with bouncing curls glided into the dining room, bringing with her the shortest skirt, longest legs, and tallest stilettos Molly had ever seen. It was Brooke Berlin in the flesh, and showing off rather a lot of it.

"I'm so happy to meet you!" Brooke squealed, hugging her before Molly even had a chance to get out of her seat. "Welcome to our wonderful home!"

Brooke had her clasped so tight, she was practically lifting Molly out of her chair. Molly, taken aback, breathed in sharply and almost inhaled a chunk of Brooke's hair.

"Brookie, it's not polite to be this late," Brick scolded.

"I know, Daddy, but Ari's wardrobe malfunction wasn't going to fix itself. I'm *super* sorry!"

Brooke dropped Molly and sailed over to her seat, shaking out her napkin with the wide smile that her suspiciously fawning Wikipedia page called "a beacon of hope for our future." Molly tried not to stare, but it was difficult: Brooke may not have been truly beautiful, but she was so well groomed that you'd never notice. The dress was designer, the eyelashes were false, the hair was either abundantly natural or expensively synthetic, and the purse she'd brought to the table was a Chloé bag Molly knew wasn't on sale yet to the great unwashed masses. Molly glanced at her own comfy hoodie and kicked herself for treating this like just another movie night with Charmaine.

"I can't believe you're really here! This is amazing! So tell me everything!" Brooke said in a mad rush of exclamatory speech. "When did you get here! How was the flight! How do you like your room! Isn't the view amazing! Your sweatshirt is fantastic! Isn't it fantastic, Daddy! So authentic! We are so glad you're here!"

"Um, thanks," Molly said, still shell-shocked by this perky onslaught, and unsure which of Brooke's statements were actual questions she was supposed to tackle. None of her varied and dramatic imaginings of Brooke included an attitude this, well, *nice*. "I'm really happy to be—"

"You are *so* welcome!" Brooke twittered. "Recognize my dress, Daddy?"

"Rodarte, right?" Molly offered, relieved to have something to contribute to this dinner after all. "*Vogue* loved that season's collection."

Brooke looked as surprised as if her tan had fallen off. "You read *Vogue*? Seriously?"

"I caught up on the flight," Molly said. "It was a long trip from Indiana."

"Look at you two. Bonding already," Brick said fondly, and bit into a giant piece of steak.

"It's like a dream!" Brooke bubbled, shooting Molly a blinding, toothy grin as she stabbed at a piece of yellowtail with the crystal-encrusted chopsticks on her plate.

"So how'd you get a fresh Rodarte like that?" Molly pressed on, encouraged by Brooke's smile. "Do you know the Mulleavys? I just read that they're from somewhere around here."

Brooke's laugh was the sound of a tiny bell on a store-front door. "So much to learn! They're in Pasadena. That's a whole other area code!"

"I met them at Fashion Week when I was doing a movie with Juliette Lewis," Brick explained. "They sent her a bunch of stuff, but this one was too big for her."

Brooke flared her nostrils. "More like, it's far too stylish for someone who wears curtains on her head."

"How *is* Fashion Week?" Molly wondered. "I've always wanted to go."

"Daddy won't let me, because—"

"Well, we'll just have to see what we can do about that!" Brick boomed at the same time, adding a dorky wink. "I bet we can talk your school into calling it extra credit."

Brooke slammed down the soy sauce with a tad too

much vigor. Molly chanced a long glance at her. Brooke's enthusiastic welcome was an extremely pleasant surprise, but Molly had read enough articles by the *Hey!* body language experts to recognize tension when she saw it. Brooke beamed at her again, though, so Molly decided to believe that whatever was making her half sister so squirrelly had nothing to do with her arrival.

"I guess Fashion Week might be a little intense, right?" Molly asked to fill the silence. "Today in the car with all those photographers was bad enough, and that was behind a window."

"Oh, you got papped?" Brooke said with sympathy. "Isn't it so inconsiderate? I mean, what if you'd had airplane spinach in your teeth? Daddy, I can't believe you let that happen to my sister."

"They're doing *My Fair Lady* at school this year, Molly," Brick said, ignoring Brooke completely. "What are your feelings about theater?"

"I used to help my mom make the costumes for our school plays, but I can't act at all," Molly said. "Guess I got her genes."

Yikes. It was probably too soon for DNA jokes. Molly shoved a piece of meat into her mouth so that she couldn't talk again for a while.

"Costumes are fantastic! So important," Brick boomed. "An actor is naked without his clothes."

"Don't change the subject, Daddy," Brooke said, her voice pure saccharine. "Don't you think it was rude of you to expose Molly to all those photographers before Saturday? She needs to be *prepared* for that kind of crazy frenzy."

Molly swallowed hard. "So what *is* happening on Saturday, exactly?" she asked.

"Only the biggest social event of your life. Let's see, we'll have the entire junior and senior classes, some industry people, and a bunch of photographers that we invited to help celebrate my sixteenth birthday." Brooke beamed. "Daddy spared no expense. He even got Fall Out Boy."

"I spared *some* expense. She asked for Coldplay."

"*Anyway*," Brooke plowed ahead. "There's an interview with *Hey!*, and everyone will be staring and taking pictures and watching everything we're doing all night long. It's kind of like being on the biggest stage imaginable."

Molly almost dropped her fork. "An *interview?*"

Charmaine would faint with joy at the idea, but Molly just wanted to faint, period. No wonder Brick hadn't wanted to lay this on her in the car. He hadn't wanted to freak her out in a confined space.

Brooke reached across the table and squeezed Molly's hand, which was slightly awkward because Brooke had to pry loose Molly's fingers from her water glass to make good on her gesture.

"Molly, if you're not ready for this, maybe it's unfair of us to ask you to come," Brooke said, her voice oozing concern.

"Nonsense! She'll be fine!" Brick insisted. "It's just a few snapshots and a quick chat with a reporter. No big deal! I was going to tell you all about it after dinner."

"Daddy, if she's not ready to be quoted in a major national magazine that's read by millions of people who will be dying to see what she's wearing, we shouldn't push," Brooke scolded, releasing Molly's hand so she could gesture wildly with her own.

"Um, well, except it's kind of not that simple," Brick hedged. "*Hey!* is sort of insisting. I guess we got a little overzealous trying to get in front of the story. Trip Kendall loved it so much, he told me that unless he gets an exclusive on Molly, he's nixing the whole thing and writing a piece about how Laurel died poor in a shanty."

Molly gasped. "But that's a lie!"

"Trip is ruthless, which is why he runs the best tabloid in town," Brick explained. "I was worried he'd exploit you unless I gave him access, and now…I can't afford to sue him with *Avalanche!* coming out next year."

Molly felt sick to her stomach. She didn't want to be interviewed by any magazine, especially not one that would take advantage of her mother's death. How had she not seen any of this coming?

Brick sighed. "Molly, I'm sorry. This is why I don't usually deal with these bastards. When it comes right down to it, I'd love to show you off to the world and give you a chance to say great things about Laurel. But Brooke is right—it's a lot to ask. So all you need to do is say the word and I will cancel this entire thing."

"The entire thing? Like, the whole party?" Brooke all but shrieked.

"The whole party," Brick confirmed. "It's just not worth it if my daughter is basting in the juices of her own agony."

Looking impressed with himself, Brick pulled out his BlackBerry again and started typing.

"Daddy, don't be so melodramatic," Brooke snapped. "All I meant about Molly being unprepared is that it was mean of you not to tell her sooner. But she seems, um, smart, and I bet we could whip her into shape in no time."

"We?" Molly asked. She felt numb.

"Of course! You don't think I'd let Daddy send you out there unprepared, do you?" Brooke chirped, her tone so cheerful it could sell tampons to a priest. "It's what sisters are for!"

"Well, that is what every father wants to hear!" Brick brightened. "It would be so wonderful to see the fruit of my loins come together in the same bowl."

"Trust me. Just do everything I tell you, okay?" Brooke cooed supportively. "You'll look fantastic, you'll sound fantastic, and it'll all be over in a flash. Everybody wins," she said, pausing and then dropping her voice into a very somber tone. "Especially your mother, Molly."

Molly looked up at Brick. Obviously, this story meant a lot to him, and Brooke was practically foaming at the mouth to help. And Molly hated the idea of the rest of America getting the wrong idea about Laurel. If there was one thing worth being brave for, it was her mother.

"You're right," Molly said finally, nodding. "I'll do it."

"Really?" Brick asked.

"If it'll keep them from saying nasty things about my mom, then yeah."

"That's my girl!" Brick crowed. "It is very touching of you, Molly, to agree to this. In fact, it is a portrait of self-lessness." He paused his fork in midair. "That would be a fantastic title for a book about all this," he mused.

Molly smiled tentatively at him, then switched her gaze to Brooke, who was radiating warmth. Okay, so maybe she seemed like she'd had one too many espressos. But after Molly had spent all this time fretting about the very concept of Brooke Berlin, it was ironic that Brooke Berlin might be the one person who wanted to help her get through this.

"Just leave it to me," Brooke said, and smiled wide.

✦   ✦   ✦

"And *then* what happened?"

Brooke paused before answering, aware she had her friend on tenterhooks and needing to swap the phone to her other side. She'd read in *Allure* that frequent ear-switching prevented oil buildup in her pores, and zits just wouldn't do if The Intruder insisted upon taking photos of her glamorous new family to send to all her monochromatic friends in the cornfields.

"Then I offered to be her best friend, of course. What's

that old saying? Keep your friends close but your enemies closer?"

Jennifer Parker was quiet for a second. "Wait, my agent told me it was 'enemas.' She is *so* fired. That was a *horrible* day. You should have seen the hose that they…"

"*Anyway*," Brooke interjected.

"Right, right. So, tell me everything. Is there acne? Does she smell like the inside of a barn?"

"Well…no," Brooke admitted. That had been the most offensive part. A hideous she-beast might've been easier to handle, but instead Princess Podunk was resoundingly *fine*—no missing teeth, no nose hair, not even a monobrow to stoke the superiority complex Brooke had assumed would nurse her through this entire catastrophe.

"But you should've seen the sweatshirt she had on— like she just tipped the cow herself," Brooke snarked. "And her bangs! So halfhearted."

"The worst kind," Jennifer whispered. "You are so brave, Brooke. If Brick only understood the sacrifice you're making."

"He's too busy grinning like an idiot. It all makes me want to puke."

"Do it if you have to, but don't force it," Jennifer warned. "When I was in that after-school special, my character used wooden spoon handles and got splinters in her throat. That can be very uncomfortable."

Brooke rolled her eyes. There was no response to Jennifer's advice sometimes.

"I just can't believe your dad is putting you through this," her friend continued. "A secret love child...if it weren't so awful it would almost be romantic!"

"Are you serious? He's turning this house into a freaking cable movie."

"Cable movies are an excellent way for an actress to hone her instrument," Jennifer said, reciting a line Brooke knew her father had fed her years ago after her Disney sitcom got canceled. "Actually, this is all kind of like *A Pocketful of Danger*."

"Is that the one where the dude from *CSI* kidnaps you?"

"Duh, no. It's the one where Susan Lucci plays my mom, and someone tries to kill us right around the time her four illegitimate children turn up."

"You think this chick is going to try and kill me?" Brooke made a mental note to lock her shoe closet. Some of her stilettos could be deadly in psychotic Midwestern hands.

"Probably not, although I guess you might want to build up immunity to arsenic, in case she's seen my movie." A hopeful note crept into Jennifer's voice. "*Do* you think she's seen my movie?"

"That was a terrible movie," Brooke said absently. "Um, except for your part."

"Oooh, or maybe you could do what my character's brother did in *Pain River*, when..."

"Jen, this is serious. It's not something your IMDb page can fix," Brooke snapped.

There was an audible gasp, which Brooke chose to ignore in favor of keeping things on her favorite subject: herself.

"I just don't trust this person," she continued. "The girl obviously hasn't had a manicure in weeks. Nobody is that *regular*."

"So you think the tragic dead mom is a scam?" Jennifer asked, her interest in melodrama overpowering the perceived insult to her résumé.

"Not really. But look how far Daddy's pity has gotten her. She has to be up to *something* and I bet she won't stop at crashing my party."

"So what now?"

"I have a plan. Don't I always?"

"You *are* an evil genius," Jennifer agreed.

"Right? If only that were a section on the SATs." Brooke sighed. "Okay, I have to run; I think the stress of dinner gave me crow's feet that I should moisturize."

"Stay strong," Jennifer urged.

Brooke hung up the phone and threw it onto the pile of gossip magazines that sat on her floor. Brick's face grinned up at her from the corner of one of the covers. She kicked at his expensively whitened mouth, creasing his incisors.

"Take that, Sperminator," she muttered.

She'd exaggerated her confidence with Jennifer. It had taken considerable effort to be friendly to Molly at dinner, and Brooke wasn't sure how long she could maintain the facade, even for Brick's benefit. Sooner or later, lines had to be drawn. This was Brooke's domain and she refused to cede territory to a dusty visitor from Planet Yawn.

Brooke needed to recharge, which meant spending some

quality time in her sanctuary: her walk-in closet. She perched on the velvet stool next to her vanity and stared at the racks of designer dresses, gleaming pumps, and towers of archived shoe boxes. Bliss. She caught her own eye in the nearest of her four full-length mirrors and cocked her head. Usually, Brooke loved what she saw: tall, thin, naturally golden blonde. Being her mother's clone had definite perks. But it hadn't escaped her that Molly seemed to share Brick's athletic build, bits of his smile, maybe even his hair color. No matter how long Brooke studied herself, she couldn't find any trace of Brick except that they used the same shade of bronzer. Her prickles of resentment became full-on stabbing pains.

She shook her head. Negative thoughts wouldn't do. She had to focus. If Brooke played these next few days right, her graceful, generous attitude would have Brick and Molly so thoroughly in the palm of her hand that they wouldn't notice the knife in her other fist.

Buoyed, Brooke fluffed her hair and allowed herself to smile. She could do this. After all, she was Brooke Berlin, dammit. She was an actress—no, an Actress, capital A— and she *would* nail this role.

SIX

"HEAVEN. Heaven."

"Seriously, this one is, like, a religious experience."

"I totally just saw God. I'm not even kidding."

Molly wished she could see what the three willowy stylists buzzing around her were talking about, but their light-speed tugging and pulling and tweaking—not to mention their enthusiastic spiritual visions, and the accompanying wild skyward gestures—made it impossible to get a glimpse of herself in the mirror. How did such scrawny women have so much energy? Obviously that half-consumed case of Red Bull in the corner had been put to good use.

"Let me see!" Brooke chirped from a couch across the room. "I bet this is the one!"

Molly returned her sister's smile. From the feel of the

skintight bandage dress crisscrossing her hips, Molly wasn't entirely sure she shared Brooke's optimism, but she was having too much fun to care. Never in all her years of reading her mother's *Vogue* had Molly imagined she'd get within sniffing distance of designer clothes. Yet here she was, just three days into her L.A. life, with a pile of garments at her feet worth more than Laurel had spent on her car.

She had Brooke to thank, just one in a string of surprising, generous acts that had wallpapered each of the days since Molly arrived. She'd been in Brooke's sole custody pretty much since that first dinner—Brick was MIA, thanks to calls from his manager, the studio, his agent, or in one case, a producer who wanted to turn *Avalanche!* into a Western—and Brooke had clearly taken to heart her task of getting Molly ready for the party. She'd insisted on making Molly practice walking in heels, giving critiques as if they were on *America's Next Top Model*. She'd chattered at length about what *Hey!* might ask—though Molly hoped her primer on tensions in the Middle East would turn out to be unnecessary—and she'd loaned Molly three different conditioners that she swore would help fight frizz.

Then there was the constant stream of cold Diet Cokes, the breathless tutorials on which colon cleanse would cause Molly to hallucinate the least, and, of course, today's styling session to prep them for the party. The attention was occasionally suffocating, but also honestly touching. For all the time Molly had spent recently thinking about having a father for the first time, she'd only considered Brooke as a sister in the most literal, bare-bones sense of the word. Now, she couldn't imagine L.A. without her. It was such a warm and welcoming relief to be taken under her wing and treated immediately like family.

Not to mention the wish-fulfillment aspect of being whipped in and out of high-fashion dresses by three tiny elves in matching skinny jeans, working just for her, and moving in such a blur Molly could barely make out their faces, much less remember their names. She referred to them in her head as Bangs, Boobs, and Botox—the latter because no matter how much she panted that an outfit was better than fist-bumping God Himself (a compliment that seemed diminished once Molly saw the jumpsuit that had spawned it), Botox's face remained a serene blank. She didn't even wince when Boobs dropped a platter of gluten-free bagels and vegan cream cheese all over a rack of Monique Lhuillier dresses, although she did spew such a creative string of expletives that Molly suspected the only reason Botox was acquainted with God in the first place was because He had popped down to warn her to watch her mouth.

"This is the exact Leger we put on Katie Heigl last week," Botox now droned, shoving Molly at a mirror.

"You'll *die*," added Bangs, stepping backward to grab her Marlboro from a nearby ashtray and sucking on it feverishly.

Molly was more afraid one of the three Bs would keel over from stress. It had been three hours and a million dresses since Stan dropped them off, and Molly still hadn't found the right one. No matter how many times she told the stylists that she wasn't comfortable in anything super tight, they trotted out ever-snugger cocktail frocks. Brooke, ceaselessly optimistic, shouted out encouraging compliments every time Molly shuffled toward a mirror (her last: "a zaftig glory"). This hot pink bandage dress was no exception.

"You look just like Kim Kardashian!" Brooke crowed.

"You think?" Molly said, scrutinizing her rear end. "I don't know. Does the camera really add ten pounds?"

"Asses are totally in right now!" Bangs drooled, picking at her overlong chestnut fringe.

"You look like ten pounds of sexy in a five-pound bag of awesome!" Boobs trilled.

"I can't move my legs," Molly said apologetically.

She felt terrible rejecting everything—it took an awful lot of strength not to fall in love with the name on the label—but she'd be hyperventilating enough at this party without her dress cutting off her air supply.

"No, she's right," Botox piped up unexpectedly. "Her butt cheeks look like two balloons fighting. Get her out of it."

Botox reclined on a brushed-metal chaise near the terrace doors, deep in thought, massaging her skull through her plum-colored pixie cut. This was her company and her house, an art deco bungalow off Wilshire in what Brooke called "the museum district," despite being unable to name which museums, exactly, were nearby. Its impeccably lit living room, a combination of smartly placed wall sconces and natural light, was full of racks of clothes, glossy foreign magazines, shoes spilling out of Barneys bags, framed photos of famous clients, and barely any furniture. What *was* there was so minimalist, it could not have been comfortable. Nor cheap.

"I'm getting the sense you don't want something snug," Botox concluded after her meditation. "Brooke, you should have told me she wasn't a sample size. Shitballs. Not you," she caught herself, waving in Molly's direction. "I just need to think."

Boobs hurried over with another Red Bull and a bendy straw, plus a red plastic cup full of string cheese. Molly thought Boobs should avoid hurrying anywhere: Running in a tank top that small exposed her large chest as the investment it was, rather than a work of nature.

"Maybe high fashion just isn't for you," Brooke said kindly. "It takes a very special physique."

"Would it be easier if I just wore something I brought from home?" Molly suggested. "I really appreciate all this, but—"

"No!" Botox blurted, sitting up so fast that Boobs had to fan her. "That is crazenuts. Brick Berlin asked us to come to the rescue, and we cannot fail him."

She snapped her fingers. "Bring me the Marchesa."

Boobs and Bangs gasped in unison. The room fell silent, as if they were in church and the sermon was about to begin. Bangs reverently walked over to a dress bag, unzipped it, and lifted out an intricately ruffled violet cocktail dress. She touched it as if God really *had* just appeared in the bodice and asked her to go easy on the fingernails.

Molly noticed Brooke had gotten up from her seat and started pacing the room and gnawing on her lip.

"That dress is *amazing*," Boobs panted.

"Major," Bangs breathed.

"Radcakes," Botox agreed. "The detailing is insane, and it's, like, a normal size." She shoved it into Molly's hands. "I pulled it for Annie Hathaway, but who cares? Just don't tell her."

Molly took the dress and shuffled back into the dressing room. She heard Brooke whisper something about a big responsibility, and inexplicably thought she made out the words *wheat combine*, but she tuned it all out in favor of slowly zipping up the snug Marchesa, centimeter by centimeter. Having Brick Berlin's DNA didn't mean she'd morphed overnight into a person who could wear a $3,500 cocktail dress without having a panic attack about ruining it.

She returned to the living room. Bangs now had two cigarettes, one in each hand, and Boobs was holding a giant binder in front of Botox and turning the pages for her. Brooke was typing furiously on her iPhone.

They all looked up when Molly appeared.

"That is freaking unbelievable on you," Botox barked enthusiastically, without any kind of assist from her forehead.

"It's so heavenly, I totally just died and went there," exclaimed Bangs.

Boobs: "*Omigod*, I fully got there an hour ago and saw Jackie O."

"I am also there," Brooke said, although her face was oddly wan.

In the light of Botox's living room, at the large three-way mirror, Molly could tell the purple hue of the dress was extremely flattering. She touched the intricate work on the skirt, then wiggled around in it, throwing her hands in the air. The strapless bodice didn't budge an inch. Molly's heart leapt. Yes, it was a lot of dress, but when else would she have an excuse to wear something like this?

Botox crossed the room and placed her hands on Molly's shoulders. That close, Molly noticed that the stylist was wearing an excess of Chanel No. 5 and dark purple eyeliner. Her breath smelled of spearmint gum and raisins.

"You look like Jessie Biel's twin," Botox said very seriously. "As a professional stylist, it would be criminal of me to let you turn this down. I'd literally get arrested."

"As a professional stylist, I'm shocked you can't see the truth, which is that she looks like a giant grape-scented loofah," Brooke said haughtily.

Molly's spirits crashed with a thud. Boobs and Bangs gasped in the background.

"Are you sure?" she asked.

"Positive," Brooke said. "You don't want to end up on *E!*

News with some stand-up comic making a crack about using you with shower gel. Can you imagine? Seriously, ladies, this simply won't do."

Boobs, Bangs, and Botox were agape. Molly got the impression nobody ever turned down a Marchesa.

Outside, a horn honked.

"There's Stan!" Brooke chirped, noticeably relieved. "Hurry up and change—that color is making me crave a Jamba Juice and I can't spare the calories."

She steered Molly back into the dressing area.

"You are fully harshing my buzz, Brooke," Molly heard Botox say. "What is your damage?"

Molly, back in her jeans, looked down at the dress in her hands. She resisted the urge to hug it good-bye, and for a second she thought maybe she didn't have the strength to give it back. But if Brooke thought she looked like a loofah…Surely, she knew what Molly ought to wear, and after three hours, she wouldn't have let Molly walk out empty-handed unless the situation demanded it.

"I have to trust Brooke on this one," she said, coming out of the dressing room and handing the dress to Bangs, who looked as horrified as if someone had just told her the health food store was out of flaxseed oil. "But thank you so much for all your help."

"Don't worry, Molly," Brooke said with a huge smile. "Fashion may have failed you today, but now that I know your tastes, I have several vintage classics at home that'll be totally perfect. Trust me."

✦ ✦ ✦

It rained on Friday, so Saturday dawned clear and bright. Even after a week in Los Angeles, Molly still hadn't quite acclimated to the West Coast, instead taking advantage of waking up three hours too early every day by hitting the pool for some laps. Brooke was appalled when she heard about it—apparently her own hair had a rare chlorine allergy—but Molly found the rhythmic smack of her arms against the water helped clear her head.

Molly was *so close* to being excited about the party. Charmaine certainly was; she had offered to fly out and live-blog it. And Brooke's enthusiasm was contagious. The previous night, they'd had Tex-Mex delivered while Brooke went over Famous Sibling Pairings in Tabloid History and how they found the optimal flattering angles when posing for pictures together. Apparently, Jessica and Ashlee Simpson had much to teach. Sometimes it felt like these first few days in Los Angeles had conspired to turn her into an alternate-universe Molly: someone who had a moderate spray tan (courtesy of Brooke), her own black Amex, and a social calendar that involved the words *red carpet*. Oh, and a private Olympic-size lap pool. Every morning, no matter how amazing it was to be experiencing all this, Molly felt a little more foreign to herself.

But maybe that's not such a bad thing. Isn't that partially why I came here, anyway? To leave sad West Cairo Molly behind?

But Molly still didn't feel quite ready for her big Hollywood debut. What if she tripped at the party and fell into the pool, in front of all of those reporters? What if she said something stupid? What if she got the name of one of Brick's movies wrong?

Brooke seemed either uncomfortable discussing Molly's nerves, or unable to relate; whenever Molly broached the subject, Brooke would digress into surprisingly impassioned tirades about things like the importance of nasal contouring. So Molly used her peaceful morning swims to work through her anxiety. There was no way she was going to allow *Hey!* to write some story about her mother wasting away on a bed of rats and cockroaches, or whatever—Laurel would have died of embarrassment, if she weren't already dead. This party had to happen, and Molly simply had to deal. The idea of being presented to Southern California like Zuckerman's Famous Pig from *Charlotte's Web* definitely made her uneasy, but it wasn't like Brick was making her give him a kidney.

Post-swim, Molly wrapped herself in the spa robe that had been hanging on the back of her bathroom door and went out on the balcony to eat her toast. It had taken her two days to work up the guts to send up for anything, but Stan promised her the cook was just happy to have something to do besides make protein shakes. She waved down at Brooke, who stood by the pool in a skimpy bikini and sarong, trailed by a mousy girl with a clipboard and directing the placement of rented tables. She smiled as Brooke's enthusiastic return wave almost knocked the glasses off her tiny friend. As intense as Brooke's fawning interest could be, she was at least an *amusing* handful.

"She's so *chirpy*," Molly said to Charmaine during one of their late-night phone sessions.

"Maybe she's a bit mentally ill," Charmaine opined.

"I think she's just lonely," Molly said. "Brick's never around and I have no idea where her mom is."

"Not even Google knows," Charmaine said, awed by the all-powerful Internet's failure to inform. "But I did find an old article on *People*'s website about how Brick married Brooke's mom at her father's house in the Palisades. They had two peacocks as ring bearers."

"Weird." Molly shuddered.

"And bad luck, because they got divorced a couple of years later," Charmaine continued. "Kelly told *People* it was time for her to find herself."

"I guess she's still off looking," Molly had said.

"Maybe she's not trying very hard."

Molly had obligingly giggled—if Laurel had known Brooke, she'd have called her a Piece of Work in the kind of tone that implied the capital letters—but she also felt guilty maligning her half sister when all Brooke wanted was to make sure Molly felt comfortable and prepared. Just yesterday, in fact, backed up with countless photos of Charlize Theron, Brooke had insisted that looking bitchy would make Molly's cheekbones appear more prominent, and then she swore posing with your legs crossed would streamline the thighs and hips. None of this made a ton of sense to Molly, but the starlets in the tabloids who did it all looked skinny and hot. Molly was beginning to suspect that Brooke was some kind of superficiality savant, whom she might be well served to obey.

Molly was mentally running through Brooke's list of tips an hour before the party as she planted herself in front of her bathroom vanity. To avoid acknowledging the din emanating from the ground level, she turned up her iPod and fixated on following *Glamour*'s advice to achieve the perfect smoky eye, giving the makeup under her lower lash an extra vigorous smudge. Brooke had said with a supportive shoulder-squeeze that this technique would diminish the appearance of eye bags. Molly had never thought she had eye bags before, but if she did, she'd better deal with them now.

"All righty, sister-friend, the moment of truth is *here*! Aren't you so, so excited?" Brooke squealed, sauntering in without knocking. "Daddy wants us downstairs in five minutes. Everyone we know is here. I think everyone in *town* is here. I can't wait to introduce you!"

Molly took a deep breath. "Almost done," she said. "How's my makeup?"

"You did it *yourself*?" Brooke said, a hand fluttering to her chest. "But Daddy paid for a hair and makeup artist! I told you about it this morning! She didn't come in here?"

Molly turned and noticed Brooke's expertly arranged blonde curls bouncing around a face that had been painted to perfection by a professional. She shook her head. She was pretty sure Brooke hadn't said anything to her about that. But it was possible she'd just tuned it out during one of Brooke's speeches about hair extensions. *That's what I get*, she thought.

"That bitch will spend the rest of her career doing infomercials," Brooke fumed, squeezing Molly's shoulders with a fervor that conveyed either sympathetic anger or homicidal mania (it seemed like a genuine toss-up). "I cannot *imagine* where she went. And it's too late to do anything about your face now."

"It's okay," Molly assured her. "The last thing I need to worry about is whether my false eyelashes are coming unglued, right?"

Brooke ran an eye over Molly. Then she smiled brightly. "I adore your optimism! And your dress is a marvel. I am a genius, if I do say so myself."

"Marvel" was right. Molly had never seen a Marc Jacobs with so many flowers and ruffles. She felt like a blooming topiary.

"Yeah, it's great," Molly finally said, patting a ruffle in what she hoped was a show of affection. If she'd known this was the "classic" Brooke had in store for her, she'd never have let go of that Marchesa. But by the time Brooke had produced it, there'd been no time for a plan C. Besides, maybe she was being too harsh. Brooke kept insisting "florals are *so* three-months-from-now," and that the dress itself had been a personal gift from the designer.

Brooke clapped her hands. "Enough! We have to go downstairs. Bad things happen when Brick is left alone with the press. He almost married that one girl from the *National Enquirer*, can you imagine?"

Molly bit back a smile and followed Brooke out the door. As she wobbled her way to the ground floor—Brooke had loaned her sky-high Manolos—Molly peeked out the window at the enormous lawn. Flotillas of pink tulips and white pillar candles bobbed lazily in the pool, and tiny twinkling lights hung from every tree, approximating the stars L.A.'s smog layer sometimes obscured. The yard had been turned into a giant outdoor living room, with huge cream couches and oversize pink velvet square ottomans clustered around low, glass-topped coffee tables, each of which bore a bucket filled with tiny splits of pink champagne. A raised stage was tucked at the back of the yard, presumably for Fall Out Boy, and buffet tables and wet bars framed the lawn like a subtle barricade, as if to note that while the budget here clearly had no boundaries, the guests certainly did.

The grounds were choked with people: cater-waiters in *Avalanche!* T-shirts under sport coats; girls wearing too much foundation and boys in popped-collar polo shirts, whom Molly assumed were her future classmates; bored-looking beefcakes lugging camera equipment and the scrawny, overtanned women they were trailing; stressed agent-types juggling four phones in the same hand; and at least three clusters of folks who were actually eating the hors d'oeuvres, and who therefore must have been gate-crashers.

Brooke led her to the shaded French doors separating the peaceful, silent living room from the mob outside, then paused and threw Molly a sly smile.

"I'll be next to you the whole time, so just look for me when you feel lost," she said. "Oh, and one last thing—make sure you stare *right at them*."

Then Brooke flung open the doors and pushed Molly out onto the patio. Her smile was the last thing Molly saw before she went blind.

"Molly! Molly, over here, sweetie! Give us a smile!"

There was an explosion of light.

"Look left, Molly! Molly, hold still! Over here, Molly!"

"Molly, how do you feel being rescued by your new father?!"

Where should she look? Was she actually supposed to answer?

"Molly, who are you wearing?!"

"Is it true your mother kept Brick's picture under her mattress?!"

Click. Where *was* everyone? Where was Brooke?

"Did you know gonorrhea could kill?!"

So this is what it feels like to need a drink.

seven

MOLLY FELT LIKE she was in the middle of that "stark naked at a pep rally" nightmare, minus the advantage of being able to burst into tears or run away screaming. Or wake up. Or *blink*.

The light from the hundreds of flashbulbs seared her skin, and there were so many loud, frantic voices that Brick's patio sounded like a stock exchange floor. Obviously, her father hadn't just stopped with *Hey!* It looked like Brick had invited every magazine, newspaper, blogger, and possibly anyone with a Twitter account to this party.

Disembodied hands propelled her onto a small swatch of red carpet, which had been tossed in front of a backdrop printed with the logos for Absolut Vodka, Williams-Sonoma Home, and, weirdly, the Greater Los Angeles

Chamber of Commerce. Cameras clicked everywhere. Molly had no idea that hundreds of shutters could be so *loud*. She whirled around frantically, trying to find any sign of Brooke, but her sister had vanished.

This is so intense. I don't know if I can do this alone.

Molly focused on Brooke's advice. But she couldn't cross her legs because they were shaking too much to move, and maintaining a crabby expression just made her feel rude. The heat from the flashbulbs was as potent as her rising panic, which made her sweaty, cold, and clammy all at the same time. She felt herself swoon.

"Mayday! She's going down!"

Out of nowhere, Brick appeared and grabbed Molly's arm.

"Let me be your life raft in the sea of humanity, precious girl," he intoned. "Also, what a turnout! So many reporters from so many magazines! *Someone* must have let them all in the back way." He winked at her and whispered, "Trip Kendall thinks he can own my story? Not so!"

He handed her a leaflet. It was all about the many glories of being a tourist in Los Angeles, called, "L.A. Story: Starring *You!*"

"Just hang on to that for a few photos," he said. "Makes the sponsor happy, and I'd rather you had that than a vodka tonic."

Brick steered her toward a tight cluster of suits with slicked-back hair who were yelling his name; the cameras followed, snapping candid after endless candid. Strangers took turns shaking her hand. Occasionally, Molly heard herself answering softball questions about her likes and dislikes; she tried bringing up Laurel, but most of the reporters seemed to find that too depressing and changed the subject. Mainly, she just listened to Brick natter brightly, and she calmed down as she finally realized this story wasn't really about *her* at all.

After about an hour of empty smiling, her cheeks began to burn. Brooke may have had a point with that tip about looking cranky.

"Cover your mouth with your hands and pretend to cough," Brick murmured. "Then while your face is hidden, wiggle your mouth to relax the jaw muscles. No one will know what you're doing and your cheeks won't hurt so much."

"Thanks," Molly whispered.

"You're doing great," he said, giving her right shoulder a supportive pat. "I'm going to find that girl from *In Touch*—once she gets a load of your dimple, she'll have to retract that ridiculous story about me getting one surgically created in Mexico. You go have some fun."

"That's okay, I—"

"I mean it, Molly. I told the press to back off unless I'm with you, because all this yada yada can get exhausting. So go relax." Then Brick brightened. "Remind me to tell you about the time Kiefer Sutherland and I were on a junket in Prague and he fell asleep during an interview with the *Herald Tribune*. It was hilarious."

He smiled wide. Molly couldn't help but return it. She

was beginning to understand how her mother ended up embroiled with Brick. He *was* charming when you had his full attention.

But while Brick thought he was doing Molly a favor by releasing her into the wild, she felt lost without him shepherding her from place to place. And Brooke was still nowhere to be found. Molly hadn't realized until now how much she'd been relying on her sister to get her through this. Sure, Brooke tended to suck up all the oxygen in the vicinity, but she was also the only person Molly knew. Where could she have gone?

Two tiny girls in shiny formal shorts scampered past her and stopped five feet away, looking back with their hands over their mouths.

"I heard she was an illegal alien," the first one giggled.

The second chortled, "Her *bangs* are illegal."

Are they talking about me?

Molly slowly looked around and saw she was at the center of a radioactive halo ringed by countless pairs of eyes openly staring right at her. Doubtless her future classmates, they all seemed to prefer to point and stare rather than come talk to her.

"And that dress! Where does she think she is? The Oregon Trail?"

"She must have left her bonnet with her oxen."

Molly suspected she was blushing. She cracked a smile and wiggled her fingers, as if to say, *Hey, I see you, and I'm not toxic*, but all she heard were more snorts.

"Look, she's not even talking to anyone."

"What a snob. Just because she's Brick Berlin's kid doesn't mean she's so great."

Molly felt herself melt under their judgment. Nobody was making an effort to lower the volume, so every insult, every half-baked rumor—a dude to her left actually just said he heard she was Brick's child bride—made it to her ears. And everywhere she moved, they seemed to follow. The grapevine was growing up around her and squeezing her to a pulp.

Frantically, she scanned the crowd again for any sign of Brooke. Nothing. Molly was all alone.

She suddenly wished she'd gone to more swim-team parties with Danny. Most of his teammates had a tendency to morph into obnoxious meatheads when they were drinking, and she'd never liked waking up the next day feeling like her brain had gone through a blender. But the consequence of being such a homebody was that Molly, unlike Danny, was lousy at small talk. He could approach anyone and make conversation; Molly tended to hang back and watch. But if she did that here, everyone would be watching *her* watch *them*, and...

"Here's your drink, ma'am. Sorry for the wait. The ice makers broke," a waiter said, grabbing a vivid pink martini off a tray full of clanking glasses. He pressed it into her hand and then wriggled off through the crowd.

The teen masses started to whisper, delighted.

"Wait, I didn't order this," Molly called after him, but he

didn't hear her. At a loss, Molly tried to follow him, pressing onward as the crowd of students parted, until suddenly she was swallowed by a crush of socializing adults who either didn't care who she was or had already forgotten. The waiter was nowhere to be found, but on the plus side, Molly felt deliciously invisible.

She looked down at the drink in her hand. It resembled the cocktails the JCMHS cheerleaders had made at their New Year's bash, when Danny had ended up dancing on the roof of someone's car, inadvertently causing a grand's worth of damage. They'd fought the next day about why he always seemed to go from zero to hammered in fifteen minutes. Molly was no stranger to alcohol, having sipped it a handful of times herself; she just didn't like it much, and Danny couldn't quite relate to that.

"It takes the edge off. It's relaxing," he'd defended himself. "Why do you think I was voted Most Friendly? Everybody loves Weekend Danny."

Retroactively, Molly felt bad about being such a nag. Finally, she got what he meant. She had never felt more tense in her life.

What the hell? she thought, and took a swig.

Plopping down on the stone bench in her father's rose garden, Brooke chewed on her lip, silently thanking God for creating flavored glosses that staved off stress eating.

On the one hand, this party sucked. Some new flunky of Brick's had shoved her out of the way before she'd so much as snuck into the background of a photograph; nobody had even batted an eyelash at Molly's bathroom-wallpaper dress; the Blahniks hadn't broken her sister's ankle; and Molly either hadn't remembered or had chosen to ignore Brooke's tip about standing with her legs crossed above the knee at all times. So much for making her look incontinent.

But Molly *was* at least acting like someone who had walked out to present an Oscar and then suddenly realized people could see her nipples. She kept wiping her palms over and over on the pockets of that heinous pinafore, her eyes were unnaturally wide, and as best Brooke could tell, the only complete sentence Molly had uttered all night was that her favorite actress was Jennifer Garner. Who *said* stuff like that, anyway? Jennifer Garner was a *brunette*.

That much, at least, was what Brooke had hoped for when she'd shoved Molly out onto the patio unaccompanied— but she couldn't fully enjoy the awkwardness because nobody else seemed to notice. It was as if they were hypnotized, like that brief period in first grade when Brooke had been so in love with Freddie Prinze Jr. that she never noticed what a terrible actor he was.

"*There* you are."

Brooke turned to face Arugula, who had appeared with Jennifer Parker by her side.

"How did you know I'd be back here?"

"Duh. It's the bench where your dad introduced you to

91

Jake Gyllenhaal," Jennifer replied. "You always come here when you're bummed out."

Brooke held her head aloft. "I am not bummed out. In fact, everything is going according to plan."

"Interesting. From where I sit, it looks like you're cowering behind a bush," Arugula said.

"I have Molly under control," Brooke insisted. "She's a nervous wreck. But everyone's so busy drooling over her that I haven't gotten any face time with the press."

"Well, then get out there." Arugula tsked. "Show a little backbone instead of sulking in the shrubbery like a vagrant."

Jennifer gasped, but Brooke saw the truth in this. "You're right. I know you're right."

She closed her eyes, inhaled hard, and repeated her new mantra: "I must be Zen. I must be dazzling. And I must not use the word *bumpkin*."

"Much better," Ari said.

Brooke smoothed her dress and shook back her hair. "How do I look?"

"Like third runner-up in the West Hollywood Miss She-Male America pageant," came a familiar voice from the mouth of the rose garden. "Too bad—I thought your shoulders made you a shoo-in for at *least* second place."

Shelby Kendall slithered into view, looking irritatingly great in the Marchesa that Brooke had made Molly reject.

"I just overheard Tom Hanks's kid saying that Molly looks like a young Jennifer Aniston," Shelby continued, twirling a lock of black hair around her finger and touching it thoughtfully to her heart-shaped mouth. "Isn't that a delicious coincidence, since you're kind of an old Lisa Kudrow?"

"Excuse us—Brooke is supposed to rendezvous with a *Hey!* reporter right now," Arugula said, grabbing Brooke's arm and hauling her away before any further sniping commenced.

"I didn't know you had an interview set up," whispered Jennifer, trotting along behind them obediently.

"She doesn't," Arugula hissed. "But why should that stop her? What do we always say? WWBWD—What Would Blair Waldorf Do?"

"Make it about herself," Brooke said.

"Exactly," affirmed Arugula. "So get out there. Be the story. You look resplendent."

Brooke knew that much was true, once she realized it was a compliment. The green dress she'd bought at Inferno looked even better than it had in the store, and when she paired it with her gold peep-toes, she looked like Diane Kruger, which trumped Aniston any day of the week.

The three girls drifted toward the locus of the paparazzi hubbub as if they were only crossing its path by accident, but Brooke had drawn a solid bead on her father. She could see the light gleaming off his hair. As she approached, she realized happily that Molly was nowhere to be found. Brick held court alone.

"Why would I take her in now? Why *wouldn't* I?" he was saying. "DNA is thicker than water. Nothing should come between me and my daughter."

Arugula grimaced. "Nobody that beefy should rhyme," she muttered.

"Great, Brick, thanks," the reporter said, snapping her fingers to signal that the camera crew could cut. "That'll be perfect for the website. Where's the kid again?"

"She's off mingling," Brick said. "When you love something as I cherish her, you set it free."

"Please intervene before I regurgitate my Slim-Fast," urged Arugula, shoving Brooke in the direction of her father.

"Ow, you're hurting—uh, I mean, hi, Daddy!" Brooke recovered in time to shoot her father a blinding, toothy grin.

"Sunshine! You look fantastic!" Brick said, giving her a hug. "Am I the luckiest dad on earth to have two such gorgeous daughters, or what?"

The assemblage of female reporters tittered adoringly. If this were a rock concert, at least one bra would be dangling from Brick's ear by now.

Still, staring up at her dad's elated face as he gently tugged on her curls, Brooke felt warm. He was all hers and he looked delighted. It was exactly what she'd pictured when she—

"Oh, Mark, hold up a sec. We need to talk to the Weinsteins about this Key West thing," Brick said, flagging down a gangly guy and disappearing with him into the crowd. This left Brooke surrounded by press girls who were all murmuring into their digital recorders and acting like the story had just left along with her father. Her skin turned cold.

"Um, Brooke?"

Brooke turned to see a small, plain woman holding up a notebook.

"I'm Ginevra McElroy," she began, tucking muddy blonde hair behind her ear. "I work at *Hey!* Well, technically, I'm an intern, but you know, hopefully there's an opportunity for upward mobility, because—"

"What can I do for you, Ginevra?" Brooke asked, ninety percent sugar and ten percent edge. She knew enough to take any and all comers, but if she had to listen to this mouse ramble about her journalistic aspirations, she'd bleed from the ears.

"Well, I asked if I could talk to you for this story," Ginevra said.

Clearly, this piteous creature was smarter than she looked.

"Of course." Brooke beamed. "Well, I'll be president of Colby-Randall's prestigious Drama Club this fall, and because I'm an actress and I have such a passion for the craft, I've got all kinds of ideas for—"

"Because, you know, this story is just so *interesting,*" Ginevra continued, as if she hadn't heard Brooke speaking at all. "Tell me what you like best about her."

Brooke's face tightened, like she was suddenly caught in a very small wind tunnel.

"What I like best…about *Molly?*" she asked.

"Yes. What is the most wonderful thing you've learned about her?"

The fact that I can murder her in her sleep tonight and get away with it because Brick is never home.

"We...well, we have very different interests," Brooke hedged. "So she can learn from watching me fulfill my destiny as the heir to the Berlin family acting legacy, and I can learn about...chickens...from hearing about her favorite, um, hayrides, and stuff."

"Diversity is so important!" Ginevra chirped. "Would you say that you are upset, though? Now that you have to share your father with her? Do you feel *obsolete*?"

The force of Brooke's shock flipped a switch in her brain. The one that controlled her behavior in public.

"You don't know me very well if you think that I would *ever* feel threatened by someone who once rode a cow topless through the streets of her hometown," she heard herself say.

"Wow," Ginevra said, a slow smile spreading across her face. "So Molly is a bit of a bad girl?"

"Just when there's gin involved," Brooke said. "But that's really only, like, sixty percent of the time." She beamed. "Off the record, of *course*."

"Of course," Ginevra breathed, pulling out a business card. "Brooke, I have to run, but you have been so helpful. And you look fabulous."

"Thank you, Ginevra, and if you ever need anything—

anything—just let me know," Brooke said, squeezing the girl's shoulder before they both walked away.

Well played, she congratulated herself. Brooke hadn't counted on a media ally, but far be it from her to look a gift intern in the mouth. Brick's irritating enthusiasm meant she couldn't go after Molly directly, but it certainly didn't preclude Brooke from finding other ways to remind her half sister exactly whose kingdom this was. If that rube wanted to run with the big girls, she'd have to learn to keep up with them.

✦ ✦ ✦

Molly tipped back the bottle of Stella Artois and drained the last few drops into her mouth. She tossed her bottle at a garbage can. It bounced off the rim and landed in the grass. Nobody noticed, because she'd hidden herself behind an unused corner settee underneath a string of lights that had burned out.

"I just missed the trash at point-blank range," she told Charmaine.

"Oh, man, you are going to be so sorry tomorrow," her friend said through the phone.

"I am fine!" Molly announced. "Liquor before beer, in the clear. Besides, I deserve a little fun."

"Then go have some. The *People* Twitter says Ashton Kutcher is there. Hang up the phone."

Charmaine was right. Hiding was stupid. And the grass was itchy. Molly hated being itchy. She popped up from behind the couch and her gaze fell on a buffet table several yards away that was still very well stocked.

"Food!" Molly squawked. "Do you want anything?"

"Yeah, I'm not there, dumbass. Seriously, if you don't hang up and go take a picture with Demi and Ashton, I will post something on the Internet that says you have a third hand growing out of your back."

Molly poked at her phone and then dropped it into her dress's pocket. In addition to being right, Charmaine was bossy. But those mini hot dogs looked awfully good.

It took forever to get to the buffet tables. Putting one foot in front of the other seemed both way more fun and much harder than normal. By the time Molly reached the finger food, two things were clear: She was hammered out of her tree, and…she forgot the other thing.

Molly slammed her hand down next to a tray of taquitos and glared at them as though they had just tried to cop a feel. How had this happened? The first martini had, as Danny was fond of saying, taken the edge off, but when it was gone Molly still felt like she needed something to do with her hands. All the other kids her age seemed to be drinking; hence the first beer, which dulled the remainder of her shrieking nerve endings. The second had been because she'd texted Danny and told him what was happening, and his response was, "Awesome, let's have a beer together." The fourth had been … wait, she'd skipped three; what was three?

Dammit. She *was* going to hate herself in the morning. Charmaine had been right about that, too.

"What did you just say about Charmin?" a girl asked.

"…I am out loud?" Molly asked.

The girl peered at Molly through a curtain of black hair, then broke into a slow smile. "Try the mini quiches," she said. "They're excellent on a drunk stomach."

"I'm not drunk," Molly insisted, standing up as straight as she could and trying to sound polite. "I'm Molly."

"Of course you are," the girl said, floating away on a purple cloud, which Molly realized was a very familiar-looking cocktail dress. "We'll meet again, Molly."

Molly tried to concoct a charming, friendly response to this while the girl was still within earshot, but her fuzzy brain didn't seem to be working right. Scooping up a handful of snacks, Molly wobbled back to her safe place and crash-landed on the grass. She shoveled several mini quiches into her mouth. After about the fifth one, her stomach started to complain, but her mouth didn't listen. She emptied her plate.

Dragging her knees into her chest, Molly leaned her head against the back frame of the couch and closed her eyes. So much for her social debut. She was wearing a dress better suited to a quilting bee, she'd let everyone point and stare her into submission, and she'd been too scared and nervous to go up to anyone and introduce herself—which is why she'd spent half the night on the phone to Indiana. And now she was wasted. And queasy. And grass-stained.

Molly felt lost and frustrated, as if she'd followed the exact directions she'd been given but still ended up in the wrong place. Her own skin had never seemed so uncomfortable. She didn't even notice the tear running down her cheek until it made a salty splash on her upper lip.

Minutes later—or hours, or seconds; Molly had no idea which—she thought she heard a girl's voice. By the time she willed a bleary eye open, though, there was no one there. Then she heard a rustling noise.

"Daddy, she's passed out," Brooke's voice all but shouted. "I can't believe she did this to you. How *humiliating*."

Molly rocketed to her feet, then instantly regretted it as her knees buckled. Brick caught her.

"Brookie, be quiet," he said firmly. "Molly, let's get you upstairs. We'll talk about this tomorrow."

Molly found the ground with her feet, then rubbed her eyes to see if that made the scene less blurry. It didn't work.

"Sounds rad, man," Molly joked feebly. But the instant the words came out, she realized how blasé and sloshed she sounded. "Oops. I didn't mean…that was dumb…this is all so…I wish I had…I want to rewind," she heard herself slur next as she wiped a fresh river of tears from her eyes.

Brick looked astonished. Molly suddenly felt hysteria

bubbling up in her throat, imagining what she must look like to him, all smudged makeup and a runny nose and breath that smelled like a brewery on a night that she was supposed to make a good impression. She had a history of laughing at inappropriate moments, like at her mother's funeral when the priest got to "ashes to ashes, dust to dust," because Laurel used to say that when she cleaned house. Tonight, as then, her nerves—this time abetted by the booze—won out. She broke into a guffaw and sagged against Brick. The trees overhead were spinning like slot-machine wheels through her vision. A face appeared among them. Molly peered up at it and smiled.

"G'night, Mom," she slurred. "See you in the morning."

After that, darkness.

eight

IN THE DREAM, Molly was two inches tall. She fought through the blades of grass in Brick's backyard, running in slow motion, trying to tell him something very important. But she was too small. He couldn't see her. Then Brooke appeared, sauntering toward Brick with a plate of mini quiches. Her shoe came down toward Molly's matchstick-size head, closer, closer, closer, making an odd rapping sound as it found Molly's skull....

She cracked a bleary eye.

Tap, tap, tap.

"Molly?" said a male voice from outside the door.

Molly pulled the covers over her head then lowered them enough to peek out without actually exposing her bedhead.

"Come in," she mumbled.

Stan popped open the door and backed inside, carrying a large silver tray with a domed lid on it. He took one look at her in her down comforter cave and smiled empathetically.

"Feeling okay?" he asked. "You seemed a bit the worse for wear last night."

Molly groaned and rolled into her pillow.

Stan reached out to where her foot seemed to be and patted it. "We've all been there. Even Brick. *Especially* Brick, since he won't eat the food at his movie premieres — says it's a caloric trap designed to make him fat and force down his salary."

He set the tray down on the large bench at the foot of her bed. "He ordered this just for you," he said. "A shot of wheatgrass juice and a vegan prune muffin bar. He swears by them. So if you lift this dome and see an Egg McMuffin with hash browns, well, I'm afraid I won't know what you're talking about."

"Thanks," Molly mumbled, and tried to summon a smile for him. It didn't exactly work. Her mouth was dry, and it tasted like the bottom of a birdcage. "It's nice of you to do this for me on a Sunday."

"No worries. It's my job. In Brick Berlin's world, there are no weekends," he said. "Why do you think I know the best hangover cures?"

Stan headed for the door, stopping just as he reached for the knob. "He does want to see you, though," he added, looking a bit grim. "Come on down to his study as soon as you feel up to it."

He closed the door behind him. Molly rubbed her face and sat up, then immediately regretted moving. Her stomach sloshed, and it felt like someone had gotten trapped inside her brain and was trying to tunnel his way out using a ball-peen hammer. It might be a long time before she felt steady enough to go downstairs, physically *or* emotionally. A week ago she'd never met her father; now he was about to punish her for crawling down the neck of a beer bottle. What a great first impression. He probably thought she got hammered all the time in Indiana, and was on the phone with Ginger asking if she'd ever staged an intervention.

Molly could barely remember what happened after Brick picked her up off the grass, though she had faint, misshapen memories—like photos accidentally sent through the laundry—of Brooke towering over her, squealing something gleeful. But she didn't want to think about that, or what it might mean. Plus, her head really hurt.

Molly burrowed through her bedding until her head popped out next to the tray, then grabbed the McMuffin and dragged it with her back under the covers. She'd face the world later.

✦   ✦   ✦

Brooke's phone rang. And rang. Irritated, she lifted her head just enough to check the clock. Eleven thirty in the morning. *Obscene.* Who called at this hour?

She groped at the nightstand until her hand found her

iPhone. Brick's name flashed up on the screen, along with a picture of him on the red carpet at the Oscars. He'd done a cameo as an unusually muscular Rasputin in *Night at the Museum III: MoMA, Mo' Problems*, which had been nominated for best costumes. Brooke smiled, remembering how funny his bit with Ben Stiller had been when they presented Best Editing. Then she heard his stern voice in her head from the previous night and recalled the disappointed way he'd looked at her—at *her*—when she brought him to Molly's slumped, drunk body.

She sent the call to voice mail.

Almost instantly, Madonna's "Material Girl" kicked up again. Brooke ignored it, still stung that Brick had seemed so put out when she was only trying to be helpful by showing him what Molly was really like. She wondered how much inertia it would take before her body forgot how to function. Once she was rendered immobile by her psychological pain, maybe Brick would see how much harm he'd done, bringing this ruinous boozehound into their lives. The question was whether he'd realize this before or after Brooke got an oozing bedsore.

Her phone tolled a third time. "Shut up, Madonna," she mumbled. But this time, it was Brie.

"Good morning!" her assistant chirped. "This is your daily tabloid report. One of the *Real Housewives of Santa Fe* threw her pottery wheel at a photographer, that new Fashion Week documentary opened huge, and one of those girls from *The City* wore the ugliest orange poncho to an

MTV party last night. And that's it. Nothing else made news. At all."

"You are a terrible liar, Brie."

"No, it's true, the poncho was awful. E! Online said she looked like the Great Pumpkin's trashy girlfriend."

"Brie."

On the other end of the line, Brie took a deep breath.

"Okay, it's actually not that bad. Most of what's online from last night are just pictures of Brick and Molly smiling. But *Hey!*..." Brie trailed off. "They got a picture of you hunched over Molly and talking on your phone, while she was passed out. It really looks like you're laughing at her."

"Dammit!" Brooke swore. "Why did you tell me that?"

"Because you—"

"In the future, please recognize when to tell me what I want to hear," Brooke huffed.

There was a loud banging on her door.

"Go away," Brooke crabbed. "I'm very busy."

"Unless what you're busy with involves being comatose, you will come downstairs right now," Brick's voice boomed.

"Um, Brie, gotta go. My trainer's here."

Shoving her feet into fluffy slippers, Brooke padded downstairs hoping she looked childlike and innocent. The last time Brick yelled at her, she was six and had spilled her apple juice on his pager; he'd been so overcome with guilt that he'd bought her a pony named Mr. Pickles. She doubted this would end as happily: From his tone, Brooke could guess that Brick had seen exactly what Brie had, and it wasn't sitting well.

Brooke shuffled toward her father's study, through the hallway that contained every certificate Brick had ever received—including one from the American Dental Association honoring his teeth as the best in showbiz—and a gallery of her school photos over the years. When she reached fourth grade, Brooke stopped, noticing a tiny, dog-eared picture that had been tucked into the corner of the frame. It depicted a little girl with crooked front teeth, brown-red braids, and a grin so earsplitting you couldn't see the color of her eyes.

Molly.

Brooke resisted the urge to rip it down, knowing that act of vandalism wouldn't actually affect anything except possibly her prospects of getting a car—though those already looked bleak. She took a deep breath and reminded herself to deny everything for as long as possible. This worked well whenever celebrity couples ran into rumors of marital problems.

"Brooke? I hear your footsteps. Get in here."

A fire blazed in the hearth in Brick's study despite it being a steamy ninety degrees outside. Brick once read on the Internet that being warmed by the heat of a burning log was great for the pores. Brooke often thought Brick was a perfect example of why literacy was overrated. He believed anything holistic-sounding as long as more than two posters on a message board agreed with it.

As she closed the door, Brooke noticed Molly already there, slumped down in a chair opposite Brick's desk and sipping from a steaming mug of coffee.

"Good morning!" Brooke all but yelled, enjoying watching Molly wince at the volume.

"Oh, don't you play the James Cameron card with me, Harvey," Brick bellowed from his wing chair, which was facing away from them. "You want him so bad? Why don't you just flush five hundred million down the toilet and save yourself a three-year shoot?"

He tossed the phone onto the rug and swiveled around to face them, drumming his hands on the desk.

"Well, well, well. Last night was interesting," he said.

"Wasn't it?" Brooke bubbled. "I overheard the movie critic from the *L.A. Times* saying he thought the *Avalanche!* script was dynamite."

"You know that's not what I'm talking about," Brick said sternly. Then he pursed his lips. "But that *is* splendid news," he added. "Remind me to send him some branded snowshoes."

"Brick…I mean…Dad…I'm *so* sorry," Molly blurted, sitting forward and slamming her coffee down on his antique oak desk in her urgency to be heard. A few drops sloshed over the mug rim. "I swear I'm not usually like that. I just…I don't know what happened."

Brick regarded Molly for a second in silence. Then he came around to perch on the corner of the desk in front of her chair, sandwiching her left hand between his two paws.

"Sweet girl, *I* know what happened," he said. "You were lost, you were alone, and you did what every teenage kid does in that situation. I asked too much of you." He hung his head. *"I drove you to drink."*

Brooke couldn't believe her ears. Was Brick seriously letting this troll off the hook?

"Daddy, you're being too hard on yourself," she began, but Brick held up a hand.

"You're to blame here, too, Brooke," he warned. "You practically took out a megaphone to announce that Molly was drunk. Where was your discretion? And who were you on the phone with?"

Brooke gulped as Brick showed her a printout of the *Hey!* photo from today's home page. The headline read SIS-TER ACT? Brooke had to admit that it looked bad—like she was kicking Molly and laughing, instead of merely prodding her sharply with her toe to see if she was still alive. In the "win" column, though, she herself looked *fantastic*.

"Why the smile?" Brick's face was stern.

Brooke let her gaze flutter down to her hands, which she kneaded theatrically. "I wasn't smiling, Daddy, I was hysterical," she said, suffusing her voice with agony. "We learned in health class last year that alcohol poisoning can kill you. So when I found Molly passed out, it was just so *frightening*. I called Ari for help."

It *had* been Arugula on the phone, but the call had been more focused on wondering if dragging Molly's semiconscious body through the yard would send too strong a message. Brooke kept her eyes down for a long period, then peeked up to see if she'd sold the half-truth. Brick picked up the photo again, studied it for a second, then patted Brooke on the head and ran it through the waist-high power shredder. It sounded like R2D2 eating lunch.

"Well, it's done now," he said. "Luckily, none of the other major magazines have decided to run with this. But a lot of the gossip blogs are feeding off *Hey!* and its photos, and there is nothing I can do about that. At least Trip agreed to ax the cover story. I can't even imagine what it would have said. I had to promise him a few *Avalanche!* exclusives and I may have to date that girl from *Beer o'Clock* for a month or so, but at least we're covered."

Brooke widened her eyes and let her lip tremble a bit.

"Save it, Brooke," Brick said. "You let me down, you let Molly down, and you let yourself down."

"By staying sober?" she taunted, unable to resist.

"By vanishing," he said. "Where were you when Molly needed a shoulder, and a friend? Where were we *both* when she needed a hand to hold instead of a beer bottle? Where were our minds, when she needed our hearts?" He got a faraway look in his eyes, which Brooke knew meant those words would eventually turn up on the big screen being uttered by a young heartthrob boasting an excess of hair product.

"No, I screwed up," Molly interjected. "It's my responsibility. I didn't mean to do this to you. *Either* of you," she added, looking pointedly at Brooke.

"I don't want it to happen again," Brick said. "But I don't blame you for it happening now. And I am going to make this right."

He stood up again and crossed over to gaze into his fireplace. "You are my daughters," he said. "You, and Netflix, represent my legacy on this planet. So I will not rest until my early work on *Cop Rock* is available on DVD, and I will not be satisfied until you are the true support system for each other that you *both* deserve to have. Expecting either of you to adjust to all these changes alone was a mistake. Fate tied you together. And that is exactly how you'll cope with this."

Brooke blanched. "You're going to tie us together?"

"No, no. Although that might make a fantastic Nickelodeon movie," he mused. "Billy Ray Cyrus could…well, hang on, let's not get ahead of ourselves. We're discussing you two. And what I'm about to do, I do only out of love."

Brooke groaned inwardly. She recognized that self-satisfied expression from *Tomorrow's Really Yesterday*, right before Brick's character announced that the only way to stop global climate change was to time travel to 1987 and freeze the equator.

"You two," Brick said, "are going to be roommates."

The entire room moved. At first Brooke thought it was because the ground was dropping out from under her feet, but then she realized she'd leapt from her seat.

"Is that…really necessary?" she croaked.

"Ladies, it's about to get real," Brick said, clearly thrilled with himself. "We will move a bed into Brooke's room. You will drive to school together, do homework together, work out together, do *everything* together. Brooke, you will be the helping hand that Molly needs, and Molly, you'll be the sister Brooke's always wanted. *Closer* than sisters."

Brooke felt herself sway. She *had* wanted a sister…when she was eight, and needed to learn how to French-braid hair. But now it seemed pointless, superfluous. Like Solange Knowles.

"And what do you plan for us to drive to school in?" Brooke asked, trying to keep her voice from inching into dog-whistle territory. "You said taking limos everywhere makes us look ostentatious."

"I was just getting to that," Brick said.

He dropped a set of keys on the desk. They bore the Lexus logo.

"Molly, those are for you," he said.

"She got drunk and she gets a car?" Brooke squeaked.

Brick raised an eyebrow. "Last time I checked, Brooke, you don't have a license."

"I do, too."

"A preordered personalized license *plate* doesn't count," Brick said.

Brooke thought she heard a snicker coming from behind Molly's coffee mug, and shot her a look so sharp it could dissect a frog. Molly at least had the good grace to seem chastised.

"Fine, Daddy. I accept this," Brooke said, grasping at one last straw. "You're absolutely right, and I bow down to—"

"Sucking up to me isn't going to get you the car," Brick said, amused.

"Well. I am offended that you think I could be so shallow," Brooke said through clenched teeth.

She turned on her heel and sailed out of there with all the grace she could muster. Then she broke into a mad sprint. Time to lock up her Louboutins. The enemy was on the move.

nine

"IS THIS THE BATHROOM?"

Brooke didn't bother looking. "No, it's the Kodak Theater."

"And this is my phone line?"

"No, it's a wet bar."

"Did this broken heel come from your Valentinos?"

Brooke's head snapped up so fast she gave herself whiplash.

"Just kidding," Molly said with a tentative smile.

"How fun for you," Brooke grunted.

Without Brick around, Brooke had lost interest in being nice. The idea of keeping up appearances 24/7 was too much to bear. She didn't appreciate her personal space being cruelly invaded, especially when she'd done nothing but alert her father—okay, a bit loudly, but still—to a dangerous piece of misbehavior on the part of their crass new tenant.

Leaning back in her desk chair, Brooke looked at the carcass of her room. The NordicTrack had been evicted, as had the couch, a chair, and a coffee table, all replaced with Molly's queen-size bed. Its tasteful Calvin Klein bedding was sullied by a giant Notre Dame throw pillow and a blanket that looked like someone blindly sewed together a bunch of knitted scarves. Muddy running shoes were tucked near the door, and in her beloved closet, two drawers hung half-open while Molly flung bras, underwear, and T-shirts inside.

"Can I put this here?"

With a huge sigh, its heft equal to the extreme effort she wanted Molly to know it required to feign interest, Brooke turned and saw Molly looking for a place to put a silver picture frame.

"No."

"What about over there?"

"I just don't see any room. It's cramped enough in here as it is," Brooke said flatly, gazing at the spotless forty feet between her bed and Molly's.

"Would you mind if maybe we moved this and I hung some—" Molly reached for the framed Vaseline advertorial.

"*Don't touch that,*" Brooke bellowed, hopping up with the speed of a lynx to protect her wall art. "That is my *mother.*"

Molly paused.

"Oh," she said. "I didn't realize. I would never…Here, this is mine."

She handed Brooke the photo she'd been looking to place. Against her will, Brooke looked down at it and was greeted with a friendly, open smile, a freckled nose, and long, straight, center-parted hair with a daisy-chain crown.

"My mom was kind of a hippie," Molly said. "She's fifteen in that photo."

The eyes were warm, and the moment—Laurel was running barefoot along a beach, laughing—seemed so perfect that it could've been one of those unrealistic prop photos on a movie set, the kind men moon over en route to winning an Academy Award for not being afraid to cry. Brooke derived some meager satisfaction from seeing that her own mother was technically more of a looker than Laurel, but she had to admit that Laurel was more natural. And she had very pretty hands.

I guess Brick has a type.

"How wholesome," Brooke said. "There might be space on the bookshelf near my pictures of Mr. Pickles."

Molly nodded and offered a timid smile. Brooke let fly another aggrieved sigh and plopped back down at her desk, staring at the e-mail she'd begun. After two hours, she'd managed to churn out only "Dear Mom." As a tiny act of rebellion, she cracked her knuckles. Kelly and her prize-winning hands would've hated that.

Brooke's restless gaze landed on the cluster of pictures Molly was sliding onto the bookshelf. One was of a hunky, apple-pie-American blond boy, arm in arm with Molly, who was wearing a floor-length blue gown. The bodice was covered in delicate, expensive-looking pleats that were repeated on the hem. It was a surprisingly pretty dress.

"Where'd you get the gown?"

"My mom made it."

It was a predictably tacky dress.

"Who's the boy?"

"My boyfriend. Well, maybe. I think. No, I guess he is. We—"

Brooke yawned. "I don't need your life story. Thanks!"

She returned to her e-mail just in time to notice the arrival of a new one. The subject line was, "Is this *the* Brooke Berlin?" and it was from some person called Ginevra. The name sounded familiar.

Dear Brooke,

What a pleasure to meet you last night. Thank you so much for sharing your time so graciously. I look forward to chatting with you further as the scintillating story of you and Molly continues to develop. You're going to be a real star!

Sincerely,
Ginevra McElroy

Of course. The reporter. Brick would be annoyed if he knew she was in touch with anyone in the media, so by instinct, Brooke made a move to delete the e-mail. Nothing good could come from being aligned with the one major magazine eager to take down Brick's happy family charade.

But her hand faltered. Maybe if she was cordial, she could get in the magazine's good graces, which would make *everyone's* lives easier. And really, wasn't it impolite to ignore a thank-you note? Wouldn't Brick prefer that his daughter exemplify good breeding and proper etiquette?

She hit Reply.

Dear Ginevra,

Thank you for the kind note. I am sure more stories will come from Molly as she sobers up and we begin to bond and I teach her to walk better in heels. (Those fabulous Manolos were mine. I just don't want you to be confused—accuracy in your line of work is so important.)

Warmly,
Brooke

Brooke double-checked it; clearly, she'd written nothing false or inflammatory. Molly *did* need to walk better in heels.

As she clicked Send, Brooke glanced over at Molly folding a pile of track pants. Brick could bunk them together like some lame *Parent Trap* sequel, but make them best buddies? Not in this movie.

Molly closed the sliding door behind her and raised her face to the sky. The L.A. air still had a little heat to it, even after sunset, but it felt so much better than the canned oxygen pumping through Brooke's room. *Their* room.

Except, no. It was still Brooke's room. The floor plan matched Molly's old space across the hall (except bigger), but Brooke oozed out of every nook and cranny—from the Barbie pink color scheme to the eleven thousand mirrors. Molly couldn't believe Brick's idea of parenting involved immersion therapy with a girl who'd spent the week smothering her, then hung her out to dry when Molly needed her most.

She'd wanted to believe Brooke's sob story in Brick's study, but Brooke's recent firm, ominous cold shoulder said otherwise. This was more than just a tantrum; it was a really bad portent for the future. She could imagine Charmaine's reaction: "What did you expect from a person who made you wear chintz?"

Dejected, Molly flopped down in the chair farthest from the bedroom window. Between moving, getting drunk, landing on a tabloid's website, and having a hangover in front of the father she'd only just met, Molly had done more living in one week than in her entire sixteen years. What was next? Flunking out of school? Immaculate conception?

Her phone buzzed.

OMG ARE YOU A HOMEWRECKER?

Charmaine had been texting her all day, as dribs and drabs of the night before leaked onto the Internet. Aside from the photo of her passed out at Brooke's feet, someone had posted a creative lie on *Hey!*'s message board that Molly drunkenly hooked up with Pete Wentz.

Molly texted back:

I WILL NOT DIGNIFY THAT.

Her head spun, partly from her hangover and partly because she was on her second bedroom in less than a week. Unpacking was taking forever—Brooke's closet was the size of a studio apartment, yet she swore it wasn't possible to clear more than a three-foot stretch of hanger space. Molly probably could've pressed the issue with Brick, but as nice as he'd been about the passing out thing, she counted that as one strike. She refused to get the other two, in case Brick decided letting her come here had somehow ruined things and then she wound up with no parents at all.

Buzz.

PETE WENTZ, HUH?

She knew Danny was teasing, but it hit a nerve. Gritting her teeth, Molly dialed him.

"I never pegged you for a groupie," Danny greeted her. "What was it like to make out with a dude who wears eyeliner?"

"Beats kissing a guy who thinks Skittles hide the taste of chewing tobacco."

"Ooh, good one," Danny said. She knew he was grinning. "Those photos online were *crazy*."

Molly just sighed. "Tell me about it," she said.

"Are you okay? Do you need me to come there and kick anyone's ass?"

The tenderness in his voice made the tension in Molly's spine ebb a bit.

"I still don't get how you drink so much beer," she said. "I feel like my head is going to explode, and I'm so exhausted."

"That's because drunk sleep doesn't count," Danny said. "You'll feel better tomorrow. What did your dad say? Was he pissed?"

"Not really," Molly admitted. "It was kind of amazing. He actually *understood*. It was probably the third time we've ever talked but he totally got me."

Danny snorted. "Lucky. My dad gets mad if I have a Coke."

"He's your coach. He's just looking out for you."

"You two always did get along. He tells me every day how much it sucks that you're gone," Danny said, lowering his voice. "And he's right, Molls. It's not the same."

"I know," she said. "I'd much rather be in your basement than all over the Internet."

"I keep trying to imagine you surrounded by all those photographers, and in every mental image, you are screaming and running away," Danny said, sounding amused.

"It was so insane. I'm starting to understand why celebrities attack the paparazzi with umbrellas."

"I'm proud of you for getting through it, babe. And you looked beautiful." He paused. "When you were upright."

"Gee, thanks." She laughed. "And thank you for not asking about Brooke."

"That one kinda spoke for itself."

"She claims the photo isn't what it looks like, but little bits of last night keep coming back to me. I think she hates me, Danny."

"You've seen too many TV movies with Charmaine," he scoffed. "I bet she's—ha-ha, stop it, Weebs, I'm on the phone!"

Molly frowned. "Where are you?"

"I'm over at Smitty's house. We're playing Mario Kart against some kids in Japan—oh, damn, Weebs, you just got smoked."

"I wish I was there," she said. "Everything is so much easier at home."

"No, you don't," Danny said. "And remember what your mom used to say—what's easy isn't always what's right. L.A. will get better, I promise."

"That's true, because I'm not sure it can get any worse," Molly said, so tragically that she had to laugh at herself. "Wait. Yes, it can. I start school tomorrow with a bunch of people who have already seen me passed out drunk on the ground."

"So you can only go up in their estimation," Danny said. "Speaking of which, Smitty wants to know how come you never went out drinking when you lived *here*. Ha! You're such an ass, Smitty."

"I should let you go," Molly said, trying not to sound lonely.

"Yeah, maybe this isn't the best time," Danny replied. "I hate that you're so far away. Wanna Skype on Thursday?"

"It's a date." Molly smiled at the balcony railing. "I love you like Pete Wentz loves his flatiron."

The distance between L.A. and West Cairo suddenly felt more like two *hundred* thousand miles. And thanks to Danny's brainiac denial strategy, Molly didn't know if she was supposed to be seeking comfort as his girlfriend or just a wronged buddy. After the last six months, Molly was so sick of trying to interpret her own emotions, she kind of just wanted Danny to take charge and tell her how it was between the two of them.

Buzz.

OK, THEY RETRACTED THE WENTZ THING.

Molly shoved her phone into her pocket. She didn't feel like talking to Charmaine about the scurrilous facts and fictions of her big Hollywood debut right now. Instead, she had real problems. Like where she was going to put her clothes. And which of them she was going to wear when she started school the next day.

Originally, she'd planned to ask Brooke. That clearly wasn't going to happen; Brooke had all but thrown her into the fire pit down by the hot tub, and that was just one party. If she was capable of doing that practically right in front of their father…well, Molly didn't want to think about what she might do next.

ten

"DON'T PARK THERE—that's *way* too far away. Walking in the heat will wilt my hair."

Molly swerved away from the offending parking spot.

"Okay," she said. "How about that one, right up front."

"Ew, no, that's *way* too close."

Molly slammed on the brakes and exhaled.

"Perhaps you should just point to where you think I should park," she said through gritted teeth.

"Like I care."

As Brooke flipped down the mirror and rechecked her lip gloss, Molly resisted the urge to speed up and then slam on the brakes, and instead pulled into a spot a few feet closer than the first one Brooke rejected.

"Interesting choice," Brooke said. "That is, if you enjoy hiking."

The whole drive to school had been like this. Molly had learned to drive on Laurel's peeling Oldsmobile, which had the gearshift attached to the steering wheel and velour bench seating in both rows, and wouldn't play FM radio unless you turned the lights on and off three times. By contrast, this car ran so smoothly, Molly thought she could probably stop steering altogether and it'd still get her to school safely. But she couldn't enjoy driving it because every time one of her hands so much as drifted past ten and two, Brooke shrieked that they were going to die.

Brooke slid out of the car and slammed her door so hard the whole Lexus shuddered. She stormed away without a word, furiously yanking down the hem of her Tory Burch minidress as she went. Colby-Randall Preparatory School technically did have a dress code—somewhere in its four-page section of the student handbook, Molly had read that skirts shouldn't be higher than three inches above the knee—but obviously Brooke felt that it, like rules of social interaction, were just piddling suggestions.

So this is how it's going to be. Molly suspected as much when Brooke killed all the lights in the room and went to bed while Molly was still trying to unpack, but she still couldn't quite believe it. The one person who could've been her life raft was ditching her. Again.

Molly launched herself into the warm Los Angeles

morning air and stared up at the grand, ivy-covered stone mansion that loomed before her. Colby-Randall's website had explained that the school—a luxe old estate hidden almost below street level at the foot of the Hollywood Hills—started as one house donated by an old studio exec, and then annexed a bunch of surrounding properties to give itself a vast wooded campus. And it *was* impressive. It looked more like an Ivy League college than a high school. Or, at least, more like what Molly *imagined* an Ivy League campus looked like, since she'd never seen one of those, either.

Molly willed her feet to move, but they didn't. She'd never been the new kid in school. In fact, they'd never even *had* a new student in her class in Indiana. People moved away, like when her friend Karen's dad got transferred to Chicago when they were in third grade, but no one ever seemed to move *to* West Cairo. She had no idea how to handle being the newbie, other than climbing back into the car and driving home to Indiana. Or into the Pacific.

"Don't just stand there—you're gonna be late."

Molly started, and turned. The tiny girl who'd spoken— she couldn't have been more than five feet—appraised Molly quickly and then pulled her green bob into a nub of a ponytail. "Gutsy call on the backpack," she said as she walked past.

Molly glanced down at her Jansport and wondered what was so courageous about it. Books needed to be carried.

But then she looked up at the fracas bubbling around the main building's arched double doors. Students were yelping and throwing themselves into one another's arms, screaming high-pitched greetings as if half of them hadn't just seen one another Saturday night at Brooke's house. Some of the girls were wearing tiny miniskirts paired with unseasonably furry boots, others sported designer jeans so tight they could've been painted on, and one familiar-looking raven-haired girl had the straps of her sandals wound up around the legs of her denim. They looked like the pages of *Us Weekly* come to life, and not a single one of them had a dingy old pack slung over her tiny shoulders; instead, they carried massive purses with shiny, elaborate buckles, or satchels stamped with the Louis Vuitton logo, which Molly doubted had been purchased out of the trunk of some dude's car. Even the green-haired girl, Molly recalled, had been carrying something made of leather.

As Molly made her way toward them, she noticed several people in her peripheral vision—and a few directly in her line of sight—elbowing each other and pointing. People stopped talking and stared, brows furrowed, like they were at the zoo and Molly was an exotic animal they'd never heard of before. *Behold, Los Angelenos, the world's only Skittish Hoosier in captivity.* It was like a really bad sequel to Saturday night.

Forget all that. You can do this.

Molly forged ahead through the double doors. Inside, Colby-Randall was breathtaking, with gleaming wood floors, lead-paned windows, and an elaborately carved ceiling. The overall effect was somewhat negated by the standard-issue metal lockers lining the walls and the smell of Lysol and pencil shavings that was apparently universal to every high school in the world, but Molly could still tell that she'd stayed in hotels that weren't this fancy. They were actually piping in classical music over the PA system.

Not that you could really hear it over the din. Molly pushed her way through the crush until she found her designated locker. Leaning against it was a chiseled Adonis-type with his arm slung carelessly around the shoulders of a pretty but pointy-faced girl.

"Hi," Molly said gingerly. "I'm so sorry—I think that's my locker."

"No problem," the guy said, rolling off it calmly. But the girl shot Molly a dirty look, then gave her the once-over.

"Is that from the Gap?" she asked.

Molly looked down at her dress—a basic, deliberately inoffensive dark gray jersey sundress—and nodded. The girl stuck her nose so far in the air that Molly could spot-check her sinuses.

"*Ew*," she said, and grabbed the boy's arm as if she was suddenly afraid this meant Molly was liable to jack her wallet. "Jake, let's go. It's so *dingy* over here."

They ambled off as the bell rang. Molly took a deep breath and struggled to open her locker. This was going to be a long day.

✦　✦　✦

Brooke sauntered into homeroom and drank in the chalky-smelling, white-walled classroom with proprietary satisfaction. Brooke wasn't crazy about lessons, but school was her domain. Students who'd been gossiping wildly in their chairs, trading stories with people in every direction, either stopped to wave or burbled enthusiastically upon seeing Brooke in their presence. A handful cowered and pretended to be fascinated with their binders. *Just the way the Lord intended.* Some people had It, and some didn't. Brooke knew which one she was, and it righted her ship significantly to see that despite recent events at home, everyone who counted still knew, too.

She dropped into her seat and surveyed the group, half of which was staring in open curiosity. Brooke was used to this treatment, even if this year she knew there was another reason for the analysis.

"God, Jen, I'm *so* exhausted," she announced loudly. "You Know Who snores like a farmhand."

Jennifer turned full around, without letting go of her boyfriend's enormous hand. "She looks like one, too," she said. "I just saw her in the hall."

"Is that who that was?" Jake said. "She seems nice."

"Oh, Jake, you're so *naive*." Jennifer withdrew her hand long enough to smack him on his shoulder.

"Settle down, everyone."

Brooke looked up at the front of the class and groaned.

"Perkins?" she whispered. "No way. She wears Crocs. I can't start my day with Crocs."

"And speaking of horrors..." Jennifer nudged her.

Brooke looked up to see Molly walk in and hand Ms. Perkins a piece of paper.

"Class, this is Molly Dix, she just moved here from Indiana, please be nice to her, take out your schedules, come to me with questions, and Mavis Moore, if you don't spit out that gum right now I'm going to make you chew the whole pack at once," Ms. Perkins said, putting her feet up on her desk and pulling out a copy of *Eat, Pray, Love*.

The room seemed to hold its breath as Molly scanned the rows for an empty desk.

"If you're looking for Hay Baling 101, it's on the East Lawn," Brooke said loudly.

"Is that an actual class here?" Jake furrowed his brow.

Jennifer patted him on the back as if to say, "Isn't he *adorable?*"

"Pipe down, Ms. Berlin," said Ms. Perkins from behind the book. "I'll have you know, California is the nation's foremost agricultural state and Indiana isn't even in the top five."

"Not for lack of trying," Molly said gamely, sliding into a front-row seat.

A couple of kids giggled. Brooke raised an eyebrow and most of them clammed up; a few others ignored her and gazed at Molly with mild interest. And a girl she recognized as one of Shelby Kendall's known associates appeared to be texting someone.

The TV set flicked on, showing Headmistress McCormack sitting at the campus news station's anchor desk, as she did every year on the first day of school.

"Good morning, Colby-Randall, and welcome to the start of what I'm sure will be another excellent and rewarding school year. Football tryouts are after school tomorrow and Wednesday...."

Jake pumped his fist and high-fived Magnus Mitchell.

"Bring the thunder, QB!" Magnus crowed.

"*Boo-ya!*" Jake shouted, and they stood up to chest-bump as Jennifer applauded with starry eyes. Brooke wanted to gag. Jocks were *so* two years ago.

"...So please report it if you see anyone handling food without a hairnet," droned Headmistress McCormack. "And rehearsals for *My Fair Lady* begin Friday in the brand-new Brick Berlin Theater for Serious Emotional Artistry. Casting took place last May, but any new or returning students who wish to audition for walk-on roles should contact Brooke Berlin via the Drama Club mailbox."

"I'll be your Drama Club mailbox," Magnus said huskily, waggling his tongue at Brooke as if this was supposed to entice her to put it in her mouth.

"Gross, Magnus," Jennifer frowned.

Next, Shelby's face filled the screen of the CR-One broadcast, pretty as ever and in newscaster mode. Brooke's reaction was so visceral she almost gagged.

"I'd be her mailbox, too," Magnus muttered under his breath.

"Don't be ridiculous," Brooke recovered. "Actual mailboxes are so passé. Like Shelby's original nose."

"I'd like to put out a call for any students willing to participate in a CR-One exclusive on neglected children," Shelby was saying. "If you're having a hard time with your parent, or you just met him, or he leaves you at home with a vacuous sibling with whom you have nothing in common, we want to know about it. But more important"—and here, Shelby leaned toward the camera, the better to give the student body a closer look at her poreless, peerless, very expensive face—"we want to *help*."

The bell tolled, marking the mad dash to first period. Brooke swept her satchel over her shoulder so hard it thwacked Jennifer in the shoulder. Seeing Shelby reminded her what a stressful semester this was shaping up to be. *My Fair Lady* was Brooke's best chance to make Brick sit up and take notice, but it was also a lot of work. She barely had time for *one* nemesis, much less two. It was clear that despite their father's idiotic attachment to making this work, Molly still had to go. Immediately.

Molly barreled through a door and stopped dead when she realized she'd not only landed in a supply closet but that the couple who'd been at her locker that morning was making out in it.

"Dude! Don't they knock in Indiana?" spat the girl.

"God, sorry," Molly sputtered, spinning around and swiping at the door handle to try to get out.

Juggling a lunch tray and the crumpled map in her fist, Molly tried to figure out where she'd gone wrong. It had been like this all day, from when she'd shown up in the chem wing when she was supposed to be at PE, to stumbling into the TV station's offices when she was due in math. She should have gone to New Student Orientation. Brooke had sworn it was unnecessary and promised that *she* would make sure Molly was sufficiently oriented, but that was before she started acting like Molly was contagious.

Correcting her course, Molly found the ladies' room. Two toilets flushed in unison.

"I mean, did you *see* how red she got?" giggled a voice from behind one stall door. "I thought she was going to have a coronary. Who'd confuse Willis Hall with the gym, anyway?"

"Clearly, they don't value literacy back where she comes from," the other snarked.

Molly scurried down to the handicapped stall and locked the door behind her before anyone noticed she was there. She dumped her stuff on the floor, closed the toilet lid, and sat down to eat her lunch. She'd seen Lindsay Lohan's character do this in *Mean Girls*. It seemed tragic at the time, but today Molly understood that it was wise (well, if she didn't think about how unsanitary it was). Overhearing nasty comments was one thing; having to endure them while the naysayers watched her eat a cheeseburger and wondered loudly whether it was one of her own cows was another story.

It would have been worse if she hadn't had her phone. Her lunch break luckily lined up with the end of the day back at Mellencamp, so as soon as the door banged behind those two girls, Molly grabbed her cell and dialed.

"How's it going?" Charmaine asked when she picked up the call.

Molly groaned, bent down to check the stalls for any signs of life, and then sighed. "I've never seen so many blondes," she said. "And everyone just looks through me. It's so weird."

Charmaine made sympathetic noises. "I wish I were there."

"Me, too. Do you think it's possible that Brick Berlin is also *your* father?"

"That would explain my movie-star charisma," Charmaine said. "I'm sorry everyone is still being so unfriendly. I thought Californians were supposed to be really nice."

"Right?" Molly peeled off a piece of her burger and popped it in her mouth. "They shouldn't have time to be mean. They should be out surfing."

"You might have to reach out to *them*," Charmaine suggested.

Molly had imagined Laurel chirping something similar, but when she'd glanced out at the open-air cafeteria where most upperclassmen ate lunch, she simply couldn't make herself do it. Everyone—especially Brooke, at her central table—seemed to be having a blast. Whenever she pictured walking out there, she knew the noise would stop, each group would hold its breath until she passed it by, and whichever one she picked would inevitably tell her there was no room, as when she'd sat down in math and was told every empty seat was reserved.

"I don't know how to do that," Molly finally said. "You haven't seen these people. They're like mini Brookes."

"All of them?"

"Most of them. The rest seem to flock to this black-haired girl who runs the TV station and is class president or something, but she keeps staring at me like she's waiting for me to apologize to her. I have no idea why."

"Well, maybe you *should* apologize," Charmaine said. "Just to make conversation. Look, I have to run—my mom needs me to babysit Eric—but remember that you're awesome. You might just need to start going up to people and beating them over the head with your awesomeness, that's all."

"You might be biased," Molly said. "But I promise I'll get on that as soon as I'm done befriending the fixtures in the bathroom."

"Call me later, okay?"

Molly recognized Charmaine's concerned tone. It was

last employed the day of Laurel's funeral, when Molly had insisted on going to Chick-fil-A on the way to the cemetery.

I have to get a grip. Things aren't that bad. I just need a better attitude.

Laurel had been fond of telling Molly, whenever she was complaining about something, that all things came to an end eventually. Molly repeated that mantra to herself the rest of the day until finally it came true and the last bell rang. She was proud of keeping her composure, but she couldn't pretend that her first day had gone well. For a student body of no doubt wealthy and well-traveled kids, her classmates seemed remarkably horrified by proof that there was human life outside the Los Angeles metro area. She felt completely isolated. And she dreaded doing it all over again tomorrow.

Molly deliberately lingered at her locker, calling Danny and leaving him a message when he didn't answer, then shuffling out to her car once the parking lot and the halls were as devoid as possible of people who wanted to stare and heckle. She had to wait for Brooke to finish some Drama Club something-or-other. Brick, who had eaten breakfast with them—aka four giant multivitamins washed down with a smoothie—greeted this scheduling problem with typical enthusiasm, waxing poetic about all the muscle-building extracurriculars Molly could explore in her free time. But there was no way Molly was going to spend an extra minute inside that school. She just wanted to turn up her iPod and sit in the Lexus, which had such aggressively tinted windows that it was the one place she could be sure absolutely no one was eyeballing her.

She dug around in her backpack for her car keys, but her hand couldn't find them.

Of course. So close, yet so far. Molly plopped her bag down on top of the Lexus and started taking things out of it with increasing hysteria—her cell phone, her notebook, her history textbook—until it was empty. Completely empty. No keys.

Molly glared at the contents of her bag, now splayed across the hood of her car and on the dark asphalt, and burst into tears.

"Looking for these?"

Molly jumped and met the eyes of a tall, dark-haired boy wearing a T-shirt that read PANTS, and holding out the Lexus key chain.

"Oh, my God, thank you," she said, trying to hide the fact that she was wiping tears off her cheeks. "Where did you find those?"

"I saw them drop out of your bag when you slammed your locker, but I was too far away," the boy said, handing them to her. "I'm sorry I didn't run after you, but you know. I run ugly." He grinned. "Plus I figured you weren't going to get too far without them."

Molly tried to laugh, but because of her crying jag it turned into an awkward hiccup.

"Rough day?" the boy asked, peering at her. "You're new here, right?"

"I must look so dumb out here, crying all over my car," Molly groaned.

"Nah, everyone cries their first day at Colby-Randall," he said, leaning against the SUV. "Take me, for example. Ninety pounds. Five feet tall. Braces. My mom? The new headmistress. It was horrible. Some senior actually tried to stuff me in my locker."

"Seriously?"

The boy nodded. "It gets worse. My mom caught him and gave him detention for three weeks. I think I would have preferred being stuffed in the locker."

"I didn't even know that happened outside of eighties movies," Molly said.

"I think all those movies were based on these people's parents."

Molly rubbed her watery eyes. "This place is so different from Indiana."

"*Oh*," he said, recognition washing over his face.

Molly nodded. "Yeah. I'm *that* girl."

"Sorry, I didn't mean to sound like a douche," he said. "I just…We've moved around a lot, but nothing like what you must be going through. My locker story seems kinda weak now."

"No, no, I thought it was very moving. Two thumbs up," Molly said.

"Next time I'm going to work in a natural disaster," he said. "And maybe a wedgie. Unless you think that'd kill the sex appeal."

"I'd normally say leave it out, but you just reminded me that a wedgie is the one bad thing that hasn't happened to me today." Molly grinned. "I always figured high school BS would be basically the same from place to place, but this"—she waved an arm at the massive mansion that marked the front of campus—"this is another galaxy."

"It's not all bad. Some of the kids here are cool, I promise. You just have to work a little harder to find them." He stuck out his hand. "Teddy McCormack."

"I'm Molly," she said, feeling a smile spread across her face. "And this is the longest conversation I've had all day."

"Well, it's a lost art," Teddy said. "I'm just proud of us for getting through the whole thing without trying to sell the other person a screenplay. It's so rare these days."

"Thanks again for my keys," she said. "Brooke would have been furious."

Teddy's mouth curled sympathetically. "Hang in there. I'm pretty sure her bark is worse than her bite."

"I'll let you know if she ever stops biting long enough to bark at me," Molly said. Then she caught herself. "Ugh, I'm sorry. That was rude of me. I'm sure this whole thing has been as weird for her as it has been for me."

Teddy looked impressed. "That's pretty magnanimous. And don't worry, it wasn't rude. Anyone can see Brooke is a tough nut. My sister Max is a junior, too, and she's…not a fan."

"Not a fan of what?" asked Brooke, stomping into view from behind a Range Rover.

"Thai food," Teddy said smoothly. "Too many bean sprouts. Anyway, it's been nice meeting you, Indiana. Brooke, a pleasure as always."

"I'm sure," Brooke said as he walked away, but she sounded unsure as to whether or not she was supposed to take offense.

Molly bent over to repack her purse and let fly a small smile. For the first time in days, weeks even, she felt almost human.

"Hurry up, Jeeves," Brooke crabbed. "Take me home now. I need some kombucha."

Almost.

eleven

MOLLY RESOLVED TO REMEMBER her conversation with Teddy McCormack if the day ever arrived when someone else was the new kid and she was the old-timer. If she'd left Colby-Randall on her first day without a single cordial moment with *anyone*, she might never have had the guts to go back for more.

As it was, Teddy's kindness had staved off any further crying jags or potential killing sprees. Instead, she'd kept her head high, ignored everyone's muttered taunts and jabs, and resisted the urge to throw a sharp elbow in response to being jostled in the hallway. Laurel would have been proud of Molly — if she weren't busy convincing Molly to slip an unlucky crystal into the perpetrators' book bags. Her mother had been a pacifist, but as Laurel was fond of saying, pacifism was the birthplace of passive aggression.

Brooke did her best to thwart Molly's efforts to rise above it all. Tuesday morning, she threw herself out of the Lexus screaming that Molly's breakfast Bloody Mary habit was going to kill them both, and her Facebook status on Wednesday—which had been read aloud near Molly by Jennifer Parker about twelve times, all while pretending not to see her—announced that alcohol had broken Brooke's family and three of her nails. Thursday, Brooke's brawny friend Magnus actually smacked a Post-it on Molly's back that said "Breathalyze me," which had sparked a series of imitators from his circle. Molly's favorite was, "I'm Molly Dix. Ask me about my middle name."

So Molly developed a morning routine: Every day, after Brooke made her customary sharp exit from the car, Molly slowly got out and scanned the crowd for one new thing to laugh about to herself whenever she needed to affix a pleasant expression to her face. Today, she noticed a girl in unhemmed jeans talking a mile a minute at her friend, then tripping over her pants and tumbling to the sidewalk. Her companion, that Shelby Kendall girl from CR-One, had simply glanced down at her fallen friend and kept walking without a word. Involuntarily, Molly shivered.

"Dude, this is the fifth day in a row you've been standing out here gawking like some freshman loser. Go inside. Face the craps."

Molly recognized the green-haired girl's voice. "Face the *what?*"

The girl grinned, pushing overgrown bangs out of her heavily kohl-rimmed eyes. "It's an acronym," she said. "Kind of. Colby-Randall Preparatory School. You'll see it on signs at football games."

"Your rivals must love that," Molly noted.

"So do our students. Our team is terrible," said a male voice.

Molly turned to see that Teddy McCormack had fallen in step alongside them. His light blue polo was only half tucked in and he was carrying a Pop-Tart.

"Want some?" he asked. "Strawberry. Max here thinks they're poison."

"I just can't believe Mom lets you eat those but she won't let me get my nose pierced," Max said, making a face. "They look like someone ran over a roll of SweeTarts."

"I love them," Molly admitted. "But I'm okay, thanks. Brick made the cook do eggs Benedict. Or in Brooke's case, grapefruit Benedict, hold the Benedict."

"Ah, an anti-Benedictite." Teddy nodded. "So sad in someone so young."

"Hey, she's obviously doing something right," Molly said. "She's got the body of a supermodel."

"Yeah, but how happy can a person be without hollandaise sauce?" Max said. "Seriously, look at Jennifer Parker. I don't think she's eaten once in the last two years and she's always complaining about something."

As if on cue, the pointy girl and her jock boyfriend from Molly's first day breezed past them, squabbling.

"You do *sometimes* use your foot on the ball," Jake was saying.

"Yeah, but, like, only one or two people!" Jennifer trilled. "Honestly, they should call it *handball*. I'm totally writing my English paper about this."

Max shook her head as the couple disappeared inside the school. "Jake tweeted something yesterday about how super hot Scarlett Johansson is, so this morning Jennifer's Facebook update said that Jake couldn't spell QB if you said it to him and asked him to repeat it," she said, sounding slightly awed.

"Jennifer isn't smart enough to have come up with that on her own," Teddy mused. "Must have been Arugula."

"Who?" Molly asked.

"Brooke's other BFF," Max explained. "The one who looks like Tyra Banks. Teddy thinks she's dreamy." Max batted her eyelashes exaggeratedly.

"Indeed, and Maxine, why are you following Jake on Twitter?" Teddy twinkled, but he'd turned a bit red.

"It's, um, anthropologically interesting," Max replied loftily.

"I bet," he snorted. "Catch you later, Indiana."

Molly waved as they followed Jennifer and Jake into the school. Max peeled off toward Headmistress McCormack's office, muttering something about reclaiming the cell phone her mother confiscated on Wednesday, leaving

Molly in the familiar position of having to navigate the halls by herself.

Squaring her shoulders, Molly marched over to her locker amid the now customary sea of faces glaring in her direction. Everyone wanted to see how she'd greet whatever new indignities were foisted upon her. This morning it was a flyer for a binge-drinking symposium at UCLA, taped to her locker next to a brochure for the famed rehab center Promises. But today she felt immune to it.

"Excellent," she said aloud to no one—and everyone—as she tore them off and pretended to read them with interest. "At least at Promises I'll have my own room."

As she opened her locker, she heard nothing. No taunts, no whispers, no barn-door jokes. It was a small victory, but a victory nonetheless.

✦ ✦ ✦

Buoyed, Molly decided to take things one step further and eat outside with the rest of civilization.

Colby-Randall's landscaped garden cafeteria was, in a word, ridiculous. With a hand-dug stream skimming the edges and a retractable roof in case a whiff of frost or rain dared penetrate their utopia, it was closer to a man-made Eden than a dining hall. Most of the best tables were taken: Brooke's was in the prime spot, of course, close enough to enjoy the giant fountain but far enough away that its trio of spitting mermaids didn't rain on her carefully shaped curls. From her central nexus radiated the social strata of people in her circle: devotees, casual followers, and then fringe riffraff. Molly noticed a similar pattern down at the end with the rock garden, which was populated mostly by student government types and academic clubs, at the center of which usually sat the mysterious Shelby Kendall — who still hadn't said a word to Molly, despite appearing to watch her intently from afar.

Molly chose an empty table as close to neutral territory as possible and sat down with her food. She fished around for her phone and sent Danny a quick text:

BREATHING FRESH AIR AT LUNCH. YOU'D BE PROUD.

Across the way, Brooke looked up from her conversation with Mini Tyra — who Molly gathered was Arugula — and narrowed her eyes. Molly ignored her and bit into her apple.

"So what's the deal? Are you radioactive, or just antisocial?"

Molly looked up at Max. "Nope, I'm a crazy, violent, unrepentant drunk. Haven't you heard?"

"That's to be expected. You're the new kid at a private school," Max said. "People here do not embrace change."

"I know the feeling," Molly said. "Do you want to sit down, or are you afraid I'm going to corrupt you?"

Max paused, her head cocked. "Well, I'm definitely bored of all the old drama," she said, her eyes flicking over to Brooke's table, where Jake had picked up Jennifer and was pretending to throw her into the fountain. "But it would make my mother, like, all tearful and proud to see me reaching out to the new kid, which could be irritating."

"She might let you get your nose pierced as a reward, though."

Max considered this. "Sold," she said, dropping her bag and sitting down next to Molly.

"So, who were you texting?" she asked.

"My boyfriend. I think."

"You think you were texting him, or you think he's your boyfriend?"

Molly shrugged. "Both, at this point. We never actually broke up, but he missed our Skype date last night."

"Skype anagrams to 'pesky,'" Max said. Then she flushed. "Sorry, dumb habit. But it fits."

"It does," Molly said, impressed. "Got one for Colby-Randall?"

Max wrinkled her nose. "Not really. The best one so far is 'carnally bold,' although sometimes when I'm talking to my mother, I prefer 'cornball lady.'"

Molly cracked up. "That's awesome. I was going to ask if there was anyone normal around here, but I think you just answered that question."

"Oh, this place is a hotbed of abnormal," Max said, cracking open a Tupperware container of what looked like wilted greens and sweet potatoes. "See that dude over there, by the soft-serve?"

147

Molly turned around to see a very short kid with a Mohawk apparently attempting to find out how high he could fill a cone with vanilla fro-yo before it overflowed.

"His dad is some bigwig at NBC, and last year, I swear to God, he brought a peacock to school," Max said. She tilted her chin toward the black-haired beauty Molly recognized from the school news. "Shelby Kendall's dad runs *Hey!* so she's all up in the TV station trying to break news, like it's genetic or something. And Jennifer Parker used to be some kind of sitcom child star."

Molly followed Max's gaze to Brooke's swatch of grass, where Jennifer was now combing through Jake's hair with her nails while he napped against her legs.

"I thought she looked familiar," Molly said, taking a bite of her sandwich.

"How could you tell? She never makes eye contact with anyone. She's like Audrina from *The Hills*. It's creepy," Max complained through a mouthful of spinach. "I don't know how Jake puts up with it."

"How long have they been going out?"

"One year, seven months, and a week," Max said automatically. "Or, you know, so I hear."

"So where do all the kids of, like, accountants and insurance agents and stuff go?" Molly asked. "Is there a special school for *normal* people in L.A.?"

"Mavis Moore's dad is an accountant," Max offered, pointing to a girl about twenty feet away who was making origami tacos out of graph paper. "But he counts the votes for the Oscars, so I guess that doesn't count. Every year he sits in a locked room for three days."

In the distance, Mavis began crushing her tacos one by one.

"I think it explains a lot," Max added. "Arugula's dad is a botanist, so that's kind of normal. Although her mom is Brick's agent, so..."

"She's the one your brother likes, right?" Molly asked, gazing at Arugula, who was splitting time between reading a chem textbook and listening to Brooke.

Max grinned. "He'll deny it, but he's totally had a crush on her since his sophomore year. She's in all the senior science classes with him, but he's too chicken to ask her out."

Molly watched Brooke and Arugula chuckle over something together. The idea that Brooke had a genius for a friend was sort of intriguing, if unlikely. Maybe there was a *Cosmo* hidden behind the textbook somewhere.

"Excuse me, do you want this?"

Max's jaw swung open lightly. Shelby Kendall, clad in a fitted navy blazer, black leggings, and black leather knee-high flat boots, was standing over them, holding out a coffee cup. Her sleek hair was braided. She looked like she was about to grab her Thoroughbred for some show jumping.

"My driver accidentally brought me two nonfat mocha lattes with foam, and it seems everyone else around here is lactose intolerant," Shelby continued. "Can you *imagine?*"

Molly looked at Max, then back up at Shelby. "Oh, are you talking to me?" she asked stupidly.

"I doubt she's talking to me." Max snorted.

"Please do take it. It'll just go to waste," Shelby said, smiling very wide. "Coffee is the number one social lubricant for youths aged fifteen to twenty-one, according to a piece I'm doing for CR-One next week. My source is Dr. Oz." She lowered her voice. "Old family friend, you know."

"I'll take it," Max said loudly, reaching for the paper cup.

Shelby steadfastly ignored her and waggled the cup in front of Molly's face.

"Um, of course, yeah," Molly stammered, getting to her feet. "Thanks for—"

"Magnus!" Shelby shouted, as heads turned to stare at her standing with Molly. "Magnus, we need to discuss your dad's lawsuit against ESPN."

Shelby swept away, straight through a bespectacled girl juggling a clipboard, some books, and her lunch tray. Everything, including her glasses, crashed to the ground. Molly saw Brooke look up and snap her fingers, dispatching a burly athlete to the kid's aid.

"Very interesting," Max breathed.

"I know, I can't believe people actually answer when Brooke snaps," Molly said, distracted by sitting down without dumping steaming hot coffee in her lap.

"That's not what I meant." Max pointed at Brooke. "*That* is."

Brooke was still staring right at where Shelby and Molly had been, and she looked distinctly unhappy. Nervous, even.

"Oh, crap. What did I do?" Molly sighed.

"Those two are mortal enemies," Max explained. "Damn, Shelby must be loving you right now. Brooke looks like she just ate a brain tumor."

The bell rang, prompting everyone to clear up their lunches. Brooke and Arugula hustled off, whispering furiously.

"Why do they hate each other?" Molly asked.

"Who even knows." Max shrugged as they walked back inside. "Brick is an actor, Shelby's dad is a tabloid guy. Never the progeny shall mix, or some shit like that."

"Well, far be it from me to look a gift latte in the mouth," Molly said, stopping at her locker. "At least Shelby isn't treating me like I'm diseased. That wins her a few points."

Molly tried to open the locker door, but it was jammed. She gave it a vicious tug, and it flew open, dumping a cascade of corn husks all over her feet and the floor.

Raucous laughter came from her left. Molly looked up and saw Brooke and her friends giggling while Magnus high-fived another giant jock type.

Molly just shook her head.

"Seriously, corn husks? That's so fourth grade," Max shouted in Brooke's direction. "Okay, I can see why you're so fixated on normal. You need a break." She grabbed Molly's notebook and scribbled something on the page.

151

"Come over for dinner tonight. We may not be any more normal than anyone else, but at least we're *sane*."

The PA system crackled. "Molly Dix, please report to Headmistress McCormack's office."

Molly waved a hand at the heavens. "You sure she'll want me for dinner? Maybe whatever I'm about to get busted for is really bad."

"She's working late," Max said triumphantly. "You're in the clear. And look, other than how you totally just tried to peer pressure me into chugging Miller behind the bleachers, you haven't done anything wrong, right?"

Molly laughed grimly, then trudged off toward the headmistress's office as just about every guy in the hallway tried to hide a joke about her last name inside a coughing fit. She *hadn't* done anything. So why did it feel like she was going to spend her entire L.A. life in trouble?

twelve

"I HEARD SHE HAS DENTAL IMPLANTS in front because she got in a bar fight."

"It wasn't a bar fight. She got dropped doing a keg stand."

"Those aren't even my favorites," Arugula said to Brooke as the two chattering students walked by their table. "I prefer the stories involving livestock. Very inventive."

"I'm sure I don't know *what* you're talking about," Brooke said airily, leaning back in her wicker chair with an innocent smile and toying gently with the sheath on her cardboard cup of organic mood-cleansing tea. But she mentally patted herself on the back for the stellar work she'd done, subtly allowing a "confidence" or two to be overheard, and making some anonymous comments on the few short blurbs that had popped up online about her and Molly. Even off campus — albeit not far; Café Munch was popular with Colby-Randall students precisely because they could get there during free periods without a car — the fruits of her labor were still the juiciest topic du jour. It was astoundingly easy to manipulate the grapevine when you knew how to find its roots.

Brooke turned her face to the sky and closed her eyes, enjoying a mood as warm as the weather (clearly, her tea was already helping). The week was on its way to ending on a high note. If Brick had any lingering doubts about that picture that ran in *Hey!*, they seemed to be fading, as he'd handed her two peanut butter PowerBars before he left for Florida that morning — which to Brick was tantamount to giving her a bag of diamonds. Shelby Kendall had been too busy at CR-One to get in her face yet. And Operation Lose the Hoosier was chugging along at a brisk pace. Molly had made no effort to join any activities, nor assimilate with the Colby-Randall crowd. Instead, she just absorbed everything that was thrown at her, by Brooke or anyone else. It would be a mere matter of time before she tucked her forked tail between her legs and toddled back to Indiana, where grody nylon backpacks were like Birkins and backbones were obviously optional.

Brooke lowered her head again and peered at the Crunch Gym across the plaza. She knew from careful attention to detail — which was different from stalking; a girl couldn't help it if noteworthy things just *happened* to take place in front of her—that Bradley Cooper favored the afternoon spinning class, and running into him there was central to her scheme to marry him someday. But beyond the other Colby-Randall students milling around the outdoor café, scarfing all-natural beverages and organic muffins, she'd only spied an Olsen twin (wearing a wool overcoat over her yoga pants even though it was eighty-five and sunny). Bradley was AWOL. It was the only thing this week that hadn't gone her way.

"I do have one query," Arugula piped up. "Do you feel at all repentant for all this enmity, given that her mother has shuffled off this mortal coil?"

"Fewer five-dollar words, please?"

"Read your SAT prep books, Brooke." Ari frowned. "What I said was, don't you feel bad about freezing Molly out? The girl's mom died. Have you even talked about that?"

"Okay, first of all, I resent the idea that I'm contractually obligated to like someone just because she had a death in the family," Brooke said, feeling the effects of her soothing herbal blend begin to wane. "And Daddy gave me no leg to stand on at home, so I need some territory to call my own. It's not like I'm *disemboweling* her."

Arugula combed her hair thoughtfully.

"I both accede to your argument and appreciate your use of a multisyllable word." She nodded.

Privately, Brooke did feel a tiny bit guilty, but that was exactly why she tried not to think about it. She didn't have time for compassion. She was on a mission.

"Besides, it's not like she's all alone in the world," Brooke continued. "Her happiness is, like, Brick's number one priority. And she's always hanging out on the balcony talking to her boyfriend. She's fine."

"She has a boyfriend?" Ari asked, furrowing her brow.

"Yeah, some dope she's got on the hook back home," Brooke said. "She tried to tell me once but I couldn't handle the number of times she said 'um' in one sentence."

Arugula stood up and brushed off her Thakoon pencil skirt. "Intriguing. A hometown sweetheart is so adorably rural."

"Wait, where are you going?" Brooke asked, checking her Rolex. "We don't have to leave for ten more minutes. I can't be on time to my first rehearsal. I have to *arrive*."

Arugula rolled her eyes and sat down again. "Five more minutes," she countered. "I told Teddy McCormack I wanted to go over some stuff from chemistry this week."

She then undid one of the top buttons on her collared shirt. Brooke giggled.

"Very studious." She nodded.

"Oh, give me a break. It's just a *little* extra epidermis," Arugula said. "Men are visual creatures."

"Dude, he drives a *Toyota*."

Ari shrugged. "He's smart. And I need to be intellectually stimulated. I don't expect you to understand." She paused. "No offense."

"Some taken," Brooke said, only half seriously. She checked her watch again and sighed. Her future first husband had obviously blown off his workout today, and she certainly didn't need to stick around to watch the constant stream of D-list starlets wandering in and out of Crunch sporting booty shorts and sports bras, as if they were just waiting for someone to notice them and ask for an autograph. When she hit it big—soon, obviously, once Brick witnessed her mastery in *My Fair Lady*—Brooke resolved never to go begging like that. Spandex was so desperate.

"Fine, let's get out of here," she said, swigging the last of her tea. "I have an entrance to make."

✦ ✦ ✦

The new Brick Berlin Theater for Serious Emotional Artistry sat near the edge of campus on an unassuming stretch of grass. Brick had chosen a nondescript setting because "the stage is a canvas to be painted by your souls, and also, if there's nothing to do outside, people are more likely to get back to their seats after intermission." The 2,500-seat building, modeled after one prong of the Sydney Opera House, sported an orchestra pit, dressing rooms, and a concessions area run by the freshman class. Even to Brooke's biased eye, it was over the top, but she liked it as a brick-and-mortar reminder of her own social superiority.

"No, Jake, you can't wear your letter jacket to play Freddy," Jennifer was saying as Brooke entered. "Freddy isn't a jock. Freddy is, like, sensitive."

"So football players can't be sensitive?" Jake asked,

combing back his blond hair with his fingers. "Tell that to my sprained pinky. It hurts like a bitch."

Brooke winced. Jake insisted he needed the diversity on his transcripts, and Jennifer swore she could turn him into a great actor—"Like Peyton Manning!"—but Brooke already suspected his casting had been a mistake. He lacked subtlety.

Still, being inside the theater got her blood pumping. They'd staged small-scale plays in the past, but this was Colby-Randall's first major production, and *she* was going to make it great. Molly could steal her precious closet space, but she couldn't take that away. Brick's approval was all but assured.

"Our Eliza Doolittle is here!" crowed Jennifer, ushering Brooke front and center. "Take a bow, Brooke."

Obligingly, Brooke curtsied as the cast applauded.

"Please, no, this is going to be a team effort. It's not just me," she said. "It's me and *Jennifer.*"

"Oh, but it's mostly Brooke; she has such vision," Jennifer gushed. "I'm just a professional consultant. My acting coach wants me to understand the other side of my art."

"Right," Brooke said dismissively. "Anyway, thank you all for coming here on a Friday afternoon. Postponing the start of your weekend is a test of your commitment as actors, and I am happy to see that you've all passed. Now, do everything we say, and this will be an enormous hit. Ignore us, and perish. Got it?"

Everyone blinked, then the applause resumed in a scattered, nervous way.

"Fabulous!" Brooke beamed. "I assume you all learned your lines over the summer. Let's do an off-book run-through to see where we are."

"I have a question." Jake put up his hand. "Why do you call it *My Fair Lady* if the book says *Pygmalion?*"

"Because *Pygmalion* sounds like a skin disease," Brooke retorted. "We're using the title from the musical. Now please, let's get started so we're not here all night. Jennifer will read the stage directions. Go."

Brooke wished Brick could see her now, running her cast with authority, jotting intelligent comments into her note-book — for instance, the more Julie Newman talked, the more obvious it became she could *not* carry off a bonnet — and basically already kicking ass. She'd spent all summer sketching out the blocking and set ideas, dropping hints to Jake that the lead actress always gets flowers....

Suddenly, she realized nobody was speaking.

"What happened?" Brooke asked. "Did we forget our lines already, people? Seriously? You had *three months*. I — "

Jennifer cleared her throat and nodded toward the spot just over Brooke's left shoulder. She turned in her seat and saw Molly standing there, a pained look on her face. Brooke clenched her jaw. Why was she always *everywhere?*

"Yes?" Brooke hissed. "Are you lost again?"

"No. I'm here..." Molly gulped. "I'm here to work on the play."

Brooke's laugh sounded tinny and hollow, like dropping an eyelash curler in the sink.

"Hilarious!" she said. "Now run along. I'm in the middle of something important here."

"I know, but...Headmistress McCormack said she'd enforce this personally," Molly told her. "I guess Brick told her I can do costumes, like my mom, and...I don't know, he said something about the trenches, I think from that Vietnam movie he did. And then he said he can't wait to see our production. So...we don't really have a choice."

Brooke felt her stomach churn. In her periphery, the cast exchanged apprehensive glances. Surely, Brick couldn't expect her to work with Molly on the play. *Her* play, that she had slaved over all summer while he skulked around the house and made plans for his secret, stupid love child to move in with them and ruin her life. How would he like it if she stormed onto the set of *Avalanche!* and told him he had to let Quentin Tarantino direct all the action sequences? (Brick and Quentin had a falling out over Uma Thurman and hadn't spoken in years. Privately, Brooke was relieved. Quentin had a habit of coming over for dinner and crashing in the pool house for three weeks.)

What's she going to ruin next? Is she going to shave my head and start wearing my hair?

Brooke felt like she finally understood what Dr. Hedge Von Henson experienced that time the flesh-eating virus went on a rampage through *Lust for Life*. Despite her best efforts at containment, Molly was contaminating every single aspect of Brooke's life, and it was beginning to seem like a fight she couldn't win. So she went with the first plan B that leapt to mind.

"Where were we?" Brooke asked the cast. "Jake, I think it's your line."

Everyone stared at her.

"Hello?" Brooke trilled. "The sooner we finish the read-through, the sooner we'll all get to start our weekends!"

"Um," Jennifer started, nervously twirling a lock of hair around her index finger. "Don't you need to finish...?"

"Finish what?" Brooke chirped.

Jake scratched his head and shot Jen a concerned glance. "Is she...*okay?*" he asked.

"Peachy!" Brooke said. "Let's get back to work!"

"I promise this wasn't my idea," Molly said. "Can't we just—"

"Jake," Brooke said, her voice getting uncontrollably higher than she'd prefer, "please continue."

Jake looked blankly from Brooke to Molly and back again.

"Or I'll give your part to Neil Westerberg!" Brooke snapped.

"But my part is better than—" Neil began.

"Are you *kidding me?*" Molly asked, from somewhere behind Brooke's shoulder.

"Brooke, I'm sure it'll only take a second to deal with her," Jen said.

"I have no idea what you're talking about," Brooke said.

She turned around and pretended to look for something, then let her gaze drift past Molly. "There's *nobody* here."

Their eyes met for a second. The hurt in Molly's, and their likeness to Brick's, was surprisingly hard for Brooke to withstand without losing her composure and apologizing. She turned around quickly and clapped her hands to avoid betraying any reaction.

"Onward!" she said.

The cast stared at her with a mixture of disbelief, awe, and a little fear. Maybe more than a little. But then Jake nervously picked up with his last line, and the read-through continued.

Brooke held her breath until she heard footsteps behind her getting fainter and fainter. The door slammed, and she knew Molly was gone. She wanted to exhale, but her body was still tense and her stomach hurt. What was wrong with her? She ought to feel victorious. This was war—an ugly, but necessary, war. And war always had casualties.

Molly let the theater door slam behind her. She'd never felt dumber. Her strenuous efforts to rise above all the rudeness, to behave in a way that wouldn't make her cringe when she looked back on her life in twenty years, were being spit back in her face. Why couldn't she have stood up for herself more? Why did she *always* have to be the one acting like an adult? She didn't look like the better person. She looked like a fool.

What am I supposed to do, Mom?

Usually, Molly could conjure her mother's voice with ease, in part because Laurel had a lot to say about a lot of random topics, and always yielded something Molly could put in her figurative pocket and apply to other situations. For instance, after an odd encounter with a guy in Whole Foods, Laurel had made Molly promise never to date a man who owned a ferret; this helped the summer she and Danny broke up and she met a fellow camp counselor who seemed awesome until he started talking about his pet rat.

But her mother was strangely silent today.

"I can't believe how rude that was."

Molly lifted her head and met Shelby Kendall's sympathetic gaze.

"You saw that?" she asked.

"The best reporters know where the story is before it even happens."

"That's...I'm sure that's true," Molly said, unsure what else to offer.

"You're incredibly brave, you know, Molly," Shelby said. "I've been watching you all week. Honestly, I'm concerned." She paused dramatically, biting her red lower lip. "I knew as soon as I heard you were moving here that her pathological tendencies would rear up and bite."

Molly stayed silent. She didn't want to fuel the fire, but

Shelby wasn't exactly wrong, either. Brooke did seem a little unhinged.

"I'm sure you're aware that Brooke and I are not close," Shelby said softly. "I don't know if it's because Brad Pitt once told me I look just like Angelina, or because her mother skipped town and she's resentful of my stable and loving family situation....But I think perhaps no one understands what you're going through quite like I do."

"She did this to you, too?" Molly asked, feeling a small flood of relief.

"Let's not dredge up ugly details from the past," Shelby said. "We're talking about you now. You need a shoulder. And I have two."

That this was a quote from one of the Dirk Venom movies—*Shoot Before Dying*—did not escape Molly's notice. *What kind of sales pitch is this, anyway?*

As if she heard the question, Shelby reached into her Michael Kors bag and pulled out a small sterling-silver case the size of a deck of cards, from which she extracted a small rectangle with one reflective gold side. She handed it to Molly and said, "Why don't you give me a call sometime? Perhaps I could be of help."

The card was embossed with the Colby-Randall crest, had the *Hey!* logo tucked down near the bottom, and read, "Shelby Kendall: Reporter, News Anchor, Student Leader." Molly had never encountered anyone her age with her own card, but then again, she'd also never encountered a teenager who treated socializing like a business transaction.

"Fancy," she said, for lack of a better reaction.

"They're terribly handy," Shelby noted. "I once ran into a *very* famous reclusive redhead in the parking lot of Gelson's, and if I hadn't had official documentation, I'd never have introduced myself, and then I wouldn't have seen that she was buying two boxes of laxatives. *Hey!* ran with that story for three weeks in a row."

"Well, thank you, I, um, I really appreciate this," Molly said.

"Don't thank me. Call me," Shelby said, reaching out to squeeze Molly's shoulder. "You won't be sorry."

She turned away, then stopped and looked back at Molly.

"See?" she said, a tiny smile playing around the corners of her mouth. "I told you we'd meet again."

The memory came rushing back: She'd bumped into Shelby, almost literally, the night of the party. While she was drunk. In retrospect, Molly remembered Shelby had seemed to be enjoying that entire fiasco. And that she'd been wearing Molly's Marchesa.

Molly glanced down at the card in her hand, then over her shoulder at the closed doors of the theater. Monday, she wouldn't have known what to do with this. But today she had a pretty good idea where to start figuring it out.

thirteen

MOLLY WENT STRAIGHT TO DINNER at the McCormacks'. She decided Brooke's behavior denied her the right to a ride home. The laws of physics supported this: If a person had to chauffeur you around town, then that person definitely existed. So if Brooke wanted to pretend Molly was transparent, then she could find another driver. Besides, it wasn't like she'd stranded Brooke at a truck stop. Someone, either voluntarily or under terrified duress, would give her a lift.

It took Molly ten minutes to decipher Max's chicken-scratch handwriting, but eventually she managed to punch an address into the Lexus's navigation system that it recognized. Molly didn't even care. Wherever she ended up, be it Max's house or a prison replete with serial killers, it would be an improvement over her afternoon.

The directions took her to the end of a cul-de-sac off a pothole-plagued road near the Hollywood Bowl and deposited her in front of a two-story shingled Craftsman bungalow. The house, which sat like a madcap anomaly between two neat little thatched cottages with tidy porches and blooming window boxes, was nearly as patchy as the street. Someone had tried, and failed, to improve it by adding a turret, and its compact, wild yard was dotted with gnarled vegetable patches and a knot of trees heavy with fruit. The effect was more romantic than run-down, though that appeared to be a fluke of nature rather than a landscaping plan.

As Molly parked behind a rusty 4Runner, a very compact bald man emerged from the garage dragging a dishwasher in a little red wagon. He squinted at Molly, then offered an absentminded salute before tugging his cargo to a dilapidated shed. An avocado fell from a tree with a thud, narrowly missing her head.

"Thank God you found it," Max said, appearing on the porch. "MapQuest usually tries to make people turn into the side of the mountain."

As she walked up the steps, Molly noticed Max's face was scrubbed clean, her hair held back by an old bandanna. She looked about twelve years old, and rather striking, almost fragile. Without the aggressive eyeliner and her shaggy green mop, Molly could see Max's eyes, which Molly had thought were dark but which actually had flecks of amber glowing in them.

"Maxine, have you seen my soldering iron?" the bald man asked, coming out of the shed and holding a disintegrating weed whacker almost as tall as he was.

"Dad, meet Molly. She just moved here. She's Brick Berlin's new kid."

Mr. McCormack looked confused. "Is he the tan parent your mother is always complaining about?"

Max shot Molly an apologetic look. "Yeah, probably."

"Right, right. Welcome!" he said, shifting the weed whacker to his other hand so he could shake Molly's. "I hope Maxine and Theodore have been helpful."

"Teddy would kill you if he heard you call him that," Max said.

"Theodore can't hear anything over that guitar," Mr. McCormack said. "Molly, I hope you like veal parmigiana. We have plenty."

"Ew. You can have mine," Max said. "Veal is disgusting. Dad, weren't you looking for something?"

Mr. McCormack clapped his head to his head. "Yes! The iron. I am never going to get this thing to work without it."

"Dad's an inventor," Max explained.

"I'm going to revolutionize the alarm clock," Mr. McCormack announced.

"Just don't test this one on me," Max grunted. "I still have a bruise from that thing with the lacrosse stick."

Mr. McCormack stared at the weed whacker. "Dinner's in an hour, girls," he said, and wandered off through the calf-length grass.

"That means anytime between half an hour and five hours," Max explained as they stepped onto the cluttered porch. "He loses track of time when he's working."

"My mom did that," Molly said. "We once had dinner at midnight because she didn't want to interrupt her train of thought on a prom dress."

"So you get it," Max said, opening the front door and shuffling through the foyer, down a hallway lined entirely with bookshelves, and into her bedroom at the back of the house.

Max's room, like the lawn, was a complete disaster. The floor was covered with library books, magazines, a tangle of indistinguishably clean and dirty clothes, and several newspaper pages folded to the crosswords—half-finished, and done in pen. There was one black Doc Marten sitting on top of Max's dresser, and the cactus on the bedside table was dead.

"I didn't know you could kill those things," Molly said, moving aside a pile of bras to sit in the overstuffed corduroy armchair across from Max's bed.

"I can kill anything," Max said, plonking down in the middle of her unmade bed. "So what did my mom want with you this afternoon? She was on a rampage this week. She called me into her office *four times.* I'm already on track to beat my record."

"What's your record?" Molly asked, grabbing a crossword and fanning herself.

Max leapt off her bed and flipped a switch on the rickety

window air-conditioning unit. It shuddered on with a wheeze. "If you think it's hot now, try sleeping in here during a real heat wave. Every summer my parents decide to get central air, and then every summer they find out it's, like, twenty thousand dollars. Teddy once slept in the backyard."

Max flopped back down on the bed, her bandanna slipping two inches down her forehead. She shoved it up impatiently. "What were we talking about?" she wondered.

"Your record," Molly prompted.

"Oh, right!" Max crowed. "Okay, so one week last year, I got called to my mom's office *nine times*! It was epic."

"How did you pull that off?"

Max looked pleased with herself. "I was helping Teddy's class boycott their fetal-pig dissection unit in biology. And that was also the week they decided they could do unannounced locker checks, which is a *total* violation of our civil rights. So I chained myself to my locker in protest. And then I ditched geometry. *Six weeks* of detention. What'd you get?"

Molly rolled her eyes. "Prison," she said. "I have to work on the play with Brooke."

"*Ew.* Why?"

"This is all part of Brick's big master plan to turn us into best friends. He's also making us share a room."

Max looked horrified. "He's making you sleep in the same room as the person who told our gym class that your drinking problem started because you were born a boy?"

That was a new one.

"Who was born a boy?" Teddy asked, appearing in Max's open doorway.

Max gestured at Molly with a lazy thumb.

"No way," Teddy chuckled. "Turns out Indiana's just full of secrets."

"I'm pretty sure she's not *really* a dude, Teddy."

"Tell me another one, dummy," he said, coming in and perching on her windowsill. "I mean, it's not like her name is *Max* or anything."

"Don't you have some T-shirts to shrink?" Max retorted. "Anyway, don't worry about it, Molly. I don't think very many people believed her."

"Well, just as long as a few of them did." Molly sighed sarcastically and rubbed her temples.

"Way to go, Max, now you've given her a complex," Teddy said.

"Oh, it's all right," Molly said. "That's not even the worst thing that happened today."

"Yeah, I heard Magnus talking about the corn husks in the hallway. That guy is such an idiot."

"No, get this," Molly said. "After your mom told me I have to do costumes for the play, I went to tell Brooke and she acted like I wasn't even there."

Teddy wrinkled his brow. "The silent treatment? At her age?"

"More like the invisible treatment. People actually asked her to acknowledge me and she pretended she didn't know what they were talking about," Molly said. "Even Shelby Kendall was surprised."

Teddy and Max exchanged glances.

"What was Shelby doing there?" Teddy asked, patting the pockets of his cargo shorts, looking for something. Eventually, he emerged with a pack of cinnamon gum. "Want some?"

"That stuff makes my tongue numb," Max announced.

"I wasn't offering it to you," Teddy said mildly. "Indiana?"

"No, thanks," Molly said. "Shelby caught up with me afterward. I guess she overheard the whole thing. She gave me her business card."

"She *would* have business cards," Max grunted. "Let me see it."

Molly dug the card out of the pocket of her jeans. Teddy hopped onto the bed with Max to examine it. Their height difference was such that he looked like he was folding himself in half just to scoot up next to his sister. But somehow they were still unmistakably related—same waves in their hair, same crooked smiles, same crinkled noses as they studied Shelby's card.

"How much do you wanna bet her dad charged her to use the *Hey!* logo?" Teddy said.

"Are you going to call her?" Max asked.

"No," Molly said. "I mean, right? She's so weird. She was all, 'I've been watching you,' like she was about to go through our trash."

"Oh, no, I'm sure she would have done that before she talked to you," Max said.

Molly peered at her and saw she wasn't kidding.

"I think you should call," Max added, after a moment.

"No, you don't," Teddy said, crinkling his brown eyes with dismay.

"It's a good idea," Max protested.

Teddy gave her an incredulous look. "In what universe?"

"Brooke hates Shelby, and Brooke is being mean to Molly," Max said slowly, as if she were explaining a complicated concept to a very stupid person. "Therefore, if Molly becomes friendly with Shelby, it will turn Brooke into a crazy person, which is going to be incredibly satisfying for all of us."

"Maybe for *you*," Teddy said. "But Shelby is bad news."

"Don't be so dramatic," Max said. "Maybe Shelby actually likes Molly. You don't know."

"Shelby doesn't like anyone," Teddy said. "Unless they can get her something she wants, and usually, that something is a story."

"Look, you can only take the high road for so long," Max pointed out. "Unless you're Gandhi, but I think we can all agree that he was exceptional."

"Hello, I'm right here," Molly said, waving her arms. "Don't I get a vote?"

"Depends who you're voting with," Max grinned.

Teddy raised his eyebrows expectantly. "Me, obviously," he said, yanking Max's bandanna down over her eyes.

Molly chuckled and sent up a silent word of thanks that the McCormacks hadn't joined the faction of the Colby-Randall student body that was filling her locker with agricultural waste products. Hanging out with them reminded her of all the long afternoons she used to spend in Charmaine's room, talking about nothing in particular. It was just easy, comfortable, like the battered old recliner her grandfather sat in to watch Pacers games and tell the same old story about the time he met Larry Bird. And now that she was grappling with this unwelcome social problem, Molly appreciated having acquaintances—*friends*, she hoped—who could give unbiased advice.

Max smacked Teddy's arm—for a whippet of a girl, she seemed awfully strong—and scooted away from him, before turning her attention back to Molly. "So what'll it be?" she asked, ripping off her bandanna and throwing it casually at Teddy's face. "Fight the Evil Empire, or be all boring and nice?"

Well, *mostly* unbiased.

"I feel like getting in the middle of this Brooke-Shelby feud might be a bad idea," Molly announced.

"Finally, someone is talking sense," Teddy said. "Well, other than me."

"I'm just saying, Brooke won't stop pushing you until she sees that you can push back," Max argued. "So, yeah, Shelby Kendall might be kind of a dillhole, but she's also a means to an end. Imagine how satisfying it will be when

Brooke chokes on her edamame because you and Shelby are palling around at lunch."

"Girls," Teddy muttered.

"What?" Max asked.

"Well, it's just that if two guys are mad at each other, we brawl and then it's over. Girls resort to psychological warfare. It seems exhausting," he explained.

"Don't be such a sexist," Max snapped. "This isn't like that."

Teddy rolled his eyes good-naturedly and flicked a tank top off the bed. "Well, what it's like, then?"

"It's...okay, it's kind of like that. But come on. Brooke deserves to get a taste of her own medicine for once," Max said. "Don't you think?"

Teddy tugged on a lock of her hair. "You're just saying that because she called you Maxi-Pad for, like, two whole years."

"Well. Maybe a little bit," Max admitted. She turned to Molly. "Seriously, though, do you want this thing with Brooke to go on for *years*? Because I feel like it could."

Molly looked down at the business card in her hand. The idea of living through Brooke's backstabbing and mind games until the day she went to college made her skin feel too tight. Besides, for an alleged dillhole, Shelby *had* been friendlier at Colby-Randall than Brooke. Molly took a deep breath and tapped the card against her mouth before smiling timidly at Teddy and Max.

"No," she said. "I don't."

fourteen

"I'M *SO* GLAD YOU CALLED," Shelby said, twisting her long black locks into a knot, then putting on a sun hat so large that its family reunions would include at least one sombrero. "You can't spend every day cooped up in your room e-mailing your friends at home. *Hey!*'s medical expert claims that too much canned air can cause lung depression."

Molly filled her lungs with sweet, tangy beach air and exhaled. "Nope, nothing depressed here," she said, letting her head roll back luxuriously.

She'd assumed that calling Shelby would lead to a few sociable encounters in the hallway, maybe a shared lunch hour or two—just enough interaction to make Brooke's brain explode and trickle out her ear. But Shelby had immediately offered to meet Molly outside the Bel Air gates—"I can't go inside. A *certain* beloved Oscar winner had us blacklisted, like it's *our* fault he went out to get the newspaper wearing a Speedo and bunny slippers"—and whisk her off to the beach. Molly had been at odds: On the one hand, Shelby's reputation preceded her. On the other, she'd never seen the Pacific.

That hand won. Actually, it wasn't even close. And now, staring at the view, not even the issue of *Hey!* she'd found waiting for her in Shelby's vintage Mercedes convertible could make her blood pressure spike—even if it *did* contain a blind item implying that Molly stole all Brooke's designer shoes. El Matador felt like a secret, tucked away in a far corner of Malibu and reached by two steep wooden staircases and a sharp, dusty hike down to the beach. The swatch of warm sand was narrow, smooth, postcard-perfect, and framed by rock formations—exactly the kind of scene Molly had imagined when she decided to leave the Midwest for California. For the first time since her flight had landed at LAX, she felt truly relaxed. At this rate, she'd be a beach bum in about three days. Maybe she'd learn to surf. Brick would like that; it was, after all, how the titular hero in *Rad Man* had dispensed most of his rogue justice.

Shelby stretched out facedown on her towel, then reached back and unhooked her bikini top.

"No tan lines." She winked. "God, isn't it just fabulous out here? I need this so bad after last week. You would not believe how amateurish most of the students at CR-One are. Don't they have any *ambition?*"

A Frisbee landed right at Shelby's elbow with a soft, sandy puff.

"Sorry," the dude said, jogging over to it while making no effort to hide his appraisal of Shelby's bare back. "My aim is bad."

"Is it?" Shelby purred, gazing up at him. Molly thought she recognized him from TV, but she couldn't be sure. Charmaine would be so annoyed, but Molly didn't know yet if it was kosher to gawk at the famous people or just let them be. It seemed rude to stare.

Shelby extracted a Sharpie from her beach bag and scrawled her phone number on the Frisbee before tossing it toward the ocean. Obligingly, the hunky actor trotted away after it.

"See? I am so good," Shelby said with a triumphant smile. "If he uses the number, *Hey!* will bust him for pursuing jailbait. Father would be *thrilled* to get someone from *Lust for Life*."

"I'm sure he thought you were eighteen," Molly said.

Shelby slid her sunglasses down her nose and cocked an eyebrow at Molly. "Did you get carded in the parking lot, honey? This is a public beach. I could be *fourteen* for all he knows. Someone in his position should really be a little bit more savvy, don't you think?" She flicked her shades back up over her eyes and rested her cheek on the sand. "Besides, it's a good reporter's duty to hold people accountable for their flaws. For their own benefit *and* the community's."

Molly just smiled. Shelby was an interesting creature.

She exuded friendliness in a way reminiscent of Brooke's initial onslaught of goodwill, but with an underlying edge that Brooke lacked, which Molly attributed to Shelby's much-professed ambition of becoming the Anderson Cooper of celebrity news. She teemed with amusing gossip, and even though fact seemed to blur with fiction occasionally— for example, Molly had a hard time believing that Shelby had a part in discovering Sandra Bullock's divorce—Shelby's entertaining penchant for embellishment made her good company.

"So, tell me about Indiana—is there a boy? Is he worth it?"

But reporter mode was never far away.

"That reminds me, I should get a picture of this beach for him. It's so gorgeous," Molly said, using her attempts to get a good shot on her phone as a way of evading this. "Thank you so much for bringing me here. Danny will be so jealous, if he ever checks his messages."

"Trouble in paradise?" Shelby wondered, concern edging her voice.

In fact, reporter mode was never away, period.

"No, it's just been hard to keep up with each other," Molly said evasively. "The time difference puts a weird kink in things."

"Maybe he's struggling with the fact that you're not *ordinary* anymore," Shelby said, her eyes glazing over as if she were already writing a headline. "I mean, what happened to you is really remarkable, isn't it?"

"I don't think that's it," Molly said. "I mean, it's only

been, like, a week. And I'm still me, you know? The only thing that's changed is my location. Well, and my dad, obviously. But *that* doesn't quite feel real yet, anyway, especially since Brick's been in Florida practically this whole time."

Shelby leaned forward. "That must be so *lonely*, honey."

"It's just quiet," Molly said. "Brooke isn't exactly speaking to me."

"And you mentioned in the car that Brick is forcing you to share a room with her," Shelby noted thoughtfully. "Far be it from me to question your father, obviously, but that seems a bit unfair."

Molly shook her head. "No, I get it. He just wants us to be friends."

"Oh, of *course*!" Shelby said. "What father wouldn't? But just think of the emotional stress it's putting on you. I hate imagining you being thrown to the wolves like that."

"Yeah," Molly sighed. "Things haven't been exactly easy."

Her voice faltered.

Shelby reached over and squeezed her hand. "Let it out, Molly," she said.

"I guess it's just that my mom hasn't really been dead very long," she heard herself confessing. "People seem to forget that part. It sucks. It's so awful."

Molly was surprised to find herself opening up like this. She hadn't intended to, but Shelby's sympathy was so unexpected and complete that once she started talking, it was hard to stop. Sort of like popping a big, painful zit.

"And I gave up *everything* to come here—my house, all my friends, my grandparents. My boyfriend," she added.

"Danny was a lifeline for you, I'm sure," Shelby said.

"And having a sister could really have helped, but Brooke doesn't want to have anything to do with me. And I don't know what I did wrong," Molly continued, feeling freer by the second. "She obviously doesn't like me very much and I don't think there's anything I can do to change it. And that hurts, too."

"That is so like her." Shelby tsked. "Afraid of change. Afraid of competition."

"But this isn't a competition."

"Oh, Molly, you are sweet," Shelby beamed. "Of *course* it's a competition. At least for Brooke. And if you just hang back and do nothing, Brooke will think she's won. You know, freshman year, when she decided to tell everyone I had plastic surgery, the only way I could manage to shut her up was by having prescription hemorrhoid cream delivered to the registrar for her."

"Wow, that is"—*brilliant? deranged?*—"creative," Molly said. "What's the deal with you guys, anyway? When I mentioned we were going to the beach today, she practically choked on her egg whites."

"Oh, the details of all that don't really matter," Shelby said, airily waving a well-manicured hand. "Put it this way:

Brooke is the Voldemort of Colby-Randall. And I'm Dumbledore. And you could be my Harry Potter. Right down to being an orphan."

Molly considered pointing out that her father was alive and sending texts from Florida that read things like, *Humidity works wonders for my pores! Let's get a steam room! Xoxoxo, Brick (Dad).*

Instead, she just said, "Brick won't like it if I cause any trouble. He just wants me and Brooke to get along, and fighting in public kind of flies in the face of that. I guess I feel like if I don't react, she'll get bored and move along to someone else. Right?"

Shelby made a doubtful noise. "Whatever you think is best. I'm just saying all this because I care," she said. "One of the first things you learn in this town is to fight fire with fire. That, and never to let the paparazzi catch you eating, obviously."

"But they get people coming out of restaurants all the time," Molly said, picking up the copy of *Hey!* on her lap. "Look, here's Blake Lively leaving Chipotle."

"Oh, yes—entering and exiting, for sure, but you almost never see them chew," Shelby said. "Believe me, we try. One of Father's top reporters tailed Renée Zellweger for two years and he never caught her putting anything into her mouth that wasn't a breath mint."

Shelby stood up and grabbed her BlackBerry. "This gives me an idea," she said, punching a few keys. "Let's grab some dinner. Nobu is right nearby. You'll die for the eel."

"Aren't we sort of underdressed?" Molly asked.

She gestured to her wrinkled white Hanes V-neck and denim skirt, which were sitting in a sandy pile on her beach towel.

"This is L.A. If you're dressed, you're overdressed," Shelby said. "And I have a few spare pairs of heels in the car." She smiled. "Come on, you'll enjoy this. I just want you to feel at home here."

Molly grabbed her stuff and tailed Shelby back to the car. She'd come this far. Dinner couldn't hurt.

✦ ✦ ✦

After half an hour of BMW-to-BMW traffic on Pacific Coast Highway, Shelby shot through an opening in the sea of cars and exited into the quaint, unassuming little strip mall where Nobu sat. A cluster of paparazzi photographers huddled outside, their backs to the valet stand. They all perked up whenever the door opened, only to deflate when the restaurant expelled someone unrecognizable.

Shelby pulled up to the valet stand at 55 miles an hour, like she was relieved to have some open road at last, then slammed on the brakes at the last possible second. The valet looked terrified as he ran off to get her a ticket.

Molly stared nervously at the paparazzi. There was a borrowed pair of Prada sandals on her feet, but they didn't make her feel much better about her non-outfit, since Shelby—despite her assurances that their attire would be fine—had changed into a BCBG dress she'd pulled out of an overnight bag in the trunk.

"I'm having total acid flashbacks from the party," Molly shuddered. "Thank God none of those guys remember who I am."

Shelby tucked away her lip gloss. "Of course they do," she said. "It's their job. Half of them were *at* your party."

"What? Wait, this is not a good idea," Molly said, peering at herself in the passenger side mirror and noticing that her nose was pink. "I don't think that Brick—"

"Brick will be delighted that you're out having fun," Shelby said, pushing open her door. "Hurry up, we're causing a traffic jam here."

Molly considered her options. If she stayed in the car, she'd look like a bratty child. If she got out, she'd be immortalized in a wrinkly, damp outfit and hair that looked like she'd combed it with an immersion blender.

Shelby made the decision for her, walking around to open Molly's door and all but drag her to her feet.

"Shelby Kendall and Molly Dix Berlin," she called out to the assembled photographers as she led Molly toward the entrance of the restaurant. Once they were smack in front of the photogs, Shelby planted her feet and turned to smile at the cameras, which started obediently clacking their shutters. Molly tried to step away but Shelby wrapped her arm around Molly and turned to her, laughing as if Molly had just said something deeply hilarious.

"Molly, one on your own, please!" called out a voice.

"Please, Molly, just one over here!"

"Come on, Molly, we love you! Step over here!"

Shelby tugged on her hand. "Enough," she said. "I'm so hungry. Let's get a table."

As she dragged Molly inside, the reporters groaned. Molly turned, offered a half smile, and waved an apology to the reporters. Their flashes went off a few more times, and then suddenly Molly was inside. The room was much better lit than she'd anticipated—she'd expected tiny tables and dim lighting, the better to rendezvous with an illicit fling, but Nobu was bright and buzzing with life. Molly noticed a crowd waiting for tables and didn't see a single empty seat.

"Table for two," Shelby announced at the podium.

"It'll be about an hour," the hostess told her.

Shelby smiled and handed her a business card. "You misunderstand."

The hostess glanced at it, then back up at Shelby. "Okay. But it'll be an hour," she said, dropping the card in the "Free Lunch" raffle jar.

"Well, then, *Hey!* won't be printing the name Nobu for the rest of the year," Shelby snapped. "Come on, Molly, let's go to Katsuya."

Molly wondered if the entire meat of her friendship with Shelby would involve firing off apologetic glances as Shelby pulled her from place to place. But as she made eye contact with the beleaguered hostess, the girl's eyes widened.

"I know you!" she gasped. "You're Brick Berlin's daughter! The one with the dead mother!"

"I...yes," Molly said.

"Why didn't you *say* that?" The hostess snapped her fingers frantically at another woman, then grabbed two menus and said, "We'll have a seat at the bar for you right away."

Molly couldn't believe it. She turned to Shelby, who blinked so quickly that Molly almost didn't notice the icy glint in her eye. Almost. *Man, she and Brooke are more alike than they think.*

"Very bold to go straight to 'Don't you know who my father is?'" Shelby said as they followed the girl to the two empty seats that had magically appeared, even though a moment ago the restaurant was packed to capacity.

"But I didn't, that was—"

"I mean it. Well played. You're going to fit right in here," Shelby said, sliding into the padded chair the hostess held out for her.

Molly thanked the hostess, then turned to the menu, but before she could even open it, one of the sushi bar chefs slid a plate of something in front of them.

"Compliments of the house," he said.

"Of course, now you'll have to tip them," Shelby said. "My advice is to buy each of them a sake bomb, and be sure and order a few of the pricier items on the menu. It's polite."

"I don't have that much cash," Molly said, scanning the

menu and watching the imaginary bill inflate before her eyes.

Shelby put down her menu and placed both hands on the table, as if summoning strength from it.

"Honey," she said. "You think Brooke feels guilty when she buys four pairs of peep-toes in one swoop? You're a Berlin now. Put it on your card."

Molly popped a slice of their complimentary tuna roll in her mouth. It was bliss—savory, spicy, perfect. The black Amex Brick ordered for her hadn't seen the outside of her wallet since Stan had handed to her. But Brick probably wouldn't begrudge her one little dinner out on the town with a new friend. Especially if keeping the chefs happy meant the Berlins maintained a generous reputation.

And the VIP seats they'd been given were only four people down from Kate Winslet and a guy who looked eerily like Steven Spielberg. Which meant it probably was Steven Spielberg. Molly was officially A-list adjacent.

"You're right." She grinned at Shelby. "It's about time I had some fun being Brick Berlin's kid."

"That's my girl." Shelby beamed.

fifteen

"SEE? It's true!"

Even with her confidence slowly returning as her second school week began, Molly wondered if the sound of Brooke shrieking in her direction would ever *not* make her seize up a little.

"Here we go," muttered Max as Brooke headed for them. "This ought to be priceless. What did you do now?"

"I must have spiked her morning grapefruit with carbs."

Max affected a deep, manly voice: "We've switched Brooke Berlin's regular skim milk with one percent. Let's see if she notices."

Brooke came to a halt in front of Molly as the hum of interest from passing students grew a little louder.

"There," Brooke wailed, pointing to Molly's feet with

the same rolled-up copy of *Hey!* that Shelby had brought Molly on Saturday. "It's just like the blind item said. Those are my favorite wedges."

Molly glanced down at her feet. She had, in fact, dug these out of the back of Brooke's closet, from underneath a pair of jellies and a tattered set of bunny slippers. She'd been sick of all the disdainful glances her Converse got from these people, and judging from the layer of dust she blew off them, she'd assumed Brooke wouldn't even remember she owned the wedges in the first place.

"Molly, my closet is not Saks," Brooke announced to Molly, but at the masses. "You can't just take stuff and figure you'll settle the tab some other time."

"That's not really how Saks is supposed to work, either," Max pointed out.

"If this bothered you so much, why didn't you say something at—" Molly stopped herself as she processed the engrossed crowd of students clustered around them. "Oh, right. Of course."

"Take them off," Brooke demanded. "I wanted to wear them today."

Molly raised an eyebrow. The wedges were black and maroon; Brooke was wearing a pastel Pucci print dress.

"No," she said.

Several people gasped.

Brooke crossed her arms defiantly and took a step closer to Molly.

"Take. Them. Off," Brooke repeated.

189

Neil Westerberg clutched at Max, who looked too surprised to do anything. "This is better than TV," he whispered.

"You know what, fine. It's not worth it," Molly said, kicking off the wedges. "Plus I'd *love* to see these with that outfit."

Jennifer wrinkled her nose at Molly. "So you're going to go to class barefoot? Like you're homeless?"

"Molly, darling," a voice called out. Heads turned as Shelby Kendall squeezed through the crowd, shouldering a quilted Chanel bag over her leather bomber jacket.

"Out of my way, Bert," she snapped at a wiry, bespectacled kid Molly recognized from the play. "FYI, I know what your brother did at Spago last night. Wonder how the producers of his pilot are going to feel about it."

Horrified, Bert backed away as Shelby finally reached Molly.

"Sweetie, you left your flip-flops in my car on Saturday," she said. "I meant to bring them over yesterday, but you know how it is—I was prepping for this morning's broadcast all day."

Molly bent down to scoop up the wedges. "Thanks, Shelby," she said, hoping she didn't sound too relieved. "Let's go get them."

Shelby looped her arm through Molly's and dragged her past Brooke. Molly stopped to hand over the wedges, then let them slip out of her fingers. The shoes dropped squarely onto Brooke's sandal-clad foot.

"Oops, sorry," Molly said. "It's probably the shakes. I haven't had a drink in two whole hours."

Laughter rippled through the crowd. She and Shelby strolled toward the parking lot as bodies parted around them. It was different from the last time this happened to Molly, at that disastrous party, when people gawked and backed away out of disgust. This felt more like respect.

"Thank you," Molly whispered to Shelby through her smile.

Shelby stopped, and they turned to see Brooke, wincing furiously and sputtering at Jennifer to pick up the wedges for her.

"You're absolutely welcome," Shelby said. "Anything for a friend."

✦ ✦ ✦

Molly's entire Colby-Randall experience changed flavor after that. The people in Shelby's social circle offered to partner up with Molly in classes and gave her accurate directions to whatever classroom she still wasn't quite sure how to find; the students on Team Brooke still radiated contempt, but in a more nervous way—like the difference between volunteering to box a punching bag versus an actual person. The people who ran with neither circle, like Max, just seemed grateful to have fresh gossip.

"It's like when *Lust for Life* got a new head writer," Max said between classes on Thursday, as about five different strangers called out greetings to Molly. "For years it was all brain tumors and boring love triangles, but as soon as the new guy showed up, sewage lines exploded during weddings and a princess got pregnant with twins who had different fathers."

"Am I the sewage line in this metaphor?" Molly asked with a grin.

"Actually, you might be the sewage," Max cracked. "Seriously, though, you know what I mean. Yesterday, Mavis Moore was telling me that ever since you got here..." her voice trailed off.

Molly followed Max's eye line across the hallway, where Jake Donovan was standing in front of his locker, in the middle of changing out of his polo and into a T-shirt.

"Yes?" she prompted.

"Huh?" Max said, turning back to her only after Jake walked away.

"So how long have you had a crush on him?"

"Spending all this time with Shelby has got you thinking like a reporter," Max said lightly. "But I'm afraid I have no idea what you're talking about."

Shelby had all but adopted Molly since Monday's wedge-sandal showdown, taking special care at lunch to make room for her—and, reluctantly, Max, whom Molly refused to ditch. She'd even shown Molly the second-floor girls' lounge, an out-of-the-way unrenovated corner of the school that the upperclassmen had appropriated years earlier and turned into a teacher-approved hangout space for whenever it was too hot or too rainy to dash off campus to Café Munch.

Molly headed there now, having promised to help Shelby with their algebra homework during their shared free period. Last week, even if she'd known about it, Molly never would have had the nerve to hang out in the lounge, but being friendly with Shelby—like her black Amex—had its privileges, one of them being increased social ballsiness.

She pushed open the door and scanned the room. In the mansion's heyday it had been a dressing area with a massive en suite bathroom, gilded crown molding, and padded brocade wallpaper. But the toilet had long ago been converted into a planter for geraniums, and the entire area was teeming with antique chairs, couches, and other furnishings that had been evacuated from various Colby-Randall rooms, deemed too chipped, torn, or timeworn to sell, yet too pricey to restore. Today, the rain dribbling down the thick glass windows made the room feel extra cozy, as did the fact that it was crammed with students chewing on pen tips as they frantically tried to finish last night's homework. Or, in the case of Brooke—whom Molly noticed sitting on a peeling velvet chair left of the makeup mirrors—nose-deep in Lauren Conrad's latest novel.

"Over here!" Shelby chirped.

Molly spied her at the center of the old sunken marble bathtub (closer in size to a shallow swimming pool, really), which had been stuffed with silk pillows. As she made her way over, Shelby elbowed the girl to her right, who was short and a bit squat, with a thick white-blond ponytail nearly the circumference of the silver-dollar pancakes Miltie used to make on NFL Sundays.

"Make room, Spalding," Shelby said. "Besides, sweetie, you really should go jog the stairs a few times if you have any hope of making the tennis team."

Spalding glanced down at her legs, then nodded and hightailed it out of the lounge.

"I'm trying to look out for her," Shelby explained as Molly sat down next to her. "Spalding's father was a big-time tennis player, and he's dying for her to follow in his footsteps. Alas." She spread her hands in a "what can you do?" gesture. "Father reported he only named her that for sponsorship money."

"He sold naming rights to his *kid?*" Molly gaped. "I guess it's a good thing he wasn't a NASCAR driver or she might be named Valvoline."

Shelby studied her for a second then smiled. "Hilarious," she said. "You're so folksy."

"I don't know why *Vogue* seriously thinks I'm going to wear booty shorts in public," a nearby senior snorted, more to the magazine in her hand than anyone else.

"Dude, this issue of *Hey!* has a whole spread of celebrities in hot pants," her redheaded friend said. "I actually think these ones are kind of cute."

"No way. You're cracked out," the first girl said, taking the magazine and flipping to the next page. "Oh, my God," she breathed.

Molly saw both of them look down at the magazine and then up at her. The red-haired one's mouth hung open slightly.

"What?" Molly said.

"Your picture is in *Hey!* See?" the girl said, pointing at a small photo of Molly. It was one of the ones that had been snapped in front of Nobu. Molly was pleased and surprised to notice that she didn't look nearly as bedraggled as she should have: Somehow, the wrinkles on her T-shirt looked purposeful, her mussed hair came off like artful bedhead, and she seemed relaxed and happy waving at the cameras, rather than apologetic and awkward. It was a total miracle.

In the reflection of the mirror above the tub, she noticed Brooke start drumming her fingers on her book's hard cover.

"You look super cute," the senior girl said. "How'd you get those leg muscles? Kettlebells? Yoga Booty Ballet?"

"Running," Molly said, still a tad nonplussed.

"Running," repeated the senior slowly, as if the word was in Urdu. "Right. Retro."

"How come you didn't say anything about this?" Molly asked Shelby.

"Oh, I've been *far* too busy with my own work to check in with Father," Shelby said, peering at the magazine over her shoulder. "This must have been taken after I went inside. Which I prefer, obviously. Being in *Hey!* would taint my objectivity."

Molly ignored her in favor of reading the blurb:

HAPPY AFTER HEARTACHE: Brick Berlin's bereaved daughter, Molly, is bouncing back! The baby Berlin, 16, had Hollywood tongues wagging after she overindulged at a recent party, but Molly looked bright-eyed and breathtaking at Nobu Malibu this weekend with a friend (not pictured), where spies tell us she smartly passed on the sake. Conspicuously absent? Half sister Brenda Berlin, with whom Molly does not get along. Is Brick too busy with his new girlfriend to notice? (See page 42 for more on Brick's rumored romance!)

"Who's Brenda?" the girl asked. "How many kids does your dad *have?*"

"Don't be ridiculous, Justine, they mean Brooke." Shelby smirked, taking the magazine out of Molly's hands. "I'll have Father fire that fact-checker, obviously. Unless Brooke just got bumped from the database. That's possible. So many *real* celebrities to keep track of, you know."

Molly saw Brooke lower her book and open her mouth. No sound came out. She stuck her book back in front of her face.

Justine shrugged and took back her magazine. "I like that shirt, Molly," she said pointing at the T-shirt Molly was wearing in the picture, with the round neck she'd snipped open with nail scissors. "It's so deconstructed. You should wear it to school instead of all this preppy junk."

"Right, thanks," Molly said, looking down at herself. Since when was a plain black tank top preppy?

"Okay, are you coming, Emily?" Justine asked, climbing out of the tub. "If we want to make it to pole-dancing, we need to blow off the next two periods."

One of the other seniors — a willowy Japanese girl — gathered their magazines and followed, but not before stopping to examine Molly closely.

"You really do look like Brick," Emily announced. "It's kind of weird."

Out of the corner of her eye, Molly saw Brooke's hands clutch her book cover with white knuckles.

"You know my dad *owns* Nobu, right?" Emily added. "Next time you come in, just tell them we're friends."

"Oh, Molly didn't have any problems getting us a table," Shelby said. "She's a natural at name-dropping."

"No! Well, I didn't — "

Emily just smirked. "Whatever. Come by sometime and we can hang out." She banged out the bathroom door, her vintage penny loafers ringing on the tile floor.

Shelby smiled, catlike. "Emily Matsuhisa is a great contact," she murmured. "So many celebrities go to her dad's restaurants. Get me something juicy from her, and I'll make sure you get partial unofficial credit."

"Oh, I don't think I'll — " Molly started. Shelby held out a hand. Molly felt like she hadn't completely finished a thought since this free period had started.

"Ugh, that reminds me, I can't do the math homework

now—I have to interview Jake Donovan about the football team's silent auction," Shelby said. She pouted prettily. "I don't know when we'll get to the algebra. Father will be furious if I don't bring up my grade."

"Why don't we do it tonight?" Molly said. "If you can wait an hour after school while I do some costume fittings, we can head back to Brick's—um, I mean, my house."

Shelby brightened. "Perfect!" she trilled. "I only need the help because I'm so busy on my next exposé, about whether children of celebrities are *more* or *less* likely to be institutionalized if their parents' movies have exclamation marks in the title."

"Obviously," Molly said. "Well, I'm happy to do it."

"Can't wait! Love you lots!" And in a flurry of air kisses and jasmine perfume, Shelby was gone.

Brooke had put down her book and was mowing through a minibag of Doritos. Molly glanced over at her own reflection. She'd gotten a bit of color at the beach that weekend, and Emily was right: She *did* look like Brick. *I bet Brooke doesn't like that at all. Excuse me, I mean Brenda.*

Stifling a giggle, Molly turned, grabbed her backpack, and plowed out of the lounge.

"Nice," Teddy McCormack said as she smacked into him and knocked him back a few steps.

Molly clapped a hand to her mouth. "Oh, my God, I'm so sorry," she said. "I wasn't paying attention."

"Are you sure about that?" he asked, retrieving the knapsack that had dropped off his arm. "I thought all the girls in school planned their days around bumping into me after band practice."

"You're in band?" Molly asked.

"I'm in *a* band," he corrected. "And we're terrible, but between you and me, that's mostly Bone's fault. Every song he writes has a parenthetical in the title."

"You're in a band with a guy named *Bone*," Molly said as they eased into a companionable walk toward the stairs, "but your mom won't let Max pierce her nose?"

Teddy grinned. "I made her promise I could do it if we came up with a name she liked. She bet me twenty bucks that wouldn't happen."

He pointed to his T-shirt. "Mental Hygienist," he said smugly. "Mom left the money tucked into my guitar fret."

"Nicely done," Molly laughed. She didn't know what it was about Teddy, but somehow, he made her feel like whatever conversation they'd been having, they'd been having for years.

"Yep. I'm a rich rock star," he said. "Are you *sure* you didn't mean to bump into me?"

"I was totally spacing out," Molly said. "This girl Emily just told me I look like Brick, and I swear, Brooke almost choked on her rage."

Teddy's face darkened a bit. "I was hoping your good mood meant all that crap was running its course."

Molly rolled her eyes. "It's not a head cold, Teddy," she

said. "I doubt it's going to be that easy. Frankly, I'll just be happy if Brooke stops telling everyone I'm on the waiting list for a liver transplant."

He let out a blast of laughter. "Damn, you're so demanding."

"I know, right?" Molly said. "Too bad Brooke is completely unreasonable. She cut off one of Shelby's pigtails during an earth sciences lab freshman year, for no reason."

"I don't think that happened," Teddy furrowed his brow. "Max would have told me."

"Shelby said she got extensions, like, immediately afterward, so maybe Max didn't know."

"Maybe," Ted said doubtfully. "Or maybe Shelby just made it up."

"Why would she need to?" Molly asked. "I'm the last person she needs to convince that Brooke is crazy."

"Okay, let me preface this by saying that I swear I'm not trying to be an ass," Teddy said, throwing up a hand. "But Shelby is bad news. If you're not going to stay away from her, then you at least need to be really careful."

"I think you're exaggerating," Molly said. "She's been very supportive. And it's driving Brooke *out of her mind*. She told me once she'd rather wear a jumpsuit than eat processed snack foods in public, but she just inhaled a bag of Doritos."

Teddy ran a hand through his hair and pursed his lips. "Congrats?" he offered.

"It's not like *that*," Molly insisted. "But don't you think she deserves it? A little bit?"

"She definitely screwed up big with you." Teddy nodded. "But I've known Shelby a long time, and she is her father's daughter, through and through. She always has an ulterior motive."

They headed down the stairs to the main hallway. The rain pounding on the domed glass ceiling was so loud, Molly had to raise her voice to say, "I can look out for myself, you know. I didn't get a head injury when I fell off the turnip truck."

Teddy didn't even crack a smile. "That's not what I was saying," he argued, stopping on the steps. "But I've seen years of back-and-forth drama between those two. If nothing else, it seems like a waste of energy to get in the middle of it. Isn't there other stuff you'd rather be doing?"

Molly felt a flash of anger. "Maybe this is *exactly* what I want to be doing," she snapped. "If I'm finally having fun and feeling better about myself—or at least not rotten about myself—who are you to judge?"

She stormed off to her locker to try to collect herself. She heard footsteps approaching quickly on her heels, and then Teddy grabbed her arm.

"I'm sorry. You're right. It's not my business," he said as his hand fell to his side. "You're a cool girl, is all, and I don't want you to end up hurt."

Molly jerked open her locker. "And I do appreciate that,"

she said, softening a little. "You and Max have been awesome to me. But the last six months really, really sucked. Like, epically sucked." Her voice was low and hard, as she fought to keep frustrated tears out of it. "I'm so tired of trying to figure out how I'm supposed to be acting, you know? I just want to…I just want to *be*. Does that sound dumb?"

Teddy studied her face for a long moment. "No, Indiana," he finally said. "It doesn't sound dumb."

Molly stopped rummaging in her locker and looked up at him. His brown eyes were warm. He did look sincerely sorry.

"But you're in a band with a dude named Bone," she said. "Can I really trust your opinion?"

He threw back his head and sighed, relieved. "Let's just start this whole conversation over again, okay? Hey, Molly, what's up?" he asked her, with excessive cheer.

"Hemlines!" she chirped back. "How are you?"

"Completely mentally hygienic!" Teddy squealed. They giggled. Molly noticed one of his front teeth was ever so slightly crooked, and his eyes had the same amber glints that Max's did, giving them an almost golden glow whenever he was happy. Like right now.

"Can we hug it out?" he asked, tilting his head sideways to grin at her.

"Yes, doofus," Molly said, and stepped into his open arms.

"Our first fight," Teddy said, over her head. "I can see the *Hey!* headlines now. 'Has Berlin Daughter…'" he trailed off.

"'Has Berlin Daughter' what?"

"Yeah, I've got nothing." He chuckled, patting her back as he gave her a harder squeeze. "Turns out I should leave the headlines to Shelby."

Molly smiled and rested her cheek on his shoulder, relaxing. It felt nice to be hugged by someone who wasn't genetically obligated to do it. The hand that had been patting her back now just rested there, warm and comforting, his thumb rubbing her shoulder blade almost absently. Her eyes fluttered closed. She realized dimly that she and Teddy were past the point where a normal hug would have ended, but she was enjoying it too much to mind. She squashed a voice deep in her subconscious that wondered if Danny would.

Then two things happened at once: Her cell phone buzzed in the front pocket of her bag, and someone yelled Teddy's name.

They jumped apart, blinking hard as if being woken up from a deep nap, to see Arugula popping out from around a corner.

"Still up for some bonus time in the lab?" Arugula asked. "One can never reach too soon for academic ascendancy."

"Oh, uh, sure, Ari," Teddy said, falling backward against the lockers and looking slightly as though he'd been caught shoplifting. "I forgot we'd talked about that."

Molly's phone buzzed again.

"You'd better get that," Arugula said. "It might be your boyfriend."

Molly felt Teddy's eyes on her but couldn't quite meet them.

"I didn't know you had a boyfriend," he said.

"Kind of. I mean, not…It's complicated," Molly heard herself say after a longer pause than Danny would have appreciated.

"No, that's great for you," Teddy said, overly casual. "The long-distance thing takes guts. I bet it's hard."

"I'm sure it is for some people, but Brooke says those two are on the phone all the time," Arugula said, tossing her hair. "It's so romantic, don't you think?"

She squeezed Teddy's arm possessively. Teddy stared down at Ari's hand, then back up at Molly. He looked like he wanted to ask her something.

"Come on, our borax crystals are looking disconcertingly anemic," Ari said. "May I steal him, Molly? Are you two finished?"

Molly heard an explanation bubbling in her throat, how she was on the phone with Danny's voice mail more than with him lately, but out of loyalty to Danny she killed it.

"I guess so," she said instead.

Ari beamed and pulled away with Teddy, but not before he shot Molly a perplexed look over his shoulder.

Her phone buzzed again. Molly dug it out of her back-pack. A text from Danny: It contained no words, just a close-up photo of a sunflower propped against one of his mother's garden gnomes.

"Perfect timing, Molls," Danny said when he answered

her call. "We were just about to go bourbon bowling." His voice indicated half of that favorite outing had already begun.

"I got your text. I just...I just wanted to hear your voice."

"Glad you liked it," Danny said. "I figure, this move is just challenging me to come up with more creative ways to give my girlfriend flowers."

Girlfriend. There it was.

So why did the word spawn more questions than it answered?

sixteen

"I'M GETTING ONE just like it tomorrow," Julie Newman whispered to the girl playing Mrs. Pearce. "I mean, it's waterproof! The rain ruined my Dooney & Bourke."

Brooke set her jaw and tried to ignore this. It was the third such comment she'd heard that day. Colby-Randall students seemed to have crowned Molly the flavor of the week, and were therefore willing not just to embrace, but purchase, the grungy backpack that always dangled from her shoulder like she was about to set up camp in a tree. Brooke abhorred camping. It was dusty, there were no bathrooms, and trail mix had, like, four thousand calories.

She returned to the task at hand.

"Jake," she began. "Your character definitely wouldn't wink at Eliza."

"What if he puts his hand on her knee?" Jake asked. "I mean, where is his mojo? I'm just trying to get a handle on this."

"Tank tops are totally on sale at Fred Segal," Mrs. Pearce — Brooke couldn't remember her real name — hissed back at Julie. "I want a red one. It'll match my new sneakers. Did you know how *comfortable* Converse are?"

Brooke shifted on the sofa that was the centerpiece of the set. She tried not to seethe.

"Jake, Freddy is from a different era," she attempted.

"I'm going to go see if Molly's done with my costume," Julie said to Mrs. Pearce. "I kind of want to ask if she'll sign my copy of *Hey!* anyway. It's so fun to be going to school with someone so famous!"

"Julie, if you don't shut up and let us focus, I swear to God I will recast you," Brooke snapped.

Julie clamped her mouth shut, her eyes bulging.

Brooke closed her eyes and exhaled. It was bad enough that Ginevra's pleasantly nasty little shoe-related blind item had been canceled out by Molly's popular appearance in the latest issue of *Hey!* Between the fact that her actors were operating at straight-to-DVD levels and all the gushy comments she'd heard lately about Molly's eyes, or her clothes, or that heinous backpack, Brooke's nerves were as frayed as a pair of tights on Taylor Momsen. She'd even been seen eating chips in public. Like a commoner. She took one more deep breath.

"Jake," she said firmly. "Freddy is simple. A bit repressed. He doesn't wink at Eliza. He is not going to grope her. And you don't need to worry about what he'd tweet about her, because none of that had been invented yet."

He hung his head sheepishly. "I was just trying to relate to him."

Brooke pondered this, then grabbed Max, who was passing by lugging a spotlight that was almost as big as she was.

"Think of Freddy as Max here: wussy, with lots of feelings nobody asks to hear," she said. "So whenever he's not onstage, he's sitting up in an attic writing in his diary and then, like, staring out the window."

"Oh. Like a blogger," Jake nodded.

"And what does any of that that have to do with *me?*" Max huffed.

"You figure it out," Brooke said. "Now run along. Jake, you're also going to need to stop flexing in the background of all your scenes. It's distracting."

"But if people get bored, they need something to look at," Jake protested.

"Works for me," muttered Max as she heaved the light into her arms.

"Thank you, Magda." Jake beamed.

Max almost dropped her cargo.

"Sure," she stammered, bolting offstage.

"Try this, Jake: Listen to your instincts," Brooke said. "And then do the opposite."

Brooke got up and left the set. "Let's take it from the top of the scene, please. Everybody, take your places. Wait, where did Julie Newman go?"

Her Mrs. Eynsford-Hill rounded the corner wearing a very large straw bonnet.

"What the hell is that?" Brooke snapped.

"It's half of my costume," Julie said, looking wounded. "Isn't it cute?"

"I specifically told that girl no bonnets," fumed Brooke. "And Bert, what is going on with your coat?"

"It's Professor Higgins's plaid suit," Bert said.

"Professor Higgins does not wear plaid, he wears tweed!" Brooke yelled, her voice nearing dog-whistle levels. "I will not allow that girl to sabotage my play just because I'm keeping her from happy hour!"

Brooke tore the jacket off Bert's back and stomped toward backstage.

"While you're back there, could you tell Molly my pants are too tight in the crotch?" Jake called after her. "I think she measured my inseam wrong."

"You let her measure your inseam?" Jennifer gasped, jealous. "How could you?"

Brooke didn't hear the rest. She was on a mission.

Molly sat backstage in her makeshift costume corner cutting fabric for Mrs. Pearce's maid's uniform. Her phone lit up with an incoming text from Max.

HE KNOWS MY NAME!!!! SORT OF.

In the distance, Molly heard Brooke's usual directorial

bellowing, but she tuned it out with ease. It was a skill she'd developed living with Laurel, who couldn't watch Molly open a jar of Jif without lecturing her on the liver-pickling toxins of nonorganic snack foods. In that sense, Molly reflected, Laurel and Brick *were* made for each other.

Max again:

YOU MEASURED HIS INSEAM?!?

Molly texted back:

A LADY NEVER MEASURES AND TELLS.

She heard very cranky-sounding footsteps coming in her direction just as Max's reply buzzed through.

PLEASE DON'T ALTER HIS PANTS.

Molly didn't have time to respond before she was confronted by a blonde banshee clutching a plaid coat.

"Plaid? Really, Molly?" Brooke seethed. "And what about 'Julie's chin can't pull off a bonnet' did you not understand?"

Molly ignored her and took a fortifying sip of the coffee she'd bought from the sophomore class snack cart. It had been like this since she was strong-armed into working on the play. Eliza's gown wasn't rich enough. Her flower-girl rags weren't ratty enough. Henry's monocle wasn't round enough.

"And Jake says his pants are so tight he'll split them in the first scene," Brooke said. "I swear to God, Molly, if you ruin this…Eliza needs to look like a goddess, Freddy Eynsford-Hill should not have a porno package, and Julie Newman cannot wear a bonnet!"

"What's so bad about it?" asked Julie from behind Brooke. "Molly has amazing fashion sense. Did you know that Katie Holmes owns that tank top? Besides, I think it's kicky." She patted her bonnet fondly.

"Well, your fake accent makes *me* kicky, so either go practice or put a plug in it," Brooke snapped.

"Brooke, I have three weeks total to pull this together," Molly said, summoning all her patience. "This is the fastest play production in the history of mankind. You'll get what you get."

"*So* nice to see you share your mother's care and attention to detail," Brooke snarked.

"So nice to see *you* share your mother's…" Molly paused. "Wait, where *is* your mother, again?"

Rarely had Molly ever come up with the exact sharp retort in the exact moment it needed to be deployed. She didn't have time to decide if this made her proud: Before Molly even registered what was happening, Brooke knocked Molly's coffee all over the maid's uniform, liberated the scissors from her hands, and—with a flourish—stabbed Julie Newman right in the bonnet.

"There," Brooke said. "Maybe *that* will challenge you to do a better job."

She walked out in a huff, leaving behind a gaping Molly and an awestruck Julie Newman, still wearing the bonnet, scissors dangling precariously over the top of her head.

seventeen

"SHE STABBED IT? Just like that?"

"Just like that," Molly affirmed, unlocking the front door and ushering Shelby inside the house. "Can you believe it?"

"Fascinating," Shelby said, her eyes darting around the Berlin family foyer. In a flash she found and popped open the secret coatroom. "Is that a bow and arrow? Does this mean Brick is actually considering doing the remake of Russell Crowe's remake of *Robin Hood?*"

"Beats me," Molly said, reaching around and clicking the door shut as nonchalantly as possible. "Come on, my room's upstairs."

Molly led the way as quickly as possible. She wasn't one hundred percent certain that Brick would approve of Trip Kendall's daughter being granted passage, much less getting a peek at the coat closet, so she thought it best to try to avoid Stan — Brick's eyes and ears — altogether.

"A bust of Brick wearing a Viking helmet," Shelby murmured as they passed the second floor, where it guarded the door of Brick's memorabilia room. "Priceless."

"Your dad must have a ton of souvenirs from work, huh?" Molly asked.

"Oh, goodness no, not in the shared spaces," Shelby said. "He wants the house to feel like *everyone's* home, you know?"

Molly prickled a bit. "Well, I like it," she said. "It's fun to see everything Brick has done."

"Of course it is," Shelby cooed. "It's like a museum of all the years you missed."

It sounded cheesy when Shelby said it, but that's exactly how Molly felt when she'd peeked into the room full of old costumes, props, photographs, and scripts. They were tangible items that lined up Brick's life with hers: When she'd broken her arm falling off the monkey bars, Brick was cowriting *Diaper Andy*; when she won the West Cairo Regional Spelling Bee, he'd been in the middle of playing Leif Ericson in *It Takes a Pillage*; when she'd gotten her braces removed in ninth grade, he'd just finished the Dirk Venom series (the tightrope from which was preserved lovingly in a Plexiglas case). It made her feel close to Brick even though, in Florida, he was currently as far away geographically as ever. But she certainly didn't expect Shelby to understand that, and she wasn't up for explaining it.

Talking about Brooke was one thing; they had her in common. Brick was personal.

When they reached the third floor, Molly turned. "Are you ready for more pink than a Barbie Dream House?" she asked, and then flung open the door to the bedroom. She knew Shelby had been dying for this kind of access to Brooke's inner sanctum, and seeing the intense curiosity fill Shelby's face, Molly felt weirdly powerful being able to satisfy it. Even if it was just to do algebra.

"So this is Brooke Berlin's room," Shelby said, her eyes darting across every surface with the quickness of a speed-reader.

"Yeah, I take no responsibility for the poster of that *Lust for Life* guy," Molly said.

"He never did call me after that day on the beach," Shelby mused. "Which means he's way too virtuous for Brooke."

"Or too sane," Molly said. "She acted like a complete psycho today."

"*Today?*" Shelby laughed.

"No kidding," Molly said. "I'm beginning to think that crazy is actually her normal state."

"She's so destructive," Shelby said. "I can't understand it. This house isn't to my taste, of course, but it's not like she was raised in a barn. *My* mother would be mortified by that sort of behavior. But then again, my mother is very involved in my upbringing."

"Oh, really?" Molly asked. "Does she work at *Hey!*, too? What does she do?"

"A little of this, a little of that," Shelby evaded, tugging on a strand of hair. "But she makes sure she's around. I don't even see any pictures of Brooke's mother in this room."

"Look again," Molly said, pointing at the wall. "Those are Kelly's award-winning hands massaging themselves with lotion."

"So she claims," Shelby said, leaning in to examine the tear sheet more closely. "I wonder what Kelly Berlin is up to these days."

"Whatever she's doing, apparently it involves staying as far away from L.A. as possible," Molly said.

She dumped her backpack on the bed and dug through it for her algebra book. "Okay, so how do you want to do this? Start the homework and just stop me when you get stuck, or what?"

"That sounds perfect," Shelby said. "But can I check my e-mail first? My phone gets no signal here and my laptop's broken. Daddy loaned it to a reporter who dropped it climbing up Heather Locklear's drainpipe."

"Why was a reporter climbing up Heather Locklear's drainpipe?" Molly wondered.

"Someone has to."

"Can't fight *that* logic." Molly curled up on the bed and hugged her math book to her chest. "I can't believe I have to remake all those clothes," she groaned. "It's going to take me forever, which is exactly what Brooke wanted. I guess she wins this round."

"You must feel so betrayed," Shelby said. "Get it off your chest."

Molly happily obliged. It *was* their favorite subject, after all.

"She obviously thinks I'm trying to tank the costumes, which is ridiculous," she began. "It's my reputation, too. Everybody knows I'm doing them."

She heard Shelby murmur her approval.

"And the cast is getting fed up with her. I can feel it," Molly said, gazing absently out the window. "She acts like she's the only person this play matters to, which is bull. Neil Westerberg came offstage practically crying the other day when she yelled that Paula Abdul would make a better Colonel Pickering."

The more she thought about it, the more Brooke's self-ishness rankled. It wasn't Brooke's play. It was *everyone's* play. They deserved to be treated with respect, not terrorized by a despot who wouldn't know the words *thank you* if they took human form, introduced themselves, and handed her a coupon for free Zone Diet Home Delivery.

"And yet no one stands up to her," Molly went on. "They're all afraid of her. It's ridiculous, seriously. Who the hell is she, anyway? She needs to be brought down about thirty pegs, I swear to God."

Shelby stopped typing.

"Brought down?" she asked.

"Okay, maybe not thirty pegs, but at least two," Molly said.

Her eyes focused again, and she noticed Shelby was using the laptop at the desk.

"Dude, that's Brooke's computer, not mine," she said.

Shelby clicked the mouse twice quickly and made a big show of recoiling in horror.

"Where is my Purell?" she retched. "I can't touch my face until I sanitize. I might grow a mustache."

Molly laughed. It felt good to have someone who just sympathized with her instead of trying to make her see the other side of things all the time, and on that score, Shelby was the world's greatest company. She didn't know what Teddy had been so paranoid about: It was just dumb high school gossiping. Nobody was getting hurt.

✦ ✦ ✦

Three hours and half the Barneys shoe department after rehearsal, Brooke's mood had improved. Nothing beat the healing power of a five-inch stiletto, especially when you tried on enough of them to fund a semester of Ivy League tuition.

"Ohhhhh, that's the stuff," Brooke exhaled, leaning back on the cream-colored banquette and admiring the hunter green croc booties gleaming below her ankle.

"Gorgeous," Brie said, jotting notes on the spree like she always did. "It's a dead ringer for the color of the car your dad got Molly."

Brooke's mouth puckered. She sat upright and practically

tore the Lexus-colored shoe off her foot, hurling it at its box. Their regular salesman, René, turned puce and swooped over to rescue its mate before it met with a similar violent fate.

"Careful, Brooke," Arugula warned as René lovingly boxed them up to safety. "You break it, you buy it, as they say."

"Let's face it, I'm probably going to buy it, anyway. Even if it is the color of *pure evil.*"

"But according to my retail journal, you have two similar pairs at home—croc booties, and dark green pumps," Brie pointed out.

"But I don't have a combination of the two," Brooke said petulantly. "Brie, it was a really bad day. I stabbed a hat. Lashing out at accessories is the first sign of a stress tumor."

"You asked me to make sure you don't double up on shoes," Brie said. "I'm just doing my job. I think these are superfluous to your collection."

"Ethical fortitude *and* an ample vocabulary," Ari said. "I approve. Maybe being plowed into by Shelby Kendall at lunch does a girl good."

"Can I go one day without hearing the words *Shelby Kendall*, please?" Brooke pouted. "They're more overplayed than the Black Eyed Peas."

"I saw her leaving school with Molly today," Brie said. "Looking very pleased with herself."

"I don't get it," Brooke said. "How are they even friends? Shouldn't our families' DNA be, like, innately allergic to each other?"

"You should be more curious about what they're doing

together," Arugula said. "It can't just be algebra tutoring, because I saw Shelby's grade on the last test and it was a B plus."

"Better grade than I'd give her summer brow lift," Brooke said. "I'm sure they're just sitting around braiding each other's hair and talking about what a bad person I am."

"And salivating over Teddy," Arugula added grumpily.

"Oh, chill. Molly has that dumb boyfriend at home, remember?"

Arugula straightened up in her seat. "Well, then explain *this* to me."

She handed Brooke her iPhone. On it was a very intimate photo of Molly and Teddy at the lockers, hugging. Molly's eyes were closed. It reminded Brooke of the time she'd spent three hours talking with Zac Efron about hair products at a party. During their good-bye hug, she'd committed the smell of his jacket to memory.

"Where did you get this?" she asked.

"I took it," Ari said. "I caught them when I was looking for Teddy to do some extra credit, and I thought it could be useful."

Brie came around and stared over Brooke's shoulder.

"Wow," she said. "I bet her boyfriend would be really upset if he saw this."

Brooke leaned forward and stared at the pile of shoes on the floor, tapping the phone against her forehead. She raised her head and met Ari's gaze.

"He would, Brie," Brooke said slowly. "He *would*."

eighteen

IN THE TWO WEEKS since the event Brooke heard the cast referring to as Bonnetpocalypse, the drive home from rehearsals had been a silent affair. Brooke preferred this: Verbal sparring took a lot out of her when she'd already spent the day bellowing in the theater, and since Molly insisted on turning on NPR—which was so ancient and menopausal to Brooke that she started feeling actual hot flashes—Brooke needed no further prompting to jam in her earbuds and disappear into an eighties dance megamix. The only thing that kept her from fully enjoying the lack of conversation is that she suspected Molly preferred it, too, and the idea of them having anything but genetics in common was too much for Brooke to stand right now.

As Brooke bent down to fish a PowerBar out of her purse,

Molly took the right turn into their driveway with enough gusto that Brooke cracked her head on the glove compartment. Clapping a hand to her head, Brooke unfolded herself and opened her mouth to scold Molly for being the worst driver in Los Angeles, then noticed that they'd pulled up behind a large truck. Workmen were lugging large slate-gray slabs with odd-shaped, multicolored knobs on them around to the side yard. It was either freaky gym equipment or bad modern art; either way, it meant Brick was back.

Brooke barely waited for Molly to apply the brakes before bolting out of the car, crossing over to the driver's side door, and opening it chivalrously.

"Come on, Sis, Dad's home!" she shouted, grabbing Molly's arm.

"What is wrong with you? Are you possessed?" Molly asked, shaking free her limb. "Although, actually, that might be an improvement."

"Shut up and follow my lead," Brooke hissed. "Brick made us move in together so that we'd bond, right? And if he thinks it worked, he might relent, right?"

Molly blinked.

"Oh, my God, what do you need? Shorter words? Hand signals? Finger puppets?" Brooke huffed.

"No," Molly said. "I was just surprised to hear you make sense."

Brooke shook off the insult. The prospect of freedom was more important. She hauled Molly up the stone steps and inside the house.

"Daddy?" she yelled. "Are you home?"

"Girls!" Brick said, bouncing around the corner with a harness in his hand. "Come give your old dad a hug."

He opened both arms and swept them into a three-person embrace. Brooke let herself enjoy the affection for a moment before cold reality intruded. *Where was all this love when it was just the two of us?*

Brick released them and held them each at arm's length.

"You both look marvelous!" Brick said. "You must have read that article I e-mailed you about the cardiovascular benefits of jumping rope! I'm so proud."

Brooke looped her arm around Molly.

"Of course!" she said. "We've been doing double Dutch every morning on the patio before school. It's our new favorite ritual!"

"See? Didn't I tell you that a little togetherness was just the ticket?" Brick beamed, rubbing his hands together. "I wonder if *Hey!* could use that story. But maybe I should wait until I've sold *Kamikaze Dad.* Don't want anyone stealing the idea!"

"So how was Key West, um, Dad?" Molly asked, trying to wiggle out from Brooke's grasp.

Brooke pinched her. *We have to sell it, you moron,* she thought, praying telepathy was real.

"It was brilliant!" Brick boomed. "We're going to make the mountain scenes work with green screen and a climbing wall. Did you see them installing our new one outside?

Turns out climbing is excellent for your inner thighs. I'm thinking of selling my own version and calling it the Berlin Wall."

"That's great, Daddy," Brooke said dismissively. "I'm so glad you're home. My Eliza Doolittle accent is coming along really well, but I need you—"

"Sure, Sunshine. Soon," Brick said. "Tonight we have reservations at Campanile."

Brooke brightened. Brick never got them dinner reservations; he always said he preferred eating at home, where he could control his butter intake.

"That sounds so fun!" she said. "I can try to pass myself off as British to the waiter, and you can critique me! It'll be like an improv exercise!"

Brooke was already imagining the server filling her water glass and begging to know if she was royalty. But before she got to the part where she invented a connection that put her eighteenth in line for the throne, Brick drew in one sharp breath.

"Ooh. Actually, honey, I meant just me and Molly," he said, grimacing slightly.

Brooke dropped Molly's arm.

"You and Molly?" she parroted.

"You and me?" Molly asked, her voice the exact opposite of how Brooke felt.

"We need some father-daughter bonding time!" Brick told Molly. "We can work on your accent all day tomorrow, Brookie, I promise. No, wait, actually, tomorrow I'm auditioning actresses to play Lark Rodkin's comely Sherpa, so maybe the next — wait, no, that day is — "

It was at times like these that Brooke desperately wished she didn't love her father.

"Don't worry, Daddy. I know you're busy," she said, her heart thumping loud, repeated objections to her magnanimity. "I'm really close to getting it perfect, anyway."

"Wonderful!" Brick said. "You can surprise me on opening night! Now, Molly, you don't have to be too formal for tonight. But just so you know, there will be a photographer there. So if I were you, I ..."

Deflated, Brooke backed away unnoticed from the family powwow. For the first time in recent memory, she didn't even have the energy for a tantrum.

✦ ✦ ✦

"Brooke? How are you doing in there?"

"Go away," Brooke mumbled. She had about ten more seconds of privacy; Stan knew her too well to take "go away" for an answer unless it was followed by, "I'm naked."

"Here, I thought this might help," Stan said, walking in and tossing her a Three Musketeers bar.

Brooke let out a pathetic moan as the chocolate hit her pillow, just to remind both Stan and herself that she was in intense psychic pain. The heat from which would probably burn off the candy bar...

"He called her 'Sunshine,'" she said, tearing off the wrapper as if punishing it for a betrayal. "I always thought that was his special name for me, but apparently, it's just some dumb thing he says to anyone."

"I know this has been challenging, Brookie," Stan said, perching on the edge of the bed. "But you've got accept that Molly isn't just *anyone* to him."

Brooke felt tears starting in the back of her throat. Real ones, not just fodder for another crocodile sob fest. She hated feeling this out of control.

"It's like he doesn't even see me anymore," she said wetly. "I know I'm supposed to be all sympathetic or whatever, because her mom is dead, I *know* that. I just don't get why Daddy can't pay attention to her *and* me at the same time. He used to tell the paparazzi he'd beat them up if they so much as asked me the time, and now he's practically paying them to photograph her. I don't get it. She doesn't even *want* that kind of attention."

"Nobody expects it not to sting a bit, sweetie," Stan said kindly. "But Brick's just trying to make her feel comfortable here."

Brooke snorted. "So you're siding with her, too. Great."

"Come on, honey. You know I've got your back. I've been your buddy since you were born," Stan said. "I just don't think Molly is the one to blame here. *Brick* is the person whose behavior is making you unhappy, right? So maybe give Molly a chance. With your dad gone so much, you might enjoy having someone to hang out with that you actually like, and who doesn't beat you at chess all the time."

"We don't play chess," Brooke pointed out, through a mouthful of nougat.

"Exactly. You're too afraid of my intellectual heft."

Brooke hurled a throw pillow at his head, but missed. On purpose. Of course.

"Your sense of humor is as stale as her face," she grumped, but her heart wasn't in it. "Don't you have a screenplay to go finish?"

Stan chuckled. "More like twenty," he said. "Don't worry, I'll be sure to slam the door on my way out. But think about what I said, okay?"

"Sure," Brooke lied, shoving the heel of the candy bar into her mouth.

All her life, Brooke had told herself that Brick's inattentiveness was an innate part of his personality—like a form of extreme absentmindedness—rather than a reflection of his feelings about her. But the way he was jumping through hoops for Molly made Brooke wonder if, this whole time, he'd just been waiting for a better daughter to come along.

That the better daughter had everyone hoodwinked into thinking she was an angel made Brooke feel even worse. Yes, Molly had a dead mother, but Brooke had photographic proof she was, at the very least, a cruddy girlfriend, and that was probably just the tip of the iceberg. The girl was a fraud.

Brooke dropped the empty candy wrapper in the trash and flounced over to her laptop. She opened her in-box and found thirty-one unread e-mails: three from various

Colby-Randall acquaintances, sucking up; a bunch of spam; *Passport to Parker*, Jennifer's fan newsletter; and some random notes from various reality TV producers who'd decided her feud with Molly would make great basic cable programming. Like Brooke needed to stoop to Kendra Baskett's level.

Bypassing them all, Brooke double-clicked on the message containing the photo of Molly and Teddy's close encounter. She'd had Ari send it to her in case of emergency. This certainly felt like one.

◆ ◆ ◆

Molly took the stairs to her room two at a time. Brick had just spent half an hour explaining that there would be a photographer from *Us Weekly* at the restaurant, snapping a "candid" of them clinking glasses for an online blurb about their father-daughter bonding. It sounded quick and uncomplicated, even to Molly. Plus, posing for photos for five minutes was worth it in exchange for some precious face time with her father.

When she reached the bedroom, Molly paused. It hadn't escaped her that, when Brick revealed dinner plans that did not include her, Brooke had crept away in total silence. This whole mansion was usually one giant china shop in which Brooke acted like the Taurus she was. But Molly hadn't heard a puff of indignation, a footstep, or even a slammed door.

But why should she care? *It's not like Brooke's ever shown me any consideration. I've already got three calluses from all the sewing I'm doing for her play.* So Molly pushed through the door, letting all her excitement show on her face. Brooke was punching away at her computer keyboard, mouth pulled tight around a pen with a giant pink feather plume exploding from the top.

"Off your diet already?"

Brooke removed the pen and tossed it into her *Diaper Andy* pencil cup.

"Don't order the short rib," she said. "It'll go straight to your hips, and you're full up."

Molly was too excited about dinner with Brick to stoke a squabble. She riffled through the dresses in her wardrobe. Too casual. Too short. Too boring. Molly wanted to wear something just right. Smiling, she thought back to how freaked out she'd been not so long ago at the prospect of being photographed in public, and how much more comfortable she was now. Molly almost felt like Brooke got some credit for that—Brooke *and* Shelby, in fact, as much as they would have hated being lumped together in anything. But the events of the last several weeks had gotten Molly accustomed to judgmental eyeballs boring into her back. Dinner wouldn't throw anything at her that she hadn't fielded before.

Molly pulled out a cute, high-necked, sleeveless black dress with intricate straps artfully woven across its open back—perfect for L.A. in mid-September, which was still comfortably warm and summery. She and Laurel had made the dress together for one of Molly's awards banquets, which was one of the happy memories she'd bottled up when Laurel got sick, so that she could uncork it when she needed it most. Laurel had looked beautiful and proud when Molly accepted the Most Valuable Athlete award; Danny had beamed like she was the only person in the room, and even rejected tequila shots at the after party in favor of making Molly feel like it was her night. It was one of her favorite nights of the last few years, and wearing that dress always made Molly happy.

"Is that BCBG?" Brooke asked.

"No, it's a Laurel and Molly Dix original."

"That explains why the back looks like a tragic rope-climbing accident," Brooke snorted.

"Well, the last time you told me you *liked* a dress, it earned me days of *Little House on the Prairie* cracks in the hallway," Molly noted. "So I'm going to follow my gut."

"Fine, but no one's going to see the back if you're sitting down," Brooke noted.

Molly ducked back into the closet. Brooke had a point, which she hated to admit. She considered a lower-cut sundress that was one of the few store-bought ones she possessed, but eventually dismissed it and slipped into the black one anyway. Giving America something interesting (like her cleavage) to gawk at was a lot less important to her than having a piece of Laurel with her.

When she popped out of the closet again, Brooke was

stretching over near the bookshelf, staring at a photo of Molly and Danny from the sophomore fall dance.

"My back hurts," Brooke said, as if answering a question. "So is the Cornbread King here the guy you're always calling from the balcony?"

"Why do you care?" Molly asked.

"I'm just making conversation. I have to keep my vocal cords warm or I'll never be able to project."

Molly rolled her eyes. "Of course," she said. "That's Danny. My boyfriend."

"You don't sound very enthusiastic," Brooke said.

"Why do you even care?" Molly asked again.

"I told you. I'm bored."

Molly sighed. "We've been on and off basically since we were kids," she explained as she tried on a couple different pairs of shoes. "And he's great. But I guess I've been wondering lately if it's really going to work out in the long run, or if we're just fooling ourselves, you know, with the distance and everything. It's hard to connect sometimes."

"You should wear my Manolos. They're fabulous with anything," was Brooke's response.

"Remind me again why I should believe anything you say?"

Brooke shot her a withering look. "I would never lie about shoes. I have morals."

It was interesting to know Brooke lived by *some* kind of code, even if it only involved footwear. Molly picked up the towering Manolos and crossed to the bed. They *were* amazing, albeit a half size or so too big for her. It was a miracle that someone as tall as Brooke didn't have Paris Hilton–like canoes for feet, but even more incredible that the Manolos seemed to forgive Molly's minor size difference and embrace her anyway. *Maybe they could teach Brooke a thing or two.*

"So, why haven't you cut the kid loose, then?" Brooke pressed.

"Excuse me?"

"Come on. You're in Los Angeles and he's in a barn or something. You just said yourself it was a problem."

"It's creepy that you suddenly have an interest in any of this," Molly said, fastening the ankle strap on her left shoe.

"It's either you or homework," Brooke retorted.

"Fine," Molly said. "If you must know, it's tough because… well, it's not like Danny's done anything wrong. It's just the mileage. He was so awesome when my mother got sick."

"What, did he milk the cows for you?"

"He brought me a sunflower every day that she was sick, right up through her funeral," Molly said hotly. "Sometimes he hid them so that they'd surprise me, like in my car or along my road-race routes. He visited my mom at the hospital. He made sure I didn't flunk out, he didn't treat me like an egg that was about to break, and he made it so that I wasn't angry and bitter all the time. It's hard to dump a guy like that even if you're growing apart. Or living apart. Or both. Is that enough information for you?"

Brooke cocked her head, deep in thought. Molly wondered if they were having a Moment.

"Yeah, you know what? I'm more bored now than I was before," Brooke said.

She skipped back to the computer and started typing with great verve, if not any increase in speed. Molly blew out her cheeks. Obviously, Brooke had just wanted to get under her skin in an attempt to ruin her evening with Brick. The girl was more transparent than a window.

It hadn't worked: Molly was jazzed. With no offense to Danny, this date was one of the most important she'd ever been on in her life. She took one last look at herself in the mirror and then checked her watch. Six fifteen. She'd be right on time.

I hope this goes well. I hope he likes me.

It felt like a ridiculous thought to have after weeks under Brick's roof, but somehow, Molly still felt like she was auditioning for a role she hadn't nabbed yet. Everything else faded into the background as Molly gazed at herself and saw Brick's dimple in her nervously smiling face and hoped he would see it, too.

Please, please *like me, Dad.*

nineteen

SOUND BOUNCED SO ENTHUSIASTICALLY off the rustic stone walls of Campanile's high-ceilinged dining room, Molly was surprised Brick even noticed his phone had rung. She was beginning to suspect that his brain worked on a special BlackBerry frequency that would allow him to hear it even if he were sitting on an exploding hydrogen bomb.

"Ryan Gosling? Are you crazy? The part is written for a woman, Caroline," Brick boomed into the phone.

Brick had sworn he had to take this call in order to meet some production deadline or other, so Molly let her gaze wander around the funky setting. Campanile was a refurbished late-twenties-era building set back a bit from the surrounding storefronts on La Brea, complete with what looked like a bell tower poking up at the sky and a dining area divided by beautiful old archways. The crowd was an interesting mix: She spied a few of the usual way-underdressed and crazy-overdressed types she was getting used to seeing out and about in Los Angeles, but mostly it was a refreshingly regular assortment of girls in jeans and guys in cargo pants, most of whom seemed like they were washing away a hectic workday by tucking into the restaurant's famous gourmet grilled-cheese sandwiches. Or, in the case of the couple seated to their right under one of the mosaics—where the woman looked dazed as the guy flicked through photos of his cat on an iPhone—a first date that wasn't going very well. Molly wondered if those two would even make it to dinner, much less dessert.

"How is Lark Rodkin going to impregnate her if she is *Ryan Gosling?*" Brick's voice interrupted her thoughts. "Try that tapenade, it's tangy!"

Molly felt like she was on a five-second delay—that's about how long it took to realize that last bit was aimed at her. Brick had a maddening ability to conduct phone and in-person conversations simultaneously, and indistinguishably. When he sighed, "Who the hell bleaches her knees?" Molly thought she was supposed to answer before she noticed Brick had his BlackBerry clamped to his left ear. Moments earlier she'd needed to explain to their jittery waiter that Brick was, in fact, trying to order the Grilled Alaskan King Salmon, and not the Grilled Deviated Septum My Ass.

"Lady Gaga is *not* doing the sound track," Brick said forcefully at poor, disembodied Caroline, whoever she was. "I don't trust people who don't wear pants."

He hung up with an aggressive punch of a button.

"I'm so sorry, Sunshine," he said. "But don't you think I'm right? Our thighs should be our greatest mystery."

"Sounds right to me." Molly passed him the bread basket.

Brick looked around as if nervous that people might see, then burrowed through it until he came up with a seeded wheat roll.

"The carbs are complex," he winked as he split it in two with his thumbs. "Even my trainer can't be too mad. Now, tell me, how is school? A good academic environment is like Bowflex for the mind."

Molly hesitated. Now that she had his full attention, she wanted to confide in Brick about how it had *really* been, thanks to the problems she and Brooke were having. But it seemed dirty to pull him into the middle of it, like she was tattling the first chance she got. Besides, maybe Brooke had the right idea earlier: The sooner Brick thought the two of them were getting along, the sooner she'd get back her own room.

"I might try out for cross-country," she said instead.

Joy washed over Brick's face. "That is a spectacular idea! We can work out together!" he said. "Exercising is one of the best ways to bond! It's like my trainer says: If you love something, sweat it free!"

"That would be—"

"I'm so sorry to interrupt you, Brick," a woman said, leaning over their table in a tank top cut so low that Molly could see the top of one of her nipples. "But that scene in *Tequila Mockingbird* where you disarmed the bomb with your teeth was amazing. Could I get an autograph?"

This was the third autograph Brick had given, and they weren't even halfway into their appetizers.

"You can just sign this," the woman said, presenting her sun-damaged right breast the way Vanna White revealed a letter on *Wheel of Fortune*.

Molly turned her inadvertent snort into a cough. Judging from the expressions of the unimpressed diners surrounding them, it had been a long time—possibly forever—since someone had her boob signed in Campanile. Although the first-date couple didn't seem to notice; he had now progressed to showing her the dry skin around his thumbs, while she focused very hard on getting one piece of lettuce on her fork.

Brick finished with a flourish. "Thank you so much," the woman cooed, reaching into her Dolce & Cabbana handbag—it was a nice try, but the letter was obviously not a G—to remove a folded piece of paper. "Call me sometime."

Brick chuckled. "That was sweet," he said, tossing the paper into the bread basket. "Now, I'm glad you'll be pursuing team-oriented cardio, but how are your studies? Education is very important, Sunshine. You can't spell 'dream' without 'read.' I learned that when I made a PSA about the Library of Congress."

"Well, I think—" Molly began, but she was interrupted by Brick's buzzing BlackBerry. He glanced at the screen and shot Molly an apologetic smile.

"This will only take a minute. It's my lawyer. Ed, talk to me."

Molly sighed. The work interruptions almost made her nostalgic for the ten ridiculous minutes Brick had spent talking to the bartender about the tragic nonexistence of low-calorie whiskey. She began to wish she'd brought a magazine—or weirder, that Brooke had come, because at least she'd be company during the lulls. As it was, she picked at her beet salad and tried to decide if that guy browsing in the wine room was Stephen Colbert.

"Are you done with your salads?" the waiter whispered.

"Incendiary nonsense!" Brick shouted.

The waiter recoiled, looking like he wanted to weep into his apron.

"It's not you," Molly whispered. "Just take the plates."

Brick heaved another exasperated sigh as the waiter scuttled away.

"I am *turning this off*," he told her, and did so with a flourish. "Precious girl, forgive me for being so distracted. Work is valuable, but family is *in*valuable."

He made as if to reach for his BlackBerry again, but stopped himself. "Remind me to write that down later."

"You can do it now," Molly offered as their server returned and slid a plate in front of each of them.

"No! This is quality father-daughter time," Brick insisted,

prodding his salmon with his dinner fork. "How's the play going? If your costuming is anywhere near as good as Laurel's was, it's going to be the best-dressed production in town. Even better than *Avalanche!*, unless Patricia Field finally comes to her senses. Do *you* think Lark Rodkin would wear manpris? Because I do not."

Molly felt a wave of affection, mixed with some residual irritation that he'd shanghaied her into doing the costumes at all. He could have simply *asked* her; Molly would've agreed just to avoid further drama. But Brick didn't know that was how she operated. He didn't know her at all, really, and at their current rate, he might never.

Maybe I should just tell him everything. Brick had been so cool after the *Hey!* party, so understanding and surprisingly insightful, that Molly was seized with optimism that he'd have the same reaction now. History was on her side. And then she could move back across the hall, and no blood would be shed.

"The play is going okay," she began slowly. "But I think… with all due respect…I know you thought if Brooke and I lived and worked together that we'd grow to love each other. And hopefully that will still happen. But right now all that togetherness seems to be making things worse. It might be doing a lot of damage, actually."

Satisfied, she chanced a peek at her father. He was tapping away on his iPhone. Since when did Brick have *two* phones?

"I should never have given Harvey my e-mail address,"

Brick said with a convivial eye-roll. "But he's trying to make us use mountain goats even though I specifically asked for yaks. It's like people don't even care."

Molly shoved a piece of coq au vin into her mouth to keep herself from screaming. Even the first-date couple seemed to be having a better time now than she was: He'd grabbed the woman's hand so she could feel what seemed to be the edge of a steel plate in his pectoral region, which, however unlikely, appeared to be the right aphrodisiac.

"Anyway, so glad to hear the play is working out," Brick said. "Now tell me where you are emotionally. Spiritually. In *here*." He tapped his heart with his fork.

"Well, I'm feeling better, I swear," she started.

"I'm so proud of you," Brick said, squeezing her arm. "You have been so brave, Sunshine. And if your mother were here, she would be so happy to see how you're thriving."

"Thanks," Molly said. "It's still hard sometimes, though."

Brick looked deeply sympathetic. "Of course it is. Tell me more," he said.

"Well, the thing is—" Molly began.

"Oh, *there* he is," Brick said, gesturing for someone at the door to join them.

Her stomach sank. It was the *Us* photographer, but Molly was in no mood to smile pretty. She just wanted five uninterrupted minutes with her father. It didn't seem like a lot to ask.

As the flash went off, Molly thought that she'd find out soon enough whether any of Brooke's old tips were worth anything, since she was pretty sure she'd look super crabby in that picture. She could see it now: *"Stars: They're Just Like Us: They Don't Listen to Their Kids at All."*

✦ ✦ ✦

Hi, Ginevra,

It's been nice getting your e-mails the past two weeks — you're right, Mischa Barton's hair does look terrible that way. Even though you don't have a byline at *Hey!*, you obviously have your finger on the pulse. I'm sure your first big scoop is just around the corner.

Molly and I are doing great. She's making friends really quickly! Just look at this candid picture that my friend showed me of Molly and our principal's son. It only took Molly, like, a week to become so incredibly close with somebody! Oh, but don't worry — I know I mentioned before that she has a boyfriend named Danny back home, but I am sure he knows all about this. Molly wouldn't cheat on someone as kind and wonderful as Danny. Why, just the other day, she was saying

A noise on the stairs interrupted Brooke. Quickly, she skimmed the rest of the e-mail. She hadn't missed a thing—it crammed in every nice detail Molly had provided about Danny, plus a few Brooke had embellished just for fun. She was a genius.

The photo took forever to attach, so when Molly walked in, Brooke pulled the laptop closer to her body and tilted the screen away from her sister's view. But Molly didn't seem to be paying any attention to Brooke at all. Strange. After a private meal with Brick, Brooke would be gloating at full volume. A victory that wasn't rubbed in your rival's face was hardly worth winning. Molly had a lot to learn.

"You have butter on your skirt," Brooke told her. Apparently, How to Use a Napkin was lesson number one.

Molly absently brushed at the spot. "Thanks."

"What's wrong with you? Didn't you *bond* enough with Daddy?"

"It's hard to bond when you're getting interrupted every fifteen minutes by people asking Brick to sign their boobs."

Brooke felt an empathetic pang. Last time she went somewhere with Brick—Gelson's, to grab Vitamin Water before a hike at Runyon Canyon—it had taken them an hour to buy two bottles because Brick kept glad-handing people, and by the time they'd left, it was too dark to hike anymore.

"Nasty," she said, trying to maintain an aura of disaffected cool.

"It *was* nasty. The woman even gave him her number."

"That happens all the time," Brooke said. "Daddy has

three People's Choice Awards and a Golden Globe. I'm *so sure* he's going to date some tragic skank from the Valley with giant boulders for implants."

"That's *exactly* who it was," Molly said as she sat down and unbuckled Brooke's Manolos.

"Daddy has a huge fan base of women who seem to think if he just sees them, he'll fall madly in love," Brooke said, warming up to the topic; after all, she *was* the world's leading expert. "They have this whole crazy website called the Brickhouse. One lady actually threw herself in front of his car."

"Well, between the ladies and the phone calls, it was hard to get a word in edgewise," Molly confessed, pulling on her pajamas. "I don't even think Brick was listening to me half the time." She sighed. "I'm sure you're happy to hear this, so...you're welcome."

Brooke hesitated. Unlike her occasional, detached pity about Molly's dead mother, Brooke knew this loneliness intimately, because she'd lived through it so many times herself.

She looked up from her desk to see Molly gazing at her with a quizzical expression.

"What?"

"I was just waiting for you to say something victorious," Molly said.

"It's like Brick always says, 'Gloat rhymes with bloat, and both are the enemy of an upstanding citizen.'"

Molly snorted as she climbed into bed with a magazine.

"Since when has that ever stopped you?" she asked. "Be careful, I might start thinking you feel bad for me."

"I do feel bad for you," Brooke heard herself say. "Um, mostly just because of your bangs. But Brick can be disappointing sometimes, I guess. I'm used to it by now, kind of, but I know it sucks the most the first time."

Wait, what am I doing?

Molly gave Brooke an appraising look, as if she was wondering exactly the same thing. On the bedside table between them, Molly's cell phone buzzed. Brooke could see Farm Boy's face pop up on the screen. Molly appeared to go through a mighty internal debate before ultimately ignoring it.

"It does suck," Molly continued their conversation. "But I guess it's been sucking for you for a long time. I'm sorry about that."

"Don't feel *sorry* for me," Brooke huffed. But Molly bypassing a call from her boyfriend in favor of saying something nice to *her* made her feel very guilty about the e-mail to Ginevra sitting open in front of her. She closed her laptop.

"I didn't mean it like that," Molly said, picking almost aggressively at the seam of her duvet cover. "It's like that old saying, where you try to walk a mile in someone else's shoes...."

"Can't have been too hard—you *were* wearing my shoes."

Molly let out a small chuckle. "True. And I still almost fell over in them. But it was...illuminating." She paused.

"My mom would be so proud. She always loved that particular cliché."

Her face turned distant. Brooke felt something bubbling up inside her throat.

"Is it totally awful?" she blurted. "I mean, your mom...is it bad?"

Brooke could tell that her question had caught them equally by surprise. About three different emotions flitted across Molly's face.

"It's getting better," Molly began slowly. "On a good day, I make it to lunch before I really start to miss her again."

Brooke didn't know what to say. For all the times she had melodramatically told herself that Kelly Berlin was dead to her, she couldn't imagine what it would be like if the words were actually true.

"I catch myself talking to her in my head all the time," Molly said, a pained smile playing at the corners of her mouth but not quite making it all the way across.

"I write my mom letters. Sort of."

"What do you mean?"

This would be a good time to shut up, a voice in Brooke's head told her.

"I write her e-mails. About everything."

I said shut up!

"Oh, well, she must enjoy that," Molly said.

"Maybe. I mean, she might, in theory," Brooke said, ignoring her inner voice and wringing her hands a little. "I've never actually sent any of them. It's just been so long, you know?"

"Oh." Molly chewed on her bottom lip. "So they're kind of like diary entries."

"Yeah, sort of. It just helps me work through stuff, even though we're not *really* talking," Brooke said. "And hey, she's a better listener than Brick."

"Why don't you send them?"

"Because they're no big deal," Brooke lied, feeling twitchy. "It's just a habit."

Molly stared at one of her pictures of Laurel. "My mother would have loved hearing about all of this," she said. "School, all those stylists, the beach, tonight's crazy skanky woman. I can practically hear her reminding me that a woman's best friend is her bra."

"That would make her the only person my dad's ever dated who has that opinion," Brooke cracked. She couldn't believe herself—now she was cracking jokes? About their *parents*? Had she suffered a head injury during gym class?

Molly laughed, then grabbed her phone to read an incoming text. *Saved by the buzz.* Brooke mumbled something about tweezers and bolted into the bathroom, closing the door behind her and rolling her forehead sideways against the cool wood.

Something was changing. It felt a bit like...having a sister. And God help her, Brooke kind of liked it.

twenty

"ARE YOU SURE she wasn't just screwing with you?" Max asked, handing Molly a thick stack of canary yellow flash cards.

Molly accepted them gratefully, then plopped down on the blue and green bench—Colby-Randall's school colors—that sat outside the main doors. Last night, while Brooke snored robustly across the room, Molly had lain awake rehashing their conversation over and over, watching the words float through her head until they suddenly looked completely foreign. It wasn't until 3:15 a.m. that she remembered she had a history test in the morning.

"Pretty sure," she said, running a tired hand through her wet hair. She'd been too exhausted to blow-dry. "Even when Brooke was being all nice to me before, there was something kind of manic under the surface. But last night she was…I don't know how to explain it. Human?"

"Curious," Max said, tapping her fingers thoughtfully against the bench. "I would have bet that I'd go blonde before you guys called a truce."

Molly just shook her head, dazed. Brooke's actions certainly implied making peace: This morning she'd said Molly could borrow those old black and maroon wedges anytime—"since I know you like them"—and told her that her bangs were really coming into their own. She'd even offered a smile and a "see you later" when she got out of the car. It was so miraculous, Molly considered reporting it to the Vatican.

Well, if she's come to her senses, then so will I.

Apparently, Brick was an accidental genius: His harebrained sibling-bonding scheme had worked, if only because his ADD frustrated them both into submission. Actually, maybe none of it was accidental at all. Maybe it was just the world's longest acting exercise.

"Hey." Max snapped her fingers. "Wake up. Last time Perkins caught me nodding off during a history test, she made me do an oral report on Rutherford B. Hayes. Do you know how boring Rutherford B. Hayes was? All those letters and no good anagrams."

"Awful," Molly yawned. "God, I just don't know how to process this."

"What, my anagram thing? It's not *that* weird."

"No," Molly said. "Like, am I friends with Brooke now? Or are we just…not enemies?"

Max shrugged. "You may not figure that out right away," she said. "First, you should probably deal with your bigger problem."

She nodded in the direction of the parking lot, where Shelby's silver Mercedes screeched into its usual spot. Shelby leapt out at top speed, wearing an oddly mature red cashmere pencil skirt, complete with matching blazer; the whole thing screamed "newscaster power suit." She hightailed it toward the small beige outbuilding that served as CR-One's headquarters.

"Oh, crap," Molly said softly, rubbing her eyes.

Being on good terms with Brooke assuredly meant ditching Shelby, and Molly didn't like that idea. Regardless of her many quirks, Shelby had been welcoming to Molly when she needed it most, and it seemed like a jackass move to drop her now just because of some feud that had nothing to do with Molly at all.

"Maybe I can be friends with both of them," she attempted.

"Nice try, Switzerland," Max said. "But we're talking about years of animosity between those two. They make the Middle East look like a Girl Scout jamboree."

Molly buried her face in her hands. "I don't know if I can deal with this on three hours of sleep."

"Just tell her you need Brooke's kidney or something," Max suggested.

"Are you kidding? Shelby would cut it out herself and call it philanthropy."

The bell rang. Molly groaned. She and Max scooped up their stuff and fell in step with the masses heading to homeroom, Molly gazing absently at her feet the whole way. The top of her right Converse was getting a hole over her pinky toe. Suddenly, a pair of purple Pradas appeared. It was Brooke, and they were in a bottleneck trying to get into the classroom.

"God, move. What, does your tractor need a jump?" barked Jennifer Parker from somewhere behind Brooke's silk-covered shoulder.

"Shut up, Jen," Brooke said, giving Molly the "after you" arm wave.

"Thanks," Molly said, squeezing inside the door and pretending not to notice the people gaping at their politeness.

As Molly took her seat next to Mavis Moore—who was knitting something that looked like small intestines—Molly spied Jennifer giving Brooke a suspicious look.

"Are you okay? Did she drug your Red Bull with one of her stolen prescriptions?"

"I'm seriously fine, Jen," Brooke replied, in a normal tone. "You're the one who left the house without washing the toothpaste off her zit."

Jennifer gasped, and clapped a hand to her forehead as Magnus Mitchell burst into braying laughter and the second bell rang.

"Everyone settle down," Perkins droned. "No parking on the sidewalk, ahem, *Magnus*. Lunch today is meatless meatballs and tofurritos, and smoking kills so don't do it on campus. Now be quiet and listen to whatever this is."

She settled behind her desk with a copy of *The Secret* and flicked on CR-One's morning newscast. Shelby appeared and began droning about a recent school board meeting at which the PTA voted five to four to expand the salad bar to include bok choy.

"I saw you on *Us Weekly*'s website this morning," Mavis whispered over the top of her innards. "Having dinner with Brick. Your dress looked great with that dessert."

"Thanks, Mavis." Molly smiled. Weird compliments were still compliments.

"And now, a more sobering story," Shelby said on-screen. "This is part one of my groundbreaking series, 'Children of Neglect.'"

A graphic whizzed behind Shelby's head of a blonde girl in giant sunglasses, standing in front of a cartoon mansion that had been torn in half.

"Hey, that kind of looks like you, Brooke," Magnus bellowed.

His jovial words echoed briefly, then died out as nobody else made a peep. Because it not only looked like Brooke, it clearly *was* Brooke. Molly's hands went clammy as she twisted to throw a shrug in Brooke's direction. But Brooke was applying lip gloss, studiously ignoring both gawkers and the monitor, sending her usual message that Shelby wasn't worth her time.

"In this series, I plan to examine how inattentive parents have impacted Colby-Randall students," Shelby continued. "To shield them from further heartbreak, I am compelled to protect their anonymity to the very best of my journalistic abilities."

"*What* abilities?" Brooke said airily. Scattered chuckles broke the tension.

"Today's subject, whom we'll call Munich, is a particularly tragic case," Shelby said. "Munich seems as if she has it all. But really, she has nothing. Nothing...but *despair*."

The twinkle in Shelby's eye made Molly's breakfast bran muffin start to rebel.

"Munich's father is a very successful, very *rad man*," Shelby said, with unmistakable emphasis. "But he's too busy to spend any time with her. Or maybe he just doesn't care. Her mother ran off years ago without any forwarding address. So Munich longs for nothing more than the loving embrace of two committed parents, but instead she's treated like they've both forgotten that she was ever born..."

Mrs. Perkins put down her book to look up at the TV.

"...and left alone to write beseeching e-mails to her mother," Shelby said, oozing insincere sympathy. "E-mails she does not send because of the certainty of rejection."

Oh, God, no. I didn't even have any coffee.

Molly was too scared to look at Brooke again. From what she could tell, no one else did, either. The difference was that the rest of the class was entranced, while Molly was trying to figure out if there was any way—short of faking a seizure—that she could stop what was happening.

"I'd like to read one of her revealing missives aloud," Shelby announced, and then cleared her throat. "'Dear Mom, Dad's been in Prague filming that movie about werewolves for six weeks. I don't have anyone to talk to. I cry all the time. I think some of it is because I'm so bloated. Where are you? I need a mom.'"

Shelby shuffled some papers and leaned forward, affixing the camera with a gaze that was supposed to be full of gravitas, but came off smug.

"According to psychologists, feelings of abandonment such as Munich's can lead to drug use, teen pregnancy, gang violence, and premature baldness. Colby-Randall, please seek help before you end up like Munich: damaged, tragic, tanorexic, and beyond help. I'm Shelby Kendall. Have an excellent day."

The screen went black. The room was utterly silent.

"Dude," Jake Donovan breathed.

Molly couldn't tell if her vision was blurred or she was in shock. Two seconds later, it was both: A heavy satchel smacked her with admirable precision right in the back of her head. As she clapped a hand to the raw spot, Molly saw that Brooke had swept past her toward the door.

"Ms. Perkins, my foot hurts, I have to go to the nurse,"

she said, barreling into the hallway — but not before fixing Molly with a look of agonized hatred.

In that moment, Molly knew the e-mail was authentic. Brooke's rapid flight, without one of her customary remarks about Shelby's mind showing the hallmarks of advanced venereal disease or something, all but proved it. Shelby Kendall had bested Brooke Berlin.

The bell rang. Slowly, the exiting students found their voices.

"I can't believe I ever thought she was scary."

"Who knew she was so pathetic?"

"Molly totally did this, right?"

"This looks like the small intestines."

That last one was Mavis Moore, studying her knitting.

"It's not that bad," Molly said, hoping no one noticed her voice was shaking.

"It's not bad at all," Mavis beamed. "It *is* the small intestines."

This was enough to galvanize Molly to get out of that classroom.

"Way to go, Molly!" shouted Spalding, bouncing so hard her ponytail whacked three people in the nose.

"You are a disgusting semihumanoid," Arugula hissed, jostling past her in the hallway with a sharp elbow.

"You are going to get killed," suggested Neil Westerberg with a sympathetic face.

Shame flooded Molly's veins. *Of course* everyone thought she was behind this. The whole school knew she and Brooke didn't get along, and Molly had made no secret of palling around with Shelby. She felt like a coward, and a rotten sister, for not running after Brooke. But what could she say? *Hey, Sis, sorry everyone thinks your mom doesn't love you. I didn't do it. Want a fat-free scone?*

"Wasn't it brilliant?"

Shelby hooked arms with Molly and smiled with great satisfaction, the way Danny did when he ate his first Big Mac after swim season ended.

Molly recoiled. "Don't touch me and don't talk to me," she said. "We are done here."

Shelby narrowed her eyes. "Excuse me?"

"I can't *believe* you just did that."

"Did what? Took Brooke down about thirty pegs, just like you asked?" Shelby said, smiling coldly as any sweetness evaporated from her tone. "You might want to watch your tone, Molly."

"I had nothing to do with this, and you know it," Molly snapped. "And I'd certainly never use her *mother*—"

"Oh, give the mommy issues a rest, little girl." Shelby sneered. "What did you think was going to happen when you started whining to me about Brooke needing a taste of her own medicine?"

"When Brick hears—"

"When Brick hears what, exactly? That I was in his house, and using a computer, with *your* permission?" Shelby said, running her tongue over her canines in an alarmingly wolfish way. "And when exactly will you tell him? Has he even bothered to come home yet?"

"You are *disgusting*," Molly breathed. "What kind of person—"

"Oh, please. You wanted this just as much as I did, sweetie. Your hands are as dirty as mine are. Maybe dirtier." Shelby examined her nails, then added with dangerous calmness, "And don't you ever disparage me in public or you're next. Okay, princess?"

Molly simply stared at Shelby for a second. Suddenly, her flawless, painstakingly crafted face no longer seemed stunning, but cold and carved and cruel.

"Shelby?" Molly said loudly, making sure to enunciate. "Fuck. Off."

The gasps of her fellow students rang in Molly's ears as she shoved past Shelby and out onto the quad. It wasn't until she paused to catch her breath that she noticed Teddy and Max jogging at her heels.

"That was intense. Are you okay?" Teddy asked.

Molly's knees wobbled and she leaned against the nearest solid object, which happened to be a tree with very prickly bark. She straightened abruptly.

"That was all Shelby, I swear," she said. "Except it may have been my fault. Inadvertently. Oh, my God."

"What did Brooke do?" Max asked eagerly. "Turn green? Start yelling obscenities? Thank God these bitches keep this place *so interesting*."

"Max, shut up and be a good friend for a second." Teddy frowned.

"I *am* a good friend," Max said. "But guys never get all the details so I figured I ought to."

Teddy had already turned his attention back to Molly. She couldn't read his face.

"Seriously, Teddy," Molly insisted. "I would never, ever have signed off on that."

"I know," Teddy said. "I was just trying to decide whether it would be piling on to say that I told you so. But you look miserable enough as it is."

"Brooke *hates* me now. And I don't blame her. I'd think it was me, too. I don't know what to do."

"You know, for all Brooke's faults, she's not stupid," Teddy said. "She'll see how upset you are and then she'll have no choice but to believe you."

"I don't know, Teddy," Max said. "I think she's more likely to go slash and burn."

Molly walked in a tight circle, wriggling her hands as she tried to breathe.

"I can't calm down," she panicked. "I can't go back in there because every time anyone looks at me, it's obvious that they think I did it, and it reminds me that Brooke is off putting my stuff through a shredder, or whatever. I have a history test after lunch, but I don't think I can make it that far without throwing up. I might throw up *now*."

"I have a better idea," Teddy said. "Have you been to Griffith Park yet?"

It took a second for Molly to realize this wasn't just a random non sequitur. "You mean...ditch?"

"Damn." Max pouted. "Principal Mom is proctoring my fifth-period study hall. She'll go postal. I'm out."

"Won't she get mad at you, too?" Molly asked Teddy.

Teddy shrugged. "I can take the heat. Besides, I'm the good child," he said.

Max sighed. "I'll just tell Perkins you started projectile vomiting or something."

"Come on, Indiana," Teddy said. "No point in waiting around here for things to get worse. Let's go."

✦ ✦ ✦

The sights and smells from where Molly lay sprawled on lush green grass more than made up for the zero she was going to take on her history test. In front of her: the exotic, blooming gardens of the Getty Center, a sprawling steel and warm stone museum nestled high in the rolling Santa Monica Mountains. Beyond that: a 180-degree view of Los Angeles stretching clear out to the gleaming blue Pacific. And directly to her left: Teddy McCormack, holding a giant Jamba Juice with an immunity boost.

"Better than class, right?" he asked.

"Amazing," Molly agreed.

When they'd left school, she and Teddy had gone straight up to the Griffith Park Observatory, where Teddy had pointed out the downtown skyline (a surprisingly small cluster of skyscrapers poking at the smog layer) and gestured in the vicinity of the Capitol Records building and a few of the major studios. Then he whizzed her down Sunset, first to browse the vinyl collection at Amoeba Records—where he'd been delighted to find William Shatner's spoken-word album, which he swore would provide great inspiration for his work with Mental Hygienist—and then past the Viper Room, where River Phoenix died.

"Who?" Molly had said.

"Joaquin Phoenix's brother? Who OD'd really young and died on the sidewalk there? He was in *Stand by Me?*"

"*Stand by Me*…doesn't ring a bell."

"Oh, come on, that's the one where they're kids and Jerry O'Connell is fat, and—"

"Jerry O'Connell, one of the great actors of our generation, was *fat?*"

Teddy gawked at her for a second until he noticed Molly biting her lip to keep from laughing, at which point he dove his hand into the bag of Flaming Hot Cheetos that sat between them and threw a handful at her head.

"Cute, Indiana," he said. "For a second there I thought we were going to have to send a humanitarian shipment of movies to your hometown."

Teddy rattled off other landmarks they passed—the Playboy mansion, the courthouse where Winona Ryder was tried for shoplifting—as he navigated his rickety old 4Runner toward the Getty. They'd whipped through a couple cool photography exhibits before collapsing on the beautiful sloping lawn.

"Sometimes on the weekend, I come here and read for hours," Teddy explained. "It's free to get in, and it's so peaceful."

"This is the kind of place that makes me want to hide until closing, and then camp out and spend the night," Molly said. "Like in *The Mixed-up Files of Mrs. Basil E. Frankweiler.*"

"I loved that book," he said. "But security here is a bit tighter. And I don't think handcuffs go with your outfit."

"Honestly, if the choice is between going to prison and having to face Brooke again, bring on the pokey," Molly said, sighing.

"You're pretty upset about this, huh?"

"She didn't even fight back," Molly said. "She could've said it was a lie. She could've said *anything*, but she just ran. She must be really, really hurt."

"Who knew her mother was her kryptonite?" Teddy mused.

"And the worst part is that last night, we kind of bonded," Molly fretted. "I was going to tell Shelby that we couldn't hang out as much anymore. And I actually felt *bad* about that. Can you believe that? You were totally right about her. I wish I'd listened to you."

Teddy shook his head, blushing a little. "It was none of my business. Afterward, I actually felt really guilty for sticking my nose in it like that."

"You were just trying to be a good friend," Molly said.

Teddy looked at his feet. "Yeah. A good friend."

The air between them became electric. Molly remembered the other day at her locker and felt a sudden urge to explain herself.

"So, about Danny—" she began.

"So, um, tell me about your boyfriend," Teddy said, at the same time.

They both looked startled and then laughed—to Molly's ears, a tad awkwardly. Molly noticed Teddy's hands twitch a little on his jeans. He must have also, because he grabbed his right hand and cracked a knuckle.

"It was kind of weird that he'd never come up before Ari mentioned him," Teddy said, trying to sound light but not entirely succeeding. "You know, since we've been hanging out a lot. You and me and Max, I mean."

Molly sighed. "I know I just brought it up, but the truth of the matter is, I've kind of been avoiding the topic, even with myself."

"Denial?" Teddy asked over his juice.

"I am a very experienced practitioner," Molly affirmed. "But when you've dated the same guy basically your whole life, and he held your hand at your mother's funeral, and now you're three thousand miles away..."

She shrugged and shot Teddy a rueful smile.

"So you're, like, childhood sweethearts," Teddy said, flicking at his straw with his forefinger. "That's tough to compete with." His ears reddened. "For L.A. to compete with, I mean. Like, it must be hard to focus on being here. Or something."

His stammering made Molly feel oddly warm. She wasn't quite sure what to do with that feeling, so she pressed on: "The problem is, when I left, he didn't want to have the Talk, and neither did I. So we ignored the issue, and now we can't even seem to talk on the phone."

"That sucks," Teddy said. "Especially because it seems, like, in a long-distance relationship, talking is kind of...it."

"I know. But honestly, back home, we didn't always talk, either. Not *real* talks," she confessed. "We were just Molly and Danny. It didn't always work, but it was so comfortable, and after a while that's all I wanted. It was kind of all I could handle. But now that I'm in L.A....I don't know. I see us from a distance and we look so different."

"But you *are* different," Teddy said. "Aren't you?"

"I don't know," Molly said. "Maybe. I guess even if *I'm* not all that different, the situation is. But...Danny saw me through the worst time of my life, you know? I feel like I owe him something." She sighed, and looked out at the garden in front of them, a riotous spiral of multicolored blossoms and spiky leaves. "Does that even make any sense?"

Teddy was silent for a long beat as he poked down all the bubbles on the plastic lid to his Jamba Juice. Finally, he looked up at her, his eyes unreadable, the amber flecks dim.

"Well, obviously, I've never been in this situation," he

began. "But it sounds like he's important enough to you that you should really *try* to say all this to him." His voice dipped a notch. "Like, before you rush into anything."

"God, you're so reasonable," Molly teased, something in her wanting to break the strange tension between them. "I wanted you to tell me that the solution would be, like, running away to a deserted island and pretending none of this is happening."

"Well, now, I can't sign off on that. I saw every episode of *Lost*. Islands are not to be trusted."

"I'll protect you," Molly said.

Teddy suddenly took such a generous slurp of his smoothie that he began to choke. Molly whacked him on the back. "Are you okay?" she asked.

Teddy closed his eyes for a very brief moment. "Yeah," he said. "I'm super smooth."

They lapsed into silence, gazing out at the city. Molly was again amazed at the sheer number of cars creeping along the road, and bodies ambling through the museum's walkways. Apparently, she wasn't the only one playing hooky. Though she *was* probably the only one with a half sister at home who was possibly, at that very moment, pouring peroxide into her shampoo bottle.

"What am I going to do about Brooke?" she asked.

"Tell the truth?" Teddy suggested. "It's a radical concept, but I learned from *Sesame Street* that it tends to be the best."

"Truth is relative to Brooke Berlin," Molly said. "She's probably rescripted this whole day in her head to the point where it was me on the TV screen, reading the e-mail and holding up her photo."

Teddy looked thoughtful. "I know Brooke has her moments. But I think this whole Mean Girl thing is a front," he said. "Like a defense mechanism. I don't know. I'm just saying, I think she's a human being underneath all that bullshit. So talk to her like one."

"You are all about me talking to people." She grinned. "I should've come here with Max. She'd be telling me to put sugar in Brooke's gas tank."

"Which would actually be *your* gas tank, which is why you should always pick me over Max in a crisis," Teddy said, returning her smile. "Look, if Brooke doesn't believe you, yeah, it's really going to suck. But at least you'll have done all you can."

"Short of killing Shelby."

"Short of killing Shelby," Teddy agreed.

Molly laughed grimly and shook her head. "Thank you for getting me out of school today," she said. "And for listening to me yammer. It felt good to get that all out— about Danny, I mean. I wanted to talk to you about it, you know, before, when…that day at my locker."

Teddy looked down at his Converse. Molly noticed for the first time that they were wearing exactly the same shoes.

"You don't owe me any explanation," he said. "I'm your friend, remember?"

"Yup. My friend," she said, feeling a vague pang.

He cleared his throat. "And as your friend, I advocate eating In-N-Out for dinner. Meat makes everything better."

"Not if you're vegetarian."

"Oh, no, I don't believe they exist," Teddy said seriously. "Vegetarians are just carnivores on vacation. Be sure and tell Max I said that."

"Well, I might have to take a rain check on the meat binge," she said. "I think Brick said he's getting lobsters flown in from Maine."

"They scream in the hot water, you know."

"Yes, indeed," Molly said. "That's why I'm going to name mine Shelby before the chef drops it in."

Teddy laughed and reached out as if to squeeze her hand, then appeared to catch himself and ruffled her hair instead. He blushed a bit.

"Why are guys so into the hair ruffle?" Molly asked to diffuse things a bit. "Brick did that to me on the day we met."

Teddy pondered this. "Maybe it's because he wanted to do something else but he didn't know how."

He turned and looked at her. Molly could swear she saw a flicker of something in his eyes. Regret? Sadness?

"I should get you back to your car," he said.

"So I can go face the firing squad."

"Chin up, Indiana. You can figure it out. *All* of it."

"Yeah. All of it," Molly repeated, knowing exactly what he meant.

twenty-one

"TERRIBLE. I look like a tornado. Get it out of here."

Brooke flung a swirling gray Calvin Klein gown in Brie's direction. Her assistant caught it with a nimble swipe of her arm.

"Are you keeping the red-and-black one?"

"And look like a dying zebra? I don't think so."

"How about the floral maxi dress?"

"Ew. It makes me look like a Wordsmith poem."

"Wordsworth," Brie corrected.

"Words*worthless*," Brooke snapped. "I would stomp all over his stupid dancing daffodils if it would make one decent outfit appear in this mess."

Brooke surveyed the Alps-size heaps of clothes on the floor of her closet and swallowed her fury. Jeans from two months ago? What *was* she, a hobo? How had she allowed her wardrobe to get in such a passé state of disrepair? Not once had Brooke gone in there and emerged anything but clearheaded and balanced. Yet today, her sanctuary had betrayed her. Just like everybody else.

"It's getting late, Brooke," Brie said. "We've been at this for eight hours. I skipped a Latin quiz."

"So? I blew off rehearsal. Are you saying that is not as important as some dumb dead language?"

"No, well, I mean—"

"Don't worry, it's fine," Brooke said, her voice rising an octave. "I just got humiliated in front of the whole school and am in tremendous psychic pain, so my play will probably fail, and instead of becoming a famous actress I'll have to move to Montana and take up ranching and smell like hay and rabbits. But don't you worry about *me.*"

Brie blinked and said nothing. Brooke smacked the wall with her palm. She knew she shouldn't take out her frustration on Brie. She just couldn't believe she'd run away instead of standing her ground. This upset her almost more than having her privacy invaded (and having to spend thirty minutes hiding out at Café Munch waiting for a cab). But she'd lost all control over anything but the flight impulse.

Brooke forced herself to do some yoga breathing.

"You may go when I say it's time," she said.

After a beat, she checked her watch.

"Okay, Brie, we're done here. I have several hours of *Lust for Life* to watch. Francesca is getting her dead grandfather's hand sewn on today so that she can still play the accordion."

The bedroom door opened and Molly sidled in, her face even paler than usual. A lump rose in Brooke's throat and she quickly turned her back and started rummaging through the piles again.

"Are you sure you don't need me to stay?" Brie asked. "Keep an eye on your stuff, maybe booby-trap your laptop so that nobody can use it *for evil?*"

Sneaking a peek over her shoulder, Brooke saw Brie level a ferocious glare at Molly, who gritted her teeth and sat down on the bed. Brooke felt a surge of pride in Brie.

"No, you'd better have Stan take you home to your parents," she said.

Brie scooped up all the offending garments Brooke had rejected and scurried out of the room.

Alone now with Molly, Brooke didn't know what to do, mostly because she didn't know at whom she was madder: herself, for letting down her guard the night before, or Molly for beating her at her own game. Summoning all her acting skills, she pasted an expression of confidence onto her face and turned around to deal with...well, with whatever it would be.

"Brooke," Molly began, sounding a bit wobbly.

"Gosh, what's wrong?" Brooke mocked her. "Did you dent your halo?"

"Brooke, it wasn't me," Molly said. "I swear."

"Why are you even here? Aren't you meeting Shelby

for a celebratory cocktail?" Brooke continued. "Be sure to put it on Brick's card."

"Would you please just *listen*—"

"Why? You win. You ruined my life. Gold star."

"Wait, I've ruined *your* life? Are you that delusional?" Molly's mouth hung open slightly. Like the mouth-breather she was.

"Nobody else knew about those e-mails. Nobody in the *world*," Brooke said, her volume rising. "And then after one night where you tricked me into opening up to you, suddenly the entire school knows? And you expect me to believe you didn't do it? *Now* who's delusional?"

"For the last time—"

"You think you're so untouchable because your mother is dead," Brooke said. "But you've been out to get me since you clomped off that airplane."

Molly threw up her hands. "Right! Because this whole situation is only about *you*."

"Name one thing in my life that hasn't been shot to hell since you got here," Brooke countered.

"I'd never have talked to Shelby if you hadn't tried to turn me into an outcast. And I wouldn't be living in your room or working on your play if you hadn't pissed off Brick by ditching me at the party," Molly listed, violently ticking off a finger with each item. "Yeah, you know what? It is all about you. Because *you* are the messed-up one here."

Brooke's heart started beating so fast against the back of her ribs that she thought it might actually burst through

268

her chest wall. She imagined this was how girls who got hooked on diet pills must feel.

"Why can't you just go away?" she choked. "We never wanted you here."

"You think I wanted this so bad myself? I'm only here because my mother *died*."

"Yeah, well—"

"No," Molly said, her voice low but strong. "You are not talking right now. You need to listen to me."

Brooke stepped backward a bit in surprise. Molly *never* spoke this forcefully.

"Do you think this has been fun for me?" Molly asked, visibly fighting tears. "I watched my mother waste away, and then I rearranged my entire life so I could get to know my father. So I could even *have* a father. Someone I didn't even know existed, for practically my entire life! Did you ever stop for one second to think about how that *felt*?"

Brooke said nothing. Of *course* she had. She was human.

"Of *course* you didn't," Molly said. "Because I don't think you're human. The only real emotion you ever feel is self-pity."

"Because you know so much about me!" Brooke shouted. "Don't get all worked up about me not feeling your pain. You didn't exactly come here and try to feel mine!"

"And what's that? The unbearable heartbreak of not having your driver's license? Cry me a river. Your mother is alive."

"You'd never know it."

"It's not my fault you don't have the guts to talk to her."

"I don't talk to her because she doesn't give a shit about me!"

The words hung between them like skywriting, dissolving only at the air's slow mercy. Molly backed up to her bed and sat down, weaving her hands into her hair. She looked at a loss for words. Whereas Brooke suddenly found that she had too many.

"She knows where I am. It's not like we moved. She just hasn't bothered with me," Brooke said bitterly. "But at least she only left once. Brick leaves me every single day, whether he means it or not. *One* of my parents is supposed to want me, and if I don't send those e-mails, at least I can pretend it might be her. But if I do try to reach out to her and she ignores me anyway, well, then I've got nothing."

Molly opened her mouth but Brooke held up her hand.

"I know what you're going to say," she insisted. "That I'm making this all about me, me, me, and I'm selfish and I'm a jerk, and my parents aren't dead and Laurel is, so I'm full of crap. If that's what you think, that's fine. But don't shout about how I don't have feelings, because I *do*. You just never bothered to ask."

"That's not what I was going to say," Molly said softly.

Brooke rolled her eyes. "Great, then, this ought to be classic. Let me have it."

But Molly didn't say a word. Instead, she got up, crossed the room, and—to Brooke's everlasting shock—pulled her sister into a tight embrace.

And then Brooke started to cry.

✦ ✦ ✦

The way Brooke sniffled and snorted, Molly wondered if it had been years since this floodgate was last opened. She hung on tight, as if to try to rein in the heaving, glad her instinct had been correct.

After a few minutes, the shuddering petered out and then stopped; all that was left was some muffled sniffs. Sensing a return to calmness, Molly released Brooke and backed away, rubbing her face with emotional exhaustion.

"Well," she said, flopping down on her bed. "We kind of made a mess of things."

Brooke scraped a mascara stream off her face and nodded.

"What do we do now?" Molly wondered.

"I don't know."

"I'm tired."

"Me, too."

"This isn't what I wanted," Molly said quietly. "I just came here to have a parent again."

"Well, there aren't any around here," Brooke muttered. "But it's not your fault, no matter how much I wanted it to be. Daddy means well. He just can't see past his own damn veneers."

"Well, they *are* pretty blinding."

The girls swapped tentative smiles. For once, Molly didn't see a spoiled, painted brat; just a kid trying to be seen. By anyone.

"Look, I want you to know that I wasn't lying when I said that I didn't leak that e-mail," Molly said. "But…really, I might as well have."

Brooke crawled onto her bed and rested her cheek against her pillow, runny makeup making a Jackson Pollock painting out of the frilly case.

"Shelby was over, and she wanted to use a computer, and I was too busy complaining about you to notice that she was using yours," Molly confessed. "I thought she'd done it by accident."

Brooke just snorted.

"I know, I know. *Now*," Molly said. "And in truth, I probably knew it then, but I didn't care. And I should have. I'm sorry."

Brooke wiped her eyes again and sat up.

"It really hurt," she admitted. "I always act like I don't care that my mom is gone, because I don't want anyone looking at me as anything but an awesome force of nature. And until up today, they did. All of them."

Molly covered her mouth to hide a smile. *Brooke will be Brooke.*

"But none of this started with you," Brooke added. "It's about Dad and Shelby and—"

"It's about all of us," Molly said. "Things just went a little too far." She paused. "And you *did* act like kind of a lunatic."

Brooke grinned. "I have to say, I have never seen anything funnier than people's faces that day I ignored you in the theater. If I hadn't been so freaked out I would've been cracking up. Neil Westerberg seemed convinced I was about to snap and murder everyone."

"That was *so uncomfortable.*" Molly half-groaned, half-laughed. "It wasn't until right then that I was, like, *Oh, my God, she really* hates *me.*"

"It was more…" Brooke faltered. "Look, this does not extend to your bangs, which we have got to fix, but I think maybe I was a tiny bit jealous."

"Because of Brick?"

"In part. But more because of your mom," Brooke said. "You have photos, you have stories. She thought you were the greatest. Mine doesn't even know what I look like now. And then Brick slobbered all over you worse than the time he found kale-flavored protein powder. So I sort of…snapped."

"Sort of? You stabbed a bonnet."

"Accessories are always the first to suffer."

"Ha! You kind of sounded like Brick just then," Molly said. "And I have to admit, it feels nice that I know him well enough to be able to say that definitively."

Brooke stared off into middle distance for a spell, then cleared her throat.

"I really am sorry your mother is dead," she finally said. "And that I made everything miserable for you."

"It's okay," Molly said. "Well, it is now, anyway. Back then I was pretty excited about dropping shoes on your feet."

"Well, at least one good thing came out of it," Brooke

said, unfurling and moving over to her laptop. "I don't know if you've heard, but we're the next big reality stars in the making. All these producers have been writing to tell me how you and I could make fifty grand an episode if we'd just let them film us."

"You mean, like *Keeping Up with the Kardashians?*"

"E! is calling it *Being a Berlin*." Brooke snickered.

"I will become a Kardashian over my own cold dead body," Molly said.

"This one is my favorite," Brooke said, opening another e-mail. "'We want to capture the excitement of the Berlin Babes' every brouhaha, as a battle over the last of the breakfast cereal becomes a hair-pulling extravaganza, or the new Stella McCartney dress is the prize at the end of the pillow fight.'"

"I assume that one is for the Playboy channel." Molly laughed.

"Right? Gross. I am not *that* desperate, *thanks*."

"Shelby Kendall would die."

"Shelby Kendall *must* die," Brooke averred, snapping her laptop shut.

Molly cocked an eyebrow.

"Of embarrassment," Brooke amended. "I'm pissed, but I'm not homicidal."

"I can't always tell," Molly said. "What is the real story with you two, anyway? Nobody will say, although Shelby did tell me she sent you hemorrhoid meds."

Brooke cocked her head. "Did she? Interesting."

"Not true?" Molly asked.

"Half true," Brooke said. "To be honest, I don't actually know how this all started, either. We went to the same elementary school, so we hung out sometimes when we were little. But then one night I remember Shelby's mom showed up here really late, and super drunk, and Dad told me I had to go upstairs."

"Wow, soapy," Molly said, intrigued. "Then what happened?"

"I never found out," Brooke said ruefully. "Shelby switched schools. Then when we all started at Colby-Randall in ninth grade, she showed up with a totally new face and a really bratty attitude. From day one she was out to get me and she never said why. Like, she petitioned the student government to have my Drama Club disbanded for tax evasion."

"That's...creative."

"I know, right? And then, I was about to start dating this one senior—he was so cute. His name was Brian. I think he ended up going to Princeton. Anyway, he was totally on the hook until she stole my training bra during gym and hung it on his locker with a sign that said 'Missing: Brooke Berlin's Breasts.' Like I can help having small boobs. And then he asked her out instead. So *I* sent *her* the medicine. It was all I could think of to get back at her." She crossed her arms smugly. "It worked. He bailed. And that was all just in the first two weeks of school."

"That sounds so exhausting," Molly said. "I don't think

I have the endurance for all that stuff. I just want to be *regular* again."

"And that is exactly your problem." Brooke tsked. "We could be on the cover of *Us* if you'd just warm up to the idea of being famous."

"We could also be on the cover of *Us* if I set your hair on fire."

"Touché," Brooke said. "But can't we just have a teeny-weeny taste of revenge? Like, retribution tapas, or something? Shelby screwed you over, too, by making you look guilty. She deserves to be punished a *little* bit."

"Please don't." Molly groaned. "I'm sick of having a nemesis."

"Really?" Brooke was shocked. "But on TV it gets huge ratings."

"Really," Molly insisted. "Promise me you won't start anything again. You and I just need to get on with our lives."

Brooke appeared to be fighting with herself for a second, then her shoulders slumped and she nodded. "Fine. You're right. I promise I won't start anything."

The girls lapsed into silence for a spell. Molly yearned to grab her phone and text Teddy or Max or Charmaine that a monumental sea change was making her and Brooke Berlin act like sisters. Like friends.

Or she could text Danny. Him, too.

Oops.

twenty-two

"NOT BLOODY *LIKELY*."

"Hmm. Try it on the last two words," Molly suggested.

"Not *bloody likely*."

"Yeah, that's good," Molly affirmed. "You're going to be funny."

"I hope so. It's only the most iconic line from the play."

Brooke reapplied her lip gloss one last time as Molly parked in her usual spot. It had been mere hours since their denouement, but so far, getting along had exceeded Brooke's expectations—she definitely preferred a compliment as she arrived at school to getting her hair stuck in the window because Molly closed it so fast.

Max caught sight of them as they climbed out of the Lexus.

"Hey!" she called out. "Is it World War III or can I put away my flak helmet?"

"Hello there, Maxwell," Brooke said, flashing her most charming smile and nodding at Max's hair. "I see your science fair project is really coming along."

"Almost as well as your lobotomy," Max retorted with equal sweetness. Then she turned to Molly. "I can't believe you missed rehearsal yesterday. Jake Donovan tweeted afterward that it felt like being poked with something pointy and sharp — that's got to be about Jennifer, right? Pointy, sharp? Like her face?"

"Jennifer is my friend," Brooke defended her.

Max looked guilty. Not *very* guilty, but enough.

"It's okay," Brooke shrugged. "I *told* her to do something about those teeth. A true friend never lies about dental needs."

"There was this one part that was so funny. Jake said — "

"Brooke!" Jennifer shrieked from afar, grabbing Jake and dragging him across the lawn toward them. "Oh, my God. I cannot deal with these actors by myself. Julie Newman's British accent suddenly sounds Russian, and Jake here told me to shut up when I explained to him that Freddy Eynsford-Hill has an iPhone, *but in his mind.*"

"Well, I don't care what your acting coach says," Jake frowned. "That sounds kind of dumb."

"Because it is," said Max.

"See?" Jake said. "Thank you, Mary."

Max started showing great interest in the concrete beneath her feet.

"You're welcome," she muttered, grabbing Molly by the sleeve and tugging her away.

Brooke flipped Molly a light wave, then corralled Jennifer and Jake and headed toward the main building. Groups of students watched her with interest, tangibly tinged with fear, as if they expected her to explode and couldn't decide if it was more satisfying to stay away from the fray, or get close enough to it so they could captivate people with a war story later.

"The buzz around school is mixed," Jennifer announced as they walked. "Some people are enjoying this, some feel sorry for you, and a few are afraid this is only going to make you stronger."

"Well, I think you're brave as hell, Brooke," Jake said, clapping her on the back. "Showing your face after that…"

"*Jake*," Jennifer gasped.

"What? I just meant, she's clearly been through a lot," Jake said, with a shrug. "Man, I'm outta here. You are so not getting a foot rub today."

"Thanks, Jake," Brooke called after him.

Jennifer smacked her.

"What?" Brooke protested. "He's right. I am brave. In fact, this gives me an idea."

She pushed open the doors to the school. As soon as

people saw her, the congenial din of student gossip tapered off into an uncomfortable silence.

"…we were working on polymers and I *missed* you," Arugula was saying to Teddy McCormack with a flirty pout. When she noticed her voice was carrying over the quiet hallway, she clammed up and sauntered over to her friend.

"She's at her locker," Ari whispered.

Head held high, Brooke smiled warmly at everyone as she cruised down toward door 131. She'd promised Molly she wouldn't start anything, but surely a tiny little conversation didn't count.

"Shelby," she cooed.

Shelby's back straightened, and she withdrew from her locker with a copy of *Crime and Punishment* in her claws. Brooke, aware that every eye in school was on her, walked right up and threw her arms around her enemy.

"Oh, Shelby, thank you!" she said at performance volume. "You've helped me see I don't have to be so damn *brave* all the time anymore."

Brooke pulled away and was intensely satisfied to see utter shock on Shelby's face.

"All that private pain made me so tired inside! Now, hopefully, others will be inspired to share their struggles with adolescence in this cold, confusing world," Brooke finished. "I'm honored you chose me to carry this torch, Shelby. I hope to do us all proud."

Dead silence.

Suddenly, Jake started a slow clap. Arugula and Jennifer joined in, and eventually—straight out of one of those terrible teen movies that are also secretly awesome—the entire hallway was cheering. Brooke beamed.

"Well played." Ari grinned as Shelby slammed her locker and shoved her way down the hall.

"I know," Brooke said out of the corner of her mouth, waving at her admirers.

✦ ✦ ✦

"I kind of miss being at war with Brooke," Max said over her plate of nachos.

"I don't," Teddy said, not looking up from his copy of *The New Yorker*.

"I don't, either," Molly agreed, glancing across the quad to Brooke's lunch table, where her half sister and Arugula appeared to be taking a quiz in *Cosmo*. Brooke glanced up and jiggled the magazine in greeting; Arugula took in the sight of Teddy sitting at Molly's table again, and narrowed her eyes. Molly felt aggravated and slightly possessive at once.

"I just felt so alive then," Max continued, oblivious. "Remember when I came up with that idea to hire a skywriter to write a bad review of the play?"

"With what money?" Teddy asked, turning a page.

"That idea was a little extreme," Molly said.

"Extremely *awesome*." Max sighed mournfully.

"Excuse me, Molly?"

Mavis Moore stood in front of her holding a giant Slurpee and an envelope.

"Somebody left this for you at the office," she said. "Headmistress McCormack caught me dissecting an earthworm on the soccer field and made me bring it to you to keep my hands busy."

"I...thank you," Molly said. "I'm sure the earthworms thank you, too."

Mavis shrugged. "They haven't said anything," she said, wandering away.

"That girl is delightful," Max said. "Okay, you need to open that thing right now, because I am dying of curiosity, and so is half the quad."

Suddenly, Molly felt the heat of eyes on her—not her classmates', but Teddy's. It unsettled her, this hyper-awareness of him sitting next to her, watching her intently. Molly opened the envelope.

"It's a *mash* note," she said incredulously.

"Wow, Danny writes love letters?" Max said. "Smooth."

"No, I mean, it's an actual MASH game," Molly said. "Danny first asked me out after he found one that I did where we ended up married with kids. I even didn't know he'd kept it."

It was as if he'd been listening to her conversation with Teddy.

"So what's the Slurpee in aid of?" Teddy asked casually.

"My mom really loved them, and when we were in

fourth grade, I spilled one on Danny at recess and ran off crying," Molly said, genuinely touched, and inexplicably having trouble meeting Teddy's gaze.

"I didn't know people could get Slurpees delivered," Max said. "Bravo, Danny."

"That's really sweet of him," Teddy said, and Molly could tell he meant it. "Danny sounds like a great guy." He swallowed hard. "I'd better bail—I'm late for practice."

Teddy got up without a backward glance and strode past the fountain. He waved at Arugula, who flashed him her brightest smile and then turned toward Molly with a glint in her eye, as if throwing down a gauntlet in a game Molly hadn't realized she was playing.

"Helloooo?"

"What?" Molly snapped back into the moment.

"You totally zoned out there," Max said. "I was asking you if Danny always makes grand romantic gestures, or only when you're away."

Molly didn't quite feel like opening up to Max about Danny, or how she didn't understand why Teddy witnessing Danny's supersized gesture bothered her so much. Or how she maybe did understand, because she might've been okay with Teddy grabbing her hand at the Getty the other day. And how confusing it was when her semiboyfriend couldn't navigate the three-hour time change for a real conversation, yet was thoughtful enough to hang on to an old game of chance telling him that he and Molly someday would get married, live in Minsk, be astronauts, and drive a Pinto.

Instead, she said, "We try to talk whenever we can."

"Well, that's nice," Max said. "Jeez, happy couples are boring, too."

"Then look who just got interesting."

Molly—happy for the distraction—pointed toward Brooke's table, where Jennifer Parker was sticking an angry finger in Jake's bright-red face.

"An hour ago, Jake's status update said he was 'over it,'" Max said, as if she'd been waiting for an excuse to share that little tidbit. "Maybe 'it' is Jennifer. She is definitely at least part creature."

"And they definitely seem miserable," Molly said.

"What if they break up?" Max said in a hushed tone. "Will I have to start believing in God?"

"No, but you might have to grow a pair and tell Jake your actual name."

"Oh, leave me alone," Max said, cheerfully. "We don't all luck out and fall in love with the boy next door. Or even with a boy who would recognize us if we ran into him at the mall."

Molly picked at her lunch. "Yeah. I lucked out," she echoed, and tried not to wonder why she suddenly felt so guilty.

✦　✦　✦

As Brooke rummaged for her production binder, Emily Matsuhisa jogged over to help keep everything else from tumbling out of her locker. The gesture itself was unremarkable in its quick simplicity, except that it was part of an unprecedented outpouring of support that had started after Brooke's big show with Shelby that morning. Brie reported that the entire sophomore class now saw Brooke as some kind of hero of the people, Bone Johnson from Mental Hygienist had announced plans to write her a song called "Girl (I Hate Your Mother)," and a tearful Perkins had patted her head for about ten seconds during history—which would've been fine if the teacher hadn't just eaten a bag of Cheetos, forcing Brooke to miss the first ten minutes of English because she had to wash fluorescent cheese dust out of her hair.

"I still can't believe you hugged her."

Brooke turned to smile at Molly.

"It's your fault," she said. "I got the idea from you. The rest was off something Jake said."

"Maybe now Jennifer will be nicer to him," Molly said. "According to Max, she put something on Twitter about how football players have cement for brains."

"Speaking of dumb." Brooke sighed. "No argument you can have in a hundred forty characters or less is an argument worth having." She slammed her locker door. "Let's get to the theater. Apparently, Bert finally learned his lines, but he also learned everyone else's and now he can't stop mouthing along."

They headed off, past the lockers and the science labs, where Teddy happened to glance through the giant window into the hallway. He and Molly exchanged waves while Arugula made an aggrieved face.

"Looks like you're giving Ari a run for her money." Brooke smirked at Molly as they burst out onto the unusually cloudy quad.

"We're just friends."

"So were Ross and Rachel," Brooke said. "And Chuck Bass and Blair Waldorf, and…"

"Brick Berlin and Ms. *Beer o'Clock?*" Molly offered.

"I blame that one on your drinking problem," Brooke said, grinning. "Anyway, he may *say* you're friends, but friends don't look like they want to vomit when their other friends' boyfriends send them Slurpees."

"You're exaggerating."

"Right," Brooke said knowingly.

She pushed her way into the dark, cool interior of the Brick Berlin Theater for Serious Emotional Artistry and down to the stage. The Henry Higgins library set looked great, if a tad historically inaccurate—too many copies of *People* on his desk—and the costumes, on the backs of cast members posing for continuity Polaroids with Brie, looked downright professional. Brooke flinched a bit from residual guilt, knowing how hard Molly had pushed to finish them.

Bert Saks sidled up to them. "Hey, um, Brooke, the vending machine gave me two Diet Cokes," he stammered. "I thought you might…you know."

He handed her one.

"Thanks, Bert," she said. "That is really nice of you."

His face turned as purple as a bruise as he backed away, nodding.

"Brooke, will you help me with my accent?" Julie called out. "Yours is really good, and I could use the advice."

"Damn, I should leak embarrassing personal stuff more often," Brooke murmured to Molly.

"Being a mere mortal isn't so bad, huh?" Molly grinned in response.

"Sure, Julie," Brooke called out to her Mrs. Eynsford-Hill. "But first..."

She propelled Molly onto the stage. Wary looks dropped onto everyone's faces, like they'd just seen a skunk wander onstage and start romancing the furniture.

Wow, they really were afraid of me. Brooke knew she should feel chagrined, but she couldn't help thinking that the efficiency of her iron fist was a little bit spectacular. Today, though, she needed to put it on hold.

"You guys look fantastic," she said. "Bert, that tweed rocks on you, and Neil, your monocle is totally dramatic. Let's all take a second to thank Molly for working so hard to get these costumes perfect."

Scattered applause built into an ovation once the cast realized Brooke wasn't kidding.

"Thanks," Molly said, seeming genuinely touched. "Although it turns out you're a genius about chins," she whispered to Brooke as the others exploded into happy chatter. "I can't find a hat that *doesn't* create problems for Julie Newman. I might just put her in a kerchief and call it a day."

Brooke giggled and hopped offstage, dumping her purse in the chair next to Brie. Her mood was lighter than the carrot soufflé she'd passed on at dinner yesterday. Last night, all she'd wanted was revenge on Shelby, but now that seemed pretty inconsequential. Molly might even have been right about leaving well enough alone.

Max burst in suddenly. "Um, Brooke?" she said urgently. "Did you…Shelby Kendall is outside with a tow truck, and she's furious and ranting about calling the cops. I guess her car is all jacked up?"

The cast stopped talking again. Molly put a hand on her hip and raised an aggravated eyebrow at Brooke.

"Not me," Brooke avowed. "I swear. On the grave of last season's Phillip Lim."

"I need better," Molly said.

"On the grave of Shelby's old face?"

Molly's face cracked into a grin. "I believe you," she said. "But then…what happened?"

"Maybe her car just got jacked up. These things do happen," Brooke said. But in her periphery, she noticed Brie slowly turning pink, tapping her pen against her clipboard with increasing speed and staring fixedly into the distance.

"Brie," Brooke said, turning to her. "You have no poker face."

Brie winced, then dragged her backpack along the floor until it was at her feet. Unzipping it, she opened it to reveal a grimy car battery. Molly clapped a hand over her mouth.

"I got the idea from *The Sound of Music*," Brie said apologetically. "I don't know. If it's good enough for nuns…"

"Oh, my God, you are my new favorite person." Max chortled.

Brooke bit her lip. "I'm going to pretend I didn't see that," she said. "Nobody in here saw it, did they?"

She looked around. Anyone who'd been eavesdropping immediately looked the other way. Neil Westerberg started whistling idly at the ceiling.

"Hey, Brooke," Jake called out with a grin. "What's that random, unclaimed bag doing sitting on the floor? I don't think it belongs to anyone. I should probably throw that out, right?"

"He rules," breathed Max, who then turned crimson, as if she hadn't meant to say that out loud.

"Yes, absolutely, Jake," Brooke said. "Dispose of it. Unattended baggage can be dangerous. I learned that at the airport."

"Oh, snap, you can totally see her from the costume room!" shouted Julie Newman.

Everyone ran back to the picture window that faced the parking lot. In the distance, Shelby Kendall was red with irritation as a tow truck driver loaded her Mercedes onto the flatbed. Gallantly, he opened the passenger door to his truck. Shelby shot him a look of purest poison before fishing a Wet-Nap out of her purse and wiping down the seat, then trying to wriggle up onto it without her Herve Leger micromini riding up over her nether regions. In the process, Shelby's ankle turned roughly in her four-inch heels, and she appeared to shout something very foul indeed.

"I'm sorry," Brie whispered. "Did I make it worse?"

Brooke opened her mouth to answer.

"No," Molly's voice said firmly. "You made it satisfying."

"Really?" Brie said, excitedly. "Because I also had an idea that we could—"

Brooke put a hand on her shoulder. "I think, for now, this is enough."

She met Molly's eyes and smiled. It was time to move on.

twenty-three

"AND BREEEEEEEEATHE," intoned Trixie, the petite blonde yoga instructor with shoulders the size of apples.

Molly sucked in a lungful of air as her right foot slipped out of position and slammed onto her mat. She'd imagined that her first weekend of being actual buddies with Brooke would involve lying out by the pool and marking up a copy of *Lucky* magazine with those cool little "YES!" stickers. Instead, she was standing in the middle of a softly lit wood-floored studio, wearing a pair of lululemon yoga pants and a snug tank top (both gifts from Brooke) that were drenched with sweat. It was over a hundred degrees in the Bikram yoga classroom, and although everyone glistened with sweat, nobody else had it raining so hard down their faces that it could qualify as class-four white-water rapids.

Molly wiped the perspiration from her face and tried her pose again. The instructor, along with Brooke and the sixteen or so other spandex-wrapped students in their class, was grabbing an ankle behind her head and pulling it forward while balancing on the other leg, but Molly couldn't even get her foot high enough to get a good grip on her toes. Her leg just didn't go in that direction.

"And now, tree pose," the instructor said in a strange half-hum.

Everyone gracefully lowered their feet and then pulled the other leg up, resting their heels on their upper thighs and raising their hands skyward. They all made it look easy: Brooke, the teacher, Matthew McConaughey up there in front, the busty toothpicks with dry, unmussed hair, and the one busty toothpick who Molly hadn't realized was pregnant until she twisted sideways and revealed a bump like a beach ball. Molly's foot slid down to her knee. She suspected even the gestating fetus was more adept at this than she.

"Beauuuuutiful," purred Trixie, coming around behind Molly. "Feel your roots."

She shoved Molly's pelvis forward and cranked her leg up high into her groin. Molly bit back a yelp and flailed as she tried to hold her balance.

"Are you maybe still out to get me?" she whispered to Brooke, who looked like she was trying not to laugh.

"Yes," Brooke whispered back. "It's murder by posture correction."

"Swaaaaay, with the breeze," Trixie said. "Beeee the palm treeeee."

Molly obliged, and promptly toppled over.

"No, you have to *be* the palm tree, Molly, not chop it down," Brooke hissed, now giggling uncontrollably.

Molly rolled onto her back and grinned. "I am being a palm tree. After an earthquake."

Brooke snickered harder, and her foot slipped. She collapsed on all fours beside Molly.

"I'm being a banyan," she said.

"I have never hated trees more than I do right now," Molly panted. "When we get home I'm going on Amazon to buy a ton of paper I don't need."

"Brick will be so happy when you become a lumberjack out of spite."

They cracked up again.

"Ladies, if you can't be *quiet* trees, then please leave us." Trixie frowned.

Brooke looked startled for a second, then threw a mischievous glance at Molly and shrugged. "Okay, then. *Namaste*, babe."

"I think I pulled every muscle I own." Molly winced as she lowered herself into her seat.

"That means it's working." Brooke beamed, setting down their tray, loaded with two coffees, a half-dozen doughnuts, and enough napkins to clean up after large-scale food fight. "Here, have a bear claw. The sugar high will distract you from the pain."

"This doesn't seem like your usual breakfast," Molly noted as she took the pastry.

"Today's my cheat day," Brooke said around a mouthful of jelly doughnut. "Besides, I sweated off, like, six pounds of water weight in that class."

Brooke shoved the rest of the doughnut in her mouth and drank in the Farmers Market's dingy but quaint open-air courtyard, edged with food stands selling everything from tacos to fresh oysters to Middle Eastern food, and packed with a similarly diverse sampler tray of Los Angeles residents. A woman dripping with gold jewelry tapped her cell phone with the tip of a long acrylic nail as she tried to eat a fruit plate. Two old men, dining on pancakes at the rickety iron table next to them, were arguing about whether the Dodgers needed better relief pitching. In front of them, a couple was cooing at each other in Spanish over crepes. And to the right, an Asian family ate bagels and passed around sections of the *Los Angeles Times* in companionable silence. It reminded Brooke of coming here with Brick when she was a kid. He would read to her from the trades while she colored.

"I like it here," Molly said, interrupting her people watching.

"I thought you would." Brooke beamed, feeling like a proud hostess whose dinner party has been a great success.

"These are the best doughnuts in Los Angeles. They even make them shaped like dinosaurs, for kids. Brick bought them for me every weekend when I was little, while Kelly had her spa mornings."

Brooke gazed down at the cruller in her hand, then shook herself like a dog climbing out of a pool. *I am tired of thinking about that woman.*

Her yoga bag buzzed. Brooke reached in and grabbed Molly's phone. Danny's name flashed on the screen, accompanied by a photo of him with an arm slung around Molly and wearing a Notre Dame baseball cap. She handed it to Molly, who bit her lip, then handed it back.

"I'll call him later."

Interesting.

"Interesting," Brooke said, deciding this was no time to censor her internal monologue. "I thought he was supposed to be your boyfriend."

"He is," Molly said. "But it's not like we could get into much of a conversation right now."

"What, you're worried those two old dudes are going to overhear? They can't even hear each other." Brooke scoffed. "Dish. What's up with the hayseed?"

"He's not a hayseed," Molly reminded her.

Brooke waved a hand. "Potato, po-tah-to," she said. "Listen, I made the decision to give up a personal life this semester for the good of my career. The *least* you can do is entertain me with your boy problems. Besides, maybe I can help."

She folded her hands underneath her chin and tried to look supportive, like Tyra Banks during the segments on *America's Next Top Model* where she counseled models to stay strong in the face of bad weaves or homelessness. Molly made a grunting noise and stuck a piece of doughnut in her mouth.

"I'm just starting to wonder if the long-distance thing is doomed to fail," she said eventually. "Not seeing him every day has been so much harder than I thought it would be."

"Should we have him come out and visit?" Brooke asked. "Ooh, we could throw a party! A *real* party. No grown-ups. We can play all those fun drinking games you were telling me about. Do you think I can get away with wearing my tennis whites for beer pong?"

"Isn't that the only socially acceptable thing to do?" Molly teased. "And I didn't mean he needs to visit right away, I meant more…I just want to *talk* to him, but it's been so hard. Like, last night, we had an appointment to Skype. But he never showed. So I call him, and he's in bed and he says he thought I meant eight *his* time, which… seriously, they're time zones, not instructions for building a particle accelerator. He felt *really bad*, though. And then I felt guilty for being so annoyed."

Brooke leaned back in her chair and stared up at the blue sky thoughtfully. Tyra would cope with this by telling a story about how modeling in Paris when she was fifteen was much harder than anyone else's pain. But the closest Brooke had gotten to Paris was using plaster-of to make a mold of her own face in art. It had taken two days to get it out of her hair. Although come to think of it, that had required great strength of character.

"And then of course there's the Slurpee," Molly continued before Brooke could share her life lesson. "It was so sweet. And so *Danny*. But if I had to choose, I would pick the phone call over the gesture, you know?"

"Hmmm," Brooke said, nodding in what she was pretty sure was a supportive and sisterly way. "I'm sure the Teddy McCormack situation isn't helping, either."

"Brooke, I told you—"

"Please," Brooke said, holding up a silencing hand. "He friended you on Facebook, like, practically the first day of school. He's into you."

Molly scrunched up her face. "You're basing this whole theory on Facebook?"

"No," Brooke said. "He also gets all moony-eyed around you when he thinks you're not looking, and he brought you a cupcake the other day at lunch. Boys don't just bring girls baked goods for no reason."

And also, Arugula gave me that picture of you guys hugging, but I can't tell you that.

"Hmm," Molly said, leaning forward in her chair and resting her elbows on her knees. Brooke detected the faintest flush on her fair skin.

"And, if I may be blunt," Brooke continued, "you're not doing Farm Boy any favors, tying him down to a girl thousands of miles away who keeps looking at another boy's arms like she wants to floss her teeth with them."

She punctuated this advice with a flourish of her hands, a move she'd picked up from Brick when he played the deputy district attorney in *Trial by Fury*.

This time there was no doubt that Molly was blushing. "I do not," she insisted. She sat back in her chair and began chewing on her thumbnail.

Brooke rolled her eyes. "Okay, if you say so. But there are at least a couple other girls at Colby-Randall who do. So, obviously, I'm not telling you what to do with What's-His-Nuts, but I think it's my duty as your sister to warn you that if you *do* like Teddy McCormack, the clock is ticking."

Brooke felt bad that she was, in essence, telling Molly to swoop before Arugula got there. But blood was thicker than smartwater, wasn't it? Plus, Brooke had long ago made a vow never to stand in the way of true love if she could help it, and Grass-fed Half Orphan Makes Painful Choice to Leave Hayseed for Adequate Guitarist was *much* more romantic than Popular Genius Seduces Lab Partner for Fun.

Molly looked thoughtful. She drained the last of her coffee. And then she said the one thing Brooke wasn't anticipating.

"Can we just go shopping now?"

Brooke jumped up, delighted. "We *are* related!" she crowed.

Besides nostalgia, one of the reasons Brooke liked the Farmers Market so much was because it was attached to The Grove, an outdoor shopping mall as artificial as the

Farmers Market was authentic—it had fountains that exploded in Vegas-style choreographed routines set to pop music, and a tram that ran from one end of the shopping center to the other, like it was too hard for car-dependent Los Angelenos to walk more than a hundred feet. But the store selection was good and it was the best place in town for celebrity sightings. Brooke once saw Sean Devlin from *Lust for Life* at the Crate & Barrel and he was so cute in person that she'd had to sit on a Blake leather lounge chair for twenty minutes before she felt strong enough to walk. (She also bought the chair.)

In fact, as Molly and Brooke crossed the street toward the Banana Republic, there was a whole cluster of paparazzi shooting someone coming out of Barnes & Noble.

"Is that Rosario Dawson?" Molly wondered, pointing at the melee.

The clump of photographers surged toward them as Rosario fought her way to the parking garage. Brooke and Molly barely had time to leap out of the way before the shouting mob trampled them.

"It's just Rosario Dawson, people," Brooke grumbled at them. "Name one good movie she's even made."

A paparazzo stopped to laugh at this and promptly got bowled over by one of his colleagues. His camera went flying. Brooke deftly reached out and caught it by the strap, rescuing it from smashing on the sidewalk.

"Hey, thanks," he said, retrieving it from Brooke's outstretched arm. Then he peered at them both. "Wait a second, I know you two. You're Brick Berlin's kids. You *hate* each other."

He whipped up his camera and snapped a picture. Brooke stared at him, dumbfounded.

"Come on, give me a smile," he shouted. A few of his buddies at the tail end of the Rosario scrum stopped trotting along and looked over at them.

"What happened?" the first guy called out. "Didja kiss and make up?"

"How does it feel to have a sister?" another guy shouted as he jogged over to them. "What are you up to? Talk to us!"

Brooke froze on the spot. This had never happened to her before—at least, not without being elbowed out of the way for Molly. She'd imagined this exact situation a million times, but now it was here and all she could do was gape.

Molly pinched her arm.

"We just came from yoga," Molly announced. "And now we're shopping."

Several more photographers abandoned Rosario's trek to the parking garage and came over, cameras held aloft. Brooke turned her head toward Molly, then felt a surge of wild joy.

Thank God I did my hair for yoga this morning.

"Are you two getting along now?" someone in the back of the pack yelled.

Brooke pulled Molly closer to her, then angled herself

slightly to the side, flipped her hair over her shoulder, and flashed a blinding smile.

"Having a sister is the best." Brooke beamed. "I've wanted one my whole life."

"Over here! To the right, Brooke! Molly, smile!"

"Brooke, over here! Give us one alone!"

She squeezed Molly and shook her hair out one more time, then stepped away. As Brooke ran through all the poses she'd seen other people do in magazines, she could see Molly grinning in her peripheral vision.

"Back together now! You girls look great!" the photographers yelled.

"Everything *is* great!" Brooke shouted at the crowd.

And, actually, it really was.

twenty-four

DRIVING HOME FROM THE GROVE, it took superhuman willpower for Molly not to laugh at Brooke, who was reacting to getting papped the way someone else might react to getting a MacArthur genius grant.

"It was just so thrilling!" Brooke bubbled. "I'm so honored to be representing our family like that! Daddy will be proud, right? Because we're all bonded now? Besides, what were we supposed to do? Run? We really didn't have a choice. We *had* to pose for them. I just hope I didn't look too bedraggled after all that yoga. And four doughnuts. Oh, my God, do I look bloated?"

She turned to Molly with such a stricken expression, Molly couldn't hold in her giggles any longer.

"You look beautiful," she said, through her laughter. "I promise."

Brooke started giggling, too. "Stop laughing at me!" she protested. "It was just so *exciting*. And so unexpected! I felt so powerful. And then Nordstorm was having that shoe sale? My horoscope was right. Today *was* a lucky day."

Brooke chattered about her shoe purchases all the way home and up into their room, where she busied herself snapping Polaroids of them, then taping the pictures to the shoe boxes and filing them in the appropriate place in the closet.

Molly flung herself down on her bed. If shopping were an Olympic sport, Brooke would have been headed for the front of a Wheaties box. It was great fun to watch — Brooke could size up any store in ten seconds and blaze through it for the best stuff in under twenty minutes — and had made for a really entertaining Saturday. Even yoga class had been amusing. And, weirdest of all, being snapped by the paparazzi hadn't been nearly as awkward as Molly's first time — or second, or even third or fourth. Seeing Brooke so excited somehow made Molly feel less exposed. It was almost enjoyable.

This was a good day, Molly thought, folding her pillow underneath her neck. She couldn't wait to tell Charmaine that Matthew McConaughey was just as freakishly bendy in person as when the paparazzi "accidentally" caught him doing shirtless yoga on the beach.

Brooke popped out of the closet and snapped a Polaroid of Molly.

"That picture is going to make some stellar blackmail material," Molly laughed. "I think my eyes were crossed."

"Constant vigilance," Brooke chirped. "Now that we're being papped, you'll need it. I wonder when those pictures will show up on the Internet."

Molly yawned and rolled over to look out the window. It was another gorgeous, cloudless day. "Do you want to go in the hot tub?" she asked. "I bet we can talk Stan into making us his famous virgin margaritas."

"I can't right now. I have to proofread the programs for the play," Brooke said, all the pep seeming to drain right out of her. "I still have so much work to do on that thing. I think it's finally coming together, though. Julie Newman's accent sounds Welsh, but at least that's better than having to explain why her character is from Moscow."

Brooke braided and unbraided the same piece of hair three times. It didn't take tarot cards and a BeDazzled turban for Molly to divine why she was suddenly so fidgety.

"It's going to be great. Brick will be so proud of you," Molly assured her. "You pulled this together in, like, no time at all."

"Yeah, well, I just hope the studio doesn't make him go scout the *Titanic* wreckage to see if they can use it in *Avalanche!* or something," Brooke grumbled. "It's the first lead role I've ever had, and it'd be nice to have a parent there."

Molly chewed on the inside of her cheek for a second and then decided to go ahead and pick the scab.

"What about your mother?" she asked gingerly.

Brooke glared at her. "Are you *new?*" she asked. "I don't even know where she is."

"So send her an e-mail," Molly said. "Send her *all* the e-mails. Let her have it and then tell her to be there for you. For once."

"I can't do that," Brooke said.

"Why not?"

"Because..." Brooke's voice trailed off. Molly could tell she was racking her brain. "Because there are limited tickets and I don't have any extras."

"Weak sauce," Molly said, shaking her head. "I was sure you'd come up with something better than that— shopping-induced amnesia, at *least.*"

"Don't push me," Brooke said, sounding both defensive and a little worn out, a combination Molly was unfamiliar with hearing from her. "I'll e-mail her when I'm ready."

"And when will that be?" Molly asked. "When you're thirty-five?"

"Please. By then I'll have faked my own death to escape my enormous fame. *She* will be desperate to find *me.*"

"Joke all you want, but I'm serious," Molly said. "There are a hundred things I wish I could say to my mother, but I can't. You still can."

"I can't believe you're playing the dead mother card,"

Brooke said, sitting down on her bed with a thump. "This is so unfair. I am telling you right now that it will eventually stop working."

"Fine. Instead of me going on and on about how you need to get everything off your chest before every opportunity is lost to the winds of time—"

"Boring."

"—then how about we make a deal," Molly finished. "You pull the trigger with your mother, and I'll face this thing with Danny."

Brooke sat up on her bed, intrigued. "I knew it! You want to dump Danny for Teddy. I'm so good. I called Tom Cruise and Katie Holmes way before the couch jumping."

"Teddy has nothing to do with it," Molly insisted, pretty sure that was true. "And it might not even be a dumping. But you were right, it's not fair to Danny to pretend everything's fine if I'm feeling ambivalent about whether this can work."

"Wait, this is a terrible deal," Brooke said, starting to sound vaguely panicky. "You're doing something you have to do anyway, and I'll get nothing but puffy eyes. I hate this plan."

"You don't know that," Molly said gently. "Maybe you'll get a mom. Whereas there's no way I'm going to come out of my end of the bargain without things getting awkward."

Brooke stared over at her laptop as if it had teeth and wanted to use them to drain her blood.

"I can't," she whispered.

Molly made a mental note to give Kelly Berlin a piece of her mind when the time came for them to meet—which at this rate seemed like it'd be the tenth of Never, so it was a pretty easy promise to make. Brick wasn't perfect, but at least he hadn't left and never looked back. Kelly's selfishness was totally antithetical to the way Laurel had been, and it upset Molly on Brooke's behalf. In this arena, at least, her sister needed a wingman.

"Do it, Brooke," pressed Molly. "Send them. Tell her everything you've ever wanted to tell her. No regrets."

"What if she never writes back?"

"Then you'll have done everything you can do, and we'll steal a bottle of Brick's Champagne and plan a serious jihad."

Silence. Molly decided to give Brooke some breathing room and went into the bathroom under the pretense of tweezing her eyebrows. Another lesson from being raised by two opinionated women like Laurel and her grandmother Ginger was that sometimes you just needed to stop yammering and let the other person process things. (She'd learned that because neither of them had *ever* stopped yammering.)

Molly killed time examining a pimple on her chin, which appeared to be running up the white flag of surrender, until she realized her hands were shaking a little. So she gave up and just stared at herself in the mirror. She still *looked* the same. But in just a month, everything about her had changed: bedroom, friends, school, Danny.

She felt like such a stereotype—the girl who gets a bit of distance from her boyfriend and suddenly decides she needs even more space. Especially because, if she was being honest, she liked the idea of being able to hang out with Teddy without feeling guilty when their skin accidentally grazed and it sent tingles down her spine. But Teddy really wasn't the issue. Danny sending her a Slurpee and a note only made him her boyfriend on a technicality; the two of them avoiding conversations the way they had been lately, like they were afraid of what they might say, was getting unbearable. Molly wondered if, that night on her front stoop, they'd both subconsciously known they'd look back someday on her last night in Indiana and realize that was supposed to be their ending. It was dumb to move away for a fresh start if you didn't actually give your-self one.

Of course, unless Brooke worked up the guts to send those e-mails—which didn't seem terribly likely—Molly might be able to mull it over a little while longer. She could hear Laurel telling her to suck it up and stop it with the dithering, but Molly was more in a mood to give sensible advice than receive it.

She emerged from the bathroom and stopped short when she saw Brooke, ghostly pale, sitting at her computer. She looked like a scared little girl.

"I did it," she said, her voice hollow. "I did it."

✦ ✦ ✦

Brooke stared at her Drafts folder. It hadn't been empty in almost four years, and now there it was, terrifyingly blank. She hadn't reread any of her e-mails, hadn't changed a thing. She'd just hit Select All and then Send All.

It had been easy. That was the kicker. For years, she'd convinced herself that sending them was an impossible act that would push her mother away for good. But suddenly, after one deep breath and a brisk figurative shove from Molly, Kelly Berlin was about to get more than two hundred e-mails—a digital time capsule of Brooke's life without her.

Molly looked just as stunned as Brooke felt.

"I called your bluff, didn't I?" Brooke asked.

"Yep." Molly grinned. "I'm so screwed. How do you feel?"

Brooke rested her elbow on the desk and cradled her chin in her palm. How *did* she feel? Jittery. Relieved. One of the toes in her right foot was numb from being crammed into four-inch heels most of last week.

"Free," she finally said. "All these years I thought writing those lightened my load, but now I realize how heavy they really were."

"That's *so* Brick Berlin," Molly said. "Quick, get out your BlackBerry and write it down."

"Yes, it'd make a perfect Lifetime movie," Brooke agreed. "I can hear the preview dude now: 'Her secret burden... was ruining her posture.'"

"Well, I think it's great," Molly said. "And you never know—she might even write back."

Brooke snorted. "I'm not holding my breath." She paused. "Molly...thanks," she said. "I think...whatever happens, I think it's better that I did it."

Molly just smiled and flipped open her biology textbook, turned on the TV, and cued up that day's *Lust for Life*.

Brooke unplugged her laptop to carry it to her bed, the better to get a good viewing angle of the wedding of fashion magnate turned bar owner Klaus Wiggins and his loyal college roommate, Bucky. According to *Soap Opera Digest*, there would be elephants. But before she scooped up the computer, a new message popped into her in-box.

No way. She did not write back that fast.

Brooke crossed her fingers for luck, then loaded the mail screen.

The message was from Ginevra McElroy, that *Hey!* reporter itching for a story. But Brooke was done with all that now. She made a move to delete the message without even reading it, but then she noticed the subject line. It read, "RE: Molly Update."

Brooke frowned. She hadn't sent Ginevra anything since right after the party, and it definitely didn't have that subject line.

She clicked on it.

Brooke, this is wonderful — I am so glad to hear
Molly is thriving, and making, shall we say, such

special friends. So pleased that you chose me to share this with. I feel that we, too, are friends.

Cheers,

G

Brooke's heart froze.

Oh, shit.

As if floating above herself, she watched her finger click over to her Sent Mail folder and scroll down to the newer stuff. There it was, nestled between her "Dear Kelly" letters: a note to Ginevra McElroy, titled "Molly Update," all about Danny, the sunflowers, and Teddy. With Arugula's stealth photo attached.

Double shit.

"What's wrong?" Molly asked. "Don't you want to watch this? Klaus and Bucky are wearing matching fur turbans."

"Oh, just…Jake and Jennifer, you know," lied Brooke. "Be right there."

But for the first time ever, fur turbans didn't matter. Nothing mattered except how the hell she was going to get out of this one.

twenty-five

BROOKE HUNG UP her cell phone and looked around the quad. She had just left her sixth message for Ginevra—one for each day since her potentially disastrous e-mail snafu—and was pretty confident that Ginevra planned to ignore this one, too, just as she had the first five calls and three e-mails Brooke sent, in which she claimed everything from the photo being doctored to temporary insanity.

Thanks to a frenzied final week of play rehearsals, it seemed like Molly hadn't noticed anything awry about Brooke's behavior, or at least, nothing she couldn't ascribe to nerves. She was also wrapped up in her own drama, having spent the last couple of days playing phone tag with Danny. *Still.* If Brooke were Molly, she would have dumped the guy over voice mail just for that. Brooke appreciated that Molly was taking her relationship seriously and everything—even if it was kind of boring from a gossip standpoint—but she hoped her half sister realized that she risked snoozing and losing where Teddy was concerned. Other people's hearts ran on their own schedule, like a train; if you found a ride you wanted to take, you had to hop on while it was at your station. Brooke learned that from Brick's character in *Tequila Mockingbird*, right before he strangled a drug lord with a shoelace.

Plopping down on an isolated bench within view of the theater, Brooke stared at her phone and shivered—partly because, as they inched into October, the last of the September heat had on cue given way to mild nights, and partly because the damn thing just wouldn't ring. However, a new issue of *Hey!* had come out since the Incident, and nothing had appeared in it, nor on its website. Maybe Ginevra, meek intern that she was, believed Brooke's outright lie about the photo being fake. Or Trip Kendall just decided there wasn't really any story there and had decided to devote *Hey!*'s resources to something more important, like whether Bieber Fever was a real medical affliction. Maybe, just maybe, Brooke was going to get away with this. She *had to*. Didn't she? Surely the universe wouldn't punish her for one tiny wee mistake, just when she and Molly were finally friends. At the very least, she must have been owed some karmic brownie points for going seventy-two hours without saying a word about how bad Molly needed a hair appointment.

So, the further away from that fateful accidental e-mail Brooke got, the more she was able to concentrate on the task at hand: It was finally *My Fair Lady*'s opening night, and she was certain—well, *mostly* certain—that Brick would be there to witness it. Caroline, Brick's agent and Arugula's mother, had called to reiterate that she would be bringing Brick to the theater personally, along with Ari's botanist father, Phil—the source of Arugula's name, interest in science, and disdain for iceberg lettuce (he called it nature's packing peanuts). Brooke was confident that Caroline would deliver, if only because Brick never passed up an opportunity to talk to Phil, the only person as fascinated by nutritional information as he was.

"What are you doing out here?" Ari asked. "Shouldn't you be in hair and makeup?"

Brooke looked up to see her friend dressed to the nines and holding her chemistry textbook.

"I thought you were driving over with your mom," she said, shoving her iPhone into her pocket. "Did something go wrong? Are they not coming?"

Ari put down the book and patted Brooke's arm.

"Relax," she said. "Brick is still coming. When I left the house, he was getting a lecture about the zucchini-daffodil hybrid my dad is working on. Brick told him to call it a zucchodil, but I think that sounds like something for your prostate."

"There's a reason Brick doesn't work in marketing," Brooke said. "What's with all the cleavage?"

"Am I not allowed to engage in exceptional ablutions in honor of my best friend's debut?"

"Don't all those syllables ever make your jaw tired?"

"The play is going to be great, Brooke," Ari said, apparently mistaking Brooke's bad mood for preshow jitters. "Trust me. I know quality. Your dress rehearsal last night was seamless."

Brooke stood up and brushed off the seat of her jeans.

"Exactly the issue," she lied. "A good dress rehearsal means a bad performance."

"That's a myth." Ari sniffed. "Come on, let's get you in hair and makeup. You need to focus."

Brooke closed her eyes. Ari knew her so well. Nothing was more calming than false eyelashes.

Relax. Ginevra has obviously fallen off a cliff somewhere, and I am going to be the most beautiful Eliza Doolittle the world has ever seen.

Still, just to be safe, Brooke superstitiously crossed her fingers.

✦ ✦ ✦

Molly climbed out from underneath Julie Newman's hem and surveyed the girl's costume. It was perfect. They were all perfect. It had taken a tremendous amount of work, including considerable neglect of her homework. But it had been worth it: She'd done Laurel proud.

"This looks great," Julie said, leaning over to examine her lace hem. "You're really good at this."

"Thanks," Molly said, tucking a strand of hair behind her ear. "Okay, take it off again real fast. I need to steam it."

Julie trotted off to change, and Molly looked around the room. The vast wardrobe area was as neat as her sewing basket—the one that used to be Laurel's, and was therefore arranged with a military precision—but in twenty minutes, it would be full of students in thick pancake foundation and seven coats of mascara. Everyone's wigs and accessories were neatly set out next to masking tape stuck to the Formica table with the corresponding actors' names written on it. Once Brooke finally stopped trying to murder her costumes, Molly had grown to enjoy the camaraderie of the theater. It was like being part of a highly dysfunctional, deeply dramatic family. Not unlike her *actual* family, when it came right down to it.

Molly glanced out the window in the cozy nook where her sewing machine lived, which overlooked the back parking lot. There, next to her Lexus and Neil Westerberg's beat-up red Vespa, was Teddy's 4Runner. She wondered if she had time to find him and give him the Danny update: They had a date to talk the next morning, after nearly two weeks of missing each other—or "missing each other," since surely nobody was that dense about basic math. It felt like he was doing that irritating boy thing where they act all obtuse until the girl breaks down and does the ugly work. Danny *had* to be avoiding the Talk again, just as much as she'd been, but it was time to face it. Molly wondered how Teddy would react: sympathy, supportiveness…excitement, maybe…

As if summoned by her thoughts, Teddy came into the window's view, looking adorable in a sport coat over one of his usual tees. Then a tall figure in a tight dress emerged from the shadow of the theater and threw its arms around him. It was Arugula, and Molly had never seen her flash so much cleavage. Teddy returned the hug, then threw back his head and laughed at whatever she said, causing Arugula to flush in a way that meant she had been trying to impress him. She hugged his arm to her ample chest, stroking it as they walked away, smiling.

Molly's heart plummeted to her knees—an involuntary reaction, like her body had already made an executive decision about something without consulting her. But she knew she had no right to feel disappointed. Technically, she had a boyfriend. *If Teddy is happy, that's all that matters. Right?*

There was a rustling behind her, and a door slammed. Max emerged from the dressing room area holding three lighting gels.

"What were you doing back there?" Molly asked, arranging her features in what she hoped was a calm expression.

"When the UPS guy delivered my gels, they put the package up here with your shipment of theatrical makeup."

"Cool," Molly said. "Um, so, hey, have you talked to Teddy?"

Max rolled her eyes. "He's coming with *Arugula*. Can

you believe it? She actually corrected my grammar in English the other day. Gross."

She smacked her hand against her head. "Oh, my God, I almost forgot the other reason I came in here! Jake. His shirt won't stay buttoned," she whispered. "So he's just walking around in there half naked. Can you please avoid him for a while? For me?"

"Molly!" Jake cried, bursting out of the dressing room. "My clothes keep falling off and I need your help!"

"Please no," Max mouthed behind Jake's back.

"Come here, Jake." Molly grinned, grateful that she had something to distract her. "I'll see what I can do."

"Awesome," Jake said, struggling with his sleeves. "This feels so *big*."

"The shirt?" Molly asked, pinpointing a loose button and a missing one. She retrieved her beat-up cardboard box full of extras from under her sewing table and fished around for a decent match—slowly, though, for Max's benefit.

"No, the play," Jake said. "I'm so nervous. This is way harder than football. There, my face mask is my mask. I mean, like, literally *and* metaphorically."

"You'll be fine," Molly said, threading a needle. "Hold still."

"I don't know," he said. "Jen said—"

Max snorted. Jake swiveled to look at her.

"Sorry," Max said.

"Hold *still*," Molly warned.

There was an interminable pause, during which Molly

could tell Max was fumbling for a way out of her faux pas. Then her friend took a long breath and actually made eye contact with Jake.

"I've been at all the rehearsals, and I think you've improved so much. You're a natural," she said. "So ignore Jennifer. You're going to be great."

Molly wanted to applaud. Jake shot Max a smile that would've tempted the angels to book a table in hell.

"That's totally what I needed to hear," he said. "Thank you, Max."

At the sound of her actual name, Max threatened to turn purple again.

"No problem," she managed. "It's all true."

She grabbed her gels and turned to go.

"By the way, I like your hair," Jake called out. "You remind me of those badass little mushrooms on Super Mario Brothers that give you extra lives."

Max flashed him a wide grin, her eyes glowing amber in the light, then practically skipped out the door.

"She's cool," Jake said to Molly.

"She's very cool," Molly agreed. "And your button is fixed. You're all set. Break a leg."

Jake recoiled. "Why would you *say* something like that? I need these legs for football!"

He trotted back to the dressing room. Molly giggled, and bent down to stow away her button box.

"Watch your head," came a voice from above. Molly was so startled by this—she thought she was alone—that she actually did jump, and cracked her skull against the under-side of the metal desk.

"Ow," she said, and crawled back out, rubbing her tender head.

She looked up. Shelby Kendall stood above her, sophisticated in a slim black cocktail dress, which Molly vaguely remembered having seen in last month's *Vogue*. Her hair was pulled back into a low, complicated knot. She looked about twenty-five years old.

"What do you want?" Molly asked.

"That looked painful. Should we take you to the hospital? An undetected brain hemorrhage can be fatal," Shelby asked, oozing false concern.

"I'm fine," Molly said shortly. "Actually, I've got a lot to do."

"I can only imagine," Shelby said. "I won't be long. When I was at Father's office, someone asked me to deliver this to you."

She held out a manila envelope. Confused, Molly took it and slid out a copy of *Hey!* that was clearly freshly printed. The cover was an alarming collage of celebrity cellulite, underneath an orange headline screaming: BUSTED: CELEB-RITY BUMS! But Molly's gaze was diverted by a Post-it stuck to the front:

> Page five is all us, Brooke! Look for this live online later tonight! Thanks for the scoop, and I can't wait to work with you again! Love, G.

"This is for Brooke," Molly said, feeling like she was pointing out the obvious.

"Is it?" Shelby said. "My mistake. I was *sure* it was for you, considering..."

"Considering what, Shelby?"

"Why don't you see for yourself?"

A slow, cold smile crept across Shelby's beautiful face. Molly's spine quivered. She hated humoring Shelby, but she was too curious to resist.

BERLIN BABE BREAKS HEART OF HOMETOWN HONEY, the headline on page five announced, and beneath it, there was a grainy photo of her and Teddy at her locker, wrapped in each other's arms. Her face was to the camera and her eyes were closed, the expression on her face very relaxed and happy. It was so intimate that Molly shivered. They looked like a couple. And the pièce de résistance: Danny's yearbook picture sat just beneath it. Molly remembered that he'd been really hung over that day thanks to a weekend jaunt out to the sand dunes, but in the photo he was the picture of apple-cheeked innocence.

Molly's breath caught in her throat, emitting a weird choking sound.

"I was sure you knew," Shelby murmured.

Molly said nothing. She was reading the blurb:

Superstar actor/director Brick Berlin is one of Hollywood's most notorious heartbreakers, and his brand-new daughter Molly, 16, is following in his famous footsteps! The troublemaking student—who's already struggled with alcohol—got caught getting down and dirty with a hunky classmate (pictured above), leaving in the dust her hometown honey, Danny Johansson, 17. "Danny thought he and Molly would be together forever," said a source close to the former high-school sweeties. "When her mother was dying, Danny was like hospice for Molly's heart. He brought her sunflowers. He was her rock." Sources confirm Danny had no idea they were even on the rocks. "She's a chip off the old Brick," the source told *Hey!* "Looks like someone left her manners back in Indiana."

It was like all the oxygen had been sucked out of the room. Molly sank down into the desk chair in front of her sewing machine and felt it rotate gently until she was facing the window again. The landscape swam in front of her eyes.

High heels tap-tapped on distant hardwood floors, the sound growing nearer with every metallic *thwap*.

"Hellllllllo?" Brooke called. "Molly? Time for final wardrobe review!"

Molly said nothing.

"Molly?" Brooke repeated, banging through the door. "Where *are* you? Aren't you going to tell me to break a leg?"

"We should be so lucky."

Even in the blurry reflection in the window, Molly could see Brooke start when she heard Shelby's voice.

"Welcome to the party," Shelby continued, grabbing the back of Molly's chair and bodily revolving it until Molly and Brooke were facing each other. "We have a present for you."

twenty-six

NOTHING HARSHES A GIRL'S BUZZ like being confronted by her mortal enemy wearing straight-off-the-runway Victoria Beckham. Brooke felt all her excited opening-night butterflies drop dead in the face of Shelby Kendall standing behind Molly, looking as delighted as if she'd stumbled upon a hot-oil treatment that also burned calories.

"Aren't you supposed to be off researching part one of another half-assed special report that will never have a part two?" Brooke asked.

"Brooke, give it up," Shelby said. "We *know*."

Brooke noticed then that Molly was staring emptily at the wall. Shelby snatched something from Molly's grasp that was rolled up so tightly Brooke couldn't tell at first what it was.

Brooke went cold. *No way. No. It can't be. Not tonight.*

Slowly, she unrolled the magazine. Molly never looked up from her seat.

"This is not what it looks like," Brooke said. "Molly, it isn't, I swear."

"*Just* like a Berlin," Shelby said. "Can't act her way out of an open paper bag."

"You're just trying to spoil opening night for us, and it's not going to work."

"*I* haven't spoiled anything," Shelby retorted. "You did an excellent job of that all on your own, wouldn't you say?"

They both looked down at Molly, who Brooke feared might have gone catatonic. Was that a 911 emergency, or could she just get Jake Donovan to wake her up by chucking her into the lake?

"Molly," Brooke said again. "Look at me. Let me explain."

Slowly, Molly lifted her head. Brooke saw a flash of fire in her eyes.

"It's not what you think," Brooke repeated. "You have to believe me."

"She doesn't *have* to do anything, except get you booted to military school," Shelby said, kneeling next to Molly's chair. "Molly, in spite of everything you've said to me recently, I am obviously your only true friend in this scenario. Let's get out of here, so I can figure out how to help you fix this."

"Fix this? Your father's magazine *did this*," Brooke retorted.

"Did what? Sent that picture to our intern in an e-mail

full of juicy little details? I'm pretty sure that was your doing, sweetie. Checkmate."

"What is wrong with you?" Brooke exploded. "Can't you just let this whole thing between us go? You already won! What more do you want?"

"So, you're conceding defeat?" Shelby pounced.

"As if. I'm just tired of it," Brooke said. "Aren't you? Listen, I'm sorry I saw your mom come over drunk that time, but that's no reason —"

Shelby rolled her eyes. "You two and your mommy issues." She sniffed, looking from Brooke to Molly. "This isn't some crappy Brick Berlin movie where everyone has a deep-seated psychological motive."

"Then what?" Brooke said. "Why are we doing this? Why are you always out to get me?"

"Because it's fun, honey," Shelby said, with a chilling smile. "What better reason is there?"

"Get out of here, Shelby."

The voice was Molly's. Brooke stared at her sister in surprise as she rose from her chair and squared off against their joint enemy.

"I don't know what part of our conversation the other day was so confusing for you," Molly said. "But your tricks to divide me and Brooke are not going to work. We are stronger together than we ever were before, not that I would expect someone like you to understand why. Now get the hell out of my costume room and stay away from me and my sister."

Brooke felt her mouth slide open a little, in shock. Shelby's nostrils flared as she drew a sharp breath.

Molly moved to stand beside Brooke, her voice pure steel. "And if you so much as breathe in this theater, I'll have Brick's security people arrest you for harassment."

Shelby's face went frighteningly smooth and expressionless. "You two deserve each other," she said. "This isn't over. And you're going to be *so sorry* when it is."

With that, Shelby turned on her thousand-dollar Fendi heel and slithered out of the costume room.

"That. Was. *Amazing*," Brooke breathed. "Man, I wish we'd been recording that. I want to play it at the cast party."

Brooke wrapped her arms around Molly's neck. "I *knew* you'd believe me. You have to understand, I—"

Brooke's voice faltered as Molly threw off her arms and turned toward her, the spark in her eyes replaced with a chilly, furious glint.

"Get away from me," she said.

Brooke had been slapped exactly twice in her life: once by Jennifer, who was practicing for a scene in *Ransom of Rage* where her character had to fend off a handsy kidnapper, and once by Arugula when she'd accidentally kicked her in the crotch while demonstrating a Tae Bo move. Each had stung, but neither felt remotely as bad as the verbal smack she'd just gotten from Molly.

"But I th-thought…" she stammered. "Everything you said…"

"Shelby doesn't deserve to get her way," Molly said, attacking any stray piece of clutter in the room with almost crazy fanaticism. "She wanted us at each other's throats, and although I am very tempted to wring yours, I will *not* give that bitch the satisfaction."

"I wasn't lying, Molly," Brooke said. "It's really not what it looks like."

"Isn't it?" Molly retorted. "Let's see, there's the sunflower stuff, for starters. Only a few people know that, and you're the only one of them likely to have a tabloid reporter on speed dial."

"I—"

"And oh, yeah, there's the note patting you on the back for your collaboration. So unless you're going to tell me you have an evil twin, I'm really not sure what the hell else it could be."

"But don't you see, this is just like when I thought you gave Shelby those e-mails!" Brooke said.

"Yeah, except you actually *did* this."

"No!"

"Great, so if I go home and check your Sent Mail, I won't see this Ginevra person's name in it?"

"Well, I mean…you will, but I didn't *mean to*," Brooke insisted.

"Oh, sure, just like a vampire doesn't mean to leave puncture wounds," Molly said, her voice getting even angrier.

"What I really want to know is, how did you spy on me that well without me knowing?"

"I didn't! Arugula took the photo, because—"

"Oh, of course, Arugula," Molly said. "I should've known. Well, good job, Brooke. You suckered me into falling for your sister act *again* and went in for the kill *again* when I wasn't protecting myself. You have officially made an idiot out of me."

"That wasn't an act!" Brooke cried. "I swear! Look, I was going to send the photo the night you went out with Brick. I was so *jealous*. But I never sent it. It went out when I sent all those e-mails to my mother. I didn't even know until Ginevra wrote back!"

Molly stopped. "Wait," she said. "You've known about this? And you didn't think you should say something?"

Dammit.

"I didn't know she was going to *do* anything with it," Brooke protested. "She's just some dumb intern. And she didn't return any of my calls and e-mails, so I just assumed..."

"You assumed an intern stumbled into a juicy scoop about Brick Berlin's family and did *nothing* with it?" Molly said. "Please. You just decided you didn't want to deal with this. Because that's how you operate."

Julie Newman poked her head around the door, then her eyes grew wide. "Um, I'll get my wig later," she said, backing away. "Ten minutes to curtain, guys."

Molly smacked her hands down on the Formica, displacing Julie's wig and a few other accessories. Brooke's breathing was in time with her heart's rapid pounding. She felt dizzy and wanted to cry. This was bad. This was *so* bad. And she already had her eyelashes on and everything.

"Half this stuff isn't even me, Molly," Brooke tried again, frantically flipping to the story and scanning it. "I never talked about Laurel to her. She made it up! Do you really think I would use the word *insouciant?*"

"You know what?" Molly shrugged. "I don't care. I'm so over it."

Brooke inched toward her. "Wait, like...you're *past* it?"

"No. Like, I'm sick of this place and you and your whole little gang of selfish schemers and liars," Molly said. "I am not a supporting character in your biography. I am a person. And guess what? I am done."

"Don't say that," Brooke pleaded. "At least, let's talk after the play."

Molly laughed, but her laughter was scary—brittle and high.

"The play. *Of course.* Of course that's more important to you," Molly said. "You may have let *Hey!* call me a skank, but at least I'm not a whore for the spotlight."

And Brooke, stunned, could only watch as Molly turned and walked away.

twenty-seven

AS SOON AS SHE LEFT, students rushed pell-mell into the makeup room, a wave of humanity breaking around Brooke's rigid, shocked body.

Great. I'm paralyzed. They're going to have to use the Jaws of Life to lift me out of this building and Brick is going to throw me into the pool house and hire a mean old nurse to sponge bathe me until I die of a blood clot.

"Brooke."

She blinked and her eyes focused on what looked like a small bonsai tree standing in front of her.

"Brooke," Max said again. "I just saw Molly run out of here like her hair was on fire. I couldn't catch her. What the hell happened?"

"She's done," Brooke said dully, handing Max the tabloid so hard that it thwacked her in the gut.

"Oh, crap," Max breathed, scanning it.

"Oh, crap," Brooke echoed.

"Let me guess. You did this," Max said.

"Please, you think I *want* the whole world to see her wearing that sad little no-name tank top?" Brooke snapped, her senses clearing a bit. "It was an accident."

Max eyeballed Brooke for a long moment.

"I believe you," she finally said. "But I can see why Molly wouldn't. I probably would've left, too. Maybe even punched you in the face on the way out."

"I don't know what to do," Brooke moaned.

Max tapped the tabloid against her palm, thoughtfully. "I think I know someone who does," she finally said. She tossed the tabloid back at Brooke and headed off toward the theater.

"Brooke!"

As if on a lazy Susan, Brooke's head turned, all motion and no emotion. Mavis Moore, who'd volunteered to be the stage manager once she'd realized she could do it while knitting and still get the credit on her transcript, appeared before her.

"Don't you go on soon, or something?" she said to Brooke. "I think it started."

Mavis was not a good volunteer stage manager.

Brooke stayed rooted to the spot. She could barely remember the name of the damn play.

"Come on," Mavis said, bodily dragging her backstage.

"Thank God," Jennifer said, taking over for Mavis and steering Brooke to the spot from which she'd make her entrance. "The curtain just went up. I almost had a stroke. Where *were* you?"

Brooke let herself peek out at the crowd. Brie sat in the second row, and there was Ari, sitting as close to Teddy as the armrest would allow. Ari's parents sat near them, with the Parkers and Jen's brother, Free, who was sporting his usual feather boa and a red wig. Stan, to their left, had shaved his chin and put on a suit and was clutching a Kleenex as if prepared to cry. Perched in the front row wearing a tiny and tight cocktail dress was the almost-A-list starlet from *Beer o'Clock*, and then—dead center with his hand on her knee—there was Brick.

He's here. Holy crap, he's here.

"Brooke!" hissed Jennifer. "Pay attention! You're on in ten seconds!"

Brooke's mind went blank. All she could see was Molly's face, then Brick's, in a never-ending loop. Every second that passed without going after Molly, Brooke felt the chasm between them get wider—and the amount of trouble she was in get bigger. But she had no idea where Molly went. And Brick was *here*, at last, supporting her. The child who'd longed for this moment stood next to the adult who knew that, for the first time ever, she'd made a huge mess that she needed to clean up herself. Fast.

It was the biggest choice Brooke had ever had to make.

✦ ✦ ✦

Thunderous applause burst in Brooke's ears. She stared up at the lights, hot and bright, and waved randomly at various parts of the theater before taking another deep curtsy. She was aware of people getting out of their chairs, not to leave but to clap harder.

She was a hit.

Brooke had surprised herself by taking those steps onstage, but it worked in her favor: Eliza was supposed to be flummoxed, having just crashed into Freddy Eynsford-Hill as he ran off to find a cab and knocked her flowers into a puddle. Once she found her footing, as Eliza did, the rest had been a triumph. The audience laughed. The cast responded with renewed vigor. Even Jake had been great.

And now, Brick was leaping out of his seat with a bouquet of roses, wrapping his arm around Brooke and weeping tears of joy.

"Brilliant, Sunshine!" he crowed. "I have never been prouder of your grace and talent!"

The crowd let out a collective coo and clapped even harder. Brooke drank it all in: the cheers, the flowers, her father's delighted eyes locked on her and only her as they stood in the spotlight, together. It was everything she'd ever wanted.

And it sucked.

Snap out of it, her inner voice lectured. *This is it. This is your moment.*

Yeah. A moment that sucked. She had picked herself over her sister, and even though she partly did it because she thought Brick would be too embarrassed if she jilted her cast and the audience—the show, as he always said, must go on, after all—Brooke knew she mostly did it for herself. And she was afraid it meant she really *was* a bad person.

But Molly understood how much Brick's attendance was worth, right? And once Brooke proved that the e-mail was sent by accident, Molly had to forgive her, right? She wasn't unreasonable. And then the two of them together could sit down with Brick and show him the magazine and present a united, adult front.

In the meantime, there was no wisdom in pretending she hadn't just brought down the house. With the rapturous approval from the audience ringing in her ears as the curtain closed for the final time, Brooke gazed up at Brick, who drew her into another bear hug.

"You are a tribute to the Berlin genes," he bubbled. "Maybe we should come out with a denim line. Kicky double meaning!"

Brooke giggled against his chest and finally allowed the glee to flood her veins. At last, after sixteen years, Brick finally *saw* her. So whatever waited for Brooke back at the house, it simply couldn't, *wouldn't*, have anything but a happy ending. Brooke simply wouldn't allow it. Not tonight.

twenty-eight

"THIS IS YELLOW CAB. Your car will arrive in approximately: Two. Minutes."

Molly hung up on the computer-modulated voice and tucked her boarding pass inside her purse. She hadn't even bothered trying to pack everything that belonged to her; she just wanted to go, fast, and she didn't want to take anything purchased with Brick's money back to Indiana. It didn't feel right. As it was, her suitcase still barely closed over the fringes of the blanket stitched together from all of Laurel's scarves.

Molly set her credit card and the keys to the Lexus on top of Brooke's laptop and slung her bag over her shoulder. She had been so angry back at school, but now she just felt numb. Soon, she'd be home again, her *real* home, away from all this endless drama. Where she should have been all along.

From deep in her backpack, she felt her phone buzz again.

"I'm coming," Molly muttered at it.

She pulled her bulky suitcase down the stairs. It clonked obnoxiously against each marble step, gaining momentum as she got closer to the bottom. Molly considered letting go of the handle and letting gravity do the rest of the work. It seemed appropriately destructive.

The doorbell rang.

"I'm *coming*," she repeated.

Molly opened the door. It was not the cabdriver. It was Teddy.

"What are you doing here?"

"Max grabbed me during intermission," Teddy said. "I came right over."

"What did she tell you?"

"Probably just the CliffsNotes version, but it was enough," he said. "I haven't seen the magazine, but...you know. I was there."

Molly forced herself to keep some distance from him. She was so glad to see him, yet so upset that he'd come. Teddy, standing on her doorstep, still dressed up from the play and looking adorably concerned, was not helping her resolve to leave.

"I'm sorry if I ruined your night," she managed.

"You didn't ruin anything," Teddy said. "The guy behind

me had awful breath, and Julie Newman's accent was all over the place."

"Why didn't you tell me about Arugula?" Molly heard herself ask, hating how petty it sounded.

"What *about* Arugula?"

"I saw you guys at the play today."

Comprehension dawned. "Is *that* what you meant, about ruining my night?" he asked. "That wasn't a *date*. That wasn't…anything. She told me she wanted to talk about our oral report before the play, and then we sat together. That's it." He frowned. "She rubbed against me a little more than usual, I guess, but that's just Arugula."

A cab pulled into the driveway and its horn blared. Molly held up one finger, as if to beg it to wait.

"I have to go," Molly said. "I'm going to miss my flight."

"Wait, what? You're *leaving*?" Teddy asked, finally noticing her bag. "Because of some stupid story in a tabloid? You're stronger than that."

Molly let go of her suitcase, which immediately gave in to physics and fell forward with a *thunk*.

"I don't think I am, Teddy. I really don't. I can't…I just can't take it anymore. And what about Danny?" she asked. "This happened to him, too. How is he going to feel when he sees that picture?"

She could feel tears beginning to burn in her throat.

"You know what the funny thing is?" she said. "He and I had a date to talk tomorrow morning. And I'm pretty sure we were going to break up."

Teddy stepped closer to her.

"But there's no way he isn't going to see this, if he hasn't already," Molly kept going, on the verge of hysteria. "It's on the Internet, Teddy. And I look like such a jackass."

"I'm so sorry, Indiana," Teddy said.

"I never wanted to be part of some stupid vendetta. I never wanted *any* of this," Molly said. "I just wanted to do the last thing my mother ever asked of me, you know?"

"Then don't give it up," Teddy said. "Not without a fight."

"But I don't have any fight left, Teddy," Molly explained, wringing her hands. "Coming here was supposed to fix me, but it's just made everything worse. It feels like my mom died all over again, except this time I have nowhere to go but backward. There's nothing for me here."

"There's me," Teddy said firmly.

"You have Ari. She obviously likes you."

"Too bad," he said. "I like *you*."

He reached out and cupped her face, flicking away one of Molly's tears with his thumb.

"You know I do. Right?" he whispered. "You have to know."

Molly closed her eyes and allowed herself one second of enjoying the feeling of his hand on her skin. It would be so easy to let him draw her into an embrace, to give in to the way her pulse sped up every time she was around him. The way it was racing right now.

No. Do not get sucked back into this poisonous place. Not even by Teddy McCormack.

She opened her eyes.

"I'm so sorry," she whispered. "I have to go."

"You don't, though," Teddy said almost pleadingly, his face full of otherwise unexpressed emotion. "Don't give up. Please, just tell me what you need and I'll be there. I'll do it. I'll be it."

His brown eyes looked so hopeful, and so sad at the same time. Through her tears, Molly reached up and ruffled his hair.

"I need my mom," she said, another tear running down her cheek.

✦ ✦ ✦

"What a night, Sunshine!" Brick said as he turned the Range Rover into the driveway and parked it behind Molly's Lexus.

"Thanks, Daddy," Brooke answered. She felt a surge of good cheer at the sight of Molly's car in the driveway. Her sister was probably just upstairs, sitting on the balcony and bitching to Clementine, or whatever her name was, while Brooke's extensive collection of vintage Marc Jacobs sundresses burned in the bathtub.

Well, she can burn whatever she wants, if it puts her in a good mood.

"I can't wait to go to the studio tomorrow and tell everyone what a talented daughter I have! *Two* talented daughters!" Brick said, sliding out of the car. "The costumes were fantastic! Why didn't Molly stay for the curtain call? You told her I made reservations at Craft, didn't you? I might even order dessert. Such tremendous accomplishments call for refined sugar."

Brooke had about twenty minutes before Brick dragged them off for what would surely be the most awful, awkward family dinner ever—worse even than Thanksgiving last year on *Lust for Life*, when Francesca's brain fog caused her to serve her own severed hand for dinner, instead of turkey. Brooke had to get to Molly first and make her see reason. See the *truth*.

"And who is this?" Brick said, crossing the driveway and walking toward the house.

Brooke looked up and noticed Teddy McCormack, who was sitting in the shadow of one of the two giant stone lions framing the front door. He looked bummed out.

This is not a good sign.

"Greetings, young man," Brick said, reaching out a hand to Teddy. "Are you here to talk to one of my girls?"

Teddy stood, and shook Brick's hand.

"I was," he said. "But I was too late."

Brick looked confused as Brooke's heart sank to the very soles of her wedges.

"Molly is gone," Teddy clarified, glancing from Brick to Brooke, and then quickly back to Brick again.

"She's *gone*?" Brick parroted. "What do you mean, she's *gone*? Where did she go?"

"She went home, sir," Teddy said. "To Indiana."

Brooke noticed that Teddy seemed to be having trouble meeting her eyes. *Of course. He blames me. I would blame me, too. I do blame me.*

Brick turned white underneath his burnished tan.

"What are you talking about?" he said angrily. "What's going on here? Is this some kind of prank?"

Teddy looked at Brooke. She poured every ounce of sincerity into her eyes and mouthed, "I'll fix it."

He nodded, almost imperceptibly.

"I'll leave you two alone," he said. "It was nice to meet you, Mr. Berlin."

"Brooke, I'm confused," Brick said, turning to look at her as Teddy disappeared down the driveway. "Who was that young person? Has he been binge drinking? *Dateline* says it's raping our society."

Brooke sighed. "No, Daddy, he's not like that," she said. "Let's go inside, okay? There's something I need to tell you, and you're not going to like it."

twenty-nine

"I'M SURE IT WON'T BE AS GOOD as the pizza you get in Los Angeles."

Molly accepted a warm, greasy bag from the kid behind the counter at Slice of Eden. She vaguely recognized him from freshman comp class, but the name tag on his T-shirt—Eddy—didn't ring a bell.

"You're thinking of New York," she said, pushing a twenty across the counter.

Eddy snorted. "Don't patronize me."

Molly stood there for a second, crumpling the waxen white paper sack in her fist, before turning and heading back out to her car. Los Angeles had felt so far removed from her hometown that she'd forgotten everyone in West Cairo was as capable of keeping an eye on her tabloid shenanigans as the kids at Colby-Randall. And it was clear they'd not only paid attention but taken sides.

No one had confronted her, exactly. But when she filled up her car at the Shell an hour ago, Bonnie Turner—who had always had a crush on Danny—whispered loudly to her friend, "I guess they ran her cheating ass out of town." Her taxi driver from the airport wanted to know why Brick hadn't provided her with a private jet. Even at baggage claim, she saw a twelve-year-old clutching *Hey!* and shooting Molly a murderous look. In L.A., Molly was just a blip, a meaningless respite between stories about legitimately famous people. But in tiny West Cairo, she was That Assy Girl Who Thinks She's So Famous but Is Actually a Disloyal Bitch. The local Osco Drug would probably have TEAM DANNY T-shirts by next week. And Molly couldn't really blame them. If she weren't That Assy Girl, she'd probably hate herself, too.

She nibbled on a garlic breadstick in the driver's seat of her grandparents' Honda, which smelled musty and airless from being parked for so long in the garage. Ginger and Miltie were still on their trip around the world—their last postcard hailed from Istanbul—so she'd had to dig the spare key out from under a potted hydrangea plant to let herself into the house. It was cold and empty without them, metaphorically and literally, since they'd turned out their pilot light before leaving town.

Molly started the car and pulled into the street, navigating her way up to the town's main park, a large oasis set against a tree-lined ridge. She and Danny had hiked up there in ninth grade and found a rock outcropping that formed a de facto bench from which you could see most of Main Street. They used to eat lunch there on Sundays.

Danny's truck was already in Pyramid Park's dirt lot. Dread tickled Molly's skin as she slowly made her way up the rough, untended slope flanking the park, left at the crooked tree onto which she and Danny had once carved their names, and out into the clearing. Danny's back was to Molly, but he'd clearly heard her coming, because he stood up in a hurry from his spot on the rock. He was bleary-eyed and his plaid shirt had what looked like syrup on the pocket, but otherwise—and in fact, in those ways, too—he was the same old Danny.

His opening salvo was, "Are we breaking up or what?"

"Wow, that was direct."

"So was this," he said, pulling out a copy of *Hey!* and throwing it onto the ground. His yearbook photo grinned back up at them, juxtaposed with the intimate photo of her and Teddy leaning against her locker. Molly kicked it to a different page. Better to stare at a story about the hot new Hollywood diet pill—horse tranquilizers from Mexico— than at that picture.

"I am *so sorry*," she said. "I never, ever wanted you to get dragged into any of this."

"Is it true?" he asked, sitting down again. "Are you dumping me for some Hollywood poser with an expensive haircut?"

She unrolled the crumpled bag and handed him a piece of pizza.

"Teddy's not a poser," Molly hedged, joining him on the rock. "And the details are totally wrong. Nothing actually happened."

"This doesn't look like nothing."

"In L.A. nothing is ever what it looks like," she said. "He's my friend. We fought, and we were making up. That's all."

"So you're home. What now? Are you coming back to Mellencamp? Because if you are, maybe we—"

His face was hopeful. Molly could feel the sad, sympathetic expression arranging itself on her face as she shook her head.

"So, it's over?" Danny asked, but he didn't sound as angry as she thought he might. "Definitively?"

Molly took a deep, quavery breath. "Definitively," she said. "If it was supposed to work, I think it would have, and we both know it didn't."

She promptly burst into tears. Danny looped his arm around her shoulder.

"Oh, Molls, stop crying," he muttered. "Honestly, it's not like we didn't break up three times while you *were* here."

Molly let out a half sob, half laugh. "You really deserved the one before this. Late to Homecoming because of a Colts game? Come on."

"It's called fan loyalty, Molly," Danny said with mock seriousness. "So, tell me about this guy. You like him, right? I can tell. I've known you long enough."

Molly looked down at her Converse. The hole that had been brewing her entire stay in Southern California was about to blossom. The metaphor annoyed her.

"Yeah," she finally admitted. "I think I do. I'm sorry. But I swear it didn't hit me until after things with us got weird."

"Well, that was my bad. I shouldn't have avoided you," he said. "But my best friend and my girlfriend was suddenly gone, and long-distance was so hard, and I just didn't want to deal. It felt like too much."

"I used to think I hated change, too," Molly said. "Now I'm not so sure. I tried going there without changing anything here, and look how well that worked."

Danny sighed. "But we didn't even make it through a semester, Molls," he said. "That's *embarrassing*."

"Well, it was kind of easy to stay together when I could skip your swim team parties, or you could skip my movie night, and we knew we'd just hang out some other time," she said. "But we're only sixteen. We shouldn't just do the easy thing all the time."

"Wow, you're so wise now," Danny teased.

"I don't feel wise. I feel really dumb."

"About what?"

"*Everything*. For being in denial about what might happen to us. For leaving L.A. without telling anyone. Maybe even going to L.A. in the first place. It's like I've become a totally irrational person since my mom died, and now everything is a mess."

"You've been through a lot. I don't think anything you

did was really that irrational." Danny shrugged. "Except breaking up with me, of course. I just broke forty seconds on a keg stand last weekend. I'm a hot commodity."

They laughed as Molly wiped her eyes. "I don't know what to do next," she admitted. "I can't imagine going back to Mellencamp, but I'm not sure I can stomach going back to L.A."

"Was it really all that bad? Is one stupid story that's eighty percent true—"

"Thirty percent true."

"—*sixty* percent true, really worth giving up everything you left here for?"

Molly fiddled with the crust of her pizza, then tossed it back into the bag. When she was in L.A., it seemed like getting back to Indiana was going to solve all of her problems. But simply being in a different time zone than Brooke and Brick didn't mean they ceased to exist. As if to rub it in, the billboard Molly could see off to the east, over the toll road on-ramp, was an ad for the *Rad Man* collectors' edition DVD.

"Brooke swore she never meant to leak that photo, but, I mean, how is that even possible?" she asked.

"Dude, I hit the damn Send shortcut in Gmail all the time by accident," Danny pointed out. "One day my sister got about ten half-finished messages from me about how if she tells our parents I use chewing tobacco I'm going to show them where she keeps her condoms."

Molly thought about this. "She did seem upset, but I guess I didn't want to hear it."

She stared down at the park and the town below it. Two kids were playing on the swings, jumping off when they got to the highest point in their arc. A cop was ticketing a car that was parked in a red zone. With a half smile, she thought about the dress rehearsal for *My Fair Lady*, where Brooke tried to convince her she could park in a handicapped spot because her Christian Siriano boots had given her horrible blisters.

"Maybe you should call her," Danny suggested. "I mean, you don't want to end up like your mom, making confessions on your deathbed because you never got around to telling people what they needed to hear."

"That's exactly what she would have said," Molly said softly.

Danny tapped her on the shoulder and pointed to a spot about twenty yards to their right. "Check it out."

A sunflower was growing on a tangled, unkempt corner of the plateau, alone and wilting.

"I would pick it for you, but…" Danny let his voice trail off.

"It's seen better days," Molly said.

"Yeah, I'd say it's near the end of its life cycle."

They traded smiles, sad ones. Finally, Danny stood up and stuffed his hands into his pockets.

"I think that's as good a sign as any that I should go," he said.

"I understand," she said. "Thanks, Danny. For going easy on me. For everything. You'll always be one of my best friends. You know that, right?"

Danny nodded. "You, too," he said. "Good luck, Molls. Don't be a stranger."

Then he loped off down the hill. Molly had watched him walk away from this spot many times in her life, but this was the first time that it felt like he was really leaving her.

But it was okay. It felt, finally, like a step forward. Their conversation had lifted some of the weight off her shoulders, but in her heart she knew it was somebody else that she had come back to see.

✦ ✦ ✦

Molly ran a hand against the curved top of the granite stone poking out of lush green grass. LAUREL DIX, BELOVED MOTHER, DAUGHTER, AND FRIEND, it read, and underneath the inscription were two quotes. One was from Joni Mitchell: I DON'T KNOW WHO I AM…BUT LIFE IS FOR LEARNING. The other was a snippet of Thoreau that read, LIVE THE LIFE YOU'VE ALWAYS IMAGINED. So many words. Typical Laurel.

Kneeling down, Molly nestled a bunch of snapdragons against the headstone.

"Well, Mom, I guess that didn't work out the way you thought."

"No kidding."

Molly turned around to see Charmaine walking toward her, two cans of Diet Coke in her hand.

"I thought I might find you here," she said, handing one

to Molly. "Of course, I already looked at your house, and Starbucks, and Danny's. And briefly at Old Navy. Turns out you weren't in the two-for-twelve-dollars tank top pile."

"Danny and I broke up. Finally," Molly said.

"So he told me just now," Charmaine said, sitting down on the grave next to Molly. "Hi, Laurel," she yelled into the grass. "I'm feeding Molly all-natural organic carrot juice!"

"It's bad luck to lie to the dead," Molly said. "Also, if she can hear you, I bet she can see you."

"Eh, she'll appreciate the effort," Charmaine said. "How are you feeling?"

Molly grimaced and cracked open her can of soda. "I don't know. Tired. I feel like I spent the last few months running away from everything, and then I turned around and ran away again."

"Well, you *were* all-state in cross-country."

"Do you think I was wrong to come back?" Molly asked.

Charmaine plucked a blade of grass and twirled it in her fingers. She held it up to her mouth and a piercing whistle sailed through the cemetery. This was one of her favorite tricks. Molly had missed it.

"Listen, Molly, I don't know what it was like out there, because I wasn't with you," Charmaine said. "But that tabloid story was pretty much a stone-cold bitch move from Brooke, so I get why you left."

"All I could think about was how much easier everything would have been if I'd never left Indiana."

"Hardly," Charmaine said. "It would have been exactly

the same. Danny still would've been the Mellencamp keg-stand champion. You'd still have had to deal with people coming up to you in the produce department and bursting into tears over the oranges. It might not have been any different, but it wouldn't have been easy, either."

"I guess that's true."

"Do you really think Brooke did it on purpose?"

"Now that I've had some time to process it, I'm not so sure," Molly admitted. "I did accidentally do something similar to her, so…Yeah. She might be telling the truth."

Charmaine looked up at the sky, as if for inspiration. "Okay," she finally said. "Do you want me to be supportive here? Or do you need Get-a-Grip Friend?"

"Get-a-Grip Friend," Molly said. "Please."

"Okay. Well, siblings fight," Charmaine said. "All the time. It's just a fact. And, yeah, this is a pretty big fight, but you of all people should know how important it is to appreciate your family while they're still around. Also, you can't just keep bouncing back and forth from West Cairo to L.A. like a Ping-Pong ball every time something goes wrong. This is your life. Don't live it in limbo with one foot here and one foot there. Pick a city and deal."

Molly was silent for a spell. "Dude," she said. "That was a good Get-a-Grip speech."

"I practiced it in the car." Charmaine grinned. "I also had a whole thing about how committing to L.A. means breaking up with Danny, but you beat me to it."

"So you think I should go back?" Molly asked.

Charmaine sighed.

"I don't *want* you to go back," she said, after a long swig of her soda. "I miss you. But I also know that you and I are going to be fine no matter what. You just need to figure out what it really means to you to be a Berlin, because you are one, whether you like it or not. And I say, go *be* one. If you're here, you never really will be." She crossed her arms smugly. "Also, if you go back one more time, you'll probably have racked up enough frequent flyer miles to buy me a free ticket to L.A. I'm just saying."

Molly laughed. "Nice to see you're unbiased."

"I just want to see Brick's Viking bust in person," Charmaine said. "But I also think you already know everything I told you, and you're just scared to lose your safety net. Which I get. But if it were me, I'd say it's worth another shot."

Molly pondered this. It was true that, when things in Los Angeles were at their most cinematically cruddy, it had always been comforting to think she could just head back to the plains. But she hadn't been thinking about running away the whole time she was there. In fact, before she'd seen *Hey!*, Molly had honestly been...happy. Brooke's vivaciousness was entertaining—when she was using it in the service of good, anyway. Brick's warmth and welcome had been genuine, if scattershot. And then there was Max. And Stan. And Teddy. *Teddy.*

"Don't just go back for the guy, though," Charmaine said, as if she'd read Molly's mind. "He's cute and everything, but I think we all learned from what happened to

Bobbie Jean on *Lust for Life* that making a decision based on a boy is hardly ever a good idea."

"I really don't think Teddy is going to give me a face transplant."

Charmaine rolled her eyes. "Bobbie Jean would've appreciated the advice."

Molly laughed, resting her palms against the grass and leaning back until her shoulders shrugged up to her ears, her fingers twining with the grass on Laurel's grave as if they were holding hands. She could stay here, with Charmaine and the ghost of Laurel and small pieces of Danny, but also with the stigma of being the girl who came crawling back because she couldn't handle Hollywood. Or she could go back and face down Brooke, Brick, and the shark tank of Colby-Randall Preparatory School, and do it better this time. There was a certain injustice in having to suck it up and go back to them with her tail between her legs, but maybe that was a part of growing up that she needed to learn—a punishment for not facing her problems head-on, the way she should have. If Laurel's death was going to teach her something, maybe it was to never leave a question unanswered, or a fight unfought.

Molly stood up and brushed the grass off her jeans.

"Where are you going?" Charmaine asked, looking up at her.

"I think I have a phone call to make," Molly said.

She bent down and hugged Charmaine, squeezing her cheek to her friend's head.

"Thank you for being my other sister," she said. "And for having the guts to tell me to get over it."

"No problem," Charmaine said. "Besides, in the movies, everyone loves the Get-a-Grip Friend. Now get out of here and go pack. Again."

The sun peeked through the clouds for the first time that day. Molly tipped her head back and closed her eyes against the light. It felt like validation from her mother that she was, at last, doing the right thing.

"A family is what you make of it," Laurel had said two days before she died, her knitting needles churning out one final scarf.

And it was time to make something real out of hers. It was time to go back to Bel Air, back to the Berlins, and make it right. For good.

epilogue

"OUT WITH IT, BROOKE. I'm not going to wait all day."

Brooke sighed. This was harder than she'd thought.

"Young lady, I do not want to hear attitude from you."

"Fine, fine," Brooke grumbled. "Um, Nebraska."

"Alaska!"

"Arkansas."

"Wyoming!" Brick crowed.

"Arkansas ends in *s*, Daddy, remember?"

Brick clapped his hands together, then swiftly clamped them back down on the wheel of the RV.

"You're right, of course," he said. "That Colby-Randall education is worth every dime. See, isn't this fun? On the journey to fix the past, we're giving each other a present."

He reached for his phone.

"Do *not* type on that thing while you're driving," Brooke crabbed. "Last time you did that, you almost ran over a VW Bug."

"Punch buggy orange!" Brick crowed, smacking Brooke in the arm. "God, I'm so glad we decided to drive!"

We?

This little trip was the opposite of what Brooke had envisioned when she'd suggested going to Indiana to beg Molly for a second chance. In Brooke's mind, they'd zip over there in a leather airplane seat, nibbling spiced nuts and drinking Champagne. Instead, Brick got a starry look in his eyes—always a harbinger of doom—and started waxing poetic about seeing America and connecting as a family. Well, first he'd made Brooke repeat the whole sordid story of the tabloid three times, delivered a stern lecture on trusting strangers, and spent ten minutes on the phone with his lawyer wondering if they could sue Trip Kendall. But once he accepted her apology as sincere and berated himself (dramatically) for not being more of a presence during Molly's first weeks there, Brick had consumed himself with how to get her back in the most normal, non-Hollywood way possible.

The radio had broken somewhere around Barstow, so Brick had made her play every corny road-trip game he'd found on the Internet, forced her to eat Tater Tots at a Sonic Drive-In, and hopped off course in Kansas to visit the famous six-legged steer at Prairie Dog Town. Brick even insisted on reading aloud three pages of Jack Kerouac over breakfast each day, because he thought it would help him "be one with the road." One night, they'd slept at a Holiday Inn that Brooke was pretty sure hadn't seen housekeeping since a murder happened in its bathtub. The whole thing was horrifying. She would never feel clean again.

Even more annoyingly, Brick was constantly delighted by these horrors, as if anything located outside Beverly Hills were the most hilarious alien oddity.

"Great news, kiddo—I decided to detour us up the 29 to see the world's largest ball of stamps!" Brick said, as if to prove her point. "Now there's a Facebook photo for you!"

"Yeah, a lot of good that'll do me. I still can't get any reception on this thing," Brooke complained, shaking her cell phone as if that would jar loose a few bars. "And the air-conditioning is jammed."

Brick balled his hand into a fist and banged on the dashboard's air vents. One of them cracked.

"Oops," he said. "Gotta talk to my trainer about cutting back on the supplements."

Brooke crossed her arms in a huff and stared out the passenger window, which was pocked with dead bugs and a thin film of dust. Brick had picked up this hideous RV on craigslist, figuring that was more authentic than buying one new and having it customized with plasma screens. "Besides," he'd said, "if we do that, we might as well just take my *Avalanche!* trailer!"

He'd laughed, like this was the most ridiculous idea ever, but Brooke had seen the trailer Brick used on set. It had a hot tub, and DIRECTV. It was paradise compared to their current monstrosity, which was beige with a metallic magenta stripe on the side that made it look like a really boxy Nike shoe on wheels. Brooke refused to sleep in it, because it smelled like cigar smoke and feet (although the Hitchcockian Holiday Inn wasn't much better), and no matter where or how she arranged her body in any of the seats, her knees hurt and her butt went numb. If this was the Great American road trip experience, Brooke saw no reason not to fly private jets for the rest of her life.

"Shouldn't we at least find a phone that *works* and tell Molly we're coming?" Brooke asked.

"No, Sunshine," Brick said. "Surprise is our greatest weapon. We're going to sweep her off her feet. She's going to be thrilled!"

She'd better. Because if this tremendous act of self-sacrifice didn't prove how sorry Brooke was, nothing would. Indiana could not arrive soon enough.

"Oops," Brick said. "We've been going the wrong way on the 29 for about an hour."

Brooke clenched her jaw. A tiny car passed them on the left. She made a fist and threw all her weight behind jamming it into Brick's shoulder.

"Punch buggy white," she said, her lips curling into a grin.

Acknowledgments

We'd like to thank our friends and families for their endless patience, love, and ability to pry us away from our computers when we need a little sunlight—especially Jim and Susan Morgan; Elizabeth Morgan; Kevin, Dylan, and Liam Mock; Alan and Kathleen Cocks; Alison, Mike, Leah, Lauren, and Maddie Hamilton; Julie, Colin, and Nicholas O'Sullivan; and the amazing Maria Huezo, without whom no words would've been written at all. We also owe a debt of gratitude to Scott Hoffman, superagent and oenophile extraordinaire; Ed Labowitz, the best lawyer and lunch date in town; and our fearless editors, Cindy Eagan and Elizabeth Bewley, for their gifts of faith, trust, and brilliant guidance. We're so grateful you all helped us bring *Spoiled* to life.

Sometimes life gets

messy.

Now that Brooke has caught a taste of fame and her movie-star father's attention, she wants to launch a blog that will position her as the ultimate Hollywood insider. But between schoolwork, party-planning committee meetings, and spa treatments, she hardly has the time to write it herself....

Enter green-haired misanthrope Max McCormack. An aspiring author with a severe case of writer's block and a terrible after-school job pushing faux meat on the macrobiotic masses of La-La Land, Max reluctantly agrees to play Brooke's ghost-blogger for an impressive salary. But how long will their lie last? Can the girls work together to stay on top, or will the truth come out and ruin everything they've built?

Hollywood lovers rejoice! Turn the page for an insider's peek at *Messy*, the snarky sequel to *Spoiled*, available now.

BROOKE BERLIN ALWAYS EXPECTED things to go her way. *Eventually.* History backed her up: The events of six months ago, when her father's secret love child moved in with them and temporarily ruined her life, could have gone *much* more horrifyingly than they did. Sure, she and Molly had gone through a rough patch that ended in Brooke accidentally chasing her back to Indiana, but they were past that now, thanks in part to her and Brick taking a nightmarishly rustic road trip to West Cairo to win Molly back. When they'd arrived, after three days without hair product and sweating oil from eating mostly Sonic Tater Tots, Molly swore she'd already decided to come back—but Brooke figured her and Brick's disheveled patheticness lent their pleas a sincerity that helped the cause. (Even so, as soon as Molly's intentions were clear, Brooke wasted no time in making Brick sell his godforsaken RV and fly them home on a private jet, like civilized people. Even sincerity had its limits.) Now, several months hence, she and Molly had slowly settled into a sisterly routine. Molly was as well adjusted as anyone could ask, which Brooke attributed to her own recent efforts to look past her sister's ill-conceived bangs and humble hayseed beginnings and find the kindred spirit within. They were, if not terribly alike, very bonded. Score another one for Brooke Berlin.

So Brooke assumed her blogographer ad would be a hit. Surely any rational, breathing human would leap at the chance to get in on a budding showbiz empire, especially once they realized she was the daughter of the man who coined the phrase *"Sayonara,* scumsucker." But getting a response after just five minutes exceeded even *her* imagination. Of course, that response had been from a guy sending her a picture of his feet, but it had started the ball rolling: In quick succession she got two e-mails from people asking if she knew Taylor Lautner, one from a girl who wanted to know if they'd be in *Seventeen* together, and then a reply from WordNerd94. It was sparse—just a brief mention of writing aspirations—but also spelled correctly. Way more promising than the one that followed, from a thirty-six-year-old man wanting to write a piece called "Dear Jake Gyllenhaal, I'd Like to Buy Your Vowel."

Max finally closed her gaping mouth. "Brooke."

"Max."

"*Brooke.*"

"Max," Brooke said again, impatiently. "Can we move on to some other words?"

"Sorry," Max said. "It's just that the ad said 'teen actress/ It Girl,' so I was expecting some sort of, you know... teen actress/It Girl."

"And *I* was expecting someone who isn't the social equivalent of menstrual cramps," Brooke retorted. "Tough day all around."

This depressing turn of events was the opposite of what Brooke had pictured. Obviously, she wanted her blog strategy to work. She *needed* it to work. But she'd envisioned it involving a bookish beauty who would be eternally grateful to Brooke for changing her life, beginning with a makeover that blossomed her into a spunky mini-Brooke, and continuing through highly nurturing shopping and social adventures. Instead, Brooke's best candidate was her high school's resident pale, acid-tongued loner whose gold-tinged eyes and green hair made her look like a refugee from some nerdy movie about elves.

A model-esque beauty in trendy glasses appeared behind Brooke's shoulder. "Max McCormack? Surely you jest."

"We covered that part already," Brooke told Arugula, relieved that her best friend had arrived to diffuse some of the awkwardness. "We're already up to the bit where I say, 'But aren't you some kind of antiestablishment shut-in?'"

Max stood up. "I have a sudden urge to go behead all my old Barbies."

"Oh, please. Don't be so melodramatic." Arugula scooted into the booth. "Maybe this is destiny. Maybe the hand of fate is trying to give you a massage."

Max glared stonily at Arugula. Brooke stifled a snicker. She and Ari had been best friends for ages, long before anyone—including Arugula—figured out Ari was the class genius. Brooke liked basking in the reflected glory of her friend's intelligence, but sometimes it was hard to keep a straight face.

"Whether fate is getting handsy or not, Arugula does have a point," Brooke opined. "Obviously you answered my ad for a reason."

Max smacked the table. "God, that ad. I am going to kill Molly for not telling me it was you."

"I don't run everything I do past Molly," Brooke said, offended. "We may be sisters, Max, but we are our own people."

"Sure. Whatever."

Brooke studied Max. There was nothing to indicate that she'd be a particularly successful writer. But then again, Brooke had always assumed from their previous interactions that Max didn't have any ambition to be anything except sarcastic, and that she would live out her days as a cranky drugstore cashier, staring pointedly at all the weird things people had in their baskets and trying to make the kids buying condoms feel really uncomfortable. The fact that she'd confided career aspirations in an e-mail to someone she thought was a total stranger made Brooke wonder if Max had hidden depths.

"Okay. I can't afford to waste the time I've carved out in my schedule," Brooke said, feeling decisive. "And since I skipped Yogilates, we might as well do this."

"Oh, no," Max said. "I'm not staying. I need an actual job."

"This *is* an actual job, and technically, you have already stayed," Brooke said. "Obviously you're not my first choice, but maybe you'll be good practice for interviewing *real* applicants."

She pulled a clipboard out of her giant leather bag and brightly clicked open a pen that said *Avalanche!* on the side.

"That's your dad's latest, right?" Max said. "The one he's shooting in Florida?"

"Yes," Brooke said, pleased as she always was when people were abreast of her father's career. "Would you like me to get you a pen?"

"It is my life's ambition to advertise such an impressive feat of cinema verité."

Brooke shook back her curls and leveled Max with a smile that said, *Nice try, but you can't provoke me.* "Let's start at the beginning," she said. "What do you think of my shoes?"

Max shook her head and rose. "They're blue. That's what I think. And since that is totally not a real question, I'm going to go home to catch the *Lust for Life* prime-time special.

Julianna is supposed to find out that her recapitation surgery is illegal and that Pip's head might get reclaimed."

Brooke put down her pen and affixed Max with a very serious look. "God invented the DVR for a reason," she said. "Sit down and respect the process."

Max appeared to be wrestling with something, perhaps a very muscular inner demon, and then plonked back down. Brooke mentally patted herself on the back. She knew she had a way of making it hard for people to wriggle out of things. She'd inherited it from Brick. It was how she kept managing to wrangle Molly into driving her places (at last count, Brooke had flunked her written driver's test six times, although it wasn't her fault—that stupid rectangular manual was ergonomically nightmarish to read).

"My shoes?" she prompted.

"They look like you left your feet outside a Siberian tree farm for three weeks."

Wrong, but at least it was creative. Brooke silently ticked the box on her form that read *Pithy Turn of Phrase*. "Favorite outfit of mine?"

"Are you ser—"

"*Respect the process.*"

"I like whatever it is you're wearing when I'm not around you."

Brooke nodded and made another mark, this time next to *Sass Factor*. The waitress slammed Max's chocolate malt onto the table.

"Interesting," Arugula murmured, reaching over to check a box with a flourish. This one read *Can I Sneak Fattening Snacks?*

"You Tyra Banks?" the waitress asked, flicking her thumb at Arugula's head.

"Yes," Arugula deadpanned. "*Top Model* auditions are in two days at 4100 Bar in Silver Lake. Seven AM sharp. Bring your bikini waxer."

The waitress skipped away, looking exponentially more cheerful.

"You sent her to Silver Lake?" Brooke whispered. "There are *hipsters* there."

"It will be character-building," Ari said primly. "Now, Max, who is your celebrity role model?"

"Brooke Berlin."

Arugula's lip twitched. "Present company excluded."

"Courtney Love, obviously."

"Style motto?" Brooke asked.

"'I shop to avoid nudity.'"

"How noble," Arugula muttered.

"Best *American Idol* winner?"

"Duh, Kelly Clarkson. I can't even joke about that," Max said.

"How many of Daddy's four Dirk Venom movies have you seen?" Brooke continued.

"Three," Max replied. "I skipped the second one because I don't believe in Kate Hudson."

Brooke looked up, surprised. "That's actually my ideal correct answer."

"Some truths are too powerful to ignore."

Brooke regarded Max curiously. "Let me just confer with my associate for a minute." She turned to Arugula. "So what do you think?"

"Well, she dresses like one of the orphans in *Annie*."

"Mmm. And she eats dairy."

"And I think her hairdresser also did my parents' hedge maze."

From across the table, Max cleared her throat exaggeratedly. "I'm *right here*."

Brooke looked at her. "Yes, you are. Tell me, why *is* that?"

"Me? Why are *you* here?" Max countered. "If you were really an It Girl, wouldn't you already have, like, *people*?"

"I am an It Girl. Unfortunately, the world just doesn't know it yet," Brooke hedged. "You saw me in the play last fall. I was a triumph. The *Los Angeles Times* wrote, 'Brooke Berlin is *on*!'"

Max frowned. "They were just listing the play in the events calendar. The rest of that sentence was, like, 'Brooke Berlin is on*stage* at Colby-Randall Preparatory School's nonmusical fall production of *My Fair Lady*,' or something."

"Details," Brooke said, waving an immaculately manicured hand. It was a favorite sentiment of hers. "The point is, my star is on the rise."

"My mother is sending Brooke's headshots around town," Arugula added.

"I'm sure that has nothing to do with her also being Brick's agent," Max cracked.

"There are two kinds of actors in this town," Ari said. "Nepotists and the unemployed."

"But I want to *get* the parts on my own," Brooke insisted. "So I need something that makes me stand out from all the other boring nepotists. Why not let people get to know me online? All the celebrities these days are pouring out their hearts on the Internet. Just look at what it's done for Kanye."

"I *did* spend a week wondering whether he ever got that cherub rug," Max admitted.

Brooke made a check mark next to the box reading *Comprehends the Magnitude of Celebrity Social Media Interaction vis-à-vis the Minutiae of Everyday Life.* (Arugula had written that one.) "Exactly," she said. "If I play this right, in a month, it could be *my* cherub rug people are worried about."

"I'm sure some lobotomized fan will find this job very fulfilling."

"That lobotomized fan could be you!" Brooke pointed out, waggling her pen in the direction of Max's face. "But you never told me why you applied."

Max gritted her teeth. "Because my job at Fu'd is making me consider taking my own life by diving into the tofu liquefier, but I still need cash for...stuff."

Arugula stared at Max intently. "It's not drugs, is it? I've always thought Teddy had a tweaker look about him."

"Was that before or after he rejected you?"

"Seriously, why do you need the money?" Brooke said, holding up a silencing hand to the side of Arugula's outraged-looking face. Her need for dish outweighed her need to defend Ari's honor. Plus, it *was* after he rejected her. "This job pays very well. Not that it's yours. I'm just saying."

Max was quiet again, staring at the countertop and tracing invisible things with her finger. Just in case, Brooke checked to make sure they weren't satanic symbols. One never knew. Being under the sway of Dark Forces might explain why Max had done that to her hair.

"I want to go to NYU's summer writing program," Max eventually admitted. "But it's really expensive."

"So it's true that you actually *want* to be a writer," Brooke said thoughtfully.

"Yeah, a writer. Not a tweeter."

"This *is* a writing job," Brooke said. "If it were tweeting, I'd have called it tweetographer. Brooke Berlin's essence is bigger than a hundred and forty characters, so I'm going old-school. I need someone to expose what a witty, enlightened asset to humanity I am, by writing blog entries as if they're me."

"You don't see the contradiction in that statement?"

"The entries will all be rooted in fact," Arugula said. "Brooke simply won't have the time. She'll be too busy going to auditions and assiduously maintaining her public persona."

"Also, I don't like to type," Brooke confided. "I inherited my mother's groundbreaking modeling hands, and everyone knows typing warps them."

"So, you already have an assistant. Dictate them to Martha."

"Her name is Brie now," Brooke scolded. "People are so callous not to respect that."

"Again with the contradictions," Max muttered into her malt. Brooke winced; every sip was, like, fifty crunches. "Can't *Brie* do this?"

Brooke shook her head. "She's terrible at keeping secrets. Last Thanksgiving, as a test, I asked her what she was getting me for Christmas and she actually told me. I need someone who will be anonymous."

"Well, good luck with that," said Max. "I'm sure pathetic minions are a dime a dozen in this town."

But her tone lacked its usual bite. Brooke tapped her pen on her clipboard a few times, deep in thought. She hadn't expected honesty from Max, who was now sitting there looking a little bit nauseated and—was she imagining it?—kind of bummed. Maybe the little troll doll needed this more than Brooke realized.

"I know we're not exactly friends, but if Molly likes you there must be *something* redeeming about you," Brooke allowed. "And you *do* share my controversial stance on Kate Hudson."

"Thanks...?"

"Look, I know what you think of me," Brooke said. "And if I were you, I might think it, too. But there's a lot riding on this for me. I'm taking it very seriously. Maybe you should consider doing the same."

Brooke slid out of the booth, ripped off a piece of paper from her clipboard, and scribbled the job's very generous salary on it. She handed it to Max. "That's my cell number, and *that* is the amount I'm willing to pay my blogographer. If you decide you're interested, and if the dozens of other applicants fail the Hudson test, maybe we can work something out."

Max took the paper and gazed at it, mutely. Ari reached around Brooke and slid a five-dollar bill onto the table.

"For the milk shake," she said. "Not *drugs*."

Max's face was full of contempt. "Right, like I would do drugs that cheap," she breezed, standing up and leaving the bill on the table for the waitress. She made a big show of dropping Brooke's piece of paper in the trash on her way out.

Well, I tried, Brooke thought, watching Max leave. Then she quickly snatched the paper out of the bin before any potential stalkers could do it. An It Girl had to be vigilant.

FOR THE LOVE OF BOOK

A place for novel people who love Young Adult books.

WE BELIEVE:

...all readers are **WELCOME**

...books can be **life-changing**

...crushes on **fictional characters** are completely legitimate

WE BELIEVE that books are the best.

 thenovl.com

 LB TEEN